PRIZE STORIES 1982

The O. Henry Awards

PRIZE STORIES 1982
The O. Henry Awards

EDITED AND WITH
AN INTRODUCTION
BY WILLIAM ABRAHAMS

DOUBLEDAY & COMPANY, INC.
GARDEN CITY, NEW YORK
1982

The Library of Congress Cataloged This Serial as
PZ1 Follows:
.O11

Prize stories. The O. Henry awards. 1919–
Garden City, N.Y., Doubleday [etc.]

v. 21 cm.

Title varies: 1919–46, O. Henry memorial award prize stories.
Stories for 1919–27 were "chosen by the Society of Arts and Sciences."
Editors: 1919–32, B. C. Williams.—1933–40, Harry Hansen.—1941–
Herschel Brickell (with Muriel Fuller, 19 –46)

1. Short stories. I. Williams, Blanche Colton, 1879–1944, ed. II. Hansen, Harry, 1884– ed. III. Brickell, Herschel, 1889– ed. IV. Society of Arts and Sciences, New York.
PZ1.O11 813.5082
Library of Congress [r50q830] Official
ISBN: 0-385-17563-9
Library of Congress Catalog Card Number: 21–9372 rev 3*

PRINTED IN THE UNITED STATES OF AMERICA
FIRST EDITION

CONTENTS

PUBLISHER'S NOTE

This volume is the sixty-second in the O. Henry Memorial Award series.

In 1918, the Society of Arts and Sciences met to vote upon a monument to the master of the short story, O. Henry. They decided that this memorial should be in the form of two prizes for the best short stories published by American authors in American magazines during the year 1919. From this beginning, the memorial developed into an annual anthology of outstanding short stories by American authors, published, with the exception of the years 1952 and 1953, by Doubleday & Company, Inc.

Blanche Colton Williams, one of the founders of the awards, was editor from 1919 to 1932; Harry Hansen from 1933 to 1940; Herschel Brickell from 1941 to 1951. The annual collection did not appear in 1952 and 1953, when the continuity of the series was interrupted by the death of Herschel Brickell. Paul Engle was editor from 1954 to 1959 with Hanson Martin coeditor in the years 1954 to 1960; Mary Stegner in 1960; Richard Poirier from 1961 to 1966, with assistance from and coeditorship with William Abrahams from 1964 to 1966. William Abrahams became editor of the series in 1967.

In 1970 Doubleday published under Mr. Abrahams' editorship *Fifty Years of the American Short Story*, and in January 1981, *Prize Stories of the Seventies*. Both are collections of stories selected from this series.

The stories chosen for this volume were published in the period from the summer of 1980 to the summer of 1981. A list of the magazines consulted appears at the back of the book. The choice of stories and the selection of prize winners are exclusively the responsibility of the editor. Biographical material is based on information provided by the contributors and obtained from standard works of reference.

INTRODUCTION

By one definition at least, we are all of us storytellers: So much of our lives, day by day, is given over to the stories we tell, anecdotes of ourselves or of others, in telephone conversations, in the course of a dinner, in moments of deepest intimacy, or a moment of confidence to a stranger—and what, come to think of it, can be more fictional, more laden with pathos or absurdity, than the gesture of telling a story to oneself, talking aloud (perhaps unconsciously) as one hurries along a crowded street, unaware of the curious or averted glances of passersby? Indeed, to calculate the number of stories that are being told now, at this moment, all over the world is to recognize that the storytelling impulse is virtually inseparable from life itself. Almost from the moment we begin to learn to talk in a semblance of sentences to the last moment we draw breath in a broken phrase we are telling stories.

But between telling and writing stories there is so obvious a difference—at best, the difference of art—that one does well to settle for another definition, another category: the *written* story. Somehow there is the need impelled from within, or the obligation imposed from without (as in a classroom assignment) to write out the anecdote, perhaps to elaborate it, transform it, so that ultimately only a kernel of truth—what really happened—remains. Or—again an immense leap—a story is imagined, which takes us into storytelling of a different order. Theoretically, anyone should be able to write as well as talk a story; the theory is not borne out in practice, however. Most of us are quite content to confine ourselves to telling the tale, improvising, keening, joking, complaining, or whatever our mood dictates. But there are the rare ones among us who write their stories, and among those, rarer still, are "the happy few"—artists of the word—whose achievements we recognize at a first reading, and remember, and return to.

We like to believe that we know a good story when we read it; and as a corollary it seems a fair assumption that the author of one good story will in due course write another and another, and ultimately will have created a sizable, admirable, enduring body of work—as we know to be true of Kipling, for example, or Katherine Mansfield, or Chekhov, or Hemingway, or Elizabeth Bowen, or Maupassant. What is troubling, however, to anyone with more than a casual interest in the continuing vitality of the story, is the appearance of a gifted writer who impresses us with a first story, and perhaps a second, and then falls silent, too often never to write (or at least to publish) again.

As the editor of an annual anthology dedicated to gathering together a selection of outstanding stories published in the preceding year, I am excited by the arrival of new or little-known writers of authentic talent. I welcome their stories and look forward eagerly to their further work. (In this respect it seems worthwhile to emphasize that in the present volume, save for the familiar presence of such established writers as Peter Taylor, Joyce Carol Oates, and Alice Adams, we have an array of writers at the beginning, or in the early stages, of what I hope will prove long and stimulating careers.) But it has to be said that in too many cases there is no further work. Why this should be so I can only surmise and therefore shan't say.

I *can* say—because I believe it to be true—that the vitality of the story as a form depends not so much on the writer who will produce a single or even an occasional story as it does on those writers who continue to write, year after year, not always achieving the standard of excellence they have set for themselves in their best work, but even in their lesser work unmistakably revealing themselves to be dedicated writers for whom the task is, in the precise sense of the word, a vocation.

It was with the intention of recognizing such writers and the invaluable nature of the contribution they make to the story, that more than a decade ago the publishers of this series established a Special Award for Continuing Achievement to be awarded at the discretion of the editor, at such times as seemed appropriate, to a writer of established reputation. It was given for the first time in 1970 to Joyce Carol Oates; and again, in 1976, to John Updike. Now, the Special Award for Continuing Achievement is being made for a third time—to Alice Adams.

A writer of uncommon excellence whose stories have gained her deserved esteem over the past decade, Miss Adams has become increasingly accomplished—hers is the art that conceals itself in a deceptive effortlessness—secure alike in what she does and in what she chooses not to do. (One finds it hard to imagine her writing an unintelligible or unintelligent sentence.) She is a writer whose achievement is particularly to be valued at a time when spectacular "effects" are too often exploited for their own sake. "Greyhound People," for example, one of the two stories by Miss Adams included here, beautifully conveys her virtues: her clear, sometimes poignant, sometimes ironic, but always deeply sympathetic view of the complexities of contemporary life. Out of the stuff of "incident," namely, a bus ride between two cities—who has not experienced it, afterwards recalling the minidramas and vignettes it offered, as a source of amusement or displeasure?—she has found the resonances that emerge from the deeper levels of feeling: a way of acceptance at once stoical and admirable. To borrow a title of her own, she has given us "rich rewards" both here and in many of her other stories. It is a pleasure to acknowledge our indebtedness to her.

—William Abrahams

PRIZE STORIES 1982

The O. Henry Awards

FACING FRONT

SUSAN KENNEY

Susan Kenney was born in Summit, New Jersey, in 1941. She attended public schools and Northwestern and Cornell universities. Besides publishing stories in *Epoch*, *McCall's*, and *TriQuarterly*, she has recently completed a novel, *Garden of Malice*, and is working on a collection of short stories. Ms. Kenney teaches part time at Colby College and lives with her husband, son, and daughter in China, Maine.

The last time my brother visited us he left a reel of film for me, the 16mm kind with no sound. "Something I found when I was cleaning out the attic at Mom's. I had a copy made for you." I just shrugged and put it on top of the refrigerator and left it for a while. It lay there, a big dark celluloid cookie, until I finally got around to borrowing a projector from the college and running it. We waited for the kids to go to sleep and then I set up the projector on the coffee table while Phil unrolled the screen we keep around to show our slides on once in awhile. I could tell the film wasn't very long, and it seemed like a lot of trouble to go to for six or seven minutes of somebody's old home movie, but I thought it might be amusing, even if it were only me waddling around in diapers squeezing mudworms through my fingers.

The big white square danced, glared, then was suddenly overtaken by the faded sepia interior of a room. The sunlight spiking through the window panes barely outlined the windows and woodwork, the folds of drapes like bleached carved stone and I could just make out in the shadows on either side of the window two tall trumpet-shaped urns full of gladiolas. A wake? A christening? The only movement was the lurching and wheeling provided by the hand-held movie camera. The room bounced for a few seconds, then the image blurred into lateral streaks and we were transported outside and temporarily overpowered by the bright sunlight. "Take your finger off the button, dummy," I muttered, while Phil sat back with arms folded, repeating gleefully, "It's a classic, a real film classic."

Then suddenly, with no transition, there they were, and I knew we were watching my parents' wedding reception at my grandmother's house in Skaneateles, New York, July 31, 1938. They just burst onto the screen, my mother and father, swaying slightly in front of the latticed area underneath my grandmother's wraparound porch, arm in arm, with big grins on their faces, my mother all dark lines and angles, black hair and eyebrows and vivid dark lips and eyes, my father blond and slim, shiny-faced and curly-haired, both proud and confident, innocent of any suspicions about their future. The breeze did something to my mother's veil, and my father said something out of the corner of his mouth, and my mother smiled even harder, put up her hand to hold down her veil, then looked up at my father and excitedly jiggled his arm with her other hand, which he pressed closer to his side. Then they both looked back at the camera. My father gazed directly into the shutter, evidently embarrassed now because the camera had been chattering away at them for what?—a minute at least—and they didn't have anything to do except grin at it and then at each other, and then back at the camera. My father bobbed his head like Charlie Chaplin, then made a swift fake grin that bounced the corners of his mouth back toward his ears and relaxed in almost the same moment. My mother hung on his arm and beamed, two large dimples shadowing her smile. The person with the camera must have said something about kiss the bride, because my father appeared startled and shook his head, and my mother lowered her eyelids and looked demure, and then they bent toward each other and briefly touched lips. Then they came to attention, eyes front, like two mechanical soldier dolls, and my father snapped a mock salute. They laughed and sidled away through the shrubbery, and the camera panned around to the other guests, my father's father, the minister, his wife, my chubby grandmother with the plain frontier schoolmarm's face, wirerimmed glasses and all, and my other grandmother, my mother's mother, stout, elegant, faded, with white hair and pale thin mouth, looking exhausted but relieved.

The whole scene had that jerky, slightly jived up tempo of old movies, but there was something else wrong. Nobody looked quite the way I remembered them; nothing matched the pictures I had filed away in my memory. Of course I hadn't been born yet, but I remembered my mother and father and most of the rest of them when they were not too much older, and these film images just weren't right. Even my grandmother's house with the high latticed porch was oddly unfamiliar.

"There's something wrong," I said. "Something's not right about the faces."

"I don't see anything wrong," Phil said. "I'd know your mother anywhere; she looked as crazy as a coot even then. It's that wild, glassed-in look in her eyes."

"It all looks strange, not the way I remember it."

"Maybe you don't remember it right because you weren't born yet."

"I don't think that's it. But never mind, let's just watch."

We watched for a few more minutes while the camera nosed around the grounds of my grandmother's house, trying to keep up with my parents as they mingled with the guests. Then the film hiccuped and my parents came out of the front door of the house dressed in street clothes, and started down the steps while the guests awkwardly hurled rice at them, and they bobbed and ducked, laughing. My father got a handful in the eye at close range from my Aunt Rozzie, and stopped to wipe the rice away like so many hard little tears. They hurried over to a car parked in the street alongside the house, got in and drove away. The film ran on rather aimlessly, forlornly, back over the wedding guests, the house, the goldfish pond, until the last frame jerked away and the film slapped around the take-up reel.

"Why did your father have an English car?" Phil asked.

"Huh?"

"The car. The steering wheel was on the right-hand side."

The white screen flooded our eyes and I flicked off the projector lights, letting the machine cool down. I thought about the steering wheel. Then I stopped the take-up reel. But this time I turned the film over, reversed it, because I thought I knew what had happened. Whoever had copied the film had rewound it inside out. My brother hadn't noticed anything wrong because he didn't know the faces of most of the people or remember my grandmother's house. It gave me a chill to think that of all the people who might ever see this movie, only I would see that all the faces in it were odd, reversed, mirror images of what they ought to be. The car alone wasn't a certain tip-off; my father might have driven a British car. Even the people in it wouldn't know, if they were still alive, which most of them weren't, because they would be used to seeing themselves that way, the way they looked in the mirror. It wouldn't occur to them that they were supposed to be seeing themselves as others saw them, and they would never miss the mild shock of non-recognition that comes with seeing all your moles and droops and quirky asymmetries in their proper places. I felt oddly excited as I waited for the film to rewind. When I started the projector again, I could see from the very beginning that everything was all right. The sepia sun-streaked room decked out with gladiolas was my grandmother's parlor where the wedding ceremony had taken place, and the slope on which the house was built ran downhill the way it always had. The faces were familiar. I sighed and settled back to watch the film again, no longer puzzled by the strangeness of it all.

At last my parents stood poised at the top of the stairs once more, then they were at the bottom, arm in arm. After one last laughing look they turned away from the camera and walked across the lawn toward the car. I watched their two young, jaunty, straight-shouldered backs as they walked away; suddenly they seemed so vulnerable, their happiness so fleeting, and I felt like a mother watching her two children walk away hand in hand into the woods alone. Then I saw that the back of my mother's dress was undone at the top, so that a small patch of white skin showed. No one else seemed to notice; nobody rushed over to do it up. My father helped her into the car and then walked around and got in himself. The two of them smiled and waved, my father leaning across my mother for one last look, and then they drove away.

Twenty years later my mother ran down those same steps, leaving behind three bewildered, underage children and the contents of every drawer, cupboard, closet, rubbish can, cereal box, flour bin and paint tin dumped out and mixed together on the floor. She had gone for three days without sleep, chattering to herself non-stop, playing jazz records at top volume on the stereo. I was seventeen, my sister twelve and my brother eleven. Worried and then frightened, finally on the third day I called the family doctor, and then the police. My mother saw the police car pull up alongside the house near the back; she ran out the front door, down the steps, across the lawn and into the fields behind a neighbor's house without looking back. The police caught her about a mile away and brought her back to the house to say goodbye to us before they took her to the State hospital. She looked at me, still all dark lines and angles, and her eyes glittered like a lathered race horse's; she looked very happy, even triumphant. Her cheeks were flushed, and her breathing shallow. She reared her head back and stared at me with her proud, satisfied, crazy eyes, and said, panting, "Did you call the police?" I nodded. "I could kill you for that," she said. The tall policeman holding her arm blinked, stared at her, at me. "But I won't. Maybe now I can get a little help around here. Get the picture?" And she turned away. The second policeman grabbed hold of her other arm and the three of them marched out of the house and down the steps to the waiting police car. She was forty-eight, and my father had been dead almost exactly five years.

II

My mother always claimed the beads were solid gold, that Uncle Ralph, my father's uncle, had bought them in France for her, and they were very valuable. The jeweler who restrung them for me said they were gold-filled and very nice, but not of any great value. My mother wanted me to have them and pass them on to my daughter Linnie, she said, as she handed them over to me two summers ago at the bottom of the stairs in the house in Skaneateles. She had gained weight in the last ten years, less running around, she thought, or possibly it was the lithium that made her so logy, but anyway the choker had gotten too small for her neck, and she wanted me to have it. I put the beads around my neck, reached back, and fastened the clasp. It was a choker all right. I gagged, not liking the feel of cold metal so close around my throat. I pulled on it slightly and the chain gave, scattering the beads on the floor. My mother and I went down on our hands and knees. "Oh, dear," my mother said, "I wish you hadn't done that. But never mind. We'll find them. They needed restringing anyway." We groped around in the dust at the bottom of the stairs, found the beads in cracks, next to the wall, under the rug, and collected them. I put them in a plastic bag, took them home to Vermont with me and had them restrung. There must have been one or two beads missing, because when I picked them up and tried them on, they were even tighter than before. The next time I talked to my mother on the phone I told her. "Oh, never mind," she said. "Just have the jeweler put a guard chain at the back, and you can wear them undone."

"But it will look funny," I said.

"But it's the back of your neck. Nobody ever looks at the back of your neck. It'll be all right; you'll see."

As I put the beads away in my jewelbox I thought about what my mother had said, and about all the years I'd lived with her, the hours I'd spent, the letters I'd written, the phone calls I'd made, trying to make some connection, trying to get her to face up to herself and her life as it really was. My father had been dead since 1953; over twenty years later she still mourned him, bitterly resented the thought that he had carelessly abandoned her to this life alone. She wouldn't give him up, and though his image wavered and changed from hero to villain and back again, it remained always at the back of her mind; he was her final audience. Of course she couldn't look behind her, because that meant facing up to what she had lost.

So often growing up I would see her walk out of the house with the hair flattened and matted at the back, her dress unzipped at the top, the hem falling down or her slip showing, her stocking seams as crooked as a hurrying snake. She would turn and smile at me, implying the question "How do I look?" and I never told her she wasn't finished behind, not after the first time, when she gave me a look of haughty disbelief, fluffed her dress in front, and stormed out of the house, insulted. The facade of her life must have seemed plausible enough to her as she skimmed past it, resisting my attempts to make her look around and see the incompleteness of it all, the flat walls propped up with angle irons and toothpicks, sandbagged into place, the doors leading into rooms that did not exist, and stairs dropping off into wild and wheeling space. And there we were, my sister and brother and I, trying to pick our way through the debris.

The other day I made my daughter a grilled cheese sandwich, and charred it on one side because I was paying attention to something else. Without thinking I flipped the sandwich over burned side down, and served it to Linnie, who took one bite and looked at me with an expression of outraged betrayal, then disgustedly spat the soggy mess onto her plate. As I threw the sandwich in the garbage I recalled all the grilled cheese sandwiches and slices of toast and pancakes my mother had served me in my life, burned side down. What an injustice it is to be served a sandwich burned side down, and not to realize it until you've already bitten in. There you sit, small and humiliated, knowing that sooner or later you'll either have to choke it down, or spit it out.

III

When my father died suddenly of a heart attack away from home in 1953, my mother was at first stunned into silence. She hardly spoke in the daytime. But I would wake at any hour of the night and hear her murmuring and crying in the dark. If I went to her room and asked her if there were anything I could do, she would just say "I'm not crying." Sometimes I would sit on her bed and try to comfort her just by being there, but the next night it would be the same thing, the precise mechanical sobs going on monotonously, even involuntarily, and after a while I gave up. Finally near the end of the summer she went to a psychiatrist who arranged a few shock treatments for her depression. But she didn't have to go away anywhere, and in fact did not seem very different to me, just sadder, and life went on pretty much the same until one day in November my aunt arrived, called a moving van, packed us all up and moved the four of us from our house in Toledo, Ohio, back into my grandmother's house in Skaneateles, where my mother and father had been married fifteen and a half years before.

Six years pass. I'm eighteen. My aunt and grandmother, with whom we've lived all this time, have both died of cancer within a year of one another, leaving my mother the sole survivor of her immediate family, and owner of the house on State Street. Since her breakdown the summer before, things have been relatively calm. My mother now sleeps in what was my grandmother's room. From my room next door, I hear again the crying in the night. I try to be enlightened about my mother's depression; she has so much to grieve for. It's summer, and the birds are chirping outside the window. In the fall I'm going seven hundred miles away, to a college I chose partly because it was so far from home.

My mother has not gotten out of bed for three days. I have already asked her several times if she feels all right, but she doesn't answer me, just lies there facing me, her eyes closed. Her eyelids flutter, pale and transparent as a moth's wing. She looks relaxed, as though she is sleeping, but she isn't. Once in a while her eyes open and she blinks, then huddles further into the blankets. I've been getting the meals and taking the children out in the afternoon to the lake, where we swim. I leave my mother alone most of the time; maybe she needs the rest. But finally on the fourth day I go upstairs and stand in the doorway of her room.

"Can I get you something to eat?"

"No thank you."

"Are you all right?"

"No."

"Are you sick?"

"No."

"Then what's wrong?" I feel impatient, irritated. If she's not sick, why doesn't she get up?

Her eyelids flutter but do not open. A tear oozes out of one corner, hesitates, coasts jerkily around the dark hollow under her right eye, then drops onto the pillow. "Oh, Sara," she whispers, so faintly it's little more than a sigh. "I hear the birds outside the window, and they're saying, 'Stu-pid, stu-pid, stu-pid.'" As if to answer her a bird chirps up, as clear as water, and I hear it say "Phoe-be, phoe-be, phoe-be." The tears roll out from behind my mother's eyelids, but she doesn't make another sound.

I call the doctor, who tells me there's not much he can do, but finally we convince my mother to commit herself to the mental hospital again for a few days. She stays two weeks. When she comes out, she seems much happier, and there's no more question of the birds telling her she is stupid. I'm relieved, because it means I'll still be able to go to college in the fall. Meanwhile there's no more crying in the night.

IV

We come down Route 20 into Skaneateles, Phil and I, past the small Gothic-style church where we were married in 1964, past the park at the head of the lake. We've made this trip quite a few times in the five years we've been married. The lake is, as always, translucent, breathtakingly, inexplicably blue. We turn right and start up the hill, passing the white houses with dark shutters stacked one after another in stately progression, their lawns trimmed, the large trees stooping protectively over the street. When I was growing up, these houses were mostly inhabited by little old ladies, many of whom were distantly and complexly related to my mother. Now there is the odd tricycle, the wading pool, but the street is still very quiet, very stately. My heart is fluttering. We haven't seen my mother in over a year, since she came back to my grandmother's house, her house now, from a brief sojourn in Massachusetts. We haven't told her we're coming, because just once I'd like to catch her when she's normal, show Phil what she's really like.

Phil looks from side to side, at all the beautiful houses. "This place is incredible. What must it have been like to grow up here?"

"I remember it was boring in the summer. And lots of little old ladies. The same thing day after day, going to the country club to swim, a little golf, a little sailing . . . you know, the usual."

"But then yours is an unusual case, I suppose."

"Not necessarily. It's a genre. Upstate Gothic. Idiots in the attic, skeletons in the closet, Uncle Hubert's drinking problem, Aunt Bertha's secret drug addiction. . . ."

"We're here." Phil turns the car into the drive, bumps up onto the two parallel concrete runners that lead to the garage, the latest thing for families with motor cars in 1926. They're a little broken down at the edges now.

The truth is, I'm anxious. Since we've been married Phil has seen most of what my mother has to offer, but it's still unsettling, to me if not to him, never to know what you're going to find when you open the door. These many years I've learned to read between the lines of letters and behind the tone of voice on the telephone, to surmise where my mother is in her wayward cycle of highs and lows, but the pattern has a disconcerting way of turning back on itself, shortening up, so that where you might expect there would be time left in the normal range, say a month or more, suddenly she's off again. Once I returned from college unexpectedly, thinking I might catch her when she had leveled out and have a little talk because all the signals were good, walked in and found the contents of a three story Auburn pawn shop spread around the house, on the floor, in the chairs, little figurines and brass objects, watches, golf clubs impishly stuffed into corners and under cushions. But never mind. The trick is, my sister says, not to let her know you're coming, because if she knows, she fidgets.

The kitchen door isn't locked; I push it open, sniffing. Sometimes the smell of the place is a clue. Even an instant's forewarning is better than none, but then what do I expect? My mother to pop out of a can like those wiggly fabric-covered springy snakes they sell in novelty shops? I tiptoe in, feeling like a spy.

"Why are we doing this?" Phil asks from behind me.

"I'm just checking. I want to see how she is."

"You know how she is. Impossible. Let's get out of here."

His message is, and has been for some time, "Give up." But I won't, not yet. "I can't," I answer. "She's my mother. I love her; I'm responsible for her." But even as I say it, I wonder if it's still true. Phil says noncommittally "Hm." He thinks the whole thing is a bad idea.

The sunlight streams into the kitchen from the dining room

windows beyond. Things look normal. It's very quiet. In the sunbeams float minute particles of dust, stratifying the rays so they slant to the floor like beams from a row of spotlights. We make our way across the kitchen. Briefly I wonder how it would be to enter unannounced and still know what to expect. But I'm suspicious now, even more than suspicious, jumpy. There is something distracted about the place, in the air, in the silence. There is no food to be seen, not on the counters, in the sink, on the stove, no dirty dishes. Then far away I hear the sound of something being abraded, an exhausted sawing noise.

"Come on," I say to Phil, who is backing away toward the door.

We find the first hole in the living room, in the chimney wall. The plaster has been chipped away, exposing the bricks for an area of about a foot square. There are several other holes in other walls, and in one place the plaster has been chipped away from the lath, and the lath broken through to expose the space between the beams. I poke my head inside; there's nothing to be seen but a pile of broken lath and powdered plaster. It's like looking at old bones. There is the sound of hammering upstairs now, and the sawing has stopped. I walk into the hall, into the parlor where my parents were married. The books have been turned out of the shelves into piles on the floor, and there are holes ranging from fist to tray size in the walls between the shelves. In the false wall in front of the old fireplace is a hole almost big enough to step through.

"What the hell is this?" Phil murmurs. His voice is awed, respectful, as though he were in a museum contemplating something wonderful. "Is she in there?" He peers into the hole in the false wall. "Nope."

But I know where she is. I walk to the bottom of the stairs and look up. She's standing at the top, silhouetted in the dim light, outlined by the white plaster dust that powders her hair, her eyebrows, her shoulders, the folds of her dress. Are her eyes glittering, or is it just a trick of the light and my expectation, knowing that the look must be there, knowing what she's done, what crazy, frantic energy it must have taken to punch and tear these holes?

"Hi, Mom," I say to the figure at the top of the stairs.

"Who is that?"

"It's Sara."

"Oh, Sara!" She sounds enthusiastic, breathless. "I'm so glad you're here." She comes quickly down the stairs, making no attempt to brush the dust from her face, her clothes. Under the white film her skin is flushed. She walks past me, then turns and faces me, and smiles. Her eyes are wild, evasive. They have a secret.

"I'm having the most wonderful time," she begins. But the rest of the sentence is lost. She falters, looks confused. "I've been looking for. . . ." She pauses again.

"I can see that." I try to sound neutral, understanding, but it doesn't work. Her expression changes from triumphant, victorious, radiant, to that of a guilty child, caught startled in the act of dismantling an expensive and forbidden but fascinating belonging of her parents.

"But I can't. . . . I haven't . . . it must be here somewhere. I just wanted to see."

"What is it?"

She stands silently, staring at me, and the guilty look dissolves into that opaque but crafty look I've seen in the glass eyes of stuffed wild animals. She's pulled the blinds down behind her eyes. She smiles and dimples her cheeks so that some of the plaster dust flakes off.

"I'll never tell."

I turn around and walk out.

As we're driving home Phil finally says, "Well?"

I feel like crying, but I don't. "I feel so sorry for her," I say. "She seems so desperate, looking for something, who knows what . . . ?"

"Desperate, hell. I thought she was having the time of her life."

"Maybe so. It's so hard to tell."

"Remember what the doctor said. Let her step in her own shit."

"Is that what the doctor said?"

"Or words to that effect."

"Oh. Words to that effect."

"Well, it's easier, isn't it? And she's survived so far. Let her have a good time. She's not hurting anybody."

"Right."

"Let's just not visit, okay?"

"Sure."

"Don't take it so hard." He reaches over and squeezes my hand. His fingers are warm.

"You don't understand. She's my mother."

"No, I'm sure I don't. But you can carry that sort of thing too far, you know."

"Thanks, I'll keep it in mind."

Phil grips my hand harder. I feel like a balloon full of hot air, straining to take off, and his hand is the rope that holds me down to earth. I hold on to his fingers. We drive in silence for a while. Before long we'll have to start looking for a place to spend the night. Phil's voice breaks in, splitting the dark. "Still," he says, "you can't help wondering what she thought she'd find behind those walls. What was she looking for?"

"Some sort of breakthrough."

"Is that a joke?"

"Not necessarily."

V

The telephone rings, dribbling into my half-asleep consciousness with the persistence of a leaky tap. It's too late to be good news. I grab the phone, hoping it won't wake up the children.

"Hello?"

"Hello, Sara?" It's my sister, calling long distance. Her voice is tense, slightly hollow, as though she were speaking from inside a tin can.

"Yeah, hi, Fran. What's wrong?"

"She's off again. Way off."

I sigh, sit up, shove the phone tighter into my ear. My fingers hurt, I'm gripping the receiver so hard.

"Up or down, and how bad is it?"

"She was high, but she got in trouble with the police because she was weaving her car all over the road—she thinks the FBI is after her—and they thought she was drunk driving. But then after she gave them this story about being an ex-FBI agent and the FBI wouldn't let her quit and was out to get her, the cops took her to the State hospital. One of the clowns there stuffed her full of heavy-duty tranquilizers and then discharged her. She took them for a week, then she crashed. She's down, really down. I stopped by the house just now and she's just sitting in a chair, staring at the wall. She must have tried to feed herself a couple of days ago and couldn't do it. There's a can of soup still stuck up there in the opener. It's gone bad. Chicken noodle."

"What do you want me to do?" I feel panicky already; the baby's only a few months old, and David's just three. I can't go anywhere.

"Well, nothing. I just thought you ought to know. I'm going to have her readmitted."

I sigh, switch the phone to the other ear and wiggle my petrified fingers. This is the fifth time in the last four years, since the day she poked all the holes in the walls of my grandmother's house. But at least Fran has taken over. But how long can she go on? Tentatively, speculatively, I say to my sister, "Don't you ever just wish she'd die? She's so miserable anyway, and then there wouldn't be any more of this. It would be all over."

There's a silence on the other end. Have I shocked her? She's a lot younger than I am. But her voice is matter-of-fact when she finally answers me, as though she's been thinking about it.

"I know how you feel, or I'm beginning to. But Sari, she is our mother, you know. Always and forever our mother. Even if she is crazy."

"I know. Sometimes I just don't care anymore. I'm tired of it. Up down turn around, and it's been going on for as long as I can remember. The doctors don't do anything that works, and she's just miserable. It's no way to live."

"How do you know?"

"Aren't depressed people miserable by definition?"

"I don't know. But there are always the highs."

"The highs are lower than the lows. How many more years of this can you take?"

"Oh, I don't know. You did ten, I'll do ten, and Vic can do ten. How many's that?"

"Not enough."

"Then we start over. You do ten. . . ."

"Leave her."

"What?"

"Leave her. Don't have her readmitted. Just let her stare into space for as long as she wants. Who knows what she sees? Maybe she'll come out of it by herself."

"Yeah, and maybe she won't. You haven't seen her. She can't do anything. She'll die."

"That might be the best thing that ever happened to her."

"You don't mean that."

"Of course I do. But you do whatever you think is right. It's your turn."

"God, you're callous."

"I'm not callous. I just happen to believe that people ought to be responsible for the consequences of their own actions. Let her step in her own shit."

"I don't believe you. I really don't." There's a long silence. The phone sounds hollow. "Goodbye," Fran says abruptly, catching me off guard.

"Good luck," I shout, but my sister has hung up before the words go down. It's several days before I hear from her. The phone rings in the daylight.

"Hello, Sara?" My sister's voice sounds tired, wrung out.

"Yes?"

"It's all over."

The words rush up against the tension in my chest like so many small birds flying headlong into glass. I'm impenetrable. For a long moment I don't know what my sister means, and I don't want to ask.

"Sari? Are you still there? Did you hear me? Everything's taken care of. Mom's all set. There's a new doctor who's got her on lithium, and he's pretty sure it's going to work. Our troubles are over. I thought you'd like to know."

VI

My mother seldom calls now, but letters come frequently, and it's been long enough since the last episode of craziness that I don't even bother to scan my mother's handwriting for signs of imminent breakup, the way I used to listen for those stomach-walloping clues of tone and catch-phrase in her voice over the phone. We're all feeling pretty secure. As long as she takes it, the lithium works for her, smooths over the hills and valleys, and at the age of sixty-seven my mother has subsided into a reasonable facsimile of an elderly, respectable widow lady who sits sedately underneath her white hair and knits sweaters and mittens for the kids.

When the letter comes it looks just like any other letter. There's nothing erratic or thready about the handwriting on the envelope, and no wild postscripts wandering around the margins, snaking back through the place and date to end in a barrage of exclamation points. This time there's just the place and date, Auburn Memorial Hospital, September 13, 1976, and "Dear Sara, I'm lying here recuperating from my mastectomy and feeling pretty good. . . ."

The phone rings and it's my sister. "Did you just get a letter?" she asks.

"I sure did."

"Could it be true?"

"I don't know. It doesn't strike me as the sort of thing you'd have for a delusion, given a choice." Silence. We're both thinking about what this means.

"Well, what do you think?" Fran finally says.

"She didn't tell us a thing, just went and took care of it all herself. 'Didn't want to worry you' she says. It's not like her."

"I know. Have you talked to Vic?"

"Not yet. But he'll check in later."

"You know what this means, don't you?" my sister says.

"What?"

"It's one more goddam thing we can inherit."

"I don't get it."

"Like being a manic-depressive. You inherit the tendency for this, too. Just one more goddam burden she's unloaded on us." My sister sounds disgusted; she's still getting over the last siege two years ago, in 1974, when my mother, having taken herself off lithium, wrecked an entire motel room and assaulted the policeman who came to get her. Fran told me it took four men to get her into the police car. That's when Fran gave up and moved to Colorado. Now everything has to be done long distance. I try to concentrate on the problem at hand.

"Well, I think we ought to consider what it's going to do to her head once the shock's worn off. I think I'll call her up and tell her I'm driving down."

"Right. You're closer."

"Sure enough, I'm closer. Okay. Thanks for calling. See you."

After I hang up the phone I try to piece together the story from my mother's letter. But there isn't enough to go on and she sounds so normal and in control. There's got to be something wrong. So I call her up at Auburn Memorial, and she's not even in the hospital anymore, she's gone home. I call her at home. She answers after a few rings, sounding breathless.

"Hello, Mom. How are you?"

"Fine, did you get my letter?" She sounds eager, as though she were ready with a piece of extra good news.

"Yes, I'm driving down."

"Oh, no. Don't be silly. You were just here a few months ago. I'm fine, just a little stiff, and the incision pulls when I breathe, but there's nothing to it. Really."

"Phil can stay with the kids and I can be there by tomorrow."

"No." Her voice is emphatic, risen slightly in pitch. I wait for the breakdown. It doesn't come. "I don't want you to come all this way. I'm all right. Really. I can take care of myself. Don't worry about me."

The question is, what to say next. All these years of bizarre phone calls, dotty letters with clues in code saying "Come and get me, I'm gone again," driving to this loony bin or that, sitting in hospital waiting rooms, three-way interviews with headshrinkers, have limited the conversation. I can't just say casually "How's your head?" All these years my mother and I have never yet spoken directly about her craziness; when she's high I can't get a word in edgewise, and when she's low she's down too deep to hear, and so self-accusatory that one more home truth about the life she's led herself and all of us would be too cruel, even if it sank in in the first place. And when she's normal, more or less, she doesn't remember, or claims she doesn't, what it's like to be around the bend. "Did I do that? I don't recall a thing about it." End of conversation.

But I recall one time when she was particularly high and obnoxious I wrote her a letter in desperation and took it to her, in an attempt to get her to face up to her erratic and irrational behavior, but she glared at me with those opaque, shiny eyes, and tore it up, daring me to say out loud to her face that anything was, had been, or ever would be wrong with her. I couldn't do it. Confronted with that blank wall of denial, what could I say? All her life since my father died—that gay, handsome, golden man who was her whole life—she's been running away, unable to see his death as anything but a betrayal, a treachery, a failure, either on his part or hers. She's never been able to put it down as just a death, one of life's accidents. It's still right there behind her, and if she reaches back to straighten her stocking seams or fix her hair or zip her dress up all the way she may just by mistake put a hand on it, that one monstrous, unacceptable, inescapable fact of his death. Listening to her now, filling in the details of her discovery and operation, I realize that all these years I've been seeing her as a paper doll, flat as a label someone's soaked off a bottle, all front, all surface, as thin and fragile as a butterfly pinned to a board. And now there's this.

"Are you still there?" she asks.

"I'm still here."

"Aunt Helen came to see me, and you know what she said?"

"What?"

"She said 'Well, dearie, you've got to die of something. Now you know.' Do you believe it? She was trying to be comforting. 'You've got to die of something!' I had to laugh." My mother laughs. "And you know, she's right. I always wondered what it would be, and now I know. It's a real relief."

"Wait a minute." The bells are clanging and the lights are flashing. Is she trying to tell me something? "Is that what the doctors say?"

"Oh, no. It doesn't have anything to do with them. The surgeon said he got it all and it was early and not to worry. But they always say that, and anyway, it's not the point. The point is, it's just a relief. You have no idea."

She's right. I don't. I've got to stop and think this one over, so I murmur something sympathetic about taking it easy, to which she answers, sounding mildly annoyed, what else does she have to do? I say I'll talk to her tomorrow, and hang up.

Such a relief. And suddenly I'm overwhelmed with pity for her, after years and years of trying to draw a line between us, not getting too close, so I won't get dragged down or hurt. For years I haven't even thought of her as a mother so much as someone I'm detached from yet still bound to in some remote way involving loyalty and responsibility, but not sympathy and certainly not love, no, never love. I'm not really prepared for this surge of sympathy, this sudden sense of connection. I'm suspicious of it, just as I'm suspicious of her stoic, matter-of-fact, accepting tone.

I sit there clutching the phone, thinking to myself this is finally the real thing. She's discovered a lump, gone to the doctor, had it biopsied, had the diagnosis, the mastectomy, made arrangements for radiation therapy, all by herself. It's every woman's nightmare, and all these years she has been the collapsing doll, dancing to a tune no one else could hear, falling in a heap or flying through the ceiling, manufacturing her own nightmares. Yet she's taken this in her stride, on her own, and is still on her feet. Of course, as my brother Vic reminds me on the phone half-an-hour later, it's still too soon to tell. So the three of us keep up the phonothon, the long-distance dial-a-vigil, the wires zinging with "Well, how did her voice sound to you?" and "What's your reading of that?" and so forth on into the third week.

But at last the wires slack off; there's been no change. Fran is running her lab in Colorado. Vic's gone back to courting his English girlfriend in Baltimore, and I'm still at home in Vermont with Phil and the kids.

It's odd, but I feel closer to her than I have since I can

remember, perhaps closer than I ever have before. Here is the reward, I seem to be saying to her in my mind, for being straight for once, for being a good soldier. I forgive you, and I love you.

Thinking of her now, for the first time in years I want to see her instead of feeling that I have to. I picture her sitting in her chair by the window, all by herself, calmly knitting up a size 56 sweater for the fat man who lives next door. She's not running and she's not falling down, she's just knitting, with a serene, satisfied look on her face, as though she's finally got everything figured out, and there's nothing to run and hide from anymore.

VII

As I pull the car into the driveway I can see her sitting in the window, so shadowy pale she's almost like a reflection. She's looking down, either reading or knitting, but as the tires crunch over the broken bits of the concrete runners she looks up and smiles expectantly. "Look, there's Grandma in the window" I say to the kids, and they both sit up and peer curiously through the car window. We haven't been here in over two years, since the summer before her operation. David barely remembers her, and Linnie not at all, but they're interested.

It's been a long trip, but I just feel tired, not particularly apprehensive. She's been so eager to see us, and I've gotten several letters in the past few weeks telling about her progress with the spring cleaning, how she's washed the curtains and all the bedding. The beds have been made for two weeks, and she's laid in peanut butter, tuna fish, and chocolate chip cookies. It all sounds good. For a while in the spring I worried that she had stopped taking her lithium again, but when all three of us questioned her about it long distance, in spite of her outrage she announced that she would continue to take it, even though it made her "feel funny," just to keep peace in the family. When I told Phil the part about feeling funny, he said "Sure, what she means is normal. She feels normal, and to her that's funny." Phil's away for a few weeks, and it seems like a good time to visit; he and my mother have never gotten along.

We all get out of the car, and in the noise of multiple doors slamming I don't hear her come out of the house, but as I come around the back of the car to get the suitcases she's standing there. I'm surprised at how gray she is now; her hair, peppery-black until just a few years ago, is suddenly almost white, and there is a gray cast to her skin, or is it just the late afternoon shadow of the sun gone down behind the house? Linnie flings her arms around her and says "Hi, Grandma," and my mother looks down, mildly startled, then pleased. David will not hug her; he is too shy, but I'm touched by Linnie's instant acceptance of this strange grandma as someone fond and huggable. For years David has distinguished her from his other grandmother by calling her "Funny Grandma." Phil and I have never dared ask whether he meant funny ha-ha or funny peculiar, but we've discouraged him from calling her that to her face. But he surprises me; seeing Linnie hug her he too with some caution sidles up to her and puts an arm around her back, lays his head briefly against her arm. She looks at me proudly, eagerly. "Hi," she says.

The children run off and I move closer to her, put my arm around her and kiss the air next to her cheek, the way we've always done. She steps back and says "I didn't know when you'd get here. How was the drive?" She sounds slightly breathless, expectant, and as she turns to go back inside I notice the flatness on one side of her dress. She has gotten rather stout in the last few years, and although she has joked to me on the telephone about not wearing a "falsie"—"I've been flat all my life and now I can see the advantage. I'll never miss it"—the difference is obvious. But that doesn't really matter. What strikes me is that everything seems so normal at last. Here I am, a grown woman with two young children, visiting Grandma while my husband is away, just like anybody else. She looks and sounds normal, and there aren't going to be any bad surprises.

Later, after the kids have settled down to watch cartoons, we're cleaning up the kitchen and she says to me casually, "Have you heard from Phil?"

"Yes, as a matter of fact. He called from London Sunday night. Everything's fine."

"I used to do what you're doing after your father died, you know."

I look up startled. "What's that?"

"Take trips with you kids. It was so lonely, especially around holidays, and no one in the family ever invited us anywhere, and I just couldn't stand it, so I'd just throw you kids in the car and take off."

I sit there flabbergasted. The last thing I want after all these years is to find out how much I'm like my mother. I remember the strange feeling I had taking the kids through Old Sturbridge Village a few days ago. I had to keep reminding myself that I was the grownup, that I had to take the responsibility for keeping everybody together and safe and happy, and I felt a strange reluctance, dragging of emotional feet. I had to force myself to assume the grownup role, and I felt that I was walking around as much in costume as all the guides in their old-fashioned clothes. One of the places my mother took us when my sister and brother and I were children was Sturbridge, and now I try to remember if what I felt there two days ago could be related to being there before, having to assume the grownup role in spite of myself, when I *wasn't* grownup. When I go there with my real children, the past haunts me, lies in wait for me in a way I don't even suspect.

"I don't like myself this way, you know," my mother says abruptly.

"Like what?"

Without a word she pulls up her sweater and shows me the hollow where her breast used to be, with the scar running across horizontally. The scar is barely noticeable—it's been almost two years since the operation—but the skin is stretched over bone, and I'm surprised to see how much flesh my mother has everywhere else in contrast to this hollow place, because I have always thought of her as a thin, angular person. I don't know what to say. She has said so many times that it didn't matter, that she hardly missed it. "Just like this," she answers, pulling down her sweater. "And old. I seem to have gotten old and gray all of a sudden. I don't like to look at myself in the mirror." I remember that not long after the operation she wrote asking me to send her giant-sized bath towels for her birthday, and I realize now they were to cover herself up, not just from everybody else's eyes, but from her own. I want to tell her I'm sorry, but I can't; it's not enough. I go around the table and put my arms around her to hug her, but she stands rigid, away from me. I hug her anyway, then sit down. Physical expression of sympathy is easier, even though we're unused to it; I can't say anything that will help. The next thing I do is turn practical, as always the problem solver, the trouble shooter, the fastest gun. So I aim for the source, or what I assume is the source.

"Why don't you get a breast form?"

She turns away from me, and her eyelids drop, but just before they do I catch a glimpse of the old evasive look. "What's the point? Why put up a false front? It really doesn't matter at my age. I just want to die and get it over with."

The words are so familiar, the refrain of so many of my years, that in spite of my determinedly practical "here's a problem and we'll solve it, where there's life there's hope" attitude, I find myself getting angry. I really thought she'd gotten past that. So I ignore the practical approach and address her last remark. "Don't tell me you still feel that way, even after all these years?"

She turns back, but doesn't look at me. "Of course. I have ever since your father died."

"Doesn't it mean something to you to have survived? Isn't there some satisfaction in that, in being a survivor?"

She looks me straight in the eye for an instant, and before she hoods them, her eyes fix me with an eagle look I've never seen before, proud, watchful, and without hope. Then the look is gone, and I'm not even sure I've seen it.

"No," she says matter-of-factly. "Everyone I ever loved except you kids has died, so why shouldn't I?"

Her words leave me speechless. I just sit there stupidly, nodding my head as though I understand, sympathize, when in fact it's all I can do to hold my eyelids apart, because if I blink the tears that have rushed up behind them will fall out, and my mother will see me cry. I take a breath, get up from the table and turn away, pretending to fold the newspaper. As I stand there, it strikes me that I can't remember when she has said to me in so many words, "I love you." This is the closest she has ever come. I want to turn and say "But if you love me, us, and we're not dead, aren't we enough, haven't we ever been enough, done enough, can't you go on from here and try to be happy with what you have left, with just being alive? Not even for us, not even for me?" I stand there rattling the newspaper, my lips clamped together, and the moment passes. I have done nothing to break through the long silence, the barrier we've put up between us down the years of crying in the night in separate rooms.

"Well, I guess I'll go to bed," I say casually. "Tomorrow is another day."

She looks at me and smiles. "You must be tired. So much excitement and such a long way. And tomorrow is another day."

"Goodnight, Mom."

"Goodnight, Sara. I'm glad you're here."

I'd planned to stay four or five days, but by the middle of the next day it's clear that things aren't going to work out. It's raining, and the kids have opened all their presents, explored the attic and basement, and now are asking for things to do. I had thought that the four of us might go someplace, visit the zoo or drive around the lake, but when I ask my mother if she wants to go, if she has any suggestions, she says no. "Don't you want to do anything with the children?" I ask, annoyed because she's urged us to come, looked forward to our visit, and now just sits in her chair as though we weren't here.

"I don't do things with children, I just like to watch them," she answers imperturbably, and goes on knitting. I begin to feel more than annoyed. As a matter of fact, I'm getting quite angry, so I turn and go upstairs, away from her, from the children bickering on the floor. How alien everything seems, how unreal—the way my mother lives. I walk through the upstairs alone and touch a crack in the plaster, and it comes away in my hand, a cobweb. Cobwebs heavy with dust festoon the corners of the rooms, the tops of the curtains, drape the lampshades. Last night I turned on the bedside lamp and smelled the dusty odor of dead flies smoldering in the heat of the lightbulb. The surfaces are clean, the tops of tables and dressers, the rugs and parts of floors that show, but under the dresser scarves my grandmother embroidered the dust has sifted through the eyelets and made a stenciled pattern on the wood, and the underneaths and corner places of the house are barricaded with dust. Nothing has changed.

As the day goes on I grow more and more irritable with the

children. My mother sits and wants me to sit, wants to talk about old times; she doesn't see people very often, and it's such a treat to have someone to talk to, she says. The children don't want to listen to our talk, they want me to play with them. They wander in and out of the room, little phantoms interrupting, and their voices wind higher and more imploring "What can I do now? Will you play with me? I'm bored." I reprove, then scold them, telling them to take care of themselves for once, not to interrupt, and after a while I begin to hear my mother's voice in mine, the same intonations of irritability, impatience, beyond what is justified by the children's behavior. I wonder if I really sound like her all the time and just don't notice when I'm not with her, or if I'm beginning to imitate her.

The weather clears, and finally I take the kids to the lake for the afternoon, and immediately the feeling of being pulled down, suffocated, mummified in cobwebs lifts, and I resume my own relation to reality, talking to our old friend who owns the cottage where we swim. But then it's time to go back for dinner. We troop into the house and my mother is still sitting; there is no dinner. She gets up stiffly, reluctantly, making odd guttural noises like a squawking bird, and stands in the middle of the room, lifting and stretching her legs. I'm standing in the kitchen when I hear Linnie let out a howl, then I hear her small feet hurrying up the stairs, accompanied by sobs. I brush past my mother, go upstairs after Linnie, who's in bed with the covers pulled over her head. The covers vibrate with silent weeping. I sit on the bed, put my hand on her little round rump under the blanket.

"What's the matter, honey?"

"I don't want to tell you."

"Oh, Linnie, you can tell me."

She claws the covers off her tear-blotched face and looks at me, lips quivering.

"Grandma slapped me in the face."

I go still suddenly, but my stomach lurches. "Why?" I say as calmly as I can.

"For no reason." She turns her face into the pillow and covers her eyes with her hands, and sobs.

And I remember all the times, the helpless, bewildered times

"With no reason" when I could not understand what my mother was doing or why, why she was so angry, what she wanted from us, how to behave so that she would be like other mothers, when my anxious questions brought only the furious answer "Because I say so" or no answer at all. I'm caught now between my mother and my children, and I'm alone, all alone, the one who has to make things right. I feel like I'm 17 all over again, standing alone between my mother and my younger sister and brother, trying to save them, save myself, and all at once I'm a climber, veering, springing away up a cliff of loose stones, scrambling and sliding, trying to get away, crying "not again, not anymore." But I stop clawing upward, let myself slide back slowly down the rock. This time I really am the grownup, not a child desperately trying to mimic one out of confusion and despair. I'm not helpless, and I won't run. I bend over and kiss Linnie's shiny cheek, hold her body under the covers.

"Don't worry. I'll take care of you. It will be all right." Linnie nods and smiles, shuts her eyes and pops her thumb into her mouth with a sigh.

I go downstairs. David is sitting at the kitchen table reading the funny papers, unaware that anything is wrong. My mother is standing at the sink, peeling potatoes.

"Did you hit Linnie?" I ask, trying to keep my voice level.

Deliberately, without looking at me, she says, "She came up and started punching me in the stomach. I tapped her lightly across the face. It was a reflex, automatic. Self-defense." Her tone implies exasperation, as if she really ought not to have to explain this, it's so simple.

My ears roar and I shut my eyes. I speak very softly. "She's upstairs crying. She's very upset. I don't think she understands the concept of self-defense. Please don't do it again. I don't care whether it's a reflex or not." My mother nods, sticks out her lower lip, and goes on peeling potatoes. I sit down at the table with David, who looks at me curiously. My mother puts the potatoes in a pot on the stove, starts past me. "I'll be right back," she says. "I just have to go to the bathroom."

I hear her go upstairs. Then David asks me to read him some of the funnies. It's awhile before I realize that my mother has not come right back. I hear the bed creaking upstairs in the room Linnie and I share. I get up from the table and go quickly, silently up the stairs and when I reach the doorway of our room my mother is sitting on the bed, holding Linnie's arms, struggling with her, shaking and pushing her, pinning her to the bed. Linnie's eyes are fixed on her face, and they are wild and panicky with speechless, uncomprehending terror. My mother is saying quietly "I just want to wrestle with you, get rid of some of that excess energy, show you a little self-defense. Come on, push me away, try to push me away." Her voice sounds gentle, but I can't see her face, and Linnie can, and she's afraid. Then Linnie catches sight of me and she takes a huge sobbing desperate breath; her eyes flood with relief. In one step I reach the bed, push my mother out of the way and snatch Linnie up in my arms, safe. She winds her arms and legs around me and buries her head in my shoulder with a trembling sigh, and I walk out of the room with her.

"Grandma was scaring me. I'm so glad you came," she whispers brokenly. I walk down the stairs, holding Linnie, and call to David in the kitchen, "Come on David, we're going out." My mother reaches the bottom of the stairs just as I am about to go out the door with the children. Over Linnie's head I look at her. She stares back, her lower lip jutting out defensively. "I was just trying to cheer her up," she says. She weaves as though she has been drinking, and her eyes are cloudy, opaque, as though the cobwebs have grown in them too. And I realize in a split second of bursting rage that I haven't forgiven her a thing. Whatever I thought or dreamed I had forgiven her for myself I will never forgive for my children. "Well, you didn't," I tell her. "We're going out."

"Are you coming back?" she asks. Her speech is slurred. It occurs to me that she has probably not been taking her pills. I turn away. She has let me down again, let my children down. "Of course I'll be back," I say crossly. "Take your pill." She blinks, then gives me that haughty racehorse look. I put Linnie down, go to the sink, dump out one of her lithium pills, fill a glass of water, and walk back to my mother, holding the pill in one hand and the glass in the other. My mother takes the pill, drinks the water, still glaring at me. "Well," she says. "I'm going to bed. I'm simply exhausted. Have a nice time." She turns and marches back up the stairs, while the children and I go out the door.

Later, after we've come home and the children are asleep, I lie in bed trying to get ahold of myself. My body feels enormous, taut and heavy with rage; my heart pounds, my chest hurts, and my forehead is tight. I feel like the stone giant I've told the children about, the carved statue supposed to be a petrified man buried in a field not far from here many years ago as a hoax. The giant lies on his side, his legs drawn up, his arms over his stomach as if in pain, but he's frozen into stone, and the weight bears him down into the earth, paralyzed, stiff, and cold. My hands and feet are numb, creeping into stone. I feel like crying out, but there's no one to call to, not even anyone to whisper to about how awful it is, Phil's not here to comfort me, there's me, just me, and then the hot tears start rolling down my cheeks and I cry silently, not wanting to wake Linnie. It's the same old pattern, nothing ever changes, and I was a fool to think it would ever be all right, if not for me, then for my children. I was a fool to risk them too. But how I've longed for it to be all right, if not for me, for them. I didn't realize it was too late.

But then a sound, a cough, some restless shifting from the next room catches my attention. On the other side of the wall my mother is awake. But what good does it do, I think to myself, even if she is awake. She's inaccessible, out of reach. I've given her up. I can't talk to her, I've never talked to her about anything that mattered, about her illness, about how I felt; it's always been just like this, the wall between us and the two of us lying here, each in our own separate distress. I toss and turn, listen to my stomach churn, trying to relax, but I'm really listening to her. And then, listening, trying to puzzle out the sounds and what they mean, I feel a sudden impulse to break the pattern. I've got to know for sure what's going on in there.

I get out of bed, walk across the room and into the hall, knock lightly and push open her door. She's lying on her side in bed, watching television. "Yeah, hi," she says eagerly. Her voice sounds perfectly normal. I feel my stomach loosen. I step forward cautiously.

"What's the matter? Can't you sleep?"

She flips a hand dismissively, then tucks it behind her head, the elbow pointed to the ceiling. I've often seen her lie like this, relaxed, expectant. "I go to sleep, then I wake up and I can't get back to sleep, so I just lie awake. Can't you sleep?"

"No, not right now." I sit down in a chair at the foot of her bed. "Does it bother you?"

"Oh, no. I don't mind a bit. I think about my life. It doesn't bother me a bit. I've got lots to think about." She reaches over and turns off the sound on the television.

"What do you think about?"

She smiles. "Oh, lots of things. About when I was a child, and my college days." She puts the other arm behind her head, lies back and chuckles. "Did I ever tell you about the time. . . ." And she begins to tell me a story about the time she was President of the Woman's Athletic Association at Syracuse, and went to the Chancellor to get the budget raised, and got it cut back instead. It's the first of several stories of her life before she was married, stories I've never heard, and she tells them humorously, without stopping, while the light from the television flickers over her face. I listen and watch her face for a long time. She's all right, she's really all right, in spite of all the bad signs and my own fierce, condemning anger. And I'm glad I came in to see for myself, glad I'm not a helpless and bewildered child anymore, afraid of what I'll find. After a while I say goodnight and go back to my room. We haven't talked about anything important, but it strikes me that we've just talked about ordinary things the way I've always imagined other mothers and daughters might do, as though all the years of struggling and wrestling back and forth between us had never existed. I lie in bed and think about my mother and me. I haven't forgiven her, but I begin to see that perhaps it's not a matter of forgiveness after all. It's not anyone's fault really, this separation, this lack, not hers, not mine. It seems so simple, and the words revolve together in my head as I fall asleep.

Finally it's time to leave, the bags are packed and in the car, my mother's arthritis is kicking up and she's coming down with a cold, but she gets up briefly to say goodbye to us, standing in her bathrobe with her hair all flat and mussed. The children both come toward her to kiss her goodbye but she fends them off, saying "Don't kiss me; you'll catch my cold." Neither of them seems particularly affected by what has gone on; Linnie fastidiously screws up her face as though shutting her eyes and mouth tight could keep out germs, but throws her arms around my mother's body and hugs her close. David does the same, ducking his head. But something holds me back. Maybe it's her own statement; I'm so tired of reading between the lines that now I'm prepared to take her at her word. If she doesn't want me to kiss her goodbye, I won't. In spite of our talk in the night I still feel alienated, separated from her. We haven't touched; our pasts don't touch; we've never admitted what's gone on between us all these years. The truth is, I've worn out the thin fabric of my unquestioning childhood love, and what is left? There are too many cobwebs here, too many echoes, cries of past and present misery, confusion and despair, and no one sees or hears them but me. My mother isn't crazy now; she's perfectly all right, but I don't like it here, and I'm not staying. The leap of sympathy I felt exists only in my imagination; in real life, face to face, it doesn't come. I can't talk to her now, I never could, and I never will. It isn't right between us and there's nothing I can do to make it so. That's not forgiveness, but recognition will just have to do. I'm on my way out the door when my mother calls out, "Sara, wait!" and groans and creaks her way upstairs. She comes back, holds out her hand to me. Rolling in the middle of the palm is a single gold bead. She smiles apologetically. "I found it in my shoe. It must have gotten stuck in there. I've been saving it for you. Maybe now the beads will fit." I take the bead and squeeze her hand. "Goodbye Mom. I'll be seeing you."

As I pull the car out of the driveway I look back. My mother stands in the driveway facing me as I'm about to drive away. I haven't kissed her goodbye, or even hugged her. She looks old, frail, bedraggled, and sad. It occurs to me that she's not serene, she's beaten. Now that the space between us is widening again, I feel once more a stab of pity. I stop the car and wave. She continues to stare into space, blankly. What's wrong? Then I realize she can't see far enough to tell I'm waving at her. I honk the horn, flail my hand out the window. She jumps slightly, then her face lights up, she smiles the ghost of that old familiar dimpled smile, that movie smile, the nearsighted public smile for the audience up front she's not quite sure is there. It's a nice smile, and she waves an odd, jaunty, flipflop wave in our direction. But not at me, not at the real me, no, never, not at me.

THE FUTURE

Joseph McElroy

Joseph McElroy was born in Brooklyn, New York, in 1930. He was educated at Williams College and Columbia University, and is the author of five novels; a sixth, *Women and Men*, is forthcoming. He has received numerous awards, including one from the American Academy of Arts and Letters.

After the event he will have his story and she will have hers. The event will amount to little more than a brief, unwelcome scare. They're the same people before and after the event, the mother and her twelve-year-old son, her "twelve-year-old." They are still there. They won't go away. But he will have his story and she will have hers. After all, they never were the same. There they are at the end of the day, at seven-thirty, quarter to eight, when she swung open the front door and he was waiting for her and tonight not on the phone but right there in front of her, standing in the entrance to their living room. He was sort of smiling, as if he had seen her coming. He was wearing the pale-orange collarless shirt she'd about decided he didn't like, and his new, expensive sneakers. He had combed his hair wetly, having apparently taken a shower. Waiting for her there between living room and front hall, he made her think of times she had come home from the office thinking, What if he isn't there?—aged ten, aged eleven. It was his sneakers that made her think of those times. And she knew now, in the instant before he said, "Can we go out to dinner?" that, getting in ahead of his mother, he was going to say what she was about to say. Her keys in one hand, in the other her shopping bag from the fruit-and-vegetable market, she went and kissed him and seemed to walk around him and into the apartment. "Shall we?" she said. She put the two pink grapefruit and the beautiful bluish-green broccoli and the watercress in the refrigerator and the bananas in the wooden salad bowl on the kitchen table. Had she really been about to say, "Let's go out to dinner"? She remembered the large, unripe avocado in her leather shoulder bag on the chair, and she removed it and put it with the bananas, laid it within the curve. She had not paid for the avocado.

In the small, narrow restaurant are two rows of tables against either wall. At one end, the kitchen; at the other, the street window, maybe fifteen feet from their table. Tonight she was facing the street.

There was the door to the street, to the vestibule, actually, and between the door and the first table, across the aisle from where she and her son sat, was a nook for the cash register. This was an ornate, old-fashioned thing that, if you looked at it, maybe didn't go with the fresh, elegant plainness of the place. It was a French restaurant, but it was cheap. A black man who she was sure wasn't French worked in the kitchen, and the owner, a tall, gray-haired, gently tense man who looked as if he had been in another profession for years, did much of the cooking. They served mainly crêpes and quiches. The tables were set with green-rimmed butter plates and a flower in a cheap glass vase. All around was a composed look of care and economy. Her son usually faced the street window and she faced the rear of the room, which gave her a view of all the tables. Tonight he put his hand on her elbow as they entered, and she went first; so she was sitting with her back to the kitchen and to most of the restaurant.

She would see her son and herself before and after the event. The event itself will be in question, come and gone along the greater event of their life together, which is also in question, and she will know that she could have predicted this—she had the power, the experience; for a long time she let her power be.

They are quite content together. On several other visits here, they never once found this table occupied; it was their regular table. When she and Davey sat down together here at the end of a long day, she didn't care about anything, not even—but in a good sense—the questions she asked him about his day, his friends Michael and Alex and the others, homework, the cleaning woman, a thank-you letter he was supposed to write. These questions he answered. Actually, tonight he had been talking since they left the apartment about his weekend arrangements. She always wanted him to tell her what he was feeling when she came home at night. It was important.

The waitress, a young Frenchwoman, who wore a white blouse and a black skirt, brought a glass of white wine and a Coke and the menus. The wine, like a lens, held a pale-saffron transparency, and for a minute it stood untouched between the butter plate and the flower in the vase while Davey drank his Coke and, changing the subject, told his mother about a new record. He had only three dollars left from his allowance. She smiled with skeptical indulgence. She liked reading the menu, which never changed.

Davey had it all planned. He laid out the whole weekend and she listened. She sipped her wine and thought about a cigarette. He would take his suitcase to school in the morning and he and his friend Alex would be picked up in the car by Alex's mother. Alex's father came out by train in the early evening. They were going horseback riding and deep-sea fishing, and Alex's parents had a tennis court and a pool. The pool was empty until next month. The weekend was a *fait accompli*, Davey's mother was going to point out to him, for she had not been consulted.

"I see we're getting something for the money we're shelling out on your tuition," she said.

"Yeah, Ann, you've got the weekend off," he said.

She liked him. He was surprising. "Yeah, Dave, I'm glad for you," she returned.

"For me?"

"For both of us."

"Are you going out?" he asked.

"Haven't been asked," she said.

"You poor thing," he said.

"But I don't need to be," she said.

"But you've got stuff to do around the house, right?"

"Don't I ever surprise you?" she said.

The waitress came, and Davey had what he always had, cannelloni with meat sauce—not exactly French. His mother decided to have marinated celery roots first, and then a vegetable crêpe. Davey asked the waitress if they had avocado. The waitress smiled and shook her head. He had developed a taste for avocado.

The waitress came back with the julienned celery roots. Ann tasted some; she held it in her mouth like wine, and her stomach seemed to contract. The taste swelled in three or four distinct waves.

Two couples came in together but sat at separate tables. The place was quiet and private. Davey asked his mother if that stuff was any good. She nodded. He broke off a hunk of bread.

She was feeling O.K., she thought. She let the marinade dilute along her tongue before she drank off her wine.

She told Davey he could have asked her before arranging his weekend. Call them, he said. She certainly would, she said; he would need money for the horseback riding. No, he said, the horses belonged to Alex's aunt, who was in the hospital with arthritis. You don't go to the hospital for arthritis, she said, and wondered if that was true. Alex's aunt had to go, said Davey; she was having an operation. One horse was a palomino.

Davey looked at the bread he was nibbling, and kept an eye on the kitchen. His mother offered him the last forkful of the celery roots, but he pulled in his chin, shaking his head. The waitress paused to see if Ann was through and discreetly crossed to the cash register and wrote something down. She came back and took Ann's plate.

"So Alex's aunt has galloping arthritis."

"My God, that's sick," said Davey, shaking his head and sort of smiling.

"You, my dear," said his mother, "mentioned the operation and the palomino in one casual breath."

"It's what Alex said."

"It's what you said."

"Well, 'galloping arthritis' is what *you* said."

"That's true."

"You just don't want me to go," her son concluded.

This wasn't true, but she didn't say so. For a moment they looked over each other's shoulders.

The waitress came with Ann's vegetable crêpe and Davey's cannelloni. She held her tray and with a napkin put Davey's dish in front of him; it was an ovenproof dish with raised edges. "It's hot," his mother and the waitress said.

A year of weekends, a future of learning the deep seas and the American trails. A back flip so slow above the blank tiles of an empty April pool that the diver holds virtually still among all his dreams of action within unlimited time, and before he finds the pool below him it has been filled.

She raised her empty glass and caught the waitress's eye.

"They have a diving board," said Davey. "I told Alex you were a champion diver."

"That's not true, dear," she said, startled.

"Well, you did it in college."

"For a while I did."

"We're going to a drive-in movie Saturday night," said Davey. "They've got a drive-in right near this golf course, Alex said."

She's already there, but it's somewhere else, and she imagines a couple passing on an adjacent highway, and the giant heads of the two romantic leads stand high to the left at an angle like that of a door ajar. And she has arranged for this night highway to run in the opposite direction at a speed of fifty-five miles an hour, so that the couple can keep driving and still see their movie from that tall and curious angle all the way to the end.

"If I give you money for the movie, you won't spend it on that record, will you?" said Ann.

"I was thinking of giving the record to Alex," said Davey. "You know, as a present. I know he wants it."

"Why don't you give his mother something; she's picking you up and driving you out there."

"I don't know what she'd like," said Davey.

Ann did not care any more than he did. They were enjoying the advantage of the menu's variety, as they would not be able to do at home, where an avocado was slowly ripening and watercress didn't need to be bought for tomorrow night's salad. Her hand dropped to feel her shoulder bag hanging from the back of her chair by its strap. She had enough money to fly to Boston and leave Davey in front of the TV set watching the game; the Yankees were on the road in a different time zone. She'd fly to a city that was part Boston, part San Francisco, and fly back before the game was over, as if Davey couldn't put himself to bed. But, once begun, the picture would not stop, and something stirred in the kitchen of her dark apartment and she heard him get out of bed and go see what it was. She kept forgetting what it was that was in Boston and San Francisco, and she kept falling asleep when she knew he was in the kitchen alone with that sound that didn't stop. It was the avocado sprouting from its pit—hard to believe but easy to hear—and he was having an educational experience in the middle of the night watching it, but she couldn't keep awake she was so mad.

"I'll give you fifteen dollars and that will be your allowance, and you can pay for your movie and you can buy them all ice cream Saturday night," she said.

"O.K., Mom, thanks. How's your crêpe?"

Her vegetable crêpe was better than his cannelloni, she was sure.

While she listened to him volunteer a progress report on what was going on in school—what was going on in science—which he almost never did, the avocado pit kept shedding light by means of the tree that grew out of it. She was sure. The light opened up the apartment house and flattened it and spread it out to become something like land, but it was more like time, and time that there was no way anymore of measuring. And the answer was that this new variety of avocado could either ripen or at its heart be totally and with unprecedented richness a pit, all pit—hence the tree, hence the light, and the apartment house turning into a land of new time. Picture all that, she thought.

She thought he was being nice to her, telling her what they were doing in science class. Yes, she knew about genes and she had heard of Mendel, but she had forgotten that it was pea plants he studied. It was about inheriting traits, and it was all about dominant and recessive. She thought of chins, she thought of personalities. Davey talked fast, looking over her shoulder, and she told him she thought he had it just slightly mixed up but she couldn't remember for sure. He said that that was how Mr. Skull had explained it.

Mr. Skull?

Mr. Skull.

She hadn't heard of Mr. Skull. Maybe they presented it differently now, she said.

Well, according to Mr. Skull, Mendel was a monk and a schoolteacher, and wasn't known during his own lifetime, and eventually his eyesight started to go; but what mattered was that he took the next step. Nowadays, they knew that Mendel didn't have the whole truth; there was a lot of stuff he hadn't gotten up to.

"But you will," she said.

"But it won't necessarily be true," said Davey, and as his mother reached in her bag for her cigarettes he opened a book of matches that had been lying in the ashtray, but she put her cigarette pack on the table and shook her head.

"True?" she said, remembering words. "Truth is just what two people are willing to agree on."

"It must be more than that," said Davey.

"Nope," she said.

"Who said?"

"Actually, your father. He said that."

"He did?"

"Yes, he did. I can assure you he said that."

She didn't like her tone. Alone with her son, Ann had gotten used to being very alert, yet she lived also with this single-minded sense of hers that she wasn't seeing everything. Yet she knew she was a good mother.

She hadn't seen the door to the small vestibule open. She was mopping the last of the oil off her salad plate with the last crust of their bread. Then she saw the young man in the white doorway. He wore bluejeans and a leather jacket. He paused, she felt, to give a person he'd come to see time to see him. He was looking toward the far end of the restaurant, where the kitchen was—the far end of what was really just a room.

The young man passed their table, and she said, "*He* didn't come here to eat."

"How do *you* know?" said her son. "He probably works here."

"Either he's the dishwasher or his girlfriend works here," she said.

"Well, he's talking to the waitress," said her son. "She's sitting at the last table and he said something to her."

"You see?" she said, observing Davey, and chewing her bread and holding and gently tilting her wineglass. She knew that the man in jeans wasn't the young French waitress's boyfriend.

"She's pointing," said her son, and his mother raised her finger to her lips in case they could hear Davey back there. "He's going to the phone. There's a phone on the wall right by the entrance to the kitchen."

"Well, that's what he came in for," she said. "He's not the waitress's boyfriend."

"Isn't he a little young for her?" said her son.

"I wouldn't be surprised," she said. The young man had long ginger hair, lank but carefully combed, and eyes like those of some animal so rarely seen that its ordinariness is what is most striking during a brief moment of exposure; his short, light-brown leather jacket looked as if it had traveled, and there was a touch of color about him she didn't identify at the moment. She looked into her son's face and was tired for the first time today.

"That was a pretty quick phone call," he said. "That was a quickie."

"Maybe he was calling his girlfriend," she said.

"He just disappeared, if you want to know," said her son. "He must have gone to the bathroom."

"I bet that's why he really came in here."

"But he asked the waitress for the phone."

"That was what he was thinking of when he first came in."

"Hey," her son remarked, looking toward the far end of the room, "that was quick. He came right out." Davey stared intimately or absently into her eyes, so she knew the man was approaching. She felt the vibrations in her feet and her chair.

As the young man in the leather jacket passed and she smelled a smell she couldn't quite place, her son looked around over his shoulder and watched the man leave after pausing once more, as if the brass doorknob in his hand had made him remember something.

"Did he get through to the person he was calling?" she asked.

"I don't think so," said her son, as the waitress came to their table and the man left.

The waitress told them what there was for dessert. The boy turned around in his chair to look at the table by the window, where there were some fruit tarts on two plates. His mother knew he would have mousse. The owner was standing by the cash register, and the waitress excused herself and turned to him. The owner raised his hand and pointed with a finger that seemed to have just pressed a cash-register key, and she went back toward another table. She returned with a twenty-dollar bill and a check.

Music got turned on and off. Ann knew Davey was aware of her mood; otherwise he'd have forgotten their little discussion about the weekend except as part of a general mulling-over that he probably didn't spell out.

They were going to have chocolate mousse and apricot—no, strawberry—tart. The waitress went to the kitchen, the owner right behind her.

"Alex's mother swam the English Channel," said Davey.

"She did not," said Ann. "That just isn't true."

"All but two miles, coming from France; if she'd been swimming the other way, she would have made it."

"Where did you hear that?"

"Alex said so," said Davey.

"Well, I doubt it," his mother remarked.

Behind him, she thought, was her dessert, on a table; behind her was his dessert, in a refrigerator in the kitchen. The two of them might be having the littlest of fights; no outsider would be able to tell. The young man with ginger hair appeared again in the doorway and entered the restaurant.

"Here he is again," said Ann softly, looking Davey in the eye so that he turned around and stared at the man, who looked at Ann, who, when her son turned back and put his elbows on the table facing her, said to him as if she were talking about anything but the young man, "maybe he's suddenly developed an interest in the waitress."

"*Mom,*" said Davey softly, embarrassed.

The young man was waiting for something to happen, she was sure, but it wasn't clear what.

"Can I have a taste of your mousse?" she said.

"If it ever comes," said Davey.

The young man strode past them toward the rear of the restaurant.

"What's he doing?" said Ann.

"He's got his hand on the phone and the owner's telling him not to keep coming in here using the phone."

"How do you know?"

"I can tell."

"Well, what's he going to do about it?"

"It's a free country," said Davey. "I'd call the police."

Ann laughed and for a moment found she couldn't stop—it was all over her face and in spasms in her abdomen. Davey smiled with grudging modesty at his remark, keeping an eye on the far end of the room. Ann started up again and stopped. She drank some water as if she already had the hiccups. "You're good for a laugh, kid," she said. Her impulse to laugh had passed.

"He's talking to the waitress," said Davey.

"What is *le patron* doing?"

"You mean the owner?" said Davey. "He's talking to the black guy in the kitchen."

"Where is our waitress?"

"She's talking to the guy who came in. Or he's talking to her. She smiled. At least, I think she did."

"She what?"

"She doesn't have my chocolate mousse."

Ann felt the treads coming along the carpeted floor, and the waitress and the young man in bluejeans passed, and the waitress went to the cash register.

"You see?" said Ann, and Davey turned to look. "She *is* his girl." For the man, who had his back to them, had put his hand lightly on the waitress's shoulder. The waitress wasn't doing anything.

"You might just be right," said Davey, glancing back at them and seeing what his mother meant. He shrugged.

"Or his sister, maybe?" said Ann, who turned instinctively to see the owner, at the back of the restaurant, step out of the kitchen.

The ginger-haired man now brought his other hand up and gripped the waitress's right arm just above the elbow, and she jerked her head around to the right, as if the street door were opening.

"No, I'm wrong," said Ann, and Davey, hearing her voice, turned to look and half rose in his chair as the man standing behind the waitress at the cash register drew her back and pivoted her away from the register and around to face back down the length of the restaurant, as if, breaking the restaurant's privacy, she were going to announce that there was a call for someone—or no, that there was a fire, no problem, or something had been lost, or the place was being closed down and the money would be refunded. And as he spoke, sharply and low behind her, there was a close moment not of ventriloquism so much as intimate agreement, when his command seemed jointly to be hers: they were about the same height, he was the roughly dressed brother or consort, and the composed life of this pleasing place derived from his behind-the-scenes industry.

His information that they were to go into the bathroom was as clear as the angle Davey's half-risen body cast in relation to his mother facing him and to the close pair on his right, three or four feet behind him.

She said, "Sit down"—was it that he was trying to be brave?—but the man, having spoken, looked away from the rest of the restaurant at the two of them and particularly at Davey, as if he could do more than speak. Ann felt the chill. And Davey was not sitting down. He had pushed his chair back and was standing up, turned to the waitress and the holdup man.

His mother had, she felt, received for them both the news that they were all going to the rear of the restaurant, into the bathroom, which was the place where you waited out this mandatory drill, which was to see how well it could be done. There must have been words; why they were so low she did not know, but what was happening was clear enough. Davey stepped away from the table and stood contemplating the young man and woman up against each other, the one somewhat hurried and scanning the room, the other rigid, and Ann for a moment didn't reach for Davey, in case the man did something. The man was saying, Hurry, with his eyes.

In one movement she rose and stepped around the table, hearing others behind her moving—she couldn't look back quite yet—and she got Davey by the elbow, his arm firm but not muscular, and drew him with her away from the waitress and the man. The man's hand, his left hand, was definitely up against the waitress's spine, and his forearm had seemed turned, as if a knife handle was gripped in his palm.

Ann had her leather bag on her shoulder. She was startled not to remember taking it. She had her arm around Davey's shoulder. The five or six customers ahead of them moving politely, as if there had been a power failure to be patient about, were people she'd hardly noticed when she'd come in—when they'd come in. Now, following them, she found them even less real to her—all except a blond woman in her fifties with a lacquered bouffant—less real to her than they had obscurely been in the privacy of her dinner with her son. Tonight Davey had had the view.

She remembered nothing and prophesied little, but she had seen finality in the alert glance the young man had given Davey. It didn't matter who Davey was—he was a person who happened to be there, there and then, from out of a field of chances. And a sudden killing in self-defense followed their backs as, the last customers to file to the rear and turn right and crowd into the bathroom, she and Davey were followed in by the owner, who shook his head gently at her and the others and raised his palm—as if any of them were going to do anything.

The little bathroom was unexpectedly long. Davey's hair was up against her nose and she put her arm around in front of him across his stomach, and she turned to look into the eyes of a short, bald man, who instantly frowned and turned away from her toward the toilet end, where there was a small, half-open window. "Where does that lead to?" he asked importantly, but the owner, whom he did not look back at, continued to shake his head. The bald man said, "Excuse me," and edged between the others and reached around them to the toilet, leaning over it. "Anyone else want to leave your wallet behind the toilet?"

A dark woman in a dark turtleneck sweater, whose shoulder was against a dark man, also in a dark turtleneck, with such firm tightness that you knew if you followed their arms downward you would find them holding hands, said, "What if he wants your wallet—what are you going to give him?"

"I got ten bucks in my pocket," the man said.

"Ten bucks," said the woman. "Are you kidding?"

The waitress had not appeared. The owner was shaking his head, but now to himself. They were close together in the narrow, longish lavatory, yet exposed by the peculiarly high ceiling. Ann didn't count how many were crowded in here. Davey whispered huskily, so the others heard, "There are ten people in here."

The dark man in the dark turtleneck looked a bit scared. The blond woman, whose lacquered bouffant seemed to be in the wrong restaurant, had pursed her lips, but she bent around and gave the bald man a kiss that just missed his mouth. The black man at the door turned on the basin faucet and turned it off. The two young men who were at the rear by the toilet and the window had given way for the bald man to stash his wallet. One of them now said, "Are your lunch receipts in that register?"

The owner hesitated. He seemed to have a clear sense of what was outside the room where they were. "There's always a first time," he said, and his accent gave a poignance to his words. "Well, it's too bad," said the other young man by the toilet. "It really is." His friend said, "My spinach quiche is getting colder by the minute," and the other said, "Remember Greece—they said you should never eat food piping hot."

Davey leaned the back of his head against his mother's shoulder and growled softly, "Where's my mousse?" He said to the owner, "Somebody ought to see what's happened to the waitress."

The owner opened the door and seemed to hear something and slipped out.

Ann hugged Davey. Her arm came around his stomach. "Did he say, 'Everyone into the bathroom'?" she asked, and she looked down at her bag, its flap covering the top but not fastened down through its leather loop.

"No," Davey said, "he said, 'Everyone get into the back into the bathroom'—that's what he said."

"I guess he doesn't want us," said the woman in the dark turtleneck.

"Beware of pickpockets," growled Davey in his mother's ear.

A terrific sadness descended upon her. The black man eased himself out the door.

"I don't think I want my mousse," said Davey.

"We'll ask for the check," Ann said. She put both hands on Davey's shoulders. *When this is all over,* she meant.

"Do you want your strawberry tart?" he asked.

The owner appeared and said the man had gone.

The man who had hidden his wallet asked one of the young men to pass it to him.

The restaurant, when they came out, seemed especially empty, because the waitress was at the far end by the window, sitting beside the pastry desserts, huddled in the chair, and the black man was comforting her. She was quietly hysterical; she was not quite sobbing. She looked as if she were waiting for someone. There were half-empty wineglasses and salad plates with forks across them and chairs pushed back. Someone said, "I wonder if he helped himself."

It had been over so soon that Ann couldn't think, except that with a pistol the young man could have made them go with him. Or killed someone just like that, so the person wouldn't be around to go through mug shots at the local precinct. She didn't know the address of the local precinct or what number precinct it was.

The waitress sat in the window crying. People were sitting down again. Ann told the owner she would have her coffee later. This sounded as if they were having hot dogs and beans in a diner. The check included the chocolate mousse and the strawberry tart. The owner subtracted the desserts.

The waitress stood up and smiled. Now it was the waitress Ann was paying; the owner was outside in the street. Davey looked up into the waitress's face. He didn't say anything.

"Are you all right?" said Ann as the waitress put down on the table the change from a twenty. "Have you ever been in a holdup before?"

The woman shook her head. She had shining blue eyes and rather curly brown hair, and she was tall and had delicate shoulders.

Davey said, "Our money is all that's in the cash register."

Ann, being a genial, alert parent in the waitress's presence, said, "Then where did she get the change from?"

"That's a good question."

"Have you seen him before?" Ann asked the waitress.

The waitress shook her head. "I hardly looked at him."

"I'd never forget him," said Davey.

Ann heard herself say, "He was wearing a turquoise belt buckle."

The waitress excused herself. Ann left two dollars and as they got up to leave Davey asked what percentage that was.

"Something over fifteen per cent."

It was the very same restaurant, except that the owner, like a neighborhood Parisian, was standing out front, looking contemplatively down the street. A cab turned into the street and came very slowly by with a passenger looking out the window.

"Do you think he was dangerous?" Ann asked.

"*Mom,*" said Davey, embarrassed.

"I think so," said the gray-haired man, his eyebrows raised.

"How much did he get?" asked Davey.

The man looked down at Davey and smiled and shook his head, but it didn't mean he didn't know.

"Are the police coming?" said Davey.

The owner gestured toward the street. "That's what they said."

When Ann and Davey said good night to the owner, the holdup was all his. At the next corner Ann looked back and he was gone. Some people seemed to be looking at the menu in the window.

"Why did you shush me when I asked if the man was dangerous?" Ann asked.

"Because of course he was dangerous. He had a gun."

"I think it was a knife."

"No, it was definitely a gun. I saw it."

"I don't see how."

"I was even closer than you."

"But they were still behind you, and when he pulled her out into the aisle his arm, his forearm, was turned around the way it would be if he had a knife handle in his palm."

"I know I saw the metal of a gun."

"I'm sure you're wrong."

"I saw it."

"You saw something."

They crossed another avenue as the light changed in the middle.

Ann took Davey's arm. He didn't crook it at the elbow.

"It's going to be a good weekend," said Ann.

They walked in silence.

"I got to call Michael and Alex," said Davey.

"You're going to see Alex tomorrow."

"I'm going to see them both tomorrow. I've got to tell them about the holdup."

"Listen, it was real, Davey, it was serious."

"You're not kidding it was serious," said her son. "We could have gotten killed."

"Well, I doubt that," she said, "but I was afraid he might reach for you, Davey, and he might have if the police had arrived." But it wasn't delayed-reaction fear that seemed now to be overtaking her.

"How could the police have arrived?" said Davey. "No one called them till after it was all over."

"You know what I mean."

"This was my first holdup. I want to tell Michael and Alex about it, O.K.?"

"We're not even sure what happened."

"I know what I saw."

"In the bathroom?"

"In the restaurant."

"But before and after the holdup."

"*And* during."

"But we can't even agree whether it was a knife or a gun."

"*You* can't agree."

"Look, let's go back and ask the waitress."

"*Mom.*"

"Why don't we phone them when we get home?"

"That's fine with me. I don't know why you don't want me to phone my friends."

"It was *my* first holdup, too," she said, taking his hand and squeezing it.

But as soon as they got home she went and ran herself a bath. It was what she should have done in the first place this evening when she came home from work. She was so tired it had to be in her head. She stepped outside the bathroom and closed the door. The water pouring into the tub seemed larger at a distance.

She listened for a moment and went to the bedroom door. She knew Davey; she pictured him. She heard him open the refrigerator, and she was sure she heard the freezer door unstick. She did not hear the refrigerator door close, but she heard a plate rattle in the closet and a kitchen drawer open. He was looking for a spoon. She heard the voice of a baseball commentator come on, and a moment later she heard Davey's voice, talking fast and excited.

She was sitting in the tub, leaning forward to turn off the water. The door was open a little, so she heard the voices in the living room.

Davey called. She called back that she was in the bathtub.

The voices continued.

Then it was only the baseball commentator's voice, rising and falling. She let it stay where it was. Somewhere in the silence around that voice, an icepick was being hammered into a stolen, rock-hard avocado. The hot water was almost too hot to dream in. She'd had the money for that avocado but would rather shuttle herself by astral projection to Boston/San Francisco—not that anyone was there anymore.

She heard Davey's voice again; it didn't sound the same. It sounded as if he were phoning the movies for the times, but the call went on longer.

Then there was only the TV again, then a knock on the bathroom door, which moved, but Davey didn't come in. "You were wrong," he said. "It was a gun."

"Well what do you know," she said quietly from the still tub.

"No, I'm only kidding, Mom; they wouldn't tell me."

"You spoke to the waitress?"

"No, he wouldn't let me, and he said they weren't discussing the matter."

"O.K.," she said very quietly.

"Hey, don't go to sleep in there."

She thought she heard steps cross the carpet. In a moment she heard Davey on the phone again. Which friend would he have phoned first? The picture wasn't clear. He was closer to Michael; their lives had some big similarities, like his father not living with him.

The bath seemed to become deeper and deeper. Her legs came up in a revolving jackknife and she did a two and a half, a three and a half, an unheard-of four and a half, the way she would do slow-motion somersaults underwater at the deep end of a pool in the summer while Davey would hold his nose and do underwater somersaults with her, though he couldn't really stay down.

She didn't want to go to sleep in the bath, but she was damn well going to. If she'd taken a bath when she'd gotten home from the office, they would never have had a holdup. They would have had broccoli and melted cheese, and green noodles, with garlic (which Davey now liked). And strawberry ice cream, which he had just been eating anyway.

She might have been asleep when she heard Davey call from the middle distance, "Are you asleep in there, Mom? Are you O.K.?" But she felt she had had her eyes open. She didn't want to talk about the holdup, didn't want to think about it. She closed her eyes. The water didn't have quite the hot fixity it had when she first stepped cautiously in. But it was good to her and she let the questions called to her go unanswered. Her eyes were closed, but she wasn't sleeping. She heard Davey come across the carpet, and though she heard the door move, she didn't think he was looking at her. She felt the water stir subtly about her; she had willed it to move for her benefit. She knew he had gone away. She massaged her dry face, and her knees broke the surface.

She listened for a while. The TV was still on. She heard Davey's voice, its quality of inquiring esteem for the other person, its habit of waiting humor. For a second she thought of her son's, any kid's, inspired account of a brush with violence—*And then you know what happened?*—and she smelled in her soap, melting somewhere near her leg, a sweeter apricot smell of freesias. (They had tried to charge her six-fifty for a small bunch last week at the supposedly wholesale flower market.) Within the scent of freesias there was a hidden, earlier, heavier vein of sweetness that she now identified as after-shave but didn't want to think about. For some moments Davey hadn't been speaking, or not so she could hear, but the TV was still on, so he hadn't gone to bed. And yet the silence beyond the TV wasn't quite silence. He would be getting away from all the city noise this weekend. A lot *he* cared about the noise.

She got herself out of the tub, and against the wash of the bathwater listened again. She ran her arms damply into the sleeves of her terry-cloth robe. She pulled open the door and put her wet foot down on her bedroom carpet.

Have a nice evening, lady, the flower man had said. Have a nice life, he said. The pale-apricot-colored freesias were doing pretty well on her bureau. The man had let her have them for six dollars.

Halfway to the door leading to the living room, she was on the point of calling to Davey that it was time for bed, when she heard his voice. "I don't know whether I can," he was saying, and then there was a pause. "Maybe I'll ask her." Then, "I will ask her; I definitely will." Then, "She's O.K." Then, "Fifteen dollars, including my allowance." Then, "Yeah, I love you too." Ann knew the voice at the other end of the line without hearing it; but she owed Davey his privacy even after he said goodbye and hung up. The commercial between innings ended, and the deep-voiced, happy commentator was back on.

She stood in the living-room doorway. Davey was sitting over near the entrance to the front hall beside the phone. He could see the game only at the narrowest angle; he could hardly see the screen.

Ann went to the set and turned it off. "Time for bed," she said. Davey just sat there by the phone. They had divided the evening between them.

She had to give them both a break, so she said, "You didn't need to call collect." They both knew what she meant.

"How did you know I called collect?" Davey asked.

"I've known for a long time, but you really don't have to."

"Thanks," he said, and stayed where he was, still dressed for the restaurant.

She didn't tell him not to thank her. "You're welcome," she said.

"So are you," he said.

"So are you," she said.

A POSTAL CREED

BEN BROOKS

Ben Brooks was born in 1948 and now lives in Cambridge, Massachusetts, where he teaches writing to elementary-school students as writer-in-residence in the Massachusetts public schools. He was a Fellow at the Fine Arts Work Center in Provincetown, Massachusetts, from 1975 to 1977. His stories have been published in *The Denver Quarterly*, *Confrontation*, *Epoch*, *Story Quarterly*, and elsewhere.

He died and a raiding party, led by his wife, scrounged through the attic so there was nothing at all left in two days. He was not that old—still active when his foot ran through a rotten board and dirty splinters shot up the inside of his pants and cut into a muscle and tore it. In the hospital they bandaged him but he developed fever, and then breathing trouble, and then he died. The moment of death seemed to teeter between light and heavy, relief but at the same time a weight, a burden, clotting inside. They ran preservative into his veins and sent him home so the neighbors could see. His wife, looking for an old hat in the attic, came across his collection. Mildewed boxes in a corner, where the roof slanted down and a board underfoot sagged. She took one look and called the authorities, and in two days it was gone. With her old pink hat on she had a sudden panic. She needed to ward off suspicion, that she saw could lick up at her like wild flames, might shoot from angry neighbors, flames with black-tipped scars. One call and it was done.

He had welfare checks, birthday cards, magazines, personal letters, advertisements, packages. Some were not even opened. Some dated back 22 years. He'd been a mailman that long, U. S. Postal Service. He never cashed checks or answered letters, but sometimes he kept what he carried. In one box they found candy gone moldy, and in another two dead mice. Odor burst into the attic when they slit the cardboard. One check was for $400, made out to Randall Grant, from the First City Bank of Trenton.

"Epluribus Jones," the minister said one morning, "a good man." He had a black robe on that came nearly to his wrists, a chain about his neck, a hat in the fashion of Sir Isaac Newton. Epluribus was in an open coffin. His hands were folded over his belt. He lay below the pulpit. They'd left him in the blue-gray uniform of the Postal Service, but clipped the shiny visor of the hat away so the coffin could close. They buried him in the early afternoon. His postal patrons came to watch.

Word of what he'd done spread through the route like fire in a droughted forest. Public outrage, so cleanly focused, does that. Telephones burst with indignation, and windows dropped so neighbors could shout through. It was too late to hush it, the first box found. People want their mail. Lines formed at the Post Office before the flowers on his grave were trampled. People want their mail. They crammed into the waiting room and hovered about the windows, watching for unusual packets. The new widow locked herself in her home, and drew curtains and mourned.

Back mail is a serious thing. One man remembered a magazine he'd never received, though he'd written an angry letter to the publisher. They owed him 12 issues. A woman recalled a welfare check, and another the time she'd been in the hospital and certain people had not sent cards. Everyone wants to know what's what. "A defunct mail-carrier," the dead man's colleague said at the window. "We cannot help now what was done. There's no one here to blame." But he had to apologize. "We're doing the sorting as fast as we can." Households along the route were strung with wire. Information sizzled. What one guessed another dreaded.

The sorting was slow work. Some of the addresses no longer existed. Some patrons had moved, others died. People were angry. Everything was opened before it was handed away. They were looking for a reason. Patrons sat on the high tables in the back of the room, where they bolt the zip code books. Some had it in mind to sue. Others made noise, and tore thick handfuls of government numbers away.

The neighborhood changed quickly in the aftermath. The outrage of mail undelivered boiled over. Consider this: A man with money went to a self-service pump at a gas station on Fourth Street and started pumping gasoline into a huge nylon-skinned balloon. He had the balloon on a trailer hitched to the rear of his car. It was blimp-shape, limp as a dead whale. He filled the balloon tight. Its sides wobbled and gasoline sloshed inside. An iridescent drip salivated down the smooth skin below the mouth of the tank. This was a time of scarcity. Cars curled around the corner and down the street waiting for gas. "I'm going to burn it!" the man shouted. "Money buys!" People shut their engines off to conserve. They froze in their cars. "Money buys!" The man handed the hose to his son, and went from window to window. "I'm going to have an explosion in my backyard and burn the whole goddam thing. Money buys!"

The blimp took shape. The sides of the balloon stretched out. The man's son held the hose tight as a lifeline. "Sheer waste!" the man yelled. "You hear?" His cries spread like dirty vapor and settled into pores. He took the hose from his son when the blimp was full and sprayed gasoline over asphalt. Little rivers formed under cars. The man who owned the station kept his eyes on the meter. He notched on paper each time it turned over. The bill came to $512.72. The man paid fast with cash. People left their cars to throw gravel (and plastic spoons from gutters) at the gorged blimp. The street ran with gas as if the earth had shifted. But the man could afford it. And every Christmas he'd handed Epluribus five dollars, and he'd been shocked that there were three packages undelivered, and a horde of mail in a shoebox.

The owner of the station rushed the rest of his customers through. Why not? He stood by the pump keeping tally on his notepad. He had a greasy blue jacket and a square gray hat with a fur rim turned up on all four sides. "OK, OK," he said, "next one, come on, help yourself now." But every patron was dripping gasoline on the ground and paying for it. Even the poorest, at least one squirt. The owner stuffed money in his pockets. His station ran out of gas, sucked dry. Waiting cars drove off skidding into curbs. The owner left for home two hours early, fat with money. And a twice frustrated customer bought a mousetrap with a razor bar, which he set for the new mailman in the letter slot of his door.

The biggest upset was never mail that had been expected but not received. That already had a niche in the brain—mail always known, finally explained. The biggest upset became mail never even suspected. There were letters from long-lost lovers, scribbled invitations, notes telling of small inheritances or announcing deaths, learned six years late.

A man from Washington came to supervise the sorting. Some pieces were impossible to identify. Epluribus had shed their envelopes. The man did not dare hang them naked on the Post Office boards. Too many prowling cats. They would fight over each piece—every claim a bullet to fire later in court. They were waiting for the whole episode to come to an end. Then it would be clear what damages could be pulled. A few brought lawyers to sit with them in the rear of the Post Office, paying out by the hour and supplying coffee.

The minister, the wife, the man himself, the neighbors. Members of the congregation signed an official reprimand, a castigation, because the minister said, "good man." Some demanded his recall by higher church officials. The wife was harassed until she nailed shut her windows and silenced her phone, and the man himself was bombarded in his box by invective and acid, and hot earth turned mucousy liquid seeped into his space. Neighbors raged and howled but never felt justice. The Postal Inspector kept turning up at their doors with new pieces of mail. The thing could not seem to end. One was a letter from an old friend suggesting a reunion, long missed, and another gave news from a hometown of four years back. Anger did not seem to affect time, and information, delayed, turned rotten like fruit and spoiled and brought bugs and worms and fast-breeding germs.

Can it be part of a man, those aspects divulged in others'

dreams and fantasies? Epluribus, melting down with spring, face still frozen in the stiff cloth hat, was here an agent of death, there nailed to a brick wall, pelted with small stones. In one dream he lay before stampeding horses, and they parted to run by, avoiding trampling him. He was little known out of uniform, and regarded only as a messenger. Is it then part of his being how he acts in another man's dream, or what role he takes in another's life? "People waiting to hear," postmen mutter. They watch the crowd nervously. The postal creed inches foolishly along the walls of the waiting room, repeated sarcastically by patrons. It is always Epluribus they picture. Tempers are short. His widow tucked his old mailbag under her mattress, out of sight. Along its cracks the leather is clean and golden. The brass buckles holding the straps are spotted. "Neither rain nor snow," they echo, as if an operator were tapping it out of them at intervals.

The coffin was shut tightly but the treated wood leaked, and Epluribus lay waiting for the ground around him to thaw. The graveyard was a new one where the grass was clipped as carefully as hair, but over Epluribus it was burned bare by chemicals. It employed two watchmen but already his headstone was knocked to the ground. The ropes that had laid him to rest had tangled so his feet were higher than his head. His widow did not dare to mourn him in public. People came by her house throwing pebbles at windows, and at night they shone flashlights, and rang the front door buzzer in calm hatred.

One piece of mail said:

> Dear Sarah,
> I love you like I never loved before. I would like to be your husband.

It was unsigned and out of envelope. The supervisor from Washington and the postal employees over his shoulder could only imagine consequences—the spurned lover, never answered; unaware Sarah, seeming cold. Was she married? Was he? Had they gotten together anyway? They tucked the little letter on crinkly blue paper into the corner of a blotter in the back of the Post Office, a reminder of duty's sacredness. Epluribus's box in the ground was mahogany, and lined with red velvet, but in the dark there were no longer colors, and his serious look, sewed on, was for none but himself. Some letters he'd burned on a wooden keg in the attic, careful with the ashes, and some he'd read in private, and others just stashed. Dead leaves from a nearby oak, brown and crisp, stuck to the bare earth above him like litter, but they were too light to be felt. The wind pulled at them, the sharp points of the leaves dancing and tickling the ground. When dogs outside the gate stopped to bark at the stillness, he could not hear, but when some of his old neighbors pissed on his grave, they slowly soaked through, and the ground, poisoned, tried to close off, pinching in on his coffin. No one would be buried near him. Former colleagues began to snicker at the letter to Sarah, malignantly glad, and they added comments around the edges of the page, obscenities penned unobserved. Is it Epluribus, really, whose spirit informs the woman her son's been killed in battle, or who withholds that information from another? Never opening the envelope he's slipped into his leather bag's side pocket, letting lies and impossible hopes bloom like deadly flowers in a mind, unwatered. Or is a messenger just a messenger—legs, a hand, a voice; blank eyes, no will?

Washington transferred the postmaster to another station, but brought no charges. He was bitter and became sloppy. He left a proud gray building deteriorating, its corners still clean and sharp, its door high, but marred with slogans in red. A window was broken, and early one morning a dozen rotten eggs were cracked over its steps. How far does a man's responsibility go? If he is unconscious of the results of his deeds, or sees them from his own perspective, can he still be blamed, or praised? If, careless, he causes an accident in his wake, and another is hurt—but he never even knows of the accident—is that guilt part of him? Behind Epluribus people grieved, and they raged, and a few laughed, looking to their day in court. And the postmaster too, the superior. The whole neighborhood changed because one simple operation, that was always taken for granted, caught on a hook and ripped, and showed the gray slimy veins of its underside. Was this Epluribus, a force of social change? Or was he just a man with a perverse delight, who took pleasure in vexing certainty, and disturbing the routine of his job?

New lawyers set up offices in the neighborhood, and unhappy people moved away. Postal patrons waited one behind the next, unsure which tack would work best: deprivation of mail, mental anguish, fraud and deceit, theft, trespassing. They multiplied damages, considered class action, tabulated fantastic figures. The rich man who'd explode a blimp in his yard felt an ulcer form in his bowels like a small planet, wondering what else he was missing—and with vengeance he set about teaching his son. The hose-bearer. His lesson was ruthlessness.

Epluribus Jones passed through seasons in his box, always rotting. His skin wrinkled and peeled back at his nails, his nose withered away, and his knee turned in the box to an almost impossible angle because its weight shifted when cartilage dropped off. His widow advertised the house for sale but no one would touch it. When the real estate woman brought out customers there was always a neighbor on hand to tell a bad story, a curse. They invented pasts more hideous than fact, and when she threatened to take them to court they laughed, saying, "try it." Neighborhood values fell daily. All about the widow Jones lots were sold. Signs stood on abandoned yards like flags, and developers and gangsters began competing for blocks, eager for control.

The whole neighborhood turned over except for the widow Jones. She took a second husband and kept her house. He was a new man in town. He yanked the nails from the windows. Values rose. Patrons relocated without suing, but remembered Epluribus and watched their new postmen with suspicion. In his grave Epluribus was down to bone and teeth. His box had rotted through and anything seeped in. The husband wanted to move but the widow Jones said no. It was their first test, a fight. Around them new apartment buildings swelled up, a storefront, a restaurant. He could have gotten a lot of money for the lot. Her own sign was still in the yard, rusting, but she rebuffed all callers.

It appeared the developers outbid the gangsters. Everything looked clean. Cold brown veneers dropped down over walls and floors, and workmen speckled red bricks with white. Men in suits came to the widow Jones, now Mrs. Martin, to talk to her about selling. They carried vinyl briefcases with polished clasps. They mentioned fantastic money, but she refused. Her new husband sat silently, listening.

Epluribus was eventually forgotten. The cemetery was plowed and developed, headstones turned under the earth with bodies. New postmen walked new routes, one after another. The new neighborhood sunk naturally into its site, as if the earth and the streets made a cradle for it. Children were born and went to school, couples fought, old men and women died. Brown walls faded gray. Floors, stepped across too often, cracked. The reputation of the neighborhood was solid. Bad citizens stood out like lights, and were watched and talked about until they moved away. Everything changed in cycles except Mrs. Martin—the old woman with a lot that stuck out like one bad debt. On real estate maps she was colored bright green. Her For Sale sign was pure rust, and its edges crumbled to the touch.

Time runs like a dump truck downhill. If the hill is long enough, and circles back, eventually everything is squashed. The mischief wrought by Epluribus mattered less and less, as the people whose mail he'd kept died, or forgot, or lost interest. A woman who might have married was now dead anyway. A book never read—so what? News, a few dollars here and there, hurt feelings, suspense. The ones left were all in their seventies and had more important things on their minds. Mrs. Martin was 82 herself. She still held on to the cracked mail pouch, which now hung on a nail on the wall. She fed old Mr. Martin, who'd had a stroke, by spoon, and listened to radio.

Epluribus's bones had been well used in cement. What was left behind fed grass. His eyes, his set face, his mind, the reasons he'd had for jettisoning expectations were as dead as he. Only the pouch remained—the old wife, the old house—to remember. But what was in her heart she never said. She pinched old Mr. Martin's chin to force open his lips, and slipped in the spoon. He'd never understood why she would not sell, and now that was too late too. He'd left his own life for hers. Even that did not matter —he was beyond caring or resenting. He waited for the spoon, eyes rolling downward: warm cereal dropped below his tongue and settled out in a pool; an occasional surprise of cold; something gristly to chew.

Then the neighborhood went to gangsters. They were a new kind, who did not worry about appearances. Pinball machines went up in lobbies, rents were raised, repairs were forgotten. Weapons became as common as shoes. Mrs. Martin added a new lock to each door, and tucked the old mailbag back under the mattress. She was old enough to remember Epluribus and wonder—not why he had stolen the mail he had been trusted to deliver, but why he'd never shared his secret with her, why he'd doubted her. Maybe he learned from himself not to trust. If you cheat, but seem not to, then others who seem innocent must be suspected as well. Epluribus must have been a suspicious man, she decided, not to have trusted her. He led her back to the past, where there were soft cushions for her mind. But she could not think what could have caused doubt, until she remembered her own secrets too.

She remembered a time she'd been unable to explain where some money he'd given her had gone. Weeks had passed, and she'd forgotten how she'd spent it. He'd shaken her shoulders with anger. Spats and fights, half-heard telephone conversations came back. Questions, denials, stone silence. The past became clear as television to her, and episodes were pictures, and voices were as they had always been. Mr. Martin had gotten worse, but she'd refused to let him leave the house for a hospital. If he needed anything he turned his wrist and a bell tinkled. It tinkled too when he died. She had her groceries delivered, her laundry taken out, and used the phone for the plumber and a cleaning woman.

Mr. Martin's funeral was in an urn. She knew there was no point in burial. They put him in a lot with sharp green grass, and gravel paths marked by flowers in spring. He had a eulogy but not much more. His body flamed nicely, nearly dried out when they lit it. His skin flaked earlier when he was on exhibit, but no one noticed. No one even walked by. In the new cemetery headstones were in rows a foot apart, nine inches between rows. Ceramic vessels were stoppered tightly to preserve ashes.

Mr. Martin had left home far away to marry the widow Jones.

He had always thought he would take her back with him. She had always refused to come. In the years that passed he lost touch back home, but never laid new roots. He worked for a time as a dress designer, and for a while he ran a store. When all the new buildings went up he got a job in one, semi-retired as desk clerk and watchman. A few people nodded hello when he gave them their messages. The gangsters left him alone.

Epluribus Jones did one unexpected thing in his life. Perhaps that is why he did it—he did not want to be only what others thought he was. Then they imagined other things of him, outrageous things, things he never was except in their thoughts. His wife clung to his memory trying to explain. He stayed clear and pink when everything else was gray. Why he did what he did, why he kept it a secret, whether it made him a different man from the one she knew. When she married she held Mr. Martin as if by a chain to her need to remember—the house, the cracked bag on the wall—until his own past withered away. Epluribus died first, victim of a long sick splinter. Then Mr. Martin, then their wife. In the end the only thing that was there to mark change was the neighborhood, turned to trash. The people who wept and the people who raged, the rich man who poured gasoline into a nylon blimp and burned it, and the lawyers who wanted to sue—they all died too. Some left children, but few remembered to pass on the story. It was old in its time. And none knew all its meanings. Even the son who held the hose for his father died, worn out in the end by greed and hostility. But the tale exists—here it is—the facts, apart from their memory. And the feelings they engendered, and the consequences, and the people who watched from the periphery, and made it a small part of their own stories. And what they learned, what they all learned. Once it occurred its permanence was assured, until such time as everything is washed over. Even death to participants, broken links in the chain of memory, have not erased past. Turn it as you will. Epluribus kept the mail, and did not tell his wife. The neighborhood festered and changed. Someone remembered.

THE PLEASURE OF HER COMPANY

JANE SMILEY

Jane Smiley was born in Los Angeles in 1949. She is the author of two novels, *Barn Blind* and *At Paradise Gate*. Her stories have appeared in *Redbook*, *TriQuarterly*, *Mademoiselle*, and other magazines. She is now teaching at Iowa State University and working on a third novel.

When Florence comes up the sidewalk toward her duplex, she can see that the large Victorian house just to the south has new owners. It is the one lovely place on her otherwise undistinguished block—porched, corniced, many-peaked and recently painted Nordic blond with piqué white trim. Each of these last few evenings, she has admired, as she does tonight, how neatly the trim glows in the twilight. She threads her way past boxes and pieces of furniture the owners have left on the sidewalk. There are two piles of women's clothing. Dishes and cutlery are stacked beside the curb, and a slender-legged plant stand supports two ferns and a grape ivy. A brown box, its lid agape, contains the *Oxford English Dictionary*, abridged edition, and two Mexican cookbooks. Draped over the back of a kitchen chair is a white dress, perhaps a wedding dress, its bodice shaped into fullness with blue tissue paper. One of its stiff lace cap sleeves has fallen off the hanger. As Florence notices this, a breeze lifts the skirt. She rearranges the sleeve on the hanger, and, unaccountably shy of being caught, hurries the rest of the way home. In the morning when she turns with her coffee cup to gaze out the window of her kitchen, the items are still on the lawn. The dress has fallen off the chair and lies spread on the green grass like a snow angel.

While she is at work, everything disappears, and that night, at last, there are lights in the windows; the stained glass she has coveted for years bejewels the darkness. There is more to covet, or at least envy, when she finally meets the Howards—Philip and Frannie. Two handmade orange rugs are flung on the hardwood floors and three or four large paintings, stretched but unframed, furnish the wide walls. There are plants. Mostly, however, there is space, so much pale floor that the rooms, as she looks through to the back porch, fit across one another like layers, inexhaustible, promising, culminating in sunlight.

Frannie has copper-colored eyes, winged brows and short, springy hair that she obviously does no more to than wash into shape. She asks Florence to sit at the round maple table for tea. Everything about Frannie, from her clumsiness with the teacups to her delight with the muffins Florence has brought for housewarming, is inviting. There is a footstep, and Frannie glances up, then takes out another plate. "Hello!" says Philip, but before he sits down, he strides around the periphery of the room, stopping twice to admire the walls and floors, to look through the open door to the front porch, to smile, and put his hands on his hips. Frannie says, "Philip still can't believe we own the place. Last night I found him out on the front porch holding on to the gingerbread and staring at the stained glass."

Philip sits at the table and leans toward Florence on his elbows. "Have you ever house-hunted? You wouldn't believe what some people do to their houses. I went to one place that looked rather charming from the outside, you know, but inside they'd cut doorways where they shouldn't have been and added on this room at the back, plastic paneling, spongy rug like fungus. It wasn't a bad house, at one time. I went outside and threw up in a trash barrel."

"Philip took house-hunting very seriously," says Frannie.

"You see how people live." He butters a muffin.

Philip, it turns out, was in high school with Florence's brother. Frannie is from Michigan; she and Philip met in college, lived for a while in the East, and only just moved back to town. Philip's youngest sister, a distant acquaintance of Florence in college, is the mother of triplets in Washington State. Philip tells them that no two strangers in the nation are separated by more than five intermediate acquaintances. When he finds out that Florence is a nurse, he asks her if she saves a life every day, and when Frannie mentions her job, directing foreign exchange programs and charter flights for the local university, he says, "Importing exotica, exporting domestica." He is obviously used to filling air and space, and he is quite handsome, but it is Frannie that Florence can't help looking at. She sits over the conversation with perfect good nature, like a child over a jack-in-the-box, waiting to be surprised into laughter. She makes Florence long to say something hilarious.

Florence goes next door, thinking that she really shouldn't be visiting again so soon. She has been there every day, sometimes twice, since they moved in two weeks ago. She brings a quarter pound of a new kind of tea, knowing that it is almost a bribe, and shouts a comical "YOO-hoo!" as she crosses the threshold. Frannie giggles from the side porch and responds in kind. The giggle is a tremendous relief to Florence, because she is ready to detect signs of boredom and exasperation in Frannie's first glance at her. The giggle allays her fears, and she grins as she pulls out a maple chair beside the maple table once again, investing the moment with her fullest, most tangible pleasure at being liked. Philip isn't there. When he is, Florence, though glad to see him, realizes that he is not the point.

Florence talks about the hospital, where she is a nurse in pediatrics. Already, Frannie has learned the names of the doctors, secretaries, and other nurses, and her evident interest renders Florence almost eloquent. She talks about the medical student she has been seeing (too young) and the photographer she is seeing now (too self-absorbed). She talks about recipes and being on the Pill and having gained and lost thirty pounds in four months. Frannie's questions and responses create such vivid images in her mind, and her smiles and rejoinders are so appropriate, that Florence grows ecstatic with conversation. She feels as though her words leap at Frannie before Frannie even finishes speaking. She follows Frannie around the house, talking. Frannie sweeps the floor, puts away the breakfast dishes, straightens one of the orange rugs, makes her bed, brushes her teeth. While Frannie is folding laundry, Florence sits on the floor of her bedroom talking and fitting the soles of Frannie's shoes along the soles of her feet. Suddenly she stops chattering and says, "I feel like I'm invading you. Are you sure you don't mind?" Frannie laughs and nods and tells her not to worry. "Do you promise to tell me to go home the first moment I get tiresome?" Florence asks.

"I promise!" Her mock exasperation is reassuring.

Florence says that her best friend in college was the most mysterious and beautiful woman she had ever met, and the only man who had ever treated her friend badly was the one she married. Florence mentions that she has saved over six thousand dollars since nursing school, and wants to buy a little house and plant raspberry canes, but the prices of houses rise faster than her savings account. Frannie says, "You know, it really was fascinating to look at houses with Philip. We went out every day with the realtor, so we really lost the sense of having our own life, and began to feel like the right house was the key to everything. On the Sunday morning after we saw this one, which we both liked, and which was empty, the agent took us to one a ways out of town. The owners were there, and they had a new baby, about ten days old. The place was spotless. There were lots of windows and awnings, and arched doorways, and the place had a sort of Provençal aura about it, maybe because the cookbooks were in French. They took us all over the house, then out into the yard, where they had planted all sorts of lilacs and dwarf apple trees and bulbs. The house was overpriced, and we would have had to replace the furnace, but Philip fell so in love that he just had to have it. Even when the realtor told him this was a better deal, Philip couldn't stop talking about how he felt there—so light and springy. I kept teasing him and saying why didn't he just call them up, since he'd made a point of writing down their name, and invite himself to dinner, but he didn't want to befriend them. He wanted to be them!" She laughs.

"I'm glad you got this house."

"It is beautiful. Philip loves it now."

Florence begins to eye Frannie closely for symptoms of retreat, but Frannie's interest and growing affection seem to meet hers on every level. Florence offers to pick up Frannie's cleaning when she is downtown. Frannie brings home butter from the market that she knows Florence needs. Florence drops by next door once a day. Frannie comes by only every other day or so, but comments spontaneously that she loves it when people drop by. Where they'd lived before, everyone was terrifically formal—always calling and making arrangements as if they expected to be entertained. Every time she sees Frannie, Florence feels intelligent. Best of all, she is witty. Her new powers exhilarate her.

Florence crosses the adjoining sideyards on a rainy Saturday morning. Frannie is intending to meet Philip at the hardware store and is waiting for the rain to let up. She pours Florence a cup of coffee. "Won't he be annoyed if you're late?" Florence asks, thinking of the photographer, but also of the fact that Frannie gossips less about her husband than anyone Florence has ever known, which is very charming.

"He'll love the chance to moon around the hardware store planning major renovations."

"Say, do you like the yellow slicker effect?" Florence gestures toward the raincoat she has left by the door. "I just bought it at the Army-Navy. It feels like a three-man pup tent, but I love it."

Frannie nods and sips her coffee. There is a letter next to her elbow, and the return address is illegible, although in a woman's hand. In a moment Frannie says, "It's odd, you know. I haven't had a really intimate woman friend since the day Philip and I got married, though I'd had three or four the day before. There's a friend I've had since grammar school, who must know more about me than my mother does, and yet there are these incredibly trivial things about my life and my feelings that I don't dare tell her, not to mention the more important things. It seems like once I let her in, even her, the door will be broken open forever, and Philip will be the loser."

Florence answers that she's never been married. She stays away a whole week, until Frannie comes over the following Saturday afternoon and asks her to go swimming with them, then stay for dinner. She and Philip husk the corn, then she and Frannie take either end of the garlic bread and butter until they meet in the middle. Philip hands her the lettuce to dry, then Frannie turns the spareribs on the grill while Florence bastes them. They drink two six-packs of beer. They eat and drink in the gathering darkness of the side porch for a long time, until at last there are only voices. Sometimes Philip and Frannie speak at once, sometimes Florence and Frannie. Later, Florence falls asleep on the new living-room couch, and in the morning, Philip wakes her with hot tea and buttered toast.

September comes, and Florence must work hard. The neonate nursery is jammed and there is a rash of school-related infections among the regular clinic patients. Late in the month she comes down with the virus herself. She spends many evenings on the Howards' wide, deep couch, sipping white wine with her eyes closed and not saying much. Philip often works upstairs in his study while Frannie reads or sews. Florence leafs through magazines and surrenders herself to exhaustion. They have gotten beyond the stage of wild talking and into the stage of companionable silence. Philip and Frannie are not perfect. Philip can be garrulous, and tends to repeat some of his jokes. Frannie breaks dates at the last minute because she never writes anything down. Florence doesn't mind even while feeling annoyed. She is glad that the honeymoon is over, and the work of real friendship about to begin.

In October there are even more newborns, and Florence has to give the hospital Frannie and Philip's number, so that she can be called when the other nurses succumb to the virus. October is the best month. It is crisp and dark outside, and the big, neat house folds them in with light and warmth. Philip teases Florence about the multitude of infants being born, and pretends not to be convinced that they are the inevitable result of winter boredom.

In November she volunteers for the second shift through Christmas because it will be more money and she needs a good excuse to get rid of the photographer, whom Frannie and Philip don't think is good enough for her. She calls Frannie at work when she can. After Christmas Frannie tells her that she and Philip are separating.

Florence is very discreet. She tries not to encounter Philip in the neighborhood, and if she sees him before he sees her, she pretends to be occupied. When she absolutely can't avoid him, she speaks cordially, but with a certain distance, as if the sun were in her eyes. She wishes she had a car, so that she might help Frannie with her moving, or that she lived in a big place across town, so that Frannie could stay with her for a while, at least.

Frannie is too happy to confide the details about the separation, and the apartment she finds is very small, very badly furnished. To Florence she says, "But I want a furnished place! It took me days to move my stuff into that empty house. I felt like I was being snapped up like a tasty morsel. This is perfect!" She installs the plant stand her great aunt gave her and hangs up her clothes. She speaks continually in the tones Florence remembers from the beginning of their friendship, as if she will abandon herself to merriment at any moment. Florence waits for her to speak about Philip, or rather, about her life with Philip (for she often says now, "Philip must have my comb," or "Philip was in the market this afternoon") but she never does, even during the intimate moments of sharing dinner preparations or cleaning the previous tenant's leavings out of the closets and cupboards. Florence reminds herself that Frannie has a basic reserve, especially about Philip, and that if anyone is to know, it will certainly be herself.

Meanwhile, Frannie's conversation is more earnest than ever. She asks Florence her views on life and death; she mentions the idea of becoming a midwife, then brings up the notion of business administration. She wants to talk about the sociological implications of a novel she is reading. She asks Florence whether we live in a decadent age, and presses her when Florence says she doesn't know. They have a conversation about sin. She makes Florence tell her about the mothers who bring their offspring into the clinic. Do they love their children? Is it because they must love them? She talks about everything except the recent past.

Some weeks pass. Florence is very curious. She brings her new boyfriend to Frannie's apartment. When he, in his comradely, once-married, matter-of-fact way, asks Frannie if she thinks she will go back to Philip, Florence sits very still and holds her breath. Frannie shakes her head without a thought. They do not pursue the subject. It is almost as if the question is dull to them, or as if they both know the ins and outs of it so well that they needn't go on. Florence bites her lip at her own curiosity, and her admiration for Bryan, both his experience and his directness, increases. The next day she asks Frannie what she thinks of Bryan, and watches her closely to detect envy in her approval. There is none.

In Sears, they pass a display of ribbed, sleeveless undershirts and baggy shorts. "Philip just loves those," says Frannie.

Such an elderly style seems so incongruous with Philip's natural elegance that Florence guffaws. "No, really!" says Frannie. "The whole family wears that stuff, and Philip's mother irons all their shorts!" After this exchange, Florence feels oddly more hostile toward Philip, which is why, when she sees him on the street a few days later, and he smiles and pauses for a chat, she walks right past him.

Florence spends many evenings with Frannie. She takes the bus, and often arrives panting and slapping in a flurry of snow, as if on an adventure. She stays the night on the living-room floor. "I wish you'd visit me!" she asserts. "I could sneak you in and out under cover of darkness." Frannie never comes, though, and it is just as well. Nothing about Florence's carefully arranged, thoughtfully acquired apartment is as hospitable as Frannie's temporary rooms.

They make popcorn and crack beers, then turn out the lights and position their chairs before the bay window. Cars and semis rush past on the main thoroughfare nearby, and they make plans to jog, to swim, to learn to cook Middle Eastern food. Florence talks about Bryan. Most of her remarks are open-ended, so that Frannie can simply fall into telling all about it if she wants to. She doesn't, even when Florence says, "If you ever want to talk about what happened, you can trust me completely. You know that, don't you?" Frannie only nods.

Florence can hardly help speculating, especially at home, alone in her own kitchen, staring out at Philip's stained-glass windows. The thumps and sawings that occasionally sound from his house seem to her not the mysteries of the moment, but those of the past autumn, when she was so often inside, but never saw what was going on.

She picks at the burned kernels in the bottom of the popcorn bowl. "You know what one of the mothers said to me today? They'd done Lamaze, I guess, she and her husband, and she said that when the pains got bad, he climbed up onto the labor table and held her head in his arms. She looked me full in the face and asked, 'How can my marriage not be perfect from now on? We were splendid together!' "

"Philip and I lost a baby." Frannie tips the beer can back and catches the last drops with her tongue. Florence runs one of the kernels around and around the buttery bowl. This is the moment. What Florence wishes to know is the story of their mundaneness: what was said over breakfast, and in what tone, what looks were exchanged, what noises Frannie could not help listening to when she was tending her own affairs, who would be the first to break a silence. "I was prediabetic without knowing it. She went full term, but when we got to the hospital they said she was dead, then knocked me out." Frannie speaks calmly, expecting Florence's expertise to fill in the details, which, regrettably, it does.

"They should have suspected." She is professionally disapproving.

"The doctor was an ass. It was a long time ago. Almost eight years."

Needless to say, it was tragic, devastating, but how so? Florence sips her beer and glances into Frannie's face. No more on the subject is forthcoming.

Bryan joins them twice, but though he likes Frannie, his pleasure in her company isn't as exquisite as Florence expects it to be. That he might sometimes be on the verge of criticizing Frannie annoys her, because she is beginning to have so much fun with him that it can no longer be called "fun." It encompasses many things other than, and opposite to, amusement.

He tells lots of stories. His past begins to assume the proportions of an epic to Florence. She likes his self-confidence and his ready flow of conversation, his thick, curly hair, and his willingness to be teased. She listens to all his stories with interest, but when he talks about his ex-wife, she can't keep her attention on what he is saying. Images of Frannie, Philip, their pale furniture and their pale floors invade her imagination. "Marriage is such a mystery to me," she says idly.

"Well, it's a mystery to me, too, even though I sometimes think I can remember every minute of my own."

"And you're going to describe them all, one by one?" She smiles.

"Only if you ask."

"And besides, there's so much else to cover." She pokes him in the ribs.

"You don't want to hear it?"

"Every word, every word."

"The past is always with you."

"God forbid." But she doesn't mean it. She will remember, for example, every moment of this talk—the fall of light through the hackberry bushes fixes his words and his tones permanently; his words and tones do the same for the light.

At the hospital, she surprises herself by recalling things she did not know she had noticed—the color of his socks, the titles of the books piled on his dashboard, what he almost ordered for dinner but decided against. When she relates these details to Frannie, Frannie's smile reminds her that she is like the one- and two-day mothers, who tell her exactly how the breast was taken, whether the sucking reflex seemed sufficiently developed, how five minutes on each side didn't seem like enough. Like the mothers, Florence smiles, self-deprecating, but can't stop.

"Another thing about him," she tells Frannie on the phone, "is that he acts as much as he talks. Don't you think that's very rare? We never sit around, saying what shall we do. When he picks me up, he always has some plan. And he thinks about what I might like to do, and he's always right. I must say that this care is rather thrilling. It's almost unmasculine!"

"I'm envious," replies Frannie, and Florence, marveling at her good luck, demurs. "He does have something of a temper, though." When Frannie hangs up the phone, she realizes that Frannie didn't sound envious. Florence smiles. She loves Frannie completely.

That evening, Bryan says, "Doesn't your friend Frannie work over at the U.?"

"Off-campus programs, how come?"

"Someone mentioned her at lunch today."

"What did they say?" Her voice rises, oddly protective and angry. Bryan glances at her and smiles. "Nothing, dear. Just mentioned her name."

Florence remains disturbed, and later decides it is because she wants Frannie, Frannie's delight, conversation, thoughtfulness, all to herself. That her name can come up among strangers implies a life that fans away into the unknown. She wonders about Frannie's activities in the intervals of her absence. She feels none of this jealousy with Bryan.

Florence rolls away from Bryan and grabs the phone at the end of the first ring. Bryan heaves and groans but does not awaken. Florence thinks it will be the hospital, but it is Frannie, who says, "My Lord, it's only ten-thirty!"

"I got up at five this morning. How are you?"

"Can you get up at six tomorrow? A friend offered me her strawberry patch. We can pick some, then have a picnic breakfast."

"Lovely. Let's just have fruit and bread and juice."

"I'll pick you up at six-fifteen."

"Mmmmm."

The morning could not be fresher. Frannie's new car is pearled with dew and smells, inside, of French bread. The strawberry patch is professionally laid out in neat rows, and among shiny dark leaves, the heartlike berries weigh into pale straw. The earth is springy and smells of damp. Two maples at the corner of the garden cast black, sharp-edged shadows; everything else sparkles with such sunlight that Florence's vision vibrates. Ripe berries plop into their hands at a touch. Frannie, it turns out, has brought champagne. "And not only jam," she is saying, "but a really delicious liqueur my friend has the recipe for. And look over there! Those two apricot trees bloomed this spring, and that peach. The one next to it is a Chinese Chestnut. She lives here alone and hates to see it go to waste. In the fall, she says she has the best apples in the county." Frannie shades her eyes and looks across the field toward the house. "I was hoping she'd come out. Anyway, last year there were seven bushels on one tree alone."

"Frannie, I've known you all these months, and I've never realized what an earth mother you are. I feel like I've missed something."

"Converts are the most ardent, you know. But don't you love the romance of the harvest?" She sucks a berry off the stem.

"The romance of putting up two dozen quarts of tomatoes and a dozen quarts of beans in one evening when the temperature and the humidity are both 95?"

"The romance of opening a jar of strawberry jam in the middle of December!"

"I'd call that the romance of consumption."

"Call it what you like. Mmmmm!" She bites into another strawberry and glances toward the still house again.

They sit under one of the maples with their shoes off, tearing hunks of bread. Champagne sizzles in their bowl of berries, and the butter is still cool, dewy. Florence is excited. She thinks she will penetrate the marriage mystery at last, then is ashamed of her unseemly curiosity. Still . . . She says, "Bryan and I saw Philip yesterday." A lie.

"How is Bryan, anyway? Are you in love yet?"

"We've agreed not to say. He's very compelling, though. Especially at six a.m., when I think he's asleep, and he grabs my foot as I'm sneaking out of bed. I thought I was going to jump right out of my skin."

"Do you talk?"

"Nonstop."

There is a pause here, where Frannie might mention her conversational history with Philip, but instead she rolls over and closes her eyes. Florence presses ahead. "I actually spoke to him, Philip I mean. I said hello, he said hello, Bryan said hello." She looks at Frannie. Nothing. "He's so boyish looking. From a distance he looks about eighteen, and getting younger. That's another thing about Bryan. Being prematurely grizzled makes him look very wise. Are you asleep?"

Frannie shakes her head and slips her hand into the bowl. "Mmmm," she says.

"Do you ever miss him?" This is so bald that Florence blushes.

Frannie shrugs. "How's Bryan's work going?" Bryan's work is to figure out how many ways the hospital can use the computer it has just purchased.

"Terrifically," says Florence. "Now they're thinking of renting time to the county and making a profit on the purchase."

"But they bought it with county money."

"The left hand doesn't know what the right hand is doing." Florence sighs. "You know, you always turn the conversation over to me, and I always rise to the bait."

"More strawberries?" Frannie holds out the bowl, and Florence gives up. They talk about a movie Frannie wants to go to, then about the seven-pound twins Florence saw the previous week. Florence begins to think of Bryan and to wonder what time it is. The champagne in the bottom of the crystal bowl is flat. Just then Frannie says, "I hate the way Philip and I admired ourselves all the time."

Florence picks up the napkins and the champagne cork and the wrappings from the loaf of bread, and then it is time to depart.

"Well, I don't think life has passed *me* by." Florence, in her bathrobe, strikes a pose on the stairs. Bryan looks up from his book, elaborately distracted. Florence lifts her chin. Lately, they have been debating whether life has passed Bryan by. "No, bitch," he says, just containing a smile. "Life hasn't passed you by." Florence exhibits an ostentatious bit of calf. "You were standing in the road, and it ran you right over!" Florence screams with laughter and gallops up the steps. At the top, she hits the light switch, plunging Bryan into darkness, then she throws herself diagonally across the bed.

When Bryan comes in, she is pretending to be asleep. He walks around the bed. "I'm so comfortable," she groans. "You'll have to sleep on the floor." She stretches out her arms. "There's no room."

"I see a spot," he says. She can hear the smile in his voice, and she feels her body contract with the tension of imminent laughter. Then he launches himself diagonally across her. The weight of his body is delightful: for a moment they are still, and she seems to feel the muffled beat of his heart. Then they are laughing and floundering across one another. They have been laughing all evening, and this laughter, Florence knows, will bloom smoothly into lovemaking. "I love you," he says. He has said it often lately.

"Do you mind if I reciprocate at once?"

"Not at all."

"I love you, too."

"Ah." They snuggle down and pull up the covers.

Just when Florence thinks it is about to begin, when her skin seems to rise to meet the palm of his hand, he squeezes her closely and says, "Speaking of love."

"Please do."

"Your friend seems to have a new one."

"Which friend?" Florence's eyes are closed, and she is trying to guess where his hands are, where they will alight.

"Frannie," he says.

Florence opens her eyes and sits up. "Oh, really?" she says. "Who?" And then, in a less casual tone, "She didn't tell me."

"A woman in the art school, I think."

"Which part do you think?"

"What?"

"What's questionable, love, art school, or woman?"

"Art school."

"Oh."

"I thought you'd be glad. They look very happy. I saw them having tea this afternoon."

"Oh."

"I'm sorry I told you."

"Don't be."

"Come here. Please. We've had such a good time tonight."

"We really have." She kisses him on the nose and smiles, but in the end they settle into bed without making love. Florence says, "I think if we hadn't had such a good time tonight then I wouldn't be able to imagine their every moment together." But she says it quietly, knowing that Bryan has fallen asleep.

She'd intended to drop in at Frannie's the next morning, a Saturday, on her way to the store, but now that seems like she'd be rushing by for the details. She doesn't know what she would say; all she can think of are challenges and accusations.

She stops on the way home, leaving Bryan's car at the end of the block. No one is around, and she sees that Frannie's belongings are in the street—the plant stand, two boxes of books; clothes in a large pile seem especially vulnerable. Florence looks around for Frannie's winter coat to throw over them, but she can't find it. While she is standing there, Frannie's car pulls up. The other woman is with her, and Frannie's "Hello!" is wildly exuberant. Florence attributes this to the presence of the other woman.

Frannie introduces them. The woman's name, Helen Meardon, is certainly conservative, even old-fashioned, and her thighs are too fat. Otherwise she is very pretty. Florence listens for Helen Meardon to say, "I've heard so much about you," but she does not, does not, in fact, smile again after the introduction, although her inspection of Florence, whose clothes are a mess and whose hair is dirty, is frank and lengthy. Helen Meardon is a person of style. "I didn't know you were moving," Florence says heartily, thinking of their recent evening together.

"Darling! It's very sudden. The house is terrific! Remember where we went for strawberries? Helen's just put in the most beautiful red enameled wood-burning stove. It's practically her place, she moved in so long ago, and the rent hasn't been raised in years, so it should cost next to nothing to live there."

"That's great."

"You'll have to come over as soon as you can."

"I'm so surprised."

Helen Meardon is moving away, toward the apartment building. She exchanges with Florence a sidelong glance before passing her and climbing the porch steps.

"Maybe I will come over," asserts Florence.

"Or we could have lunch together downtown."

"Can I help you move? I've got Bryan's car."

"We can handle it, I think," announces Helen from the porch. "We're nearly finished." She goes into the building.

"Helen's terribly shy," says Frannie, looking after her.

"You must be good friends with her to be moving in."

"We met almost my first week on the job last fall. Sometimes I feel like I've known her since kindergarten, and sometimes I feel like we've just met."

"Mmm."

"Frannie! What about this?" Helen is holding an object up at the window screen. Frannie turns to squint at it.

"I better go. Bryan will be expecting his lunch," Florence says.

Frannie smiles at her.

"Not that I'll make it for him, I mean. I'm not his slave, of course. I just went to the store."

Frannie continues to smile. "He's a nice man."

"I think we're in love now."

"You told me that last week."

"Yes, right." It is impossible to leave. At length, Florence simply turns away and runs down the street to the car. She imagines Frannie and Helen meeting in the doorway of the empty apartment, the same height, kissing. Florence could have said to Frannie, "I love you, too."

Florence is drawn outside by the odors of cut grass and privet. Bryan should be coming soon to take her swimming. It is a glorious day, and Philip is snipping his hedge, his back to her, his progress slow and neat. The grass he has mown is already bagged and sitting on the curb. Before going back inside, Florence watches him for a minute. She hasn't spoken to him since her spring antagonism. Now she fears that she has found out the secret of his marriage, and he would know by looking at her.

He sets down his shears and wipes his face in his shirt. When she turns to go inside, he calls to her, "What do you think, Florence, shall I trim it into birds and perfect spheres?"

"What is that called again?"

"Topiary. How's the baby business?"

"Bouncing. How are you?"

"Sorry not to see you more often. And this is your slow season."

"I haven't been home much, I'll admit."

"Ah, love." He speaks with only ordinary irony.

"I've been around enough to hear a lot of thumps and bangings across the way. Are you haunted over there?"

"Only by the spirit of remodeling. I took out the kitchen bar and put down new linoleum, and let's see, put in some new windows and repainted a little."

"My goodness!"

"Would you like to see it?"

He has also had the new sofa recovered in a pattern of green leaves and lemons. The place is even more spacious now than before, if that is possible. Philip's furniture, director's chairs and yellow canvas deck chairs, recalls the ocean. His floors recall sandy beaches. Nothing recalls Frannie, and Florence feels suddenly calmer. He has brought his desk downstairs and set it up where he can survey his solitary realm. There is an air of satisfaction about the furnishings and their arrangement, as if they have spread themselves this way and that, unhindered. "I should have come over sooner," Florence says, not remembering till then that she wasn't invited to come over. Still, she feels that she has missed the transformation itself, and having missed it, she will never know what it was that has been transformed. "You know how nosey I am," she adds.

But Philip has gone to the kitchen window. "Look over there. See that little building? I bought that at a farm sale for thirty dollars. It's an old chicken house. Sound, though. I'm insulating it, and putting down a tile floor, then I'm going to install a Franklin stove and run lights out there and make it into my study. No phone, no nothing. Grapes growing all over it, a couple of easy chairs, a nice rug."

"You've got all this space to yourself right here!"

He glances at her, amused that she hasn't gotten the point, and shrugs. "The spirit of remodeling is pretty persistent you know."

"It's so different from the way it was," she says, because Philip's cool realm oddly invites confidences in a way that Frannie's hospitality did not, "and it's not that I don't like it. It's refreshing. But I loved the rusty-red sofa, and all the chairs drawn up around the coffee table. That kitchen bar was so ugly—awful nineteen-fifties modernizing—but it really made the place cozy." Philip is looking at her quizzically. "Don't you think it was nice to just sit around in the evening with most of the lights off and drink brandy and talk? I loved it! Especially when it rained or snowed those times, and even my apartment seemed too far away. Didn't you like it?"

"Our friendship was very pleasant."

"I didn't feel like just your friend. I felt like your child or your sister, or something. Should I be embarrassed? Those nights seemed so self-contained."

"Frannie mooning over Helen, me mooning over Frannie." He speaks with a teasing edge. "And others. I don't think we were very kind to you, Florence."

"Weren't you? I thought you were." Florence swallows bitterly.

"We needed someone else to talk to, about unimportant things."

Florence turns away quickly and peers energetically out the window so that Philip won't see her eyes. "We needed you, Florence; what Frannie and I talked about with you wasn't unimportant, exactly, but it wasn't the central issue for either of us. Do you understand what I mean?"

"No one was happy but me?" She looks at him again and he shakes his head.

Bryan pulls up next door and gets out of the car. Florence does not move. "Is that the secret of marriage?" she asks.

"One of them."

Bryan takes off his sunglasses and throws them on the seat, then steps around the car.

"What's another one?"

"Maybe that all the secrets are never disclosed."

"And another?"

"That it's worth finding out for yourself."

Bryan raises his finger to her doorbell. She shouts, "Here I am! Bryan, I'm over here!"

CHARYBDIS

T. E. HOLT

T. E. Holt was born in Philadelphia and now lives in Ithaca, New York. He is a graduate student in English at Cornell University, where he received his master of fine arts degree in 1979. He is working on a collection of short stories, a handbook for amateur astronomers, and a dissertation on myth in nineteenth-century English poetry.

I shall from time to time continue this journal. It is true that I may not find an opportunity of transmitting it to the world, but I will not fail to make the endeavor. At the last moment I will enclose the MS in a bottle, and cast it within the sea.

POE

There is something I can't recall. It has a name, like "farther," or "whom," but these are wrong. It was in the dream that woke me this morning, we call it morning when I awaken here, but I couldn't remember the dream: only the shape of the word dissolving, a pair of lips parting, puckering "shh." I told this to mission control, I don't know why. Maybe because the way they say "good morning" annoys me: it's afternoon in Houston, and it's nothing you could call anything here. So I said there was something I couldn't remember, ate breakfast, and turned on the reader. My coffee was cool by the time the reply came, breaking into their recitation of today's schedule: which of the systems did I think it was in? Without pausing they returned to their list and read on. I lowered the gain, said "No, it's nothing real, it was in a dream. It sounds like 'hips,' or maybe 'warm.'" I mixed more

Originally published in *The Kenyon Review*, Vol. II, No. 4 (Fall 1980). Reprinted by permission of the author and Kenyon College.

coffee and started a new story, one of Stern's mysteries: murder and incest, funerals, gunfire, somebody floating face down.

Mission control muttered softly, static on the air. "Say again, Prometheus?" They hate to ask for confirmation, now the line of sight has stretched to twenty minutes. The distance makes communication between us strained, as I have come to suspect the lengthening pause between question and response. It makes their rising panic, their politeness sound too deliberate to be genuine. This is only an illusion, the effect of distance.

"It was in a dream," I told them, and looked from the reader out the port. Jupiter was off abeam, a featureless star so bright its light seems heavy. I can feel it in my eyes. Soon the image will spread, form a disc. I try to imagine what it will look like: a marble, a banded shooter, a catseye: I have seen pictures, but it will not be the same. There will be a salmon-colored eyespot, which I'm looking forward to seeing. It was our mission's objective. At least it is something to wait for. Return transmission was eight minutes late. "We've asked Dr. Hayford to discuss this with you. If you'd like." If I'd like: back at Houston, Hayford could have driven halfway home by now, leaving a string of words slung through the ether from mission control: I could no more shut him up than I could stop this ship. Since Stern and Peterson walked out on me, there's been a lot of empty deference on the airwaves, mostly incoming. Dr. Hayford claims to know me better than my mother does, and this may be so, but I think he feels inadequate to this situation. "We've reviewed your transmission," he says. "I gather it's not your nightmare. So I'm glad. You mentioned a sound in this dream. That's a good sign. Would you like to talk about it? I'll wait."

I told him if I remembered it I wouldn't have bothered them in the first place, I didn't care about it anymore, let's quit wasting time. I let him think it was only a sound, but it was more: it was a word.

Here's a list of mission control's euphemisms:

the burn
the event
the incident

the accident
the unfortunate [all of the above]
the spontaneous ignition
the midcourse miscorrection
the transorbital overenhancement. This one was my favorite, but the one they preferred was "the accident." I have started to ask them, "which one?"

And they say I've lost my sense of humor.

I still need to explain. We slept afloat, adrift like tethered fish, hugging ourselves to keep our arms from feeling awkward. My mouth opens in my sleep, sometimes saliva wells around my tongue, forms a sphere inside my mouth, and then I inhale it and wake, choking. I hack on the gob of spit, cough it out, and when I can breathe again I look around and see only dark, drifting shapes, I cannot remember who or where I am. I see Stern and Peterson afloat on their tethers; I hear them breathe, first one, then the other, a soft sound like water flowing into a drum. The ship cycles air, water; servos whine on and off around the hull, all these sounds are very close, and though I would awake immediately if they stopped, waking now gagging in the dark these sounds are stifling, and I think first I have awakened with a fever in my bedroom in my parents' home, I have heard the horn of a freighter on the lake; but then a window drifts in front of me, a light shines far beyond the pane, and I see stars, so thick they seem a solid mass, and the cabin walls could dissolve in an instant.

Sickening plunge through roaring; darkness; twitch at my belly the tether snapped; falling aft: down: we tumble together on the after bulkhead, Stern feet first and shouting, but the roar of the main engine drowns his voice, the darkness defeats us as we struggle. Peterson is motionless. The cockpit and controls now up against acceleration a dozen meters never meant to be climbed, I feel the distance stretching each second the ship leaps farther and faster ahead, leaving behind the fuel we need to get home. Banging my head against stanchions, losing my grip and slipping in the dark, alone, there is only one sound, and no progress upward: the ship is climbing away with us, and its gathering speed strips each moment out past measuring.

Suddenly there is light and I am blinded, blinking at the workbench I hug. Stern hangs from the opposite wall. We look up. A speaker squalls ". . . status . . . cut-off . . . manual": gibberish. I freeze, but Stern climbs again, barking more noise into air already too burdened to carry sense.

Nineteen minutes and some seconds pass before we can override the impulses that somehow opened the fuel system. Silence, and we fall freely again through space, faster now: I can feel the pace in my pulse. Peterson drifts forward through the cabin, his head trailing a pennant of blood.

Now that the cabin is empty, there is no reason to float around in bed any longer than the moment I awake: off tether, off to the head, breakfast, mission control like the morning news on the radio. I read more and more each day: deserts, dry gulches, buzzards circling. Jupiter stands off to starboard, brighter than before, and now I see a disc. I realize what I said in my first entry was a lie: I can't compare its size to anything we know, the head of a pin, an egg, my eye. If I had a penny, I could hold it to the glass and compare, but there's not a cent aboard, isn't that odd? I'm glad I can't: the comparison would show me nothing but a penny in my hand, and beside it, so far away I count the space in months, not miles: a planet. Its image is as clear as if etched on the glass, its satellites are perfect points of light beside it, all on a line, balancing. I envy them. I feel heavy and obtuse.

But I am weightless: an overhand pull swung me out of the cockpit and back into the cabin. Gone these months and not once thought of cash, but I spent the rest of the afternoon tearing through Stern's and Peterson's effects, rifling the ship just to see. Not a cent.

Mission control has many suggestions: about me, the ship, our mission. They are like bachelors babysitting. I sense fear in their omissions: "In theory . . ." they say, and skip ahead to speak of

Jupiter. While I hang here listening, they weigh the orbits open to me there, and plan for my survival until rescue comes. They appear to have made a decision: they offer to make me a constellation, translate me into the sky with Io, Europa, and the rest. I am unwilling. But it is not mission control who forces me; it is ahead, Jupiter growing broader and brighter by degrees so small I never see the change, whom I must answer to. In practice, I doubt that I will have much to say in the matter.

There is one group that wants me to stop these recordings, and another wants them transmitted instead. A third thinks I should carry on, and one lonely man is horrified at the prospect. I suspect he knows what he is talking about, and wish he would shut up.

The ship moves on, and forces me to choose. Here, the choices are simpler, the rules are clearer: action, reaction; mass acting on mass; an object in motion tends to stay in motion, unless. . . . But this kind of clarity is useless to me now, since I can clearly see Jupiter ahead, and know how all of these equations balance, what answers they will come to: something very like a zero. I could crash there, of course; I could orbit it and wait for mission control; or I could crack the whip around it, shoot out in any direction I choose: how much more poignant to fly past earth on my way out into darkness, moving too swiftly to say goodbye. I'd prefer to keep on the way I've come.

I prefer: the choices stay with me; but in none of the equations for action, mass, and motion have I ever read a term for my capacity to choose. There are more things in heaven than in earth, I see that now, and clearly. I am not *in* theory anymore; philosophy is not a dream: I am alive; that star behind me is the earth, and there is no "unless" in Jupiter. But there are choices.

While the balance of its mind was disturbed, mission control brought my parents in to talk to me today. I mean that. I think they have taken leave of their senses, lost their marbles, gone off the deep end. My parents are in their eighties, and have not left the nursing home since I put them there ten years ago, and I do not visit often. Dad is aphasic; Mom talks, but how much is there to say? She asks me how my work is going, and I tell them—Okay—and she says, brightly—Good. Once, when I told her I had just returned from Mars, the eyes she turned on me were disappointed: so old, and still lying to his mother. But for an instant the maternal mask had slipped, and I saw there: fear, and how much of it had come to me as my inheritance.

And now they've sent an airconditioned sedan to fetch them to the airstrip, bundled them on a NASA jet, transshipped to Houston. Here. For a moment it seemed the radio was eavesdropping on my childhood, the voice in the speaker calling from the kitchen door, come in for supper, put on your jacket, it's getting late, time to come home. I shook my head, wondering if this were one of Hayford's radio dramas, and I the only one without a script, hearing her say—Your father's here. His voice saying—Where is he? and then the cabin walls, the stars outside, all fell away and I could see them, lost in mission control's white glare, shivering in the chill in their Florida clothing, their heads quivering on their delicate necks as they turn to watch technicians passing, voices hurrying, saying nothing they can understand, and Dad's whisper.

"Get them off. Get them out of here. Take them home."

I cut the connection.

I have been floating here in silence since, thinking of my alternatives, to stop at Jupiter or travel on: the journey outward, into silence so thick as to become something: a pressure, a presence here with me. As weight surrounds a mass, so silence would fill the air around me, falling in, rising from blood rustling in my ears to become a whisper, a word spoken, a cry, the roar of burning and finally the crash of everything that falls forever. How loud? Beyond Pluto, silence would be more than absence of speech: even zero has meaning, but what is zero taken to an infinite power? And on what fingers do I count it?

I reach up and touch my ears: they are cool. I try to trace their infoldings with my finger, picture the pattern there, but my mind won't follow: "pinna," "auricle," these words drift through my thoughts, and I don't know where I learned them. No. Though I could hear the spheres sing lullabyes, see colors off the spectrum, touch nothing: how could I tell? and whom? No. I will not go. I am Jupiter-bound.

But by how long a chain?

Stern and Peterson left in that order, on successive days. The initiative was Stern's. We did not talk much in the days following the burn. At first, I attributed this to simple shock, and fear for our survival. Conversation seemed at first a burden, then a risk. But just as we no longer sensed our new velocity once acceleration ceased, so our increased risk became a piece with the fears we'd shared since liftoff and before. Still we found it hard to talk, even to meet each other's eyes: as if the sudden return to free fall, the leap from acceleration to silence, had shaken something loose and left us trying to remember how to talk.

Stern started mumbling after a week, odd things, as if he thought we wouldn't hear: "elucidate," "supernal," "ineluctable." He prowled like a pregnant cat, carrying objects to and from the hold: I remember his back receding through the hatch, shoulders hunched and holding something precious: a hand-vacuum, binoculars, a hair-dryer. On a Monday I heard him mutter "terra matter," and on a Tuesday he was gone. He left in the lander, leaving us its portable seismometer and a set of digging tools, a deeper silence, and then the voice of mission control, advising us of a change of plans.

He left at night. The whine of servomotors woke me and Peterson to wonder why the hold bay doors had opened, and where was Stern, and then, befuddled, why the hold-hatch was dogged: through the deadlight we saw nothing, then stars burning in vacuum, and we understood, slowly, why the hatch wouldn't open, why we were locked in, and as we floated there, feeling like children at a bedroom door, we saw through the glass the lander, poised, Peterson croaked "wait"—to Stern, to himself or no one—concussion echoed through our hands, knees, noses, whatever touched metal, and the hold was filled with fog, swirling, clearing: empty.

We tracked Stern by the light of his main engine until he faded in the stars, and then by radar. He dropped rapidly astern, but before we lost him we learned his trajectory. He would fall into the sun sometime in May.

Naturally Peterson was hurt. He and Stern had trained together, shared naval academy ties and a series of backyard barbecues in Houston, of which there is still a Polaroid taped over the galley microwave: two men, two women, the men wearing dark glasses, the women with the loopy shut-eyed look that comes from too much sun and a fast shutter. Their arms are mostly hidden: here and there a hand appears, disjointed beside someone's neck. There is no indication who took the picture, but in my imagination I am the photographer, and I think this prevents my tearing it up. I am surprised Peterson did not take it with him: it was Stern's second wife, but Peterson's first.

Jupiter was active on the decameter band this afternoon, crackling and hissing like a witch and her caldron. I piped it back into the hold all day while I worked there on one of the instrument packages. I have been dreaming again, a nightmare in which I am unable to awake. This makes the silence in the ship nerve-wracking: hence Jupiter. It reminds me of surf, and the hold can be my boathouse, my Ogygya. I may leave the radio on tonight, a mood record, like those used in nurseries, to lull the babies with big soft noises—but something stops me. This is not a record.

At the suggestion of mission control, who want one instrument package sent to Io in place of the lost lander, I work in the lighted hold, holding onto handgrips with my toes as I modify the contents of the capsules—three featureless shells. They shine in the floodlights, smooth as pills rolling under your tongue, as hard to hold onto; so blandly polished their scale is as hard to grasp as their surfaces: from across the hold they can look as small as BBs and the hold no wider than a mailing tube; sometimes they could be worlds, and at the hold-hatch I cling to the top of a well dropped down from heaven. The weightlessness does this.

I prefer to work inside them, where I curl comfortably. Their brushed-metal interiors give back no reflections (outside, the distortions are immense), only a dim shape that moves with me in the corner of my eye. Jupiter's speechless hissing comforts me then, a voice tongueless as a radio wave. But I know when the cabin lights cycle off tonight and I float to sleep, I will not have the courage to keep a radio turned on in this ship. I possess already—perhaps I have dreamed it—a sense of how it will be when I wake suddenly to Jupiter's voice pronouncing words, whole sentences, my name. I have enough trouble with my dream.

In my dream I am Peterson, or with him in his suit, and we are looking back at me, at the ship, as Peterson drifts away. His tether gone or never connected, tumbling through the stars revolving, looking out, looking back, we do not see my face in the cockpit window. In my dream I know the ship is deserted, and although it is I who have left it, I feel abandoned. Lights burn in every port along its length, and every port shows empty in the light. The hold bay doors stand open, open on a two-car garage, lined with lawn mowers, ladders. The cars are gone. Oil gleams darkly from the center of the floor, unreflecting. I change my mind. I am too sad, too tired or sick or small to go, and I want to turn back, but it is too late.

He took no means of rescue with him. Once he stepped outside the airlock unattached, once he jumped, he was committed. I think he knew the limits of his resolve, and surrendered himself to physical law before he could recant. In my dream, I open my mouth to speak but I cannot. There is no air. Tears puddle in my eyes but won't fall. The absence of air, the suspension of gravity: I recognize these things. They return to me, as if I knew them once but long ago forgot. Breath, weight, those are spells finally broken, exceptions now set aside. This is real.

And only when I pass beyond denying this can I awake and remember the rest of the story.

I don't know what woke me, the night Peterson left. The operation of the airlock is almost silent, and unless he made some sound, I cannot explain how I came to witness his leap of faith. I suspect he did signal me, deliberately, banging a wrench against a bulkhead until he saw me move, and then he turned to the open hatch, to crouch and spring. He was not far when I reached a porthole. When I saw a spacesuit in free fall beside us, I turned to summon Peterson, to tell him there was a man out there, should we shoot a line? There was something terrifying about the absence of an umbilical between the suited figure and the ship—my mind refused to supply the missing connection, I was afraid to look behind me. Long seconds passed, in which the image of a human form, tumbling in somersaults, shrank. I floated, I froze, I gave no thought to rescue, to fear or pity, to anything but the gradual diminution of the figure, until I recognized his waving arms, and remembered the man they signified: I bolted overhand—away from the airlock, my eyes clenched shut. Blind momentum carried me to the cockpit, and the radio.

His frequency was full of speech when I found it. A sob rocked the room before I could back off the gain, and then, gasping, Help me, and, I'm sorry.

I sat in my couch and looked out the windshield, where the galaxy slanted across the ecliptic, between Gemini and Orion. I tried to find the lines between the stars that make a pair of twins, a hunter, but the figures crumbled, forming trapezoids, triangles, and finally single stars burning red, blue, gold at the bottom of the black. "What's wrong?"

Nothing moved.

"What is it?" Only stars far away, and his voice coursing on unnoticing, his remorse weighting me, and I stayed and watched the stars beyond the screen and listened, as if the voice were a lost memory, a dead child, a dream.

And even when I moved to ask the proper questions, he did not respond. I knew his receiver was finally *off*, and it didn't matter. I saw nothing when I returned to the cabin port, but his voice remained, lingering in the radio, where it cried and cried. His signal followed, fading too slowly, for hours: time enough to return, and return, to the sorrow and the emptiness. He thought it was a trick, an exercise, a game, but he was wrong, it's only empty space and I'm sorry. Help me.

I switched it off.

So I am alone. Mission control approached me later with a surprising delicacy, a care to avoid certain words. Perhaps my inaction on Peterson's behalf disturbed them; or perhaps out of the three they most expected me to jump. They may no longer feel sure of whom they're dealing with, and their delicacy is the caution demanded by a dawning sense of ignorance. Perhaps they no longer think me trustworthy. I think when they failed to take this up with me, they stopped being entirely candid.

The silence has burrowed deep into my dreams. In them, human forms flash by, and I see their faces turning as they pass, their lips moving, forming one word. Always it is the same word, but the sound I hear is not speech, nor is it ever the same. One figure passes, my mother, who tells me it is a car's horn honking. My physics teacher says it is a hissing fire, a gas jet. To my father, it is the sound of stones dropped in deep water. I call after them, but can make no sound at all until I wake, tangled in my sleep-tether, whispering "wait" into an empty cabin.

I wake from dreams into memories, moments long submerged resurfacing: the beach ball I took into the pool to stand on, wanting to walk it, roll it with the soles of my feet across the bottom of the pool, but it would not sink: no matter how I thrust it down, it bobbed back. I tried to force it down against the weight of water and it floated; tried to balance and it burst upward. I threw myself on it, and it threw me off. I clutched it to my belly and it bubbled out and up, leaving me to flounder after.

Years later, in school I learned about specific gravity, the opposing forces of air and water, how the nature of the ball is to float and, by extension, how ships sail and planes fly, how any closed sphere, even if of rock, can reach its equilibrium and float—in air, if need be, if air be dense enough. And I thought: this is why I like science; and I had my triumph over that ball. But coming to space taught me again. I unlearned, and science is a consolation only to the ignorant.

Consider the names of ships: *Mercury*, *Gemini*, *Apollo*; *Ares*, where I earned my wings, and now *Prometheus*. Think how the missions lived up to their names: *Mercury*, an aery theft of thunder from the soviets; *Apollo*, to a chaste sister giving sacrifice by fire; *Ares,* and the terror it brought us to. God save the man who rides on *Kronos.*

The computer is my timekeeper, it is my courier and my library. It stores in its memory the pages I call up on the screen of the reading machine. For my collection I chose Shakespeare, Poe, Melville, the old myths. My crewmates left their libraries with me: Stern loved mysteries; Peterson was more a Western man.

I spend hours with the reader now, and though I am grateful for the machine, it leaves me skeptical. I wish often for the weight, or at least the solidity, of a book, instead of the image of words cast on a screen. The transience of the picture worries me, and I have caught myself calling back earlier pages, comparing them to my own memory to see if the text has been altered by the computer's traffic with so much other information. Sometimes, I am tantalized by a suspicion—surely that word was not "noses," but something starting with "g"; and that was "cave," not "save"; not "screen," but—I catch myself, and read on.

Mission control wants me to go out and look at the communications antenna, which is a paraboloidal dish big enough for a man to lie in. Servomotors aim it constantly toward mission control, so the dish faces back the way I've come, my Janus. They sound more worried than usual, and although it could easily be an act, put on for reasons I may no longer guess, it seems they really are having trouble understanding. Somewhere in the system something's wrong, but at their end or mine no one can tell: they want me to go outside and see if, perhaps, something grossly physical (and therefore beyond their power to control) has come unhinged. They sound desperate.

I switch on the aft external video, and eye the dish. It eyes me back, pointed steadily at earth, which is a white crescent, off to port and well astern. The dish looks fine to me, I tell them, and wait. No, they insist, someone there believes a meteor may have knocked the antenna off focus: I must see for myself. Here are the tools I will need. I listen as the list clips through the cockpit speakers, each syllable enunciated so sharply it stands alone. I am not paying attention. Jupiter has crept into the forward section of the windshield, striped and swirling, closer, and suddenly the pattern I have watched for weeks snaps, and as if a picture has jumped off a printed page and rolled into my lap I see the planet's marblings turn, and turn into clouds, winds: weather. It is a place, not a pattern. The red spot stands dead center, a catseye blinking back at me. I feel exposed.

"Wait a minute. If there's something wrong with my antenna, how can I read you so well?" The voice in the speakers will not hear for forty minutes. By the time they can answer, it will be too late.

There is a kind of vertigo which is purely intellectual. It starts as a shudder in the cognitive processes, a refusal to proceed from a phrase to its logical finish. You're at a mental chasm, teetering. Only then does the physiology of dizziness occur: we want our senses to serve us before they serve the world. When their loyalty is divided, I feel it in my stomach. I stopped, half out of the airlock, holding the hatchcoaming, my belly whirling counterweight to my head until panic gripped it: death by vertigo, suffocated inside a helmet full of undigested food, is no more arguable an end than any other. I tried to find a reference point. I tried to think.

Empty space. Stars swarming in: I heard them humming in my headphones. I closed my eyes: darkness, stars shining through. I put my hands to my eyes, but the gloves fell flat on my faceplate. My head afloat in its helmet, sweat stung my eyes; I leaned my skull against the globe and through the glass heard nothing. No, there, between Castor and Capella, something flashed, faded, flashed again. Something whispered in my ear. Something reflected the sun as it tumbled. "Peterson." I whispered, and it flashed. I watched, and the light neither grew nor faded, nor moved against the stars. It was following.

I turned and held hard to the ship, and though I felt the light flash behind me, counting its rhythm against my pulse I crawled along the hull. I passed portholes through which I saw the cabin, lighted and calm, where objects waited as if left by someone else. I passed over lettering painted on the hull: signs and insignias lay like shells on the seafloor, like fossils found in rock. I waited for one of them to move.

When I reached the dish I turned to look. There was the lander hovering, there was Peterson's mummified face pressed close to mine, gibbering in his helmet—for a moment every direction was down. Then there was nothing, just my tether trailing back to the open hatchway, and the slow revolution of stars.

The dish was fine. I crawled around it, gripping the tripod that held the antenna at its focus, and my shadow fell across its face. Radio traffic was passing through my body, my computer talking to theirs, and probably them talking to me, making excuses; static. I gripped the antenna boom and stared at it: instructions for removal, the NASA insignia, but no clue, no hard fact explaining what was going wrong between us: nothing. Nothing: I had come to the end of my tether and found—I turned and faced the flashing following me: nothing. Only the on and off of it, on and off. Static; and in my helmet, my breath, and the sound of swallowing. "You have nothing to say," I said into the space between my face and the helmet's glass, and the sound bounced back in my face and died. Silence spread. My heart beat, my lungs suspired, but in their intervals I felt a tension slacking off, untuning, my body finally adrift, no longer seeking a weight to stand against. My senses may have left me. I may have slept.

With a slow return of pain my thoughts assembled out of silence, but whether to preserve the peace or to rake up again the coals of sense I could not say, only that from these thoughts my hands could move now to the antenna, to tear it off, to do away with mission control and their evasions. Fools or liars, I can no longer tell the difference: everything they say sounds empty, void of sense; or in this void of sense, nothing they can say will help. It does not matter. But as I reached I looked and saw flash, fade, and flash again, and my heart leapt up again.

"No." I said, and it vanished. No: and it never reappeared. No. I would not rip out my tongue for mission control.

I went inside and overrode antenna guidance, steered it away from earth. Mission control faded in midsentence like a dream. I swiveled the dish 180° in azimuth, faced it forward, until the decameter hiss of Jupiter filled the room.

I keep the radio on, now the time is free for me to fill, metered only by the tripping in my chest. I have shorted out the cycle on the cabin lights, and gone to manual. Sometimes, I work in the hold, removing instruments from one of the capsules. The instruments are useless to me now; I want the shell. Sometimes, on ship's radio, I transmit: music, I have not spoken yet. Jupiter has not answered. It grows oblate ahead, and I wait for word.

Ahead has become beneath.

We thread through satellites too fast to read Europa's lines, past Io's peacock eyes, the radio snarling static from the radiation belts. We dive down deep, into Jupiter's sphere now filling the sky, now out of sky we fall toward a land, and a horizon encircles us, flattens to a wall we climb, a ceiling we cling to, striped with fire, clay, cream, rust, slate, straw, snow. I doubt my calculations, doubt the sense of reckoning with anything this huge. The whole world hangs above, a few dim stars below. We soar or swim, I do not know. We must be close enough to see, or it was all for nothing. I will have all or nothing.

The computer chatters beside me, parroting the terms I fed it weeks ago, but my eyes are pulled from its screen out past our bows, to the end of the broad brown ridge of cloud we follow, ahead where a darkness rises. It sweeps up and over us in a second, and the sun is gone: the aft camera shows a rim of red stretching from horizon to horizon, then, dizzying, the computer swivels the ship to face the sunset where light filters like an infection deep into the planet's limb, until Jupiter seems lit from within by fevers, forges; moonsglow falls ashen on cloudtops. The computer throws a series of numbers across its screen, countdown glowing green in the darkened cabin, gleaming across my knuckles where they grip the armrests, and as the numbers reach zero and turn to the word "ignition" we have ignition and the world is flattened.

Our orbit is low, in secular decay, mission control would have said, leaving me to wonder how much weight to give which meaning of the word.

I am grateful already for the silence they finally surrendered me: I no longer hear their echo mocking in my ears. Only Jupiter fills them now, the voice proper to the scene I see, if only I could fit the sounds to sight, and make some sense of both, strain an answer from the chaos below. I need new words for what I see, and as we pass low over the cloudtops, the hazy regions where my decaying course will drop me, spiral me down in a week or a month, I don't care to calculate, somewhere in my chest I sense the suspension—above or below—of a crushing weight.

Jupiter speaks syllables, sibilants, subsides. I no longer need direct the antenna: the sound seems to pierce the cabin walls, rising from the chaos below. I have broadcast nothing since we entered orbit, but hourly I feel silence grow gravid around me. I have moved Stern's couch from the cockpit, and fitted it in the empty capsule.

Below, finally, it spreads over the horizon and advances, the Great Red Spot I called it, but now I see only a tide of red swallowing everything. The nose of the ship bleeds pink, the light in the cabin suffuses dim red. We have arrived, and nothing is as I expected. Spot? A continent swirls below me, the skin of a world stripped off and spread still dripping across the flanks of Jupiter. I look down and see clouds churn, swallowing, the whole so huge we seem to slow in our passage, or else the ship is drawn lingering toward the shadowed hollow at the center. The hollow passes off our starboard wingtip, and leaves me wondering what to call it now that I have seen: a cyclone, monsoon, typhoon—metavortex like the dozens I can see spun off and shattered below, as much in size to them as they are like a hurricane. No. I do not know. This storm will blow for a million years, as it has blown since before a man worked stone, learned fire, or sketched the shadow of his hand against a cave wall. And at its center, a hazy depth, calm blue, blue as eyes, leading in. I must see closer.

The radio is silent.

It changes hue with every revolution: now an ember, now a rose, a sore, the underside of my tongue. We pass far north of it on one orbit, and it lies on the horizon like the glow of a city. We pass over its center, and the dark center, its rim raised, is a caldera: Etna, I think: Olympus. My chest aches. Ten years ago I stared down the throat of Olympus Mons on Mars, alone at the controls of a ship much like this, while Stern descended to the surface, and returned with eight charred bodies, five women and three men, my crewmates. Through twenty orbits returning like a tongue to a broken tooth I looked down, I wanted to see, there, on a piece of soil irrevocably so, the place where the rocks had burnt blacker, the shards of the ship shining. I looked down, fearing to see the flame of the lander ascending, dreading the quiet at our reunion, a stillness still unbroken. Now I see. I look down on the eye of the storm, and though the resemblance is uncanny I feel nothing: I am careful not to move: the word was balanced within me, but down the vortex I see nothing. A drop of water drifts before my eyes. In it I see reflected all the colors that are on Jupiter. I find I have been sobbing.

It drifts away, and I sleep, undreaming. When I wake my chest feels emptied, the cabin is filled with light, and I lie quiet.

I spent this day at the telescope, watching the surface, setting up a trajectory on the computer. I returned to the instrument capsule, the hollow shell of it, and began again, piling on the couch inside it some things I should jettison: the program manual, two photographs, some tools. Each thing suggested a dozen more alike in their absurdity, their profanation of this place, and then I worked through a time that passed unnoticed, until I found the capsule almost full and the hold, the cabin, the cockpit stripped, a free space almost like the one outside, bounded only by these featureless walls, this steel painted white. I had not thought the shell would hold so much.

I heard it then at last. Whispered without lips, spoken speechlessly by this voice inside that I have heard more clearly since I left the earth behind, the word I came so far to learn.

I heard no signal, saw no blinding flash; the heavens did not open, nor the rocks: but as I fitted in the sphere an ordinary shoe —a sneaker, made by Converse, but the name no longer matters: names are in the capsule now, and only now that they are gone and my world is empty do I understand: nothing. Only nothing: and nothing is a name and nothing more. It is the word, the only word that lies, the only one that tells the whole unholy truth. It was before my beginning, it will be beyond my end, but these words too are nothing. All or nothing: I threw in the object I held, but before I seal them all inside I must complete my mission: all or nothing.

I have not dismantled the ship itself: I need it to live in until I die; but I will make an exception now, and open the panel where the computer's memory lies. On tapes, spiraled on spools, how many million words are stored, my library, they all must go. Reel follows reel into the capsule, until only one remains, still spinning: listen. I will not touch it. I can jettison the rest, drop every souvenir of earth, every memory of mission control into the eye, and cleanse myself of the last of my earthly inheritance. And on the necessary air, food, fuel, and water, and this small store of words, my own, await my story's end.

In the echoing emptiness left in the ship I watch and I wonder as the capsule drops shining away, sun lighting its limb, a crescent moon, Diana, what would I see and what hear had I gone, as it sounds down into the eye of the storm darkly blue. I see the capsule turn in its fall, a slow dreaming spin, a top's sleeping. I see its porthole come round, a flash in the sun blinking back at me. What would I see? This ship, winged V, Nike, Styxdaughter, attending. No more. The noise of our fall would grow, swell, soaring. Down faster now, through thin keening, clouds whipping: it hazes a minute and I fear it lost. Then again suddenly smaller it flashes falling silver into the indigo center, one bright swimming in violet falling and deeper. The sound would be shaking now as it slows, heated and glowing dull red from the wind, the action of sounding. Weight grows on it, pound on pounding, and I think of a bubble in water, unsinking, and see: it is gone. See no splash. Silent.

THE JUNGLE OF INJUSTICE

NORA JOHNSON

Nora Johnson was born in Hollywood, California. She is a short-story writer, critic, and novelist, author of *The World of Henry Orient*, *A Step Beyond Innocence*, and other books. Her most recent work, *Flashback*, is a memoir of her father, Nunnally Johnson.

Standing by the pool, Mandy Rivers was singing along with her own voice on stereophonic tape, watched and admired by her mother and her lover. She wore a black string bikini and an old felt fedora, and on her feet were cork-soled wedgies that laced up her ankles. She had long, honey-colored hair which flopped around as she sang, for she performed with a good deal of energy. She had a strong voice, and the double sound of it poured across the pool and patio and over the other pools and patios carved out of the side of the mountain. The arrangement was precarious, and during heavy rains (which always astonished the inhabitants), houses, or large sections of them, sometimes slid down the side and buried the property below. But John and Anita Rivers had propped up their notch with three tons of cement, which was the most that could be done short of moving down into the flats. It was worth it to live up here where there was always a breeze and the traffic on the freeway was only the faintest murmur, almost soothing, like white sound. Far below, under a perpetual dark golden haze, lay Hollywood.

Anita, stretched out in a lounge chair on the other side of the pool, watched her daughter fondly. Mandy had been endowed with every physical glory that Anita, at her age, had just missed having. Her legs were long and beautiful (Anita's were only long); her breasts were perfect, proportionate globes—inherited from some buxom ancestor, for Anita was flat-chested; the line of her gleaming tanned body from her half-naked behind up the curve of her back to her shoulder was an artist's dream. Her shoulders were straight, her neck was long; if her nose and mouth were a little large, that gave distinction to her face, set her apart from the hundreds or thousands of her kind, struggling up the same constantly narrowing ladder of success. She had a smile that could melt the cruelest heart, and that, along with her considerable talent as singer, dancer, and actress, plus her years of training, gave Anita hope for her in what she knew was a jungle of injustice. It was a world Anita could negotiate fairly well, and John excellently, but she feared for Mandy, who was only twenty-three, and whose dear, funny way of putting her foot in her mouth could be disastrous with the wrong person, and whose tendency to lateness could cost her a job.

Sprawled on a towel at her feet, Mandy's lover, Flash—*Flash*—smiled up at her through his aviator glasses, missing not a curve or a wiggle. He wore a small, shiny, white bikini, and he lounged alongside the pool in almost permanent appreciation of the situation he found himself in, one which Anita regarded alternately as natural and incredible. John thought Flash should be thrown the hell out, but Anita, first at Mandy's urging and then for her own reasons, kept staying his hand.

"They'll just go live in some rathole together," she told him.

"Well, then there's got to be some deadline. I'll put up with him for another week, period. Does he ever have any auditions?"

"He had one yesterday. He didn't get the job."

"Naturally not."

It was natural, inevitable, and annoying that Flash's career didn't move, but it was natural and understandable that Mandy was having a difficult time. There were a million Flashes, there was only one Mandy. To Anita, an eastern emigrant, Flash was some strange indigenous fauna. John had grown up in southern California, and didn't find anything remarkable about him, but

Anita, even after twenty-five years in the southland, was still fascinated and horrified by that quality known as *laid-back*. Flash's presence in this family of achievers was disturbing; he was a lazy butterfly in a colony of ants. When they all got up at seven in the morning, John to be on the set at eight, and Anita to be in her office in the Valley, and Mandy prodded into action for a class when she had one or an early audition, Flash lazed naked on the twin bed he and Mandy shared in her room or floated in the Jacuzzi at the far end of the pool. Mandy would kiss him goodbye tenderly before jumping into her Fiat to go to dance class, and he would frequently be there when John and Anita got home. What he did in the meantime was unclear—the occasional audition, some surfing, a certain amount of hanging around the right places hoping to be noticed.

"Noticed for what?" John asked.

"Oh . . . just noticed," Anita replied. She and John were old-fashioned believers in hard work, and Anita particularly had gone to great lengths to instill this value in Mandy—not so easy in a place where success (whatever that meant) did often come for not much more than simply being noticed at the right moment.

"But it doesn't last," she had told her daughter. "The really great careers, every one, were built on dogged determination and an obsession to be better than anybody else. There is a certain rough justice, you'll see."

"But Tina Reynolds has already done two *Barettas* and a Mary Tyler Moore special and she's a no-talent screw-up."

"You can never afford to sit back and say you're better than the next girl. Assume she's better and see what you can learn from her."

Anita had learned this, as she had learned a great many things, from John. At Mandy's age, she had lived in a sleazy little two-room apartment on Vine Street with a Texas beauty-contest winner named Gardenia Vance. Anita, who had worked all her life for the things she had, never took Gardenia seriously until she got a part that Anita wanted.

"But it's crazy," she had said to John, whom she was "dating" at the time. "We aren't the same type at all. She's Mitzi Gaynor. I'm Rosalind Russell. Besides, I'm ten times as talented and I work ten times as hard."

John said, "She has something you don't, or she wouldn't have gotten the part. My advice to you is, find out what it is."

John Rivers was so serious and intelligent, so unlike the rest of the men she had met in California, that she took his advice to heart. She examined Gardenia as she lay sprawled on the couch covering her nails with hot-pink polish. She watched her panther walk as she went into the kitchen in her blue rayon negligee, flicking on the radio as she filled the basket of the percolator. She listened to Gardenia's stupefyingly dull phone conversations and her brainless comments on the state of the world and her flutelike soprano in the shower. She looked at Gardenia as she wandered naked around the tiny bedroom, fishing through the piles of clothing for a clean bra, digging her toes with their hot-pink nails into her marabou-trimmed mules, admiring herself in the mirror.

One day, with a dreadful sinking feeling, Anita realized what Gardenia had—she had everything. Not only was she beautiful, but because of a certain unselfconscious detachment, she allowed you to stare at her without feeling like a voyeur. It was a trick she played on you, or a deal you made together. Every star that Anita could think of engaged you in the same complicity, or had the same self-framing quality, for it was quite unconscious. You couldn't take your eyes off her. It didn't matter that she was a moron and could hardly read a line—heroines were morons in those days. Thin-faced, intelligent girls like Anita were always the wise-cracking best friend who couldn't get a man, and they got parts only if they had a good comic talent. Girls like Gardenia became stars.

But Gardenia didn't care; after the picture came out she married somebody and went off to live in a trailer camp near Thousand Oaks. She had had very good reviews, and Anita, who had long gotten over being angry about losing the part, was now angry at her for not using what she saw as a precious gift. A couple of years later, when Gardenia came down for a visit, she told Anita that she had never believed she could be a success and wanted to get out while she was still ahead, rather than end up dead in the pool of the Chateau Marmont.

Now that treasured quality could be seen in her own daughter, as unmistakable to Anita as a caul. She watched as Mandy finished the song and dove into the pool, shoes and all, followed by Flash. Together they splashed and plunged about in a giggling effort to get Mandy's shoe-ribbons unwound from her legs and the shoes off her feet, which Flash tried to do with his perfect white teeth while Mandy, unbalanced, ducked and sputtered. It was a Sunday afternoon and the mountainside was quiet except for other splashings in other pools and the occasional shift of gears as a car roared up the steep road. The flame trees rustled and billowing purple bougainvillea on the roof moved in the slight breeze. John, a director, was at a preview in Santa Barbara. The moments of rest were few and dearly bought, and Anita had worked so hard for most of her life that she hardly knew what to do with them when she had them. Even now she had to make a conscious effort not to get up, go inside, and work on the script she was supposed to be revising. When the telephone rang she started to jump up, but Mandy was already out of the pool, one heavy clog still flopping from her ankle by its ribbons. Mandy opened the big glass sliding door that led into the living room and picked up the phone, turning her back to the patio and closing the glass door behind her. Anita made herself lie back again and Flash slowly swam toward her. He leaned his elbows on the side of the pool and smiled up at her.

"Want me to turn on the sprinklers, Anita?"

She shook her head and smiled musingly at him. Strangely enough she liked Flash, disapproval struggled with a little core of affection. He seemed to be entirely without guile or suspicion. If life were like her television scripts, she and Flash would sleep together, thereby destroying her marriage and her relationship with her daughter. Then he would callously go off to wreck another home. Flash was such a willing and good-natured houseguest (though the term didn't seem quite accurate) that she imagined he could be seduced, if that was what she wanted of him, out of sheer politeness, the desire not to be rude to his hostess. But

Anita's hungers lay elsewhere, and Flash tried to please only by watering the garden in the late afternoon and occasionally straining the leaves and bugs off the surface of the pool, as well as being agreeable to his elders.

"Thanks, I did it before."

"You're going to have a few tomatoes out there," said Flash. He had a pleasant cowboy twang which went oddly with his bleached hair and chest-bangles. "And some more of those baby lettuces are ready."

"I don't know why I bother with that vegetable patch."

"Just one more thing to fuss with, Anita." He had her number. "I went back East last year," he went on. "Visited a guy I know in New York. Man, I was glad to get out of there. Everybody was in too much of a hurry."

"That's how they get things done."

Flash grinned and suddenly submerged. She watched the water close over him and then he surfaced again in another spot, still grinning. "You got to go with the flow, Anita."

"If John and I had gone with the flow all these years you wouldn't be splashing around in that pool."

Flash laughed. "I don't *need* this pool," he said. "I like it, but it sure isn't worth killing myself for."

Behind the door Mandy put the receiver down and went over to the bar on the other side of the room. She took a handful of ice cubes out of the plastic bucket, put them in a glass, opened a can of Fresca and poured it in. Then she took the glass to the telephone and continued talking. She sat on the back of the sofa, legs hanging down, picking with one hand at the shoe-ribbons. Finally she hung up, opened the sliding door, and came out onto the patio, where she lay down in the lounge chair next to Anita. She rested the Fresca on her satiny brown stomach, where tiny hairs marched in a delicate golden line, and closed her eyes.

Anita had grown up in Connecticut, in a place where communication was as sharp and clear as the winter air. In her parents' white clapboard house there were bulletin boards, note pads with pencils next to them, magnets on the refrigerator to hold messages, and a telephone in the small front hall where all conversations could be easily overheard. Everyone announced his or her comings and goings—"I'm going to town to get eggs, back in half an hour." "That was Jane on the phone—she's returning those books on her way to the dentist. Oh, and she said Bob Davis is coming next week, his mother's seriously ill." The conversation at dinner was mostly about what everyone had done all day—dull though it might be, it was considered to have a place simply because it had happened.

"I'm going in search of stimulating conversation," Anita had said when she left. Of course that wasn't true; she was going in search of acting jobs. But she assumed that people who did interesting things would talk about them in an interesting way. John did, about being a director, but he had said that when it came to making pictures, the single perfectly chosen action could be more telling than the best dialogue. He told her that after she had given up trying to be an actress and had decided to try her hand at script-writing.

She watched Mandy, waiting for the announcement that never came of its own accord. Then, as always, she gently pried.

"Was it anything about Bronstein?"

Bronstein held Mandy's fate in his hand: he was considering her for a part in a feature film. He was "hot," he was "top enchilada" at Fox. The mention of his name broke glass at twenty feet. The air shimmered, and Mandy said nothing for a moment. Her eyes pressed closed more tightly, and then she sighed and reached under the chair, groping around on the concrete for her pack of thin black cigarettes.

"Tomorrow," she said, without opening her eyes. Slowly she pulled one of the cigarettes out of the package and lit it, then inhaled and blew out a great lungful of smoke in a kind of sigh.

"Oh, Mandy, darling." Anita excitedly reached over and pressed her daughter's inert hand.

Flash had gotten out of the pool and now he walked over to where they were sitting, sprinkling diamond drops of water around. He bent down and kissed Mandy's silken middle.

"You feel good about that, baby?" he asked.

"Sure," Mandy said from behind her sunglasses. "I love to have my head chopped off."

The lighting in the kitchen was indirect, coming from under the cupboards, and it created a bright circle at the end of the long, dark living room. Outside the rough surface of the pool water picked up little points of light from the interior rooms, all of which opened with sliding glass doors onto the patio. There were tatami blinds for privacy, but Mandy's were open, and as Anita put the few dishes in the dishwasher she could see her daughter sprawled on the bed watching television. She had eaten alone. Flash had gone out to meet some people who "might help" and Mandy had said she was tired and didn't want dinner. Mandy's face was devoid of expression, her room a spectacular mess, and Anita was glad that fastidious John wasn't around to see it. She would pick it up later tonight, or first thing in the morning.

Anita closed the dishwasher and sat down at the butcher-block table with a cup of coffee. At the same moment Mandy flicked off the TV and walked toward the kitchen. She was wearing a white terry cloth robe, her hair untidily tied back with a ribbon, and she looked rather sleepy and cross.

"Is there anything to eat?" she asked, opening the refrigerator.

"I'll fix you something."

"Oh, I'll do it." She took out the makings of an enormous Dagwood sandwich, and Anita smiled. "God, I feel really weird. Dizzy, kind of. Maybe I'm just hungry." She piled salami, cheese, lettuce, pickles, and hard-boiled egg slices on a piece of bread and put mayonnaise on top.

"What do you have to do for the audition?" Anita asked. "Read a scene?"

"I guess so." Mandy's voice was low as she poked the monstrous sandwich together and opened a can of Fresca. Then she laughed. "Maybe I'll get laryngitis again. Remember that time in Pasadena, at that amateur night, and the time at CBS when I couldn't warble about the margarine?" Her eyes were bright as she took a huge bite of the sandwich. She chewed and then gulped some of it down. "I'll never forget Jimmy What's-his-face's expression when I opened my mouth and out came this croak."

Exasperation settled over Anita's head like a lowering cloud. "My God, Mandy. You laugh at the strangest things. Now if you're nervous, I don't blame you a bit. When I had my audition with Zanuck . . ."

Mandy's eyes glazed over. "I'm not nervous," she said. She held the monstrous sandwich in her graceful hands, one piece of lettuce dangling down between two long, lacquered nails.

"How about a glass of wine, to relax?" Anita submitted to a violent urge to get up and move around. She took out a jug of wine and poured them each a glass.

Mandy said, "It's not such a big deal."

"Jesus," Anita said, "it is *so* a big deal."

"But I mean, if there wasn't any audition on Monday, we'd all live, wouldn't we? We wouldn't just lie down and die or anything, would we? We'd keep on going to the studio and swimming in the pool and driving on the freeways, we'd eat and sleep, we might even be able to *smile*. The sun would rise and set, wouldn't it?" Mandy's voice was accusing, but her eyes were lowered. "I'll be all right, Mom. Okay? Everything'll be just *fine*."

The next morning John said, "Flash has to go."

John was a bald, fattish, serious man with sunbaked skin, full of energy and an exuberance that was a life force to the rest of them. As he finished dressing, Anita said worriedly, looking out of the bathroom, "All right. But not until after she sees Bronstein."

"Oh, is that this week? All the more reason he should go right away."

"Let him stay two more days, John."

"I don't want him here another hour."

"But she needs him somehow. He's a nice kid. He's sweet, really."

John laughed. "I told you that when he first came. But enough's enough."

Through the blinds a shadow moved. Anita went over and looked out, but no one was there. The surface of the water was ruffled by tiny breezes and a yellow towel lay in a soggy ball.

Under one of the lounge chairs were a plastic glass and an ashtray full of cigarette butts. John looked over her shoulder.

"When are you going to make her pick up after herself?"

"I can't *make* her do anything. She's twenty-three."

"She's a slob," said John cheerfully, going out into the hall. "Hey, Mandy! Come and have breakfast with me!"

Anita finished dressing hurriedly and went down the hall to Mandy's room. Delicately, she knocked on the door and waited—for order, for a pretense of respectability—and to her surprise Mandy opened the door fully dressed in jeans and a plaid shirt.

"Daddy wants Flash to leave," Anita said. "I'll try to get him to change his mind."

After a slight pause Mandy said, "Never mind. It's all right."

"I'll try to talk him into a few more days."

"Oh, don't bother, Mom. Let's not hassle about it."

"But don't you want . . . ?"

"Flash knows he's supposed to go, just stop worrying. Okay?"

She was elusive, this prized daughter, as hard to catch as a raindrop and as strangely, frustratingly formless. When she was small she had begged for a certain talking doll that was exhaustively advertised on television, and after Anita had driven all over Los Angeles to find it (supplies having been snapped up quickly), Mandy received it listlessly and said she wanted a rubber raft for the pool.

"Where is Flash?" Anita asked suspiciously.

"He's out somewhere." Mandy pulled a comb through her hair. She didn't invite Anita into the room, rather in the most subtle way blocked her every time she tried to move forward. Anita felt a surge of unexpected disappointment.

"Will he be back?"

"Oh, sure. He wants to thank you for being so nice to him."

"I'm sorry," Anita said. "I'm sorry he can't stay."

"Mom, it's all *right!*" Mandy's tone was impatient. "I don't blame Daddy or anything. It's cool, okay?" She edged out the door and closed it behind her. "Had breakfast yet?"

Why doesn't she fight? Anita wondered, sitting at the kitchen table with her coffee, while John made them all an omelet. Her own growing up had been shaped by the violent pull away from her parents and the fighting off of their values, and so, as a matter of fact, had John's. Why was this child so different? Mandy's mouth was stretched over a piece of Granola toast while she read, with the intense preoccupation of the young, the entertainment section of the Los Angeles *Times*. Anita relaxed a little, her tight shoulders lowered. Mandy had her own style, that was all, and a more mature one than hers had been. She saved her energy for work and she worked hard. She talked less. Maybe she and John pressed her too much, she had to be allowed to become her own person. Anita looked at Mandy and asked silently, What do you want of us? Do you love us? Hate us? Can I do anything for you? And if so, won't you tell me what it is?

"How many girls are auditioning?" asked John from the stove.

"Just three," Mandy said.

"Wow. It's that close."

Mandy put down her toast. "I can't eat," she said. "I'm sorry, Daddy, I don't want any." He stood over her with the omelet pan.

"Are you all right, baby?"

"I'm fine. But I don't even want to *smell* it."

John gave Mandy's share to Anita. It was a glory of mushrooms, cottage cheese, and parsley, and she didn't want it either, but she began eating it anyway.

"Do you want me to go with you?" Anita asked.

"No," Mandy said, "and for Christ's sake don't just happen to drop by."

"Is Flash going?"

Mandy's green eyes met hers. "Flash says screw the whole thing," she said, and before they could say anything, she turned and left the room.

By three o'clock Anita knew she could do no more work that day, and she left to go home. There was no way she could spy on Bronstein without looking like an ass, or without Mandy's finding out, and the frustration of the day lay curled up in the pit of her stomach in a small tight ball. She would have stayed home, had not John almost pushed her out the door. The driveway of the house was visible shortly after leaving the Hollywood freeway, and as Anita's BMW crept down the white street late that afternoon she looked through the tops of the eucalyptus trees to see who was home. John's Mercedes wasn't there, nor was Mandy's Fiat, but Flash's Mustang was.

She parked and went quickly inside. The house was dark in contrast to the glare outside, a place to hide. In the hall stood Flash's suitcase. She went down the hall to Mandy's room, which was empty and quite neat. The bookshelves were empty, the bare sheets smooth, the blinds closed.

She opened the glass door and went out onto the patio. The pool was quiet, sun-dappled turquoise, a vast, opaque eye that gave away nothing. She walked around it to the living room doors and slowly opened them. It took a moment for her eyes to adjust to the darkness, and then she saw Flash sitting on the sofa. He wore white jeans and a Hawaiian shirt knotted over his middle, and he held a can of Sprite.

"Hi," he said.

She looked at him in his gay getup—except he wasn't gay, he was her daughter's passionate lover, given to lying around in the sun with lightener in his hair. Slowly he stood up.

"Did she go to the audition?" Anita demanded.

"I haven't the faintest idea."

"Damn you," she said, "I don't believe you."

He looked at her in surprise. "Man, I can't help *what* you believe. I don't *know* where she is." She stared at him uncertainly. "Her suitcase is gone. And her drawers are empty. Go see for yourself." While she did so he took another drink from the Sprite can and lit a cigarette with John's leather table lighter.

Anita came back slowly and sat down in a chair. She felt weak and faint, and there was a dreadful pressure in her throat, the pressure of imminent tears. He wasn't kidding. Only a week ago they had all had dinner together, the four of them. She had cooked steaks outside on the grill and Flash had made the salad out of vegetables from the garden, their own tomatoes and cucumbers and parsley grown in a sandy patch on the mountainside. John had told stories and they had drunk two bottles of wine, and Mandy had laughed and laughed.

"You did it," Anita said, and her voice broke. "You never wanted her to audition with Bronstein. 'Flash says screw the whole thing.' With one eloquent sentence you destroyed everything, so she could go with the flow like the rest of you. Damn you, why did you ever come here?"

Flash, at the bar with his hand in a can of peanuts, turned and stared at her. "I didn't want her to audition? You think I'm crazy? I *pushed* her. You think I like sleeping on the beach, spending my time with losers?"

Anita said slowly, "But didn't you say . . . ?"

"I never said it. She *wanted* me to say it. She'd say, 'This thing with Bronstein is making me crazy. I can't sleep. I have pains in my chest. I'm not right for the part. If I don't get it my mother'll kill me.' I said, 'If you don't go, *I'll* kill you.' We're a good pair, Anita. We drove her right out of the house." Anita, sitting in the darkness, was silent. "Listen, there's a million like me out there. But Mandy's something special. I'd have to be *nuts* to want to stop her." He looked at her. "Oh, come on, don't cry. Kids disappear all the time. She's probably in Venice." He came over to her. "Listen, I want to thank you for putting me up all this time. You and your husband and Mandy are the first things in this town that didn't turn out *rotten*."

"I'm sorry," she said, and her voice shook. "I'm really sorry."

"Hey, nothing to be sorry about, man." He looked around the pleasant room and gave a small, involuntary sigh. "Well, I'd better split."

"Don't you want to . . . wait for her?" The abruptness of this announcement and the ease with which he was ready to depart their lives was a little startling. "Would you like a drink? I mean, she might phone. She might even come back." She turned on the lamp. "You know, she might even have *gone* to Bronstein and not want us to know."

Flash looked at her for a moment. "You're crazy," he said, matter-of-factly. He got out two glasses and began putting ice in them from the ice bucket, and then Scotch—he knew what she liked to drink. "Some cheese?" He went into the kitchen and got a piece of Brie out of the refrigerator, and put it on a plate with crackers. "It's always so damn hard to leave," he said.

The last fiery rays of the sun burned over the Pacific and across the white beach, so wide and magnificent that it made the tiny, rocky little edgings in the East seem hardly worthy of the name. The sand was dented with thousands of footprints, and a few late stragglers were gathering up towels to go home. Along the boardwalk floated the roller-skaters on their plastic skates, bending and dipping, ducking back and forth like ghostly birds in the fading light. The oldest people in sight were a pair of silver-haired, bronze-skinned gays strolling along the boardwalk, but everyone else was young and lovely limbed, children playing at dusk in some never-never land.

Mandy left her Fiat in a parking lot and walked along the boardwalk for a while, then sat down on the edge and looked out over the beach. She lit a joint and smoked it slowly, enjoying it as she enjoyed the warmth of the fading sun and the heat of the sand between her bare toes, the smell of the sea and of french fries from a fast-food stand. She felt as though the cold of the pool were being baked out of her, slowly thawing whatever it was that made her feel so hard and chilly in the daytime and so terrified at night—that sapphire coolness she dipped in again and again until she was coated all over with something she didn't understand. In a few minutes she'd get a hamburger from the stand, and some of the fries, and after she had eaten she'd go and find Liz, or Ralph and Dicky, and stay with them for a while till she got her head together. Not too long—you had to be careful about staying with people too long—it could do funny things to you, as it had to Flash. She knew that, and now she also knew the precious power of splitting.

She leaned back against one of the pilings and smiled, her eyes half closed. Somebody's radio was playing Billy Joel's "Movin' Out." The longer you stayed the harder it was to leave, the more you hated yourself for staying there, helpless and half strangled and exhausted from the effort of not telling them to shove it. When the time came to get in touch with her parents, in a few months or whatever it took, her explanation would be very simple: "You wore me out." Not that they'd have any idea what she was talking about. But possibly, if she worked on it in the months to come, by that time she'd have a better way of putting it—though it was stupid to think that at twenty-three there had to be an explanation.

She looked down the boardwalk, half expecting to see her mother barreling along in her big sunglasses, her well-cut pants, her gigantic leather handbag full of checks and credit cards, her mouth pulled into that tense smile. How had she gotten like that? She called it "drive," and said the rest of the Connecticut relatives had it too, but none of them were as bad as Anita. If that was drive, Mandy didn't want it, though she didn't know what she wanted instead—except, at the moment, to sit here and get stoned. She hadn't done it for a long time, since about three years ago when she used to smoke dope all the time to get her mother, before she had become a "serious actress."

She got up and went over to the hamburger stand and bought herself some dinner, and as she sat down to eat it she felt a little twinge of loneliness. She would sleep alone tonight, for the first time in weeks—alone on somebody's couch or in somebody's sleeping bag. It would be so easy for Flash to find her, if he wanted to. She was in this obvious place, hanging out like a sore thumb. Part of it was, probably, a test—the kind most people never dared make. She thought how strange it was that the strongest statements people made to each other were silent—acts or the absence of acts—and how you knew in some gut way what they meant before your head understood them. He might come, it was possible—just stroll along the walk in his white jeans and say, "Hey, babe, let's find some place of our own to live. I don't care if we're poor." Now that was the real fantasy, the ultimate dream.

I THOUGHT OF CHATTERTON, THE MARVELOUS BOY

KENNETH GEWERTZ

Kenneth Gewertz was born in New York City and spent most of his childhood in Floral Park, Queens. He received a bachelor's degree in English from Queens College and a master's in English from Princeton. Since then he has worked as an editor, writer, and teacher and is now a public relations writer for the University of Massachusetts at Amherst. His stories have appeared in *The Massachusetts Review*, *Ploughshares*, and the *Carleton Miscellany*.

Martin Sobel had his coronary in November. The month was significant. He took it as a sign—the most recent in a long, discouraging series—of the inherent shoddiness of the stuff of which he was made. "I couldn't wait for winter and get it shoveling snow like the rest of the old geezers," he complained. "I had to get it in the autumn raking leaves."

As a joke the remark was a great success. Herb Green, his neighbor, threw back his head and gave a bellow that brought the nurse stamping in, indignantly demanding silence. And Anne Pelegrino, who taught Spanish at Monroe, gazed at him with such pained sympathy that he thought she might actually gather him in her arms and press him to her vast bosom. The problem was, though, he meant it quite seriously. The doctor had assured him that it was not a severe attack, not one of those that are called "massive." Nevertheless, during those first few days in the hospital, he could think of it in no other way than as the beginning of the end. And, like the final step in a flight of stairs one has miscounted, the end announced itself with unseemly abruptness. He was only fifty-seven. He had imagined a lifetime as being roomier than this one seemed to be.

The sense of doom receded when he returned home and began to absorb himself in the discipline of convalescence. His doctor, who, minus his condescending air and Cardin jackets, could have passed as a student in one of Martin's senior English classes, was big on preventive medicine, and he outlined elaborate dietary rules as well as a progressive exercise program that were to be followed to the letter. Martin had rafts of sick leave coming to him, and the doctor thought it best for him to take off not only the remainder of the fall term, but the spring term as well and, as he phrased it, "Put some real effort into getting healthy again."

Martin took up this suggestion with fierce enthusiasm. Once he realized the second chance that was being handed to him was the real thing, he clung to it like a drowning man. His fatless meals, his digitalis, and his timed constitutionals became exacting daily rituals. "You're going to live," he told himself, staring at his face in the bathroom mirror. "Believe it, Martin; you're going to live."

Single-minded as his pursuit of health was, it still left him with many free hours. Most of these he spent reading. Having once published several poems, he would claim, particularly to junior colleagues, that he was a poet first, a teacher only second, but that mundane affairs kept him from his original love. Now he could afford to think about writing again, and to reacquaint himself with contemporary verse. And hunting up books and periodicals at the public library provided an occasion for the walks his doctor had enjoined.

He spent so much time at the library that it became a kind of second home. Often, while he was reading, students from Monroe would come by to pay their respects. He was speaking one afternoon with a boy and girl from his senior honors class who, by all indications, were "serious" about each other, when he happened to look past them and notice a woman at the next table smiling pleasantly at him. He smiled back. The young people turned to see who had captured his attention, gazed at the woman for a moment without interest, then turned back to resume their talk.

But Martin continued to dart glances at her, even after she had gone back to her own work, filling a notebook page with extracts from a ponderous volume open on the table before her.

Her gray hair was cropped short, framing her broad, pale face like a helmet. Martin put her age at about fifty, possibly a little older. She wore a dark blue acetate blouse with a strip of the same material tied in a bow around her neck. Encased by the clinging fabric, her arms and shoulders had a rounded, compact sturdiness that Martin was surprised to find himself attracted by.

He had not been with a woman since Mae's death. Even while she was alive, sex had not played much of a part in his life. She had little appetite for it, and he had adjusted. Only now, suddenly, he had a premonition that this was all to change, and that it was the heart attack that had done it, the thing which, logically, should have slowed him from a walk down to a crawl.

He kept his eye on the woman through the rest of the afternoon, and when she got up to go he followed. He caught up with her on the steps outside the library and found her rummaging distraughtly in her bag. She glanced up at him for an instant, then resumed her search. "My fountain pen," she muttered. "I must have left it inside."

"Stay here, I'll get it," Martin said.

"No, no, really."

"Please, it's my pleasure." He re-entered the building and went to the seat she had occupied. There was a Schaeffer pen lying on the table top. He took it and brought it out to her.

"Thank you. You shouldn't have done that." She had a pronounced eastern European accent.

"I wanted to."

They walked in silence to the sidewalk, then she stopped and turned toward him. "I smiled at you before because it was nice to see you talking with that young couple. They were relaxed with you and yet I could see that they respected your authority. Are you a teacher?"

"Yes, but I'm on the shelf now."

"Sabbatical?"

"No, coronary thrombosis."

"Oh?" she said. "Not serious, I hope."

"I was never in real danger. At least that's what they tell me. But while it was happening, I was prepared for the worst. Or rather not prepared, if you know what I mean."

"Of course, that is natural. I only asked because I have seen you walking, and, I don't know, perhaps it was your posture, a certain vigor, you did not strike me as a sick man."

"Why, thank you. You've seen me before then?"

"We live on the same block. You didn't know?"

"No," he said. "Do you really? I'm sorry, I can't imagine why it is I've never noticed you before."

"Please, there is no reason why you should have. I have only been there a few months. I am in the last house across the street from you, on 76th Road. I rent the upper floor."

"Mrs. Shaughnessy's house?"

"Yes, my landlady."

"Martin Sobel," he said, putting out his hand.

"And I am Lola Kaufman." Her handshake was firm.

It was unseasonably warm, far above the melting point. Snow piles veiled with soot decayed slowly into wetness, soaking the crumbling pavement. Three little boys chased by, yelling shrilly, their coats flapping open. Martin felt tongue-tied, out of place as well as out of practice. Like the old joke, he thought: I know you're supposed to whistle, but I can't remember why. The woman came to his rescue.

"Do you teach at the local high school?" she asked.

"Yes, James Monroe. I've been there twenty-six years."

She smiled ruefully. "That seems such a long time to be in one place. It must be quite a good school."

"Not as good as it used to be. It used to be topnotch. Now it's just the best of a bad lot."

"I asked," she said, "because I was wondering how well my son would fit in there. He is at a private school now, and it is very good, of course, but it is also very expensive, and I wondered, now that we are in this neighborhood, whether the public school might be all right for him."

"Has there been some problem?" Martin asked.

"No, not a serious one. Only he is very . . . high-strung. He is a creative boy, only his life at home has not been . . . but you are not interested in such stories. You must know thousands of them. Tell me, what subject do you teach?"

Martin tried to assure her that he was, in fact, interested in her son's problem, but she absolutely refused to speak of it. At last he was persuaded to talk about himself, and, once he warmed to the subject, found it an unusual pleasure. She was an astute interrogator, and she showed such unfaltering interest that he found himself divulging information which ordinarily he considered rather private.

He began to talk about his poetry. He had started writing in the army and continued after he was discharged and returned to college. Those early poems—wry, wistful reflections on camp life tinged with romantic longing—seemed quite immature and remote from him now. Yet they had been published while his later poems had not. He had never been able to understand it. In any event, the rejections discouraged him, and, as his responsibilities grew, his poetic output diminished. Finally, it shrank to nothing.

"And you have given it up entirely then?" she asked.

"To tell you the truth, no. Since the attack I've decided to go back to it. It's a little late in the game, but who knows? Only this time I'm going to be smart about it. Not like some young excuse me, schmuck, who thinks he's a genius that no one can teach anything. This time, before I even start, I'm familiarizing myself with what's been done. I'm reading all the collections, the studies, I'm going to back issues of magazines, I'm giving myself a real education in the subject, and when I feel that I know what's what, then I'll start to think about writing something of my own."

She began nodding in agreement before he finished speaking. "Yes," she said, "I think it is a very good plan. And it will help you as a teacher as well, isn't that so?"

"Yes, of course," he said. "But primarily it's for me. I've decided that for once in my life I have the right to be selfish about something."

They walked in silence for half a block. Martin was dressed too warmly, and the oppressive weight of his many layers of clothing made him short of breath and slightly faint. It frightened him, and he felt his heart begin to pound. He stopped and ripped off his scarf and opened the top buttons of his overcoat.

"Are you all right?"

He turned, aware of how alarming his distress must be to her. "I'm okay," he said. It came out a hoarse gasp, hardly as reassuring as he had intended.

"My house is only a block more. You can rest there."

"It's really nothing."

"Please, I don't mind."

He was carrying a small shopping bag full of books. She took it from him and thrust her arm through his. "There," she said. "You can lean on me if you feel unsteady. I am strong."

There was nothing wrong with him, he realized, just fatigue. That bursting pain he had experienced the first time was absent. But he let her guide him, leaning against her shoulder, their hips brushing together through the thicknesses of cloth.

They reached the house. Keeping her arm in his, she opened her bag and took out the key. "Can you manage the stairs?" she asked as the door swung open.

"I think so."

He mounted the stairs slowly, the woman close beside him in the steep, narrow compartment. They reached the top, made a right turn, and entered the living room. She helped him off with his coat, then led him to the sofa. "Do you want something to drink?" she said. "Some tea, coffee?"

"Just a glass of water would be fine."

While she was in the kitchen running the faucet, he took a look around. It was obviously a furnished apartment, filled with the carved mahogany and lumpy brocade of forty years ago—Mrs. Shaughnessy's cast-offs. But it was so clean and orderly, the puckered veneers so polished, the old oriental, nearly worn through in spots, so carefully vacuumed, it was as if the room considered itself a showplace in spite of the shabbiness of its components. She returned with a glass of water and placed it in his hand.

"Thank you," he said, taking a sip. "You know, I really am all right. It's just this weather, so warm and muggy. I was a little overdressed and I got overheated. But I'm fine now, I really am."

"Good," she said, obviously relieved. She sank into the armchair across from him. "But it is best to be careful, I think, yes?"

Her overcoat was open. She wore a gray, belted skirt and a pair of low-heeled black shoes. The lower half of her body had the same sturdy solidity he had admired in her arms and shoulders. Her calves and ankles were rather thick, and a vein or two bulged through her nylons, but there was a vitality about her, an indomitable self-respect which, like the room, seemed to hold signs of age in disdain.

Martin gave a laugh. "Being careful is the story of my life," he said. "It's what I do best."

She looked away, and he sensed that his self-pity had discomforted her. He changed the subject. "I noticed in the library that you were very industriously taking notes. Are you taking a course or . . . ?"

"I am a student," she said brightly. "I am going for my bachelor's degree."

"In what subject?"

"Mathematics."

"Really? I'm barely able to handle simple arithmetic myself. I'm impressed."

"I went into it because it interested me," she said. "Not for any practical reason. Now that my husband and I are separated, I wonder if I chose wisely. I have been thinking of taking the necessary education credits so I can teach, but I have been told that the schools prefer not to hire those who speak with an accent."

"That's nonsense," Martin said hotly. "Whoever told you that doesn't know what he's talking about." The thought of this charming woman being turned down for reasons that were so patently discriminatory distressed him. Yet when he mentally reviewed the staff at Monroe he could think of only two teachers with accents, and they were both Puerto Rican and under twenty-five. No, Lola would not have much of a chance.

"It may be just as well," she said. "Possibly I will go on to graduate school. That is what I really want. It is only the financing that is still in question."

"Doesn't your husband help?"

"Yes, when he can." She looked down at her lap. There was an uncomfortable moment. Then she looked up again with a determined smile. "Can't I get you something else? I have some excellent coffee cake in the freezer."

He gave in. She took him into the kitchen and sat him at the table. He examined the room admiringly while she bustled around, measuring coffee into the percolator, slicing the cake. Like the living room, it was spotless and orderly to an extreme. But here, with less to begin with, she had expressed her personality more fully. Using the most inexpensive materials—contact paper, art prints, common craft items—she had managed to create an environment that was warm, tasteful, inviting. Martin's own kitchen was virtually the same as Mae had left it—a kind of anonymous Sears Roebuck modern. He had thought of changing it, but somehow a kitchen needed a woman's touch.

She brought the cake and coffee to the table and sat down across from him. The conversation flowed on. Martin felt a profound contentment, but at the same time he was quivering with excitement and anticipation. What senseless fastidiousness had ever induced him to deny himself pleasure such as this?

Downstairs the front door opened, and suddenly she was no longer with him. Her eyes shifted focus, and she seemed to attend to the sounds of knob-turning, lock-clicking, and foot-shuffling with her whole being. There were footsteps on the stairs. As they neared the top she lowered her cup and gripped the table edge, ready to stand. "Andrei," she called. "Is that you? We are in here, sweetheart, in the kitchen."

There was no sound, just the sense of a sullen, wary presence.

"Aren't you coming in? There is someone here I want you to meet."

He heard the squeak of a rubber sole, then a series of heavy footsteps. He looked up. A giant appeared in the doorway. He was about six foot six, a huge, rawboned boy. He wore a blue down jacket, and if he had stood straight, his shoulders would have filled the door frame. But he had the adolescent's need to minimize himself. He not only slouched, he presented his body edge-on, tucking his blond, touseled head behind his shoulder like a timid pugilist. His mother rose from the table, went to him, and put her arm through his. "Come," she said to Martin with a proud smile. "Come and meet my son."

He came toward them.

"Andrei, this is Martin Sobel. He is a teacher of English at the high school. Martin, my son Andrei."

The boy's face was pale and somewhat indistinct. His eyes, however, were extraordinary. They were a warm brown flecked with amber and viridian like some exotic mineral. Almond shaped, rimmed with long brown lashes, they would have been conspicuous on a woman. On this pathetic Goliath they seemed an exercise in incongruity, a grotesque collage. Martin forced a smile and held out his hand.

The boy stammered something that might have been hello. The magnificent eyes squeezed shut and the head twitched to one side. The moist, flaccid hand briefly enclosed Martin's, then dropped away. The boy glanced pleadingly at his mother. Something passed between them, rapid, private, then he turned and shuffled down the hall and out of sight.

Childless himself, Martin nevertheless had had plenty of experience with parents and their offspring, and he knew some compliment was in order, even a comment on the boy's size would have done. But all he could feel was a towering revulsion. "I think I really must be getting home now," he said.

She accompanied him down the stairs. The street lamp drenched her in white light as she held open the door. She gave him a cheerful smile, and Martin was filled with admiration for her. To soldier on, to keep up an unflinching front, when upstairs lurked that spastic golem whom the genetic grab-bag had foisted on her—that indeed was admirable. Reaching the sidewalk, he turned to wave. She waved back. A movement above drew his attention. It was the boy. Unaware that he could be seen in the window as clearly as an actor on a stage, he stared down at Martin boldly. Martin looked up frowning, and the boy quickly slipped from view.

Martin was at the library early the next morning. It was a fine, clear day, not too cold, and the crisp air seemed to sing in his blood. It was the first time since his heart attack that he had experienced a sense of physical well-being. He couldn't make himself concentrate. Each time the door opened, his eyes bobbed up from the page. He spent hours dreamily wandering among the shelves, picking up books at random and absently riffling their pages. Lola arrived at two. He caught her eye and gave a little wave as she went to her seat. She smiled warmly, but immediately absorbed herself in her work and took no more notice of him for the rest of the afternoon. By the time she began packing up her notes and returning her books to the shelves, the sky had turned a majestic violet. Martin was waiting for her when she arrived at the door.

"Are you on your way home?"

"Yes."

"Do you mind if I walk with you?"

"Not at all. I would like that very much."

They walked slowly, enjoying the beauty of the evening. A single bright star shining above the silhouetted turrets of the railway station was like part of a stage set, too gorgeous to be real.

"There is a favor I wish to ask you," Lola said, turning to him.

"Of course, anything."

They were within sight of her house. The windows on the second story were dark. She slowed her pace, looking down at the sidewalk as though collecting her thoughts.

"It's about Andrei. I don't know if it is fair of me to ask this. Perhaps, with your own work, you do not want such a bother. If this is so, please tell me. I mean this sincerely. Andrei has written quite a lot of poetry. Whether it is good, bad, I really do not know. My English is not sufficiently good for me to tell, I think. Some pieces seem excellent to me, but I don't know, maybe I am reading them as a proud parent. I have told him to show them to his English teacher, but he says that he has no rapport with her, and he refuses. Finally he has given me permission to bring them to one of my professors at the college, but now I think that I would rather give them to you because, I don't know, I think you would be kinder, more understanding. It has been hard for him these past years, and now he has found a way to express himself, but he needs encouragement."

Martin nodded understandingly. The idea of the creature he had met the day before composing poetry was a bit startling at first, but he soon adjusted to it. As a teacher he had seen the most unlikely cases bloom suddenly into would-be Byrons and Shelleys, only to lapse back to normalcy by the following semester. In a sense, poetry was one of the diseases of adolescence, like mononucleosis. There was no reason why it shouldn't strike anyone who was not absolutely a vegetable. Nor was it likely that Andrei's efforts would be the worst he had encountered in his long career. He assured Lola that he would be happy to read her son's poems.

"You are terribly kind," she said. They were in front of her house. "Wait here, I will run up and get them for you." She entered the house, emerging a minute later with a green folder. She thrust it into his hands. "I will say nothing about them," she said. "I will let you read them and judge."

He tucked the folder under his arm.

"Does Saturday give you enough time?" she said. "Andrei will be visiting his father over the weekend, and I thought that if you wished you could come for dinner and we could discuss the poems then."

"I would like that very much indeed."

"Would six o'clock be all right?"

"Fine."

"Good. Until Saturday then, and once more I thank you."

Martin did not get around to Andrei's manuscript until the following evening when he took it to bed with him, expecting to give the poems a quick once-over before going to sleep. What he found amazed him. He had anticipated dog-trot rhythms, forced rhymes, some effusions in *vers libre*, perhaps a haiku or two. Not finding these things, he was at first somewhat baffled and annoyed. It took some time before he was able to understand that he was in the presence of genius.

In terms of technical proficiency the poems were the work of a mature artist. Andrei knew literature, and he had learned from it. When he wrote a sonnet, he not only got the rhymes in the right places and the right number of beats to each line; you could tell that he had read Shakespeare and Spenser and Milton and even Berryman. When he used free verse, you heard Yeats and Williams and Pound.

But he was no parrot. He did more than imitate, much more. There was a unique sensibility in these poems, a definite voice. While technically he showed remarkable precocity, his themes, his imagery, were those of anguished adolescence. That was what made them so remarkable—all the torment and humiliation of growing up was here, the obscure longings, the immoderate gestures, but raised to such verbal heights that they achieved a kind of monumentality. It was as if, Martin thought, groping for a simile, as if a god had been afflicted with acne.

It was past 3 A.M. by the time eye strain and drowsiness finally got the better of him and he put the manuscript down and switched off the light. But he was unable to sleep. Passages from the poems had embedded themselves in his memory and kept sounding through his mind. Andrei's face appeared, not the stammering, twitching boy he had met the day before, but the face of the poet. The eyes, like great warm gems, peered into the bare unprotected spaces of Martin's soul. Ease my pain, they pleaded, help me to be born.

Martin awoke the next morning cramped, stiff, a moist, insistent ache behind his eyes. The green folder lay on the night table. He propped himself up and reached for it. A part of him hoped that his initial judgment would turn out wrong, but if anything the poems were finer in the light of day. There were subtleties, hidden meanings, music he had failed to notice the first few times he had read them.

He put the folder down, turned over, and buried his face in the pillow. He felt a hollow pain in his chest, and for one furious moment he wished that the clotted valves in his heart would constrict and finish him once and for all. What was the point of nurturing this remnant of life when he was condemned to a bland mediocrity to the end of his days? He had wanted to be a poet, but in half a century of effort he had produced nothing of value, not even one really good line. As for his current plan to build himself into a poet through study and imitation, that was a waste of time. This child made language obey him in ways Martin couldn't hope to duplicate if he lived to the end of time.

He lay there a long time, his eyes open, staring at the wall. Finally he rolled over, sat up, and planted his feet decisively on the floor. Standing, he picked up the folder. "I'll marry her," he said aloud. Then again, more positively, clenching his fist, "I'll marry her!"

At six that evening he rang Lola's bell, the folder in his hand. She came downstairs in an apron, flushed from the heat of the kitchen. "Come in, come in," she said. "Please excuse me, dinner is a little late."

The apartment had been tidy before; now it seemed to shine. The wooden surfaces were like mirrors, the upholstery looked shampooed. Martin sat on the couch and put the folder beside him.

"How about a little something to drink? I have scotch, brandy, vodka."

He put his hand over his heart. "Nothing too strong, I'm afraid."

"A spritzer then?"

"Fine."

She disappeared into the kitchen. He heard the wrenching of an ice cube tray, then the whoosh of seltzer in glasses. In a moment she was back with the drinks. Martin waited for a chance to mention Andrei's poetry, but she did not give him one. She kept her eyes off the folder, chatting about her classes, about gossip she had picked up from Mrs. Shaughnessy. After a few minutes she excused herself and went back to the kitchen, returning with a tray of pickled herring, a stack of cocktail napkins, and a little cut-glass jar filled with toothpicks.

"This is delicious," Martin said, patting his lips with one of the little napkins. "Why doesn't the herring I buy taste this good?"

"I made this myself," she said with a pleased twinkle. He heard a pot boiling over. "Please excuse me once again," she said, running back into the kitchen. Martin settled back, took a fresh toothpick, and speared another chunk of fish.

The meal was lavish and superb. They ate by candlelight from heirloom china. The silver shone with a soft gleam, and the wine sparkled in crystal goblets. She waited on him so assiduously that his wishes were met before he had half thought of them. The folder remained on the sofa while they dined.

By the time she brought out dessert, Martin was feeling more exquisitely satiated than he had in years. The rich sauces had alarmed him, but one time wouldn't hurt. Besides, he had the feeling that if he so much as hinted at his dietary restrictions, the cholesterol would vanish from her cooking like magic. He would tell her for next time.

They went into the living room for coffee. "Did you have time to read my son's poems?" she asked, trying to hide the apprehension in her voice.

"Yes, I did," he said, relishing the moment. "And I think they're extremely good—more than good, I think they're extraordinary."

Her face lit up. "Andrei will be so pleased. I too felt they were good, but I was not sure. My English . . ."

He was about to pick up the folder when the doorbell rang.

"Excuse me, please," she said and went downstairs to answer it.

It was a man. Martin could not make out what was being said, but he sensed an intimacy between the two speakers. They conversed rapidly, snapping at one another with accusations and denials. He was alone for quite a few minutes. Finally there was a sound of footsteps on the stairs, and Lola came back into the room, followed by her visitor.

"Martin," she said, "I want you to meet Andrei's father."

"Julius," the man said, stepping forward and thrusting out his hand.

Andrei's size remained as much of an enigma as ever. Julius Kaufman was a bantam of a man, no taller than his wife and a good twenty pounds lighter. His face was small, wizened. A sparse, wispy beard grew on the delicate chin. His graying hair was brushed back and hung in greasy curls over his collar. His right upper incisor was made of gold. Still in his overcoat, he threw himself into the armchair and breathed out stertorously through his nostrils.

Lola stood in the center of the threadbare carpet, wringing her hands. "I'm sorry, Martin, but there is a problem. Andrei is gone. We do not know where he is."

Julius made a disparaging noise. "He'll be fine. Seventeen years old and she treats him like a baby." He took out a pack of Gauloise and lit one, staring disgustedly at the floor lamp beside his chair.

Lola took the glass ashtray from the coffee table and placed it beside him. "Will you tell me what happened?" she said. "What did you do to make him run away?"

"What did I do?" he exploded. "I didn't do anything! I talk to him like a mensch and he can't take it because you coddle him all the time."

"What did you say?"

He shrugged and sucked on the fat cigarette. "Nothing."

Martin started to rise. "I can go if you want to deal with this by yourselves."

"No," Lola said, taking a step toward him, hands raised as if she meant to push him back onto the sofa. "Please, that is not necessary. Would you like some more coffee?"

"No, thank you." He settled back reluctantly.

Julius turned toward him. The pungent smoke from his cigarette tickled Martin's nose. "Do you have any children?"

Martin shook his head.

"You're a lucky man. You won't find many people honest enough to say that, but it's true. Maybe once upon a time it was different, when a father was someone you listened to. My own father, rest his soul, I would sooner bite off my tongue than talk back to him. He used to whack me across the shins with his cane. I could still show you the scars. Of course he was from the old country." He turned away, gazing across the room, the cigarette between thumb and forefinger. The ash fell off and landed on his fly. He brushed it absentmindedly onto the carpet.

Lola glared at him, then turned on her heel. "I am going to call your apartment to see if he is there," she said, walking toward the bedroom.

Julius turned back to Martin as soon as Lola was gone. "Are you one of my wife's professors?" he asked.

"No, I'm a neighbor."

"What do you do? Businessman? Doctor? Lawyer?"

"High school teacher," Martin said. "English."

"Very good. You've met my son?"

"Yes, briefly."

"I call him my son because he bears my name. As Shakespeare tells us, 'It's a wise father that knows his own son,' which I'm sure you know, being a very well-read man. But since you've seen the boy, I don't have to tell you he looks about as much like me as I look like a Chinaman."

Martin was at a loss. He shrugged consolingly.

"No, it's all right, it's all right. I can face facts. I learned to face facts at a very young age." He jerked his thumb in the direction of the bedroom. "She's the one who's trying to run from reality."

Lola returned, as though summoned by the accusation. "He's not there," she said. "Julius, tell me what you said to him to make him run out."

The little man thrust out his lower lip and spread his hands palms up. "I gave him some constructive criticism."

"What exactly did you say?"

"We were sitting at the table. I made him a nice dinner—chicken livers and noodles. You remember the way I used to make that. Every Sunday. It used to be my specialty."

"Will you get to the point, please?"

"All right, all right! He was sitting there jerking around, you know? I know he does it just to get my goat, I've watched him very carefully."

"He does it when he's feeling tense. Go on."

"So I told him to stop it, that's all."

"That's all you said?"

"That's all. I swear, it's the God's honest truth."

"That's all, just 'Andrei, will you please stop doing that?' "

"Well, I may have put it a little stronger than that, just to get him to listen to me."

"A little stronger. What do you mean, a little stronger?"

"You know, a little stronger choice of words, so he'd pay attention to what I was trying to say to him."

"What were the exact words, Julius?"

"The exact words? Okay, I'll tell you the exact words. I said he looked like a drunken ape and if he didn't cut it out he was going to end up in the loony bin, that's what I said."

Lola covered her face with her hands.

"It's the truth!" Julius cried. "He needs someone to tell him what's what, not the fairy stories you've been feeding him ever since he was in the cradle."

Lola's arms dropped to her sides. She leaned over him, trembling with anger. "I only hope you haven't done it this time," she said. "I only hope you haven't finished it."

"What are you talking about?"

"Just the other day," she said in a low, even voice. "I found him in the bathroom. He was holding a razor blade and he was staring at his wrist."

"No!"

"No? Julius, I saw it."

"He was doing it for the effect. He was trying to frighten you. All this time and you still don't understand him."

"I understand he's in pain and that you with your insensitivity may have pushed him over the edge."

Julius squirmed in his seat, silently fuming. At last he burst out, "If he's so close to the edge, then let him fall over! Let him go! It's too much already, it's too much!"

With a muffled cry, Lola raised her fist and came toward him. Julius rose from the chair and caught her by the wrist. They stood locked together, glaring into one another's eyes. Martin got up and tried to pull them apart. "Stop it, stop it!" he pleaded. The phone rang. They broke apart and Lola ran into the bedroom to answer it. Martin sank back onto the sofa, his chest on fire.

She was gone about five minutes. When she came back she seemed calm but preoccupied. She was carrying her handbag. "That was Andrei," she said. "He was calling from the Port Authority Building. He tried calling you, but you weren't in. He didn't want you to worry about him."

"Port Authority, what's he doing there?"

"He was going to take a bus, go away. I convinced him to give it one more chance."

"So where are you going?"

"I told him to wait there for me. I'm going to bring him home."

"He got there by himself, he can't come home by himself?"

"Not in the state he's in. I didn't want to take the chance."

"You won't let go, will you, Lola?"

"Not when I'm needed." She went to the closet and took down her overcoat. "Martin," she said. "I'm sorry this had to happen. Martin, are you all right?"

"Yes, I think so," he said. "I thought my heart was acting up, but it's nothing. I'm fine."

"Are you sure? I can walk you home on my way to the subway."

"No, really, I'm all right."

She got him his coat and the three of them went downstairs and out into the street. It was snowing. Large, soft flakes drifted past the streetlight, slow and relentless. They melted into the wet pavement like ghosts passing through a wall, but on the lawns and on the branches of the evergreens they were starting to form a ragged net of white. Lola gripped Martin's hand. "I will call you," she said. "Again, I am sorry." She turned and walked off purposefully, her heel taps sounding sharply through the moist air.

"Quite a woman," Julius said, looking after her. "Yes, even now I can say that." He raised his arm oratorically, the coat sleeve falling back to expose the skinny forearm. "She leaves hearth and home. She goes into the world alone, alone on a wide, wide sea. Robert Frost, right, English teacher? She looks for a new harbor where she can find shelter. You'll be next, you know. I can tell by the way she looks at you. You're the new harbor she's steering her boat into. And when she makes up her mind to do something, she does it, whatever the consequences. You'll be next. I know what I'm talking about." He nodded, grinning, his gold tooth flashing dully in his mouth.

"We're just friends," Martin said.

"That's what you say now, but things will change, you'll see."

"I don't think so," Martin said, and turned to go.

"You'll see," the voice called after him, rising to a cackle. "Good night, brother!"

True to her word, Lola called the next day. She apologized

again for the interruption at dinner. Martin said he understood. He hoped that everything had turned out all right. Things had in fact turned out quite well. She had found Andrei sitting on a bench on the main floor of the terminal, studying the crowds and looking rather pleased with himself. On the way home he told her that the experience had been an important one for him, a turning point, he thought. He had seen himself for the first time not as a child, a dependent, but as an individual in the stream of life. He believed that he could take responsibility for himself in a way he had been unable to do before. He was now writing a poem on that subject.

Lola had told him how much Martin liked his poetry, and he had been, as she put it, tickled by the news. He was eager to meet Martin again and discuss his work. Lola suggested dinner the following evening—nothing fancy this time, just a relaxed everyday meal where they would be able to get to know one another better and talk. Martin told her that he had an appointment with his cardiologist and couldn't make it. She suggested the day after that. He said he had some cousins visiting from Los Angeles and that he would be tied up for a while. "Why don't I give you a call when I'm free?" he said. "You see, I'm not sure exactly how long they'll be staying."

His hand trembled when he put down the receiver. He wasn't in the habit of telling lies, particularly to someone as perceptive as Lola, and the experience had been an unnerving one. But he was glad he had gone through with it. Very glad.

He had returned home the night before determined to pay no attention to the ugly scene he had witnessed, but it was impossible. A feeling of repulsion grew in him like mold. The more he thought about it, the more convinced he became that it was wise to be on guard. The woman was taking advantage of him, using him. There was no doubt about it, Julius was right. With his salary, the pension he had coming to him, his house, his bonds and mutual funds, his savings account, he was a safe harbor, all right. Marry him and her troubles were over.

And his heart condition, was that an added incentive? How could it not be? He thought of an insect he had read about once, a kind of wasp. The female laid its eggs inside the body of a certain species of beetle, and when the eggs hatched, the young devoured the beetle from the inside out. Then they broke through the empty shell and set out on their adult lives. During the next few days Martin avoided the library. He did his reading at home, and when he had to go out he took care not to walk near Lola's house.

The weeks passed. He did not call Lola and she did not call him. The weather grew warmer. Spring was really on its way now; each day the sun mounted higher in the sky. Then for a time it rained heavily almost without letup. Between showers the sky was a remote steely blue with shreds of cloud that the wind whipped mercilessly from horizon to horizon. When the weather allowed, Martin kept up with his walking program. When it did not, he exercised on a stationary bicycle in his basement. He began to feel stronger, better in fact than he had for years. His doctor promised that in a month or two he would start jogging.

Lola called at about nine one evening while he was watching TV. He had been half expecting her to contact him; nevertheless, his heart jumped when he heard her voice. The receiver to his ear, he lunged forward and snapped off the set.

"I'm fine. Yes, the cousins are back in L.A. Sorry you didn't get a chance to meet them. I've been quite busy. Preparing for fall classes. Yes, raring to go. I've got the creative writing class next year and that takes a lot of work. My own writing? It's been subsumed, I guess you might say. I suppose I'm basically a teacher after all. And how are you?"

He could tell from her tone that the estrangement he had been feeling was mutual. He was glad. There remained only the question of what she wanted. She did not leave him in the dark very long about that.

"Martin, what has happened between us is water under the bridge. I think I know why you have been avoiding me, but there is no need to speak of it. One thing I must say to you, however. You took on the responsibility of helping my son, but you have not fulfilled your obligation. For myself I do not care. But for his sake I must insist that you finish what you began, that you meet with him and discuss his work with him as you promised. If it was not so important I would not put pressure on you in this way.

It is not easy for me, but Andrei needs this from you. It is so damaging to leave him hanging in this way, you do not know."

He agreed readily. Distasteful as the prospect was, he was cheered by the knowledge that it was the last they could require of him, the final payment. Andrei was home for spring vacation, so they arranged to meet the following morning at the library.

It was raining heavily when Martin awoke. The rain must have begun the previous night because already the sidewalks were flooded and the runoff burbled in freshets along the curb. He breakfasted, then read until it was time to go. Dressed in a raincoat, galoshes, and carrying a black umbrella, he walked to Queens Boulevard and hailed a cab. He kept his eye out for the mismatched forms of Lola and her son, ready to call out to the driver to stop and pick them up, but he saw no sign of them.

They had arrived before him. They sat at the table where Lola usually did her work. Both of them looked drenched to the skin. Andrei's blond hair clung to his head in moist ringlets. The green folder lay on the table in front of him.

"Pretty wet out," Martin said, removing his coat and hat and sitting down across from them.

Lola shifted in her chair, looking down at the folder. She was not going to be lured into small talk. Andrei stared at him with his variegated eyes, his head jerking sharply to one side every few seconds as though pulled by an invisible wire. There was something stupidly mechanical about the habit that made it extremely irritating. He fully understood Julius' outburst.

"Andrei," Lola said. "Mr. Sobel told me he liked your poems very much. Perhaps there is more he can tell you about them."

Martin opened the folder and began to speak. The vocabulary of poetics was second nature to him, and he had only to glance at the pages before him to summon forth a series of formal comments. Metonymy, onomatopoeia, feminine rhyme—with each technical word he felt a growing confidence. He spoke much longer and more fully than he had intended, scarcely conscious of the twitching young man before him or the grim woman by his side. When he was done with the last poem, he closed the folder and forced himself to look at Andrei's face. "What more can I tell you?" he said. "They're excellent. You have a great deal of talent. Keep writing, and some day I expect to come in here and find your books on the shelves."

Andrei opened his mouth to form a word, but his impediment seized him powerfully. His face became flushed and his eyelids fluttered like moth's wings. Still, all he was able to get out were tiny gulping sounds from deep in his throat. Martin leaned forward slightly, staring at the boy's writhing lips. Andrei took a breath, then seemed to break through the obstacle by main force. The words came out in a barely comprehensible tumble. "Thank you very much," he said, then flopped back in his seat.

"You're welcome," Martin replied, and as he looked at Andrei's face, serene for the moment with an expression of confidence and satisfaction, he wondered whether this pitiable boy, talent aside, was not in essence finer, braver, healthier than he was himself, and thus deserving of a kind of fealty, without regard for the merely personal. But the thought was too painful, as well as utterly useless to him. He dismissed it. "Well," he said. "I've got to be going now." He got to his feet and gathered up his hat, coat, and umbrella.

Lola nodded to him with a look that said plainly, you have paid what you owed; you are dismissed now. He walked past the card catalogs and out the door.

The rain had stopped. The street wore that cleansed look which a residue of fresh water can lend to the most contaminated of surfaces. Using his furled umbrella as a walking stick, Martin started on his way home.

It was pleasantly warm, but he felt no discomfort. The sun appeared, and the droplets on the roofs of the parked cars sparkled in its rays. He filled his lungs with fresh air. He was free. He had survived.

LA VICTOIRE

KATE WHEELER

Kate Wheeler was born in Oklahoma but was raised in various parts of South America, including Venezuela, Colombia, Peru, and Argentina. She attended Rice University in Houston, Texas, and received a master's degree from Stanford's creative writing program. She is now working on her first novel.

The 707 bus is behind schedule, and jammed with men from the downtown Buenos Aires racetrack, the kind of men who smoke harsh short cigarettes and expose themselves to young girls. Victoria stands close to the driver, pressed among swaying bodies, wishing she did not have to breathe and that the bus would go faster.

A block ahead, she sees the railroad barrier suddenly fall across the road. That's it, she thinks, a sign. I will die before I see Paris. As the bus lurches to a stop, the slick-combed head of a seated man bumps against her fingers. He is blond; a book lies open on his lap, but he is gazing out the window with an expression almost of sadness. It appears that he has not noticed anything, so Victoria does not apologize.

A yellow train passes but the barrier remains closed for the northbound express.

Victoria's first French lesson begins in ten minutes and she will be late. She is wearing all new clothes for the occasion, and in her purse she carries ninety thousand pesos, full advance payment for six weeks of classes with Monique Gilbert, who holds a license from the French government. Sixty thousand of these pesos came from typing the manuscript of a dull book about multinational corporations; thirty thousand from a report about insect parts found in the tomato paste produced at a provincial factory. There were so many charts and tables that it took Victoria two weeks of nights to finish the work even though she has a year's experience as a typing teacher at the Pan American Academy of Secretaries and Office Workers.

Here is her dream: a man waits for her on the runway in Paris. He wears a wrinkled suit of white linen and a blue shirt; the breeze from jet engines has flung his thin tie back over one shoulder. She descends from the airplane and they kiss eagerly, using their tongues. Together they ride to the hotel in a shiny black car. Later, silver drops of condensation run down the sides of an ice bucket while they lie close together, touching each other's bodies under a thin sheet.

The bus ride lasts for an unbearably long time. Victoria and the man in Paris buy a house in the country and drive downtown each day in a Peugeot 504. They visit the Eiffel Tower and, at the top, he photographs her in profile as she looks out over the city.

Someone is breathing softly on Victoria's neck.

"Oh," moans a man's voice behind her shoulder, "oh, to be the sun and make you thirst for water." The voice gains volume. "Oh, to be a fork and pierce that potato." Victoria feels that her body has been instantly transformed into something as cold and deadly as the blade of a sword. These things do not happen to me! Without looking around she pulls the bus's stop cord.

As she moves to the door, her skirt catches on the metal edge of a bus seat. She half-notices but does not stop: her right hand crosses over the left to catch a handrail; her feet shuffle sideways like a crab's. Soft green fabric pulls, stretching along one thread into a mortifying line of puckers. Everyone stares. The bus driver races the engine and plays a few notes on his scale of electric horns. Someone, perhaps the young blond man, releases Victoria; she finds herself on the pavement and the bus roars away, belching insolent fumes.

Alone on the sidewalk, she hunches, scratching one plum-colored fingernail along the pulled hem. Three weeks ago, her mother gave her two new outfits and said, "Happy twenty-ninth birthday. We were wearing the same styles when I was your age, isn't that funny? You were just learning to walk." Victoria has forgotten what she said to her mother, but now in the empty street she continues the conversation as though her mother could hear her. "I know you want me to catch a man in these new clothes, Mama. I know you think it's too late. But what about you? Your husband has run away and you say you don't understand."

A woman pushing a baby carriage is coming around the corner. Victoria bites the thread, exposing for an instant the dark tops of her stockings. Brushing the skirt into smooth folds, she raises her head and hurries off down the pavement, her purse bumping, bumping away from her hip. She will have to walk six blocks to reach the French teacher's respectable suburban address.

There is no doorbell at Number 986, Street of the Viceroys. Victoria opens the front gate and walks timidly up a row of sandstones to knock at a heavy wooden door.

A tanned young woman's face appears at the open upstairs window.

"Monique is in the back," the woman says. "Go out again and in on the other side of the hedge."

Here, at a gate of twisted wire, is a buzzer. Victoria pushes the black button and then walks in, down a narrow muddy path between shoulder-high hedges. She steps over a child's stick horse and a little red shoe. In the back yard she can see a thatched hut, a few trees and a beach umbrella. The hedge is infested with snails.

"Watch out for the dog!" cries the voice of Monique Gilbert. "Come here, Froufrou!" There are dog noises and scufflings.

"It's all right, now I've got him. I'll lock him up." The voice is hoarse, dark, deep for a woman's; it rolls R's in a thrilling way. The long, fine hairs on Victoria's arms stand out. She wonders what French word she will learn to say first: the word for love? the word for the toilet? Good afternoon? She stands helpless on the scrap of lawn.

"*Bonjour, Mademoiselle Victoire,*" says Monique Gilbert,

emerging from behind the thatched hut. "Or are you *Madame?* I am Monique. You are late."

"Yes," says Victoria in a voice so meek it could have come from one of the snails. The French teacher is naked. No, the French teacher is wearing a black bikini, three tiny pieces of cloth connected by threads and gilded rings that cut deeply into pale, slack, aging flesh.

The French teacher is also wearing high-heeled slippers of gold plastic and an ankle bracelet. She looks fifty-five years old. Victoria closes her eyes and receives small dry kisses on both cheeks.

"This is how we greet in France," says Monique Gilbert. "Now, come in, sit down and excuse me while I put on some clothes. I was just sunning myself; I thought you had changed your mind about me."

I think I am changing it now, thinks Victoria, trying not to look at the teacher's sagging buttocks. Have you no shame, to walk around like this?

At least, she thinks more generously, this Monique has the decency to pull a curtain while she dresses.

Sitting very composed in a canvas chair, Victoria inspects the hut's single room like a spy looking for evidence. The woman obviously lives here: there are windowshades and the thatch has been coated inside with cement to keep out the rain. A small gas bottle with a burner for cooking. Two canvas, one wicker chair that hangs by a rope from the ceiling; a couch that must be used for sleeping, and a huge green and white map of France. Except for one ashtray overflowing with filterless cigarette butts, everything is very clean.

Books on a small shelf: *Madame Bovary*, dictionaries, French books, *The Oriental Manual of Love with 57 Positions and Photographs*. The French teacher sweeps aside the curtain. Now she is dressed in blue jeans, a man's shirt, and the same gold sandals.

"*Voilà!*" she says. "Now if my feet will kindly stop hurting me we can get down to business, *Mademoiselle Victoire Fernandez.*" Victoria has never heard her name pronounced this way before, with accents in the wrong places and one syllable chopped off altogether.

"Is something wrong with your feet?" she asks politely.

"Oh, they are deformed," says the teacher, settling heavily into the hanging chair. "They hurt all the time, and the heels won't go down flat, see?" She removes the sandals, one with each hand, and waves her legs at Victoria. "They don't look so bad. But I have this curse, that I may never wear low shoes. At least I am not a man."

"No," says Victoria. "Should I have brought some paper?"

The chair groans and twists on its rope; the teacher throws down her shoes and places her feet in them.

"First you must learn to say your name and then we will have coffee, Vic-toirrre. Say after me, Vic-toirrre."

"Victwad."

"Veek-toirrrre. In the back of the throat. As though you were going to spit."

"Veek-twagh." Is this how people will say my name in Paris?

"Better. Do you take sugar? I have no milk."

"Yes, please."

"Yes, please, Monique, is easy to say."

"Monique . . . Did you ever live in Paris?"

"Once, as a child." The teacher stands up, walks slowly to the sink and begins filling a pan with water. "But I wouldn't go back for all the money in the world. Why? Because life is more interesting here."

Maybe your life is more interesting, Victoria thinks. I hate it here.

"Victoire, how old are you?" asks the teacher warmly as she settles again in her chair. "Myself, I am forty-eight. *Divorcée.* I have no secrets."

"I am twenty-nine and my boyfriend works in a bank," says Victoire, the lie rolling off her tongue almost of its own accord.

"Ah, you have a fiancé. Say it, *un fiancé.*"

"*Fiancé.*"

The word hangs in the air like a perfect rose.

"*Très bien!* and now I must grind the beans."

Victoria sets her purse on the floor. "Who lives in the front house?" she asks while the teacher's back is turned.

"My sister and her husband and the children live upstairs. My mother lives on the bottom, and she allows my father to use one room. She says he never takes a bath."

"Oh," says Victoria.

"Now. *Ma mère,* my mother. *Mon père,* my father. Say them. I will write them down for you. I do not use books because we learn, first, by talking. Like babies. *Comme les bébés.* Now say: *Ma mère. Mon père. Les bébés.* We are starting with the facts of life. And yes, you must bring a notebook next time."

At the end of three weeks, Victoria can see the map of France in her sleep. She can make sentences for combing hair, riding the bus, detesting tomatoes. At the Pan American Academy she gives her pupils secret French names and thinks in French about them as she listens to their hesitant clacking on twenty-four ancient black typewriters: "*Je déteste Léonie. J'aime Suzanne. Hélène est belle.*" She finds it strange that the same word is used for loving a man, liking a woman, and liking to eat meringues.

Once, she calls her mother a species of hairy cucumber and then runs out of the room, choking with laughter.

Victoria also knows that Monique's husband was a secret homosexual for fifteen years before he asked for a divorce. She has seen Monique's nephews and niece prance naked through the yard on their stick horses. She has seen Monique's mother chase her husband out of the house, throwing shoes at his head and screaming things that Monique patiently translates: "Filthy beast," "Vile creature," "You stink of shit."

Monique had a lover who was a martyr of the Communist cause in Chile. A poster of his face with one of his poems hangs in the hut: "Brothers I have beyond counting," it begins, "and one very beautiful sister whose name is Liberty." Gerardo, Monique's newest lover, is a doctor with a heart condition. His skin has a greenish tinge and he wears a large gold and silver crucifix around his neck: he comes to visit Monique one afternoon during the lesson and sits on the bed looking at magazines. He does not speak French. Victoria wonders how many of the positions Gerardo and Monique have tried, sure that they could not perform some of the contortions demonstrated by the manual by two, sometimes three, acrobatic-looking Orientals in leotards.

And somehow, with the regularity of taxis setting out from a crowded stand, lies upon lies have come out of the mouth of Mademoiselle Victoire. Her fiancé is named Ramón; he likes to make love with the lights on. Her father died accidentally while hunting boars on the pampas: he was shot by one of his friends. Her mother, no longer the principal of a grubby nursery school for the children of laborers, has become a pale wraith of a woman who spends all day at a wooden prayer stand, begging the saints to prevent Victoria from marrying Ramón. Ramón, who is growing a mustache; who has stopped wearing hair oil because Victoria said it made him smell like a prostitute.

It seems to Victoria that the more outrageous the history of Mademoiselle Victoire, the more eagerly Monique believes and presses for details. "But how can you go on seeing such a monster?" Monique demands when Victoria complains that Ramón does not want her to use birth control in order that she will become pregnant and force their marriage.

"He does not control everything I do," says Victoire, calmly blowing a smoke ring. "Besides, he is a fantastic lover."

That Friday night, Victoria and her mother decide to go out to dinner together at The King of Beefsteak, where they always go. Under the purplish neon lights her mother's lips look unnaturally bright, pinkish-orange. Roaming among the tables, a scrawny photographer proclaims: "Everybody comes out good-looking!" For two thousand pesos he takes their portrait with his American camera, mounts it on cardboard and presents it to them with a flourish. Their four eyes have turned out red, like beasts'.

"I wish your father would come back," says Victoria's mother, inspecting the picture as though she might find him in it, seated at a table in the background. "I don't care if he has been living with naked Indians in the jungle." Victoria imagines her father sitting on a low wooden stool, smiling at the caresses of a dozen pygmy women whose bodies are smeared with different-colored paints. She places a hand on her mother's arm.

"Ah, Blessed Virgin," sighs Victoria's mother dabbing wine and tears from her chin with a napkin, "ah, Holy Heaven. He was a fool, but I loved him."

Victoria allows for a short interval of silence.

"Mama," she says softly, "I have always wondered whether I should tell you this. You never knew it, but Father had a lover. Here in Buenos Aires."

"What!" Her mother's face seems ready to break into several pieces. Victoria continues. "I saw them on the river beach one day. At first they were kissing on the sand, lying down. The woman had on a black bathing suit and gold sandals, but she took them off when they went into the water. Father was smiling. They played tag in the water, but they didn't see me."

Her mother draws a shaking breath; tears squeeze from under her closed eyelids and wash clean lines through the powder on her cheeks.

"You are lying to me," her mother says. "Take me home."

In the jungle, Victoria's father joins hands with the pygmy women and they all dance in a circle around his empty throne.

Set aside for conjugations, the fourth week of classes is the hardest so far for both teacher and student. Monique writes down all of the tenses and persons for the verbs to love, because it is so amusingly regular in grammar at least; to be and to have, which are very complicated; and to suck, because Victoria wants to speak French to Ramón.

"*Ma chérie!* But you are funny sometimes," exclaims Monique indulgently.

Victoria takes the lists to the Academy and types them over and over. She also finds more work to pay for a second six weeks: the studies of a woman naturalist in Tierra del Fuego, the new budget and by-laws of a small riding club.

On Thursday afternoon, Monique pronounces Victoire's progress extraordinary and says it is time for a little celebration.

"Some friends of mine are having a party Saturday at a club downtown. I invite you to come," she says. "All of them speak Spanish, so you can bring Ramón. And you can tell your mother you'll be spending the night with me: she'll believe that, won't she?" The two of them have discussed Victoire's difficulties in finding times and places to make love with the fiancé; in fact, Monique herself seems to have a talent for scheming, and together they have kept Mademoiselle's mother almost completely in the dark.

"Well," says Victoire. Luckily, that very day on the bus, she made a plan in case Monique should ever try to arrange a meeting with Ramón. "That would be, um, *merveilleux?* But I have to see if I can drag my fiancé away from his psychoanalytic theater group. They are meeting on Saturdays this month." She sets her mouth in a little smile.

"I would like to be introduced, so try," urges Monique. "Tell him he'll shrink his brains to the size of a raisin. But, if he insists, maybe you will meet someone who does not want you to have babies."

That night, Victoria locks herself in the bathroom at home while her mother is cooking. She takes off her clothes and stands on the toilet, inspecting her naked body from all angles in the mirror above the sink. She has never had a man. She wonders what she will say to Monique's French friends. I am not yet a woman, so how can I have children?

In the morning she stops to buy cigarettes at the candy stand across the street from the Academy. Felipe, the owner, gives her a free packet of violet-scented breath mints.

"Such a lovely creature should not go around with breath like an anyone's," he tells her. "Suck one of these and the men will come flocking around your mouth like bees around a flower."

"Thank you very much," Victoria says, "I will take them even though I do not need them. You see, I have been stung before."

"I see," says Felipe, leering. "At least you did not swell up." He laughs and makes a large encircling gesture with his arms in front of his stomach.

Je suce le bonbon, thinks Victoria in class, I suck the candy. It tastes like perfume and she spits it into the wastebasket.

But I will keep the rest of the packet, she thinks, as a reminder of the sweetness we had together, my lover and I, before our destinies tore us apart. He was North Korean; he looked very much like the Indians of the southern Amazon. Last year his government assigned him to spend the rest of his life in Paraguay as an underground Communist agitator, and I refused to go with him. Once he wrote me a letter with no return address: he was spending his days in a village bar, telling the peasants about oppression. These were his favorite candies, but he could not get them there. Now I do not know where he lives, or even if he lives. This is how I was stung. This is why I must go to Paris and forget.

Just then Lourdes the shorthand teacher comes to knock at the open door of the typing classroom. "Would you like to have coffee after work?" Lourdes asks. "I am meeting my new boyfriend, a Sicilian, a sergeant in the army, but he can't come until four-thirty and I want someone to sit with me until then."

"All right," says Victoria. "I should be finished here at a quarter till."

At the sandwich shop next door, she and Lourdes chatter and laugh over cups of syrupy, bitter espresso. Lourdes is the biggest gossip of all the Academy teachers. She has just found out that the owner of the school, a plump and balding man in his late thirties, is probably having an affair with Leoncia Jimenez, the tallest of the students and one of the least intelligent. What is more, Lourdes is having an interesting time with the Sicilian: he is married, and he says his wife always undresses in the closet. Victoria agrees that nothing could be worse than that.

"I think it is better not to get married, ever," Victoria is saying as the Sicilian walks into the restaurant. "You should have seen the way my father behaved. Is that your boyfriend? He's handsome."

The Sicilian introduces himself as Luis, orders a coffee and then lapses into an awkward silence.

"What were we talking about?" Lourdes says. "Oh, your family."

"Yes," says Victoria, tossing her hair. "It's just that my father was always giving things away. He gave everything away."

"Really? Like what?" says Luis.

"Oh, he would come home in winter and take away the gas heater for a friend he had met in a bar the night before, things like that." Victoria takes the last sip of her espresso and then places the cup carefully back on its saucer. "No one could make him see reason until the day the living-room couch disappeared. That night my mother kicked him out of bed and he had to sleep in the armchair. In the morning he spat on the floor at her feet and announced he was taking the car on a trip to the North, to sell a load of plastic-coated tablecloths. We didn't know where he got them."

"How awful," says Lourdes. "And you haven't seen him since?"

"No," says Victoria. "He called my mother up from a public telephone to say that the car had blown up and he had sold it. Nothing after that, and that was two years ago."

"How awful," Lourdes repeats. "And your poor mother!" Luis nods.

Sometimes I go beyond myself, Victoria thinks. "Not really," she says. "She was glad to get rid of him. My mother is easily bored. It is a trait I must have inherited from her."

"We have to go," says Luis.

"See you Monday," says Lourdes.

"I hope you two enjoy yourselves," says Victoria. As soon as they have disappeared she walks to the counter and asks the waiter for a glass of mineral water. She chooses a seat near the wall and begins reading a row of signs posted above the menu: "Mother, the only light in the dark clouds of this world." "May God give you twice what you desire for me." At the pay telephone next to her, a young man is shouting into the receiver with one finger stuck in his ear.

"Listen!" he screams. "You can't do this to me! It's barbarous!" He slams the telephone into its cradle and stands still for a moment, looking around at the tiny tables. Most of them are occupied. He sits down on the stool beside Victoria and orders a fried steak and a beer. Victoria tries to read more signs through the water in her tilted glass, but the letters are wavy and indecipherable. The young man is blond and bearded, like Ramón: like the young man who helped me get off the bus that day of my first lesson with Monique, Victoria suddenly remembers. His eyes are wide and blue, and the white shows all the way around, as though he has just had a surprising idea.

Suddenly he hides his face in his hands. "I have been betrayed," he moans so that Victoria can hear. "Beasts in human form." Victoria reads through the bottom of her empty glass: "Cash only." "I love the tango because it tastes of Death."

The young man clutches her arm.

"Tell me," he says. "Have you ever given everything you had for something? And then . . . And then been crucified?"

"No!" shrieks Victoria. "What do you want?" The young man blinks; slowly, he releases her arm. There is bitterness in his smile, Victoria thinks.

"I have made a fool of myself," he says and turns his head toward the wall. "Two plus two is four but the heavens are empty." The waiter brings his beer and he takes a large gulp. Victoria lifts the strap of her purse over one shoulder.

"No, please, wait," says the young man, grabbing her arm again. "Will you let me explain? I don't always behave like this." He stares at Victoria. He is a well-bred man caught in some desperate situation. He is intelligent and deeply emotional; he has values. Perhaps his fiancée has left him.

"I should go home," she says, looking pointedly at the hand on her arm.

"I'll come with you. I have to talk to somebody. I can't sit here alone just now."

Victoria places her purse on her lap. The young man releases her arm and places his two hands side by side on the counter, palms down; his long fingers dance in order, as though he were a piano player gently practicing.

"My name is Raimundo," he says. "I have just suffered a tragedy." He pauses, looking up from his fingers into Victoria's eyes. "Will you listen to me?"

"I guess so," says Victoria, thinking: Yes.

The young man continues slowly. "A political tragedy. Personal, in a way." I was wrong about the girlfriend, Victoria thinks, and wonders whether she should ask if he is a Communist. He looks like one, she decides: his hair is not quite combed and he wears a dark blue military jacket that once had insignias sewn on the sleeves. The jacket is too big: he is on the thin side, Raimundo.

"It was something like a coup d'etat," Raimundo begins, slicing off a bite of steak and stabbing it with his fork. "Conspiracy among the lieutenants." He puts the meat in his mouth and chews it gloomily. "Am I boring you?" Victoria can think of nothing interesting to say.

"Are you a Marxist? No, I am not bored," she says.

"Not exactly," he says. "Are you?" Victoria shakes her head. She is watching the motion of his lips. Like bees around a flower, she thinks.

"Yesterday I was the chairman of the Union of Radical Students at the National Faculty of Agronomy and Veterinary Science," he says. "Today I am nothing. I have just been deposed."

"Monstrous," Victoria says. "Why?"

Raimundo's pink tongue darts out to lick the golden hairs of his mustache. He makes a small, exasperated smacking noise, then sighs and says, "They are calling me a revisionist. I thought we could get what we want by talking." For a year now, he explains, veterinary students have been agitating to get a new laboratory and buildings of their own. He himself had reached an understanding in private conference with the Ministers of Education and Agronomy. But his followers were not convinced: and this very afternoon they have called a student strike.

"Even now," Raimundo says, "the Radical Students are slaughtering a sheep on the steps of the university and building a fire to roast it. Oh, the thought is unbearable." He pushes his plate away. "Do you want to go to the movies?"

"I should go home," Victoria says without conviction.

"I'll pay for you. Please? I am in your debt."

"Well, all right." Victoria's heart beats very fast. I like you, Raimundo, she thinks, even though I know what Felipe would say, I know what my mother would say, I know what the waiter must be thinking. She imagines herself at the party telling someone that she has found a new lover, a man whose kisses are like apricots.

As they walk to the cinema she remembers something Monique has told her: that for the past hundred years, architects in Buenos Aires have copied their designs from Paris.

"Buenos Aires looks a lot like Paris," she says in a conversational tone.

"Have you been to Paris?"

"I lived there as a child," says Mademoiselle Victoire. "But I wouldn't go back there for all the money in the world."

"That's interesting," says Raimundo. "Why not?"

"Bad things happened to me there," she says.

In the darkness of the movie house, the face of John Wayne looms on the screen like a huge moon. Raimundo's arm touches hers on the shared seat rest; Victoria cannot pay attention to the film. She sighs and moves lower in the seat.

Somewhere in a red canyon he kisses her. His mustache prickles softly on Victoria's upper lip; behind the barrier of her teeth, his warm tongue surprises her own. Raimundo's eyes are closed; his long eyelashes rest like a flickering shadow on his cheek. Sweetness, thinks Victoria. She trembles. Raimundo puts his arm around her shoulders.

"You have a wonderful mouth," he whispers.

On the way to the lobby they hold hands. It is dark outside; under the blinking neon he says: "I always feel strange when I come out of the movies and find that night has fallen, don't you? It's as though a part of our lives has been lost and we can never get it back."

"I never go to movies at this time," says Victoria. "I like to be outside at the hour when you can't tell if it's night or day. When the sky is light, but it's dark down here."

"I am falling in love with you," Raimundo says. "Can we go have coffee somewhere?"

"Yes," says Victoria, "but not right now. I really have to go."

"Do you have a boyfriend?" he asks. "No? Can I have your telephone number?" On the back of a bus ticket, Victoria writes her name, her address and, for no reason, a false telephone number.

"Come to a party with me tomorrow night," she says.

He agrees to pick her up at eight, at her apartment. They will have dinner together and then ride downtown on the train.

At ten minutes to eight the telephone rings. Victoria is standing on one foot, then the other in front of her mother's full-length mirror, trying to decide whether her black pants hang better over a high shoe or a low one.

"Vicky, it's for you," shouts Victoria's mother from the living room, where she is watching the Saturday night soap opera. "I think it's your French teacher." Victoria turns down the volume of the television set as she hobbles unevenly into the room.

"The high one," says her mother as she hands Victoria the receiver and turns to look out the dark window. I know you are pretending not to listen, thinks Victoria.

"Hello, Monique?"

"*Allo,* my cabbage, yes, it's me." The connection is bad, crackling and tangled with many voices.

"I can't bring my lover," Victoria says loudly. "But I can spend the night anyway." Her mother's shoulders rise and stiffen.

Through deepening static, Victoria strains to decipher words. Monique sounds very small and far away, as though she were a dwarf shouting across the central hall of an airport. She seems to be saying that she has arranged for Victoria to meet one of her friends, a young man, tonight.

"Can you hear me?" Victoria shouts. Monique's voice dissolves into a roar. It is the sound of airplane engines, Victoria thinks: I am landing in Paris. And my shoes are mismatched. She wants to laugh.

"You see, Ramón and I had the most awful fight," Victoria says into the deaf receiver. "He didn't want to share me with anyone else and I am not about to adopt his politics. Plus he never gave up about the babies. So it's over, what can I say? He told me he's going to join the guerrillas because he doesn't want to live any more. But wait until you meet Raimundo."

"Why don't you tell her he's a Marxist," Victoria's mother says.

Suddenly the teacher's voice speaks, as clearly as though Monique were standing in the same room.

"*Allo? Allo?* Who is there?"

"*C'est moi, Victoire.*" The French R comes smoothly, with a little rasp.

"You are coming tonight, aren't you? Oh, I have had it up to here with these telephones! Did you hear that Jules is dying to meet you?"

"I am coming at ten or so," says Mademoiselle Victoire. "But I will probably be bringing someone, if that's all right."

"Who? Not Ramón! Oh, Jules will be so disappointed! But I am pleased anyway, the whole world knows that Ramón is a pig. And you have just told me all about the other one while I was listening to an old lady complain about the sick canary. I tell you, I will never be like that."

"Someone is at the door," says Victoria. "I will tell you everything tonight."

"I refuse to open the door for a terrorist," says Victoria's mother.

"Good," says Victoria.

As Raimundo helps her put on her coat, Victoria looks into the living room. "See you tomorrow," she calls to her mother.

Walking down the hall to the elevator, Raimundo takes her hand.

"I have a confession to make," he says.

"Already? What is it?"

"I'm not really the chairman of the Radical Students. I mean, I never was."

"Then why were you shouting at the telephone?"

"I wanted to meet you," he says. "Do you forgive me?"

"Never," says Victoria. "Yes, on two conditions."

"Anything. I submit to your mercy."

"I will tell you the second condition within six hours."

"Agony is delicious," Raimundo says. "Tell me the first one now."

"You must promise in advance."

"I do."

"That we shall always lie to each other."

"I am telling you the truth right now," he lies. They kiss while the elevator rises to meet them. They kiss again inside, descending.

LAYAWAYS

STEPHEN DIXON

Stephen Dixon's third story collection, *14 Stories*, was published in 1980 by Johns Hopkins University Press as part of its Poetry and Fiction series. He teaches in the Writing Seminars at Johns Hopkins University and has published short stories in various magazines in the last fifteen years, plus two other collections (*Quite Contrary* and *No Relief*) and two novels (*Too Late* and *Work*). His "Mac in Love" was included in *Prize Stories 1977*. Mr. Dixon now lives in Baltimore.

Mr. Toon says goodbye and goes, keeps the door open for two men who come in. Wasn't a very good sale, pair of socks, layaway for a couple of workshirts. Two men look over the suits.

"Anything I can do for you, fellas?"

"Just looking," shorter one says.

"Harry, mind if I go to the bathroom?" Edna says.

"Why ask? You ask me almost all the time and I always say yes. —You don't see anything you got in your mind you're looking for, just ask me. We got things in back or different sizes of those."

"Thank you," same man says.

"Why do I ask?" Edna says. "Because I like to ask. Because I have to ask. Because I'm a child who always has to ask her daddy if she can make."

"You're my wife, talk to me like my wife, not my child."

"You don't get anything I say. You're so unclever, unsubtle."

"What's that supposed to mean?"

"You don't pick things up."

"I pick up plenty. I picked you up 32 years ago, didn't I? One pickup like that, I don't need anymore."

"Well that at least is an attempt at cleverness. What I meant," she says lower, "is those two men. I don't want to leave you out here with them alone when I make."

"They're okay."

"I don't like their looks. They're too lean. No smiling. One has sneakers on."

"So they're lean and don't smile. Maybe they got good reason to be."

"They're swift, they do a lot of running, I don't like it."

"They're okay I'm telling you. You work here Saturdays, you think you know everything. But I've been in this neighborhood for how many years now, so I got a third eye for that."

"Your third eye you almost lost in the last holdup."

"Shut up. They might overhear."

"And get ideas?"

"And get scared out of here thinking we always get holdups."

"We do get holdups."

"But not always. You want to go to the bathroom, don't be afraid. You got my permission. Go."

"Call Joe out first."

"Joe's taking his break."

"Let him take his break out here."

"He's taking it in back because he wants to get away from out here. —Sure nothing I can do for you, fellas? You're looking for a suit, sport jacket? Just what size exactly are you?"

"If we see anything, we'll tell you," shorter one says. Taller one's holding a hangered suit to his chest.

"Big one doesn't speak much. He I think we got to be especially beware."

"You're paranoid, you know what it is?"

"No."

"It means you're paranoid. You know what it is."

"I was just testing you if you do and you didn't. You couldn't define it."

"I can too. You're paranoid. *You.* That's my defining it. To every lean looking man not smiling if he has sneakers on you're paranoid."

"So what's a man with sneakers buying or looking at a suit for?"

"To buy for later. If he buys a suit from us, he'll go to Clyde's or Hazlitt's and buy a pair of shoes to match. He's in a buying mood. These guys, they get a paycheck Friday, they spend it all at once the next day and mostly on liquor and clothes. What do you think they're here for? Leave me alone with your being paranoid. One robbery this month—"

"Two."

"One. That second we didn't know was a robbery."

"That one last week? Call Joe out here and let him tell you how much a robbery it wasn't. That was a knife that man pulled out of his newspaper on Joe, big as your head."

"But he was crazy. He carries the knife and makes threats so he can feel like a big man. He does it to a lot of stores around here and they just tell him 'Sure, here's a penny, all we got, it was a slow day,' and show him the door."

"Okay, that one doesn't count. But what does? When they stick it in your heart?"

"Shush, will you? They'll hear. You're going to the bathroom, go like I said, but don't worry about bringing out Joe."

"No, I'll stay here. I don't want to leave you alone with them."

"Do what you want."

"At least say thanks."

"Why should I? I don't think you're right."

"My heart's in the right place."

"Okay, your heart. You're a dream. You saved my life. You made me live 20 years younger, oh boy am I lucky. But scare these two away with your robbery and knife talk just before my antennas say I'm going to make a big sale with them and I'll be mad as hell at your heart because we need every cent we can get. —That one's a real good buy and a beauty. Want to try it on?"

"Yeah, that's a good idea, where can I?" shorter man says. They come over to the counter Edna's behind and where I've been talking to her and he holds out the suit to me. "How much?"

"Tag's right on the arm cuff. Sometimes they're hard to find.

I'll get it for you. Size 44? This is for you? I say that because it's more of a size for him. You can't be more than a 36, and besides, this one is a long and you're a regular."

"I'm regular, 36, you're right, you really know your line," and from under the suit he's still holding he points a pistol at me. Other one opens his jacket and aims a sawed-off shotgun at Edna and cocks it. "Don't scream. Whatever you do, don't. You'll both be nice and quiet now and you call out your friend Joe. But call him out nice and quietly, don't startle him. Just say—"

"I know, I know how to say it," I say.

"Shut up. Listen to me. Just say 'Joe, could you come out and help me with this fitting for a second?' Exact words. Got them?"

"Yes."

"Repeat them."

"Joe, could you come out and help—"

"Okay, say it."

"Do as he says," Edna says.

"I will, you think I'm crazy? Joe, could you come out and help me with this fitting for a second with this gentleman please?"

"I still got ten minutes," Joe says.

"He's a nice boy," Edna says. "He's my son. He's his son. He won't do anything. Don't touch him."

"We just want him out here, lady. Now call him too, same kind of words but harder."

"Joe, will you please come out here a second? Your father—Harry's got two customers at once and it's too much. For a fitting."

"You can't do it?"

"I don't know how like you yet."

"You don't know how. You'll never know how. I worked my butt off on stock today and want to rest. Oh hell," and he comes out holding a magazine and coffee container.

Taller one holds his shotgun behind him, other one inside the suit.

"Which one needs the fitting?" Joe says.

"Just keep it quiet, baby," shorter one says pulling out the gun and aiming it at Joe. Other one has the shotgun on me, Edna, then keeps it on me.

"Don't hurt him," Edna says about Joe.

"I won't if he does everything we say."

"Everything," Joe says to him. "Give them it all, Harry."

"You think I won't? Look, gentlemen. Come behind here and take everything, please, take it all. Edna, get out and let them in."

"No, lady, you dish it out for us in one of your stronger bags."

"As you say," she says and rings No Sale, he looks over the counter into the bill and change tray and says "Okay" and she starts putting the money into a bag. They keep their guns on us, their backs to the store windows. Joe has a gun on the shelf under the cash register but deep in back. He got a permit for it last month because of the three robberies so far this year when each time we got cleaned out. Edna drops a few change rolls and bills on the floor.

"I'll get it," Joe says.

"You'll get nothing," shorter man says. "Pick them up, lady."

"She's too nervous. She went through a robbery just last week with a guy with a knife here."

"I am very nervous," she says.

"Then you pick it up and empty the rest in the bag but make it quick."

"Just be careful, Joe, and don't do anything silly," I say.

"Like what?" shorter man says.

Man taps on the door, shorter man waves to him, holds up one finger and the man goes.

"Like not making any wrong moves which you might think suspicious," I say, "that's all. We're not armed or anything like that, I wouldn't allow it here, and no burglar alarms to the police. We'll only cooperate. Do just what they say, Joe, but nothing more."

"I know."

But I can see by his look he doesn't. "Let me get the money."

"Why you want to get it?" taller one says.

"Because Joe seems nervous too. He went through the war. He still has tropical illnesses."

"I'm not nervous. I want to give them all the money and for them to leave right away with no trouble."

"Why you two talking like you're up to something?" taller one says.

"We're not," I say.

"They're not," Edna says.

"No, we're not," Joe says.

"What do you have back there?"

"Nothing," Joe says. "Come back and look."

"Pick up the money, old man," shorter one says to me. "You come away from there" to Joe. "Go into the middle of the room. You stay back there, lady."

Joe goes to the middle of the room. People pass on the street. A couple look inside as they walk and I guess don't see anything but don't hesitate or stop. Radio music from in back is still playing. I hear a dog barking nearby and from somewhere far off a fire engine siren. I bend down and pick up the money and put it in the bag and empty the rest of the tray money into the bag and lift the tray and stick the big bills under it into the bag and say "I guess you want our wallets too" and shorter one says "And her pocketbook money and your watches and rings too."

"Give it to them all," Edna says. "My purse is under the counter. Can I reach for it?"

"Go ahead."

"You want the personal checks from today too?" I say.

"Forget the checks."

We empty our wallets and watches and rings and purse into the bag and the shorter one says "Good, now go in back. The two men, right now. Lady stays here. We're not taking her so don't worry. Just want her standing here between you and us so you don't do anything stupid, now go."

We go in back. Joe looks through the tiny two-way glass to the front he had me install last month. I say "They taking her? What are they doing?" I hear the door close. Joe runs out and goes behind the counter and gets his gun and yells "Both of you, flat on the floor" and Edna shouts "Don't, let them go" and I shout "Joe, what are you doing?" when I know I should be shouting "Don't, put down the gun." The men aren't even past the store windows yet. They're out in the street flagging down a cab with that man from the window before joining them when they see Joe opening the door and turn all the way to him and shorter one fumbles for something in his belt and other in the bag and Joe's yelling "You goddamn bastards" and the two from before have their guns out and Joe's shooting the same time they're shooting or almost, I think Joe before, and our two windows break and Edna screams and blood smacks me in the face and across my clothes and the two men fall and Edna bounces against the wall behind the counter and falls and glass is sprayed all over the store and clock above me breaks and Edna's jaw looks gone and face and neck a mess and Joe's alive and the one from the window gets up from where he dived and starts running across the avenue and Joe fires at him and runs over to the men on the ground and I yell "Joe, stop, enough" and kicks their guns to the curb and runs a few feet after the man and then back to the store and jumps through the empty window and sees his mother on the floor and screams and drops to his knees and says "Mom, mom" and I hold his shoulders and cry and mutter "Edna, Joe" and he throws my hands off and runs to the front and opens the door and shouts "You bastards" and one of the men on the ground raises his head an inch and people who have come near them now scatter every which way and Joe puts two bullets into the man who raised his head and grabs the pistol and shotgun from the curb and puts the one shotgun round left into the taller man's head he just put two bullets in and about five bullets from the pistol into the already unconscious or just dead shorter man and then he kicks their bodies and whacks the shotgun handle over the shorter man's head and throws the broken gun away and pistol-whips what's left of the taller man's head and gets on his knees and sticks the pistols in his pockets and pounds the ground with his fists and some people come over to him and the bell from the door tells me someone's coming in the store while I get a pain in my chest that shoots from it to all four limbs and sudden blackness in my head that's only broken up by lightning-like cracks and fall on Edna and feel myself going way off somewhere and in my blackness and lightning and going away I feel around for her hand and find it and hold it and then pass out from whatever, maybe the chest pain.

I ask to be in the same room with her but they say we have to stay in two different intensive care units at opposite ends of the hall, one for serious gunshot injuries and other for coronaries and strokes and the like. Joe sits by my bed for the five minutes they give him and says "I hope mom dies, it's not worth it to her or you if she lives. The bullets went—"

Nurse puts her finger over her mouth to him and I nod to Joe I understand.

"How's the store?" I say and he says "I think I better go in tomorrow. We got all those layaways for Easter. The customers will be disappointed last day before the holidays start not to get them and they won't want them after and will want their money back."

"You better go in then."

"I'm not afraid to."

"Why should you be?"

"People says those two men got friends who'll want to get revenge."

"What do the police say?"

"They say what I did will act as a deterrent against revenge and more robberies but what am I going to be a deterrent with? They took away my permit and gun."

"For the time being?"

"They got to investigate if I couldn't've not used it. But who knows."

"Don't go in then. I don't want you getting killed."

"But those customers. They got layaways and it's our best two days."

"Do you have to talk about business now?" nurse says to him.

"It's okay," I say. "Store talk relaxes me and I feel all right. Don't go in," I tell Joe. "Go back to college. Stay away from business. I just made up my mind for you."

"I like the business. I got my own family to support too. I want to keep the store."

"We'll get insurance from the robbery and the sale of the merchandise later on. You can have half of it. You deserve it. You have to go back into business, open a store in a quieter neighborhood."

"In a quieter neighborhood the store will die."

"Go into another business."

"What other business I know but men's clothes?"

"Once you know retailing you can open up any kind of store."

"I like men's clothes."

"I don't think your father should be discussing this now," nurse says.

"I feel much better, Miss. Anyway, it wasn't a heart attack I had."

"It was a heart attack."

"It was, dad."

"It was indigestion. It was that, doubled up with nerves. I didn't deserve them? My own wife? Him? That whole scene?"

"You'll have to go," she tells Joe.

"I'll see you later." He kisses my forehead and leaves.

"Could you call him back?" I say.

"It'd be better not to."

"I want to ask him something I never got an answer from. If I don't get that answer I'll be more worried and heartsick than if I do."

She goes outside the room and Joe comes back. "Yeah?" he says.

"You going back to the store?"

"I guess I have to."

"You really aren't afraid?"

"A friend of mine, Mac, has offered to stay with me. He's a big guy and will take care of the register and look after the door."

"Call Pedro also. He called me just a week before the accident and asked if business was going to be good enough to hire him back. Call him. His number's in the top drawer of the counter."

"I know where it is. We have money to pay him?"

"Even if you have to take it out of my pockets. The glass fixed?"

"They put it in yesterday. We had to. Cops didn't want it boarded up if we're going to still occupy it and other storeowners complained it looked bad for everybody else."

"They were right. Don't keep more than 300 dollars in cash there any one time. You get one dollar more, deposit it—it's worth the walk."

"I know."

"I still have to tell you. Two guys like those two come in, even one who looks suspicious, don't take unnecessary risks. No risks, hear me?"

"I won't."

"Give even a ten year old boy who's holding up the store whatever he wants."

"A ten year old I'm not giving in to."

"If he has a gun?"

"That's different."

"That's what I'm saying. But any older person who says this is a holdup—even if he or she doesn't show a gun, give them what they want. Remember, you're only going back to be nice to the layaways, right?"

"I'm going back because I also need the money, me and my family, you and mom, and to tell the goddamn thieves they're not shoving me out."

"They know that already. Listen to me, don't be so tough. I can tell you stories about other tough merchants. I'm not saying what you did caused your mother like she is. But if you didn't get so crazy so suddenly, not that you couldn't've helped it—well right?"

"Don't make me feel bad."

"I'm not trying to."

"Don't blame me because I got excited. Sick as you are, I'm telling you this now for all time."

"I understand you. In your own way that day, you did okay."

He waves.

"Where you going? Give your father a kiss goodbye. He needs it." He kisses my lips. He never did that before. I also never asked him to kiss me any time before. My own father asked me to kiss him hundreds of times and I always did. But only once on his lips did I kiss him and that was a few minutes after he died. I start to cry. Joe's gone. Nurse asks me what's wrong. "Got any more news on my wife?"

"You know we're not allowed to speak about her."

"What am I supposed to think then, she's dead?"

"She's not dead. Your son told you. She's holding her own."

"That isn't much, right?"

"I can't say. She also has the best equipment to help her. You can talk about it more tomorrow with her doctors when they move you to a semi-private."

I'm released three weeks later and go back to the store a month after that. Joe's had another robbery. He gave them what he had without a fuss. Pedro was there that day and later said he'd never let anyone take anything from him again, even if it wasn't his store. Pedro got a gun. Two of the merchants on the street stood up for him for the gun permit. Because Joe's not allowed to apply for one again for two months, he told the police Pedro needed the gun to take the store receipts to the bank. Pedro keeps the gun in back. He told Joe "It's no good keeping it under the counter or in the register, for where's the first place they look? They find it, they might just kill you. I've been robbed three other times besides my twice here and in back's where they always send you or want to either tie you up or lock you in the mens-room so they can have as much time they can to get away."

Edna's in a nursing home now paralyzed from the neck down. Even if she comes out of her coma she'll be paralyzed like that for life. She'll never be able to speak and if she gets out of the coma she hardly won't be able to think. She should've died in the hospital or in the store but more in the hospital because there's more dignity to dying there. The doctors say she won't last another few months. So I go back to the store just to have something to do, though my own doctor says I shouldn't. I say hello to Pedro and he says "I'm really sorry what happened to you, Mr. Sahn."

"It was a long time ago."

"It isn't a long time for something like that and it's still happening to you with your wife, right?"

"Maybe it isn't too long ago at that. But you've been a great help, Pedro, to my son and me and if we could afford it, we'd double your hourly salary and also put you on for all six days."

"I'm glad I got what I got, so don't worry."

"But we'll give you 40 cents more an hour starting today."

"Hey pop," Joe says, "what are you trying to do, rob us? We haven't got 40 cents more to give."

"Twenty cents will be fine," Pedro says, "and I can really use it."

"Twenty then," I say.

I go to work every other day and on Saturday of that same week two men come in when Pedro and I are reading different sections of the newspaper and Joe's taking care of the one customer in the store. The men don't bother like the rest of them with looking for a suit or slacks but take out their guns before the door's even closed and the thinner one points his at Pedro and I and the heavier one at the customer and Joe and that one says "Holdup, nobody go for anything or step on alarms." The customer says "Oh my god" and Pedro says "We freeze, fellas, no worry about that, we're no dopes" and the heavier one goes to the register and starts emptying it into a briefcase and the thinner one says to me "You there, owner, hold this" and gives me another briefcase and says "Your wallet and everything else in it and get the same from the rest" and we all dump our wallets and watches and rings in it but I don't have a ring because mine was taken the last time and for some reason never recovered though everything else in the bag outside was. The heavier one comes around the counter and runs in back and comes out and says "They got no storerooms to lock themselves in and bathroom has no door" and says to us "All right, you all go in back but way in back and don't come out for five minutes minimum or I swear one does you all die" and Pedro says "Don't worry, we've been through this before and we all go in back for ten minutes not five, I'll see to that" and we go in back and Joe goes to the two-way and says "They've left" and Pedro reaches behind a pile of shirtboxes and pulls out a gun and I drop the phone receiver and say "Pedro, don't" and he says "I'm not letting them get away with it, Mr. Sahn, I told your son" and the customer sticks all his fingers in his mouth and says through them "Oh no, oh no" and Joe says "Let me have the gun" and Pedro says "No, I'm licensed for it and get in trouble letting anyone else use it" and Joe says "But I know how to use it" and Pedro says "I know too, the police showed me one day in practice" and Joe says "One day? You crazy? Let me have it" and I say "None of you, let them go, nobody goes after them" but Joe reaches for the gun and Pedro shouts "Watch out, it's cocked" and jerks it back before Joe can get hold of it and the gun goes off and bullet into Pedro's chest and we hear shots from outside and windows breaking and duck to the floor, customer's already there bawling, and Joe yells "You goddamn bastards" and grabs the gun and runs to the front but the men had only shot out the windows because I suppose they thought they were being shot at by one of us and by the time Joe gets to the street they're in a car and gone.

I close the store and sell the entire stock. Joe goes back to pharmacy college for the next year with me paying all his bills. Pedro dies from the bullet through his lungs. Edna lives on in a coma for another month before she succumbs in her sleep the doctor says, I have another heart attack and move South into a single room by myself among a whole bunch of much older people in the same crummy hotel, living off my social security and Edna's life insurance and savings and maybe not in a better hotel till Joe graduates and can earn a salary large enough not only for his family but to begin paying back me. Then I get a phone call from his sister-in-law who says Joe got in an argument in the park with three men who were mugging an old couple and they beat him in his kidneys and head till he was dead.

I return for the funeral and because I don't like the South much with all that sun and beach and older people having nothing to do but wait for death and me with them, I move back for good and open another store but a much smaller one for candies and greeting cards and stuff like that and in a much safer neighborhood. I ask Joe's wife Nancy if she and her kids want to share an apartment with me to save money and because I'd also like to be with them more and she says "Actually, I don't want to, not that I don't like you, dad. But with us not having much money and all and the kids for the time being so small, maybe for the next four years and if I don't get remarried or move in with some guy, it's probably the best of ideas."

So we live like that, me not making much in my store in a neighborhood that only rarely has a robbery, my grandchildren asking me questions and wanting me to play with them like I'm their dad, Nancy working part-time and going out with different men and sometimes staying overnight in their apartment but not really being attracted to any of them just as I think they're not attracted to her. Some days we go to the two graves in the plot for eight I bought 30 years ago and that's the only time we all just hold one another, the kids not understanding it too much, and say some prayers from a little book the cemetery provides and cry and cry.

THE GIFT OF THE PRODIGAL

PETER TAYLOR

Peter Taylor was born in Trenton, Tennessee, in 1917. He has spent most of his life there and in Virginia. He is married to the poet Eleanor Ross Taylor and has two grown children—both of whom are writers. The Taylors live in Charlottesville, Virginia, where Mr. Taylor teaches in the English Department of the University of Virginia. Mr. Taylor is the recipient of numerous awards, including a Guggenheim Fellowship, a Fullbright Fellowship to study in France, and several previous O. Henry Awards. He is the author of a novel, *A Woman of Means* (1950), several plays, and many short stories.

There's Ricky down in the washed river gravel of my driveway. I had my yardman out raking it before 7 A.M.—the driveway. It looks nearly perfect. Ricky also looks nearly perfect down there. He looks extremely got up and cleaned up, as though *he* had been carefully raked over and smoothed out. He is wearing a three-piece linen suit, which my other son, you may be sure, wouldn't be seen wearing on any occasion. And he has on an expensive striped shirt, open at the collar. No tie, of course. His thick head of hair, parted and slicked down, is just the same tan color as the gravel. Hair and gravel seem equally clean and in order. The fact is, Ricky looks this morning as though he belongs nowhere else in the world but out there in that smooth spread of washed river gravel (which will bc mussed up again before noon, of course—I'm resigned to it), looks as though he feels perfectly at home in that driveway of mine that was so expensive to install and that requires so much upkeep.

Since one can't see his freckles from where I stand at this second-story window, his skin looks very fair—almost transparent. (Ricky just misses being a real redhead, and so never lets himself get suntanned. Bright sunlight tends to give him skin cancers.) From the window directly above him, I am able to get the full effect of his outfit. He looks very masculine standing down there, which is no doubt the impression his formfitting clothes are meant to give. And Ricky *is* very masculine, no matter what else he is or isn't. Peering down from up here, I mark particularly that where his collar stands open, and with several shirt buttons left carelessly or carefully undone, you can see a triangle of darker hair glistening on his chest. It isn't hard to imagine just how recently he has stepped out of the shower. In a word, he is looking what he considers his very best. And this says to me that Ricky is coming to me *for* something, or *because of* something.

His little sports car is parked in the turnaround behind this house which I've built since he and the other children grew up and since their mother died. I know of course that, for them, coming here to see me can never really be like coming home. For Rick it must be like going to see any other old fellow who might happen to be his boss and who is ailing and is staying away from the office for a few days. As soon as I saw him down there, though, I knew something was really seriously wrong. From here I could easily recognize the expression on his face. He has a way, when he is concerned about something, of knitting his eyebrows and at the same time opening his eyes very wide, as though his eyes are about to pop out of his head and his eyebrows are trying to hold them in. It's a look that used to give him away even as a child, when he was in trouble at school. If his mother and I saw that expression on his face, we would know that we were apt to be rung up by one of his teachers in a day or so or maybe have a house call from one of them.

Momentarily Ricky massages his face with his big right hand, as if to wipe away the expression. And clearly now he is headed for the side door that opens on the driveway. But before actually coming over to the door he has stopped in one spot and keeps shuffling his suède shoes about, roughing up the smooth gravel, like a young bull in a pen. I almost call out to him not to *do* that, not to muss up my gravel, which even his car wheels haven't disturbed—or not so much as he is doing with his suède shoes. I *almost* call out to him. But of course I don't really. For Ricky is a man twenty-nine years old, with two divorces already and no doubt another coming up soon. He's been through all that, besides a series of live-ins between marriages that I don't generally speak of, even.

For some time before coming on into the house, Ricky remains there in that spot in the driveway. While he stands there, it occurs to me that he may actually be looking the place over, as though he'd never noticed what this house is like until now. The old place, on Wertland Street, where he and the other children grew up, didn't have half the style and convenience of this one. It had more room, but the room was mostly in pantries and hallways, with front stairs and back stairs and third-floor servants' quarters in an age when no servant would be caught dead living up there in the attic—or staying anywhere else on the place, for that matter. I am not unaware, of course, how much better that old house on Wertland was than this one. You couldn't have replaced it for twice what I've poured into this compact and well-appointed habitation out here in Farmington. But its neighborhood had gone bad. Nearly all of Charlottesville proper has, as a matter of fact, either gone commercial or been absorbed by the university. You can no longer live within the shadow of Mr. Jefferson's Academical Village. And our old Wertland Street house is now a funeral parlor. Which is what it ought to have been five years before I left it. From the day my wife, Cary, died, the place seemed like a tomb. I wandered up and down the stairs and all around, from room to room, sometimes greeting myself in one of Cary's looking glasses, doing so out of loneliness or out of thinking *that* couldn't be *me* still in my dressing gown and slippers at midday, or fully dressed—necktie and all—at 3 A.M. I knew well enough it was time to sell. And, besides, I wanted to have the experience at last of making something new. You see, we never built a house of our own, Cary and I. We always bought instead of building, wishing to be in an established neighborhood, you know, where there were good day schools for the girls (it was before St. Anne's moved to the suburbs), where there were streetcars and buses for the servants, or, better still, an easy walk for them to Ridge Street.

My scheme for building a new house after Cary died seemed a harebrained idea to my three older children. They tried to talk me out of it. They said I was only doing it out of idleness. They'd laugh and say I'd chosen a rather expensive form of entertainment for myself in my old age. That's what they *said*. That wasn't all they *thought*, however. But I never held against them what they thought. All motherless children—regardless of age—have such thoughts. They had in mind that I'd got notions of marrying again. Me! Why, I've never looked at another woman since the day I married. Not to this very hour. At any rate, one night when we were having dinner and they were telling me how they worried about me, and making it plainer than usual what they thought my plans for the future were or might be, Ricky spoke up—Ricky, who never gave a thought in his life to what happened to anybody except himself—and he came out with just what was on the others' minds. "What if you should take a notion to marry again?" he asked. And I began shaking my head before the words were out of his mouth, as did all the others. It was an unthinkable thought for them as well as for me. "Why not?" Ricky persisted, happy of course that he was making everybody uncomfortable. "Worse things have happened, you know. And I nominate the handsome Mrs. Capers as a likely candidate for bride."

I *think* he was referring to a certain low sort of woman who had recently moved into the old neighborhood. You could depend upon Rick to know about her and know her name. As he spoke he winked at me. Presently he crammed his wide mouth full of food, and as he chewed he made a point of drawing back his lips and showing his somewhat overlarge and overly white front teeth. He continued to look straight at me as he chewed, but looking with only one eye, keeping the eye he'd winked at me squinched up tight. He looked for all the world like some old tomcat who's found a nasty morsel he likes the taste of and is not going to let go of. I willingly would have knocked him out of his chair for what he'd said, even more for that common look he was giving me. I knew he knew as well as the others that I'd never looked at any woman besides his mother.

Yet I laughed with the others as soon as I realized they were laughing. You don't let a fellow like Rick know he's got your goat —especially when he's your own son and has been in one bad scrape after another ever since he's been grown and seems always just waiting for a chance to get back at you for something censorious you may have said to him while trying to help him out of one of his escapades. Since Cary died, I've tried mostly just to keep lines of communication with him open. I think that's the thing she would have wanted of me—that is, not to shut Rick out, to keep him talking. Cary used to say to me, "You may be the only person he can talk to about the women he gets involved with. He can't talk to me about such things." Cary always thought it was the women he had most on his mind and who got him into his scrapes. I never used to think so. Anyway, I believe that Cary would have wished above all else for me to keep lines open with Rick, would have wanted it even more than she would have wanted me to go ahead in whatever way I chose with schemes for a new house for my old age.

Because the house was *our* plan originally, you see, hers and mine. It was something we never told the children about. There seemed no reason why we should. Not talking about it except between ourselves was part of the pleasure of it, somehow. And that night when Ricky came out with the speculation about my possibly marrying again, I didn't tell him or the others that actually I had already sold the Wertland Street house and already had blueprints for the new house here in Farmington locked away in my desk drawer, and even a contractor all set to break ground.

Well, my new house was finished the following spring. By that time all the children, excepting Rick, had developed a real enthusiasm for it. (Rick didn't give a damn one way or the other, of course.) They helped me dispose of all the superfluous furniture in the old house. The girls even saw to the details of moving and saw to it that I got comfortably settled in. They wanted me to be happy out here. And soon enough they saw I was. There was no more they could do for me now than there had been in recent years. They had their good marriages to look after (that's what Cary would have wished for them), and they saw to it that I wasn't left out of whatever of their activities I wanted to be in on. In a word, they went on with their busy lives, and my own life seemed busy enough for any man my age.

What has vexed the other children, though, during the five years since I built my house, is their brother Ricky's continuing to come to me at almost regular intervals with new ordeals of one kind or another that he's been going through. They have thought he ought not to burden me with his outrageous and sometimes sordid affairs. I think they have especially resented his troubling me here at home. I still go to the office, you see, two or three days a week—just whenever I feel like it or when I'm not playing golf or bridge or am not off on a little trip to Sarasota (I stay at the same inn Cary and I used to go to). And so I've always seen Ricky quite regularly at the office. He's had every chance to talk to me there. But the fact is, Rick was never one for bringing his personal problems to the office. He has always brought them home.

Even since I've moved, he has always come *here*, to the house, when he's really wanted to talk to me about something. I don't know whether it's the two servants I still keep or some of the young neighbors hereabouts who tell them, but somehow the other children always know when Ricky has been here. And they of course can put two and two together. It will come out over Sunday dinner at one of their houses or at the Club—in one of those little private dining rooms. It is all right if we eat in the big dining room, where everybody else is. I know I'm safe there. But as soon as I see they've reserved a private room I know they want to talk about Ricky's latest escapade. They will begin by making veiled references to it among themselves. But at last it is I who am certain to let the cat out of the bag. For I can't resist joining in when they get onto Rick, as they all know very well I won't be able to. You see, often they will have the details wrong—maybe they get them wrong on purpose—and I feel obliged to straighten them out. Then one of them will turn to me, pretending shocked surprise: "How ever did you know about it? Has *he* been bringing his troubles to *you* again? At his age you'd think he'd be ashamed to! Someone ought to remind him he's a grown man now!" At that point one of the girls is apt to rest her hand on mine. As they go on, I can hear the love for me in their voices and see it in their eyes. I know then what a lucky man I am. I want to say to them that their affection makes up for all the unhappiness Ricky causes me. But I have never been one to make speeches like that. Whenever I have managed to say such things, I have somehow always felt like a hypocrite afterward. Anyway, the talk will go on for a while till I remember a bridge game I have an appointment for in the Club lounge, at two o'clock. Or I recall that my golf foursome is waiting for me in the locker room.

I've never tried to defend Rick from the others. The things he does are really quite indefensible. Sometimes I've even found myself giving details about some escapade of his that the others didn't already know and are genuinely shocked to hear—especially coming from me. He was in a shooting once that everybody in Farmington and in the whole county set knew about—or knew about, that is, in a general way, though without knowing the very thing that would finally make it a public scandal. It's an ugly story, I warn you, as, indeed, nearly all of Ricky's stories are.

He had caught another fellow in bed with a young married woman with whom he himself was running around. Of course it was a scandalous business, all of it. But the girl, as Rick described her to me afterward, was a real beauty of a certain type and, according to Rick, as smart as a whip. Rick even showed me her picture, though I hadn't asked to see it, naturally. She had a tight little mouth, and eyes that—even in that wallet-sized picture—burned themselves into your memory. She was the sort of intense and reckless-looking girl that Ricky has always gone for. I've sometimes looked at pictures of his other girls, too, when he wanted to show them to me. And of course I know what his wives have looked like. All three of his wives have been from good families. For, bad as he is, Ricky is not the sort of fellow who would embarrass the rest of us by *marrying* some slut. Yet even his wives have tended to dress themselves in a way that my own daughters wouldn't. They have dressed, that is to say, in clothes that seemed designed to call attention to their female forms and not, as with my daughters, to call attention to the station and the affluence of their husbands. Being the timid sort of man I am, I used to find myself whenever I talked with his wife—whichever one—carefully looking out the window or looking across the room, away from her, at some inanimate object or other over there or out there. My wife, Cary, used to say that Ricky had bad luck in his wives, that each of them turned out to have just as roving an eye as Ricky himself. I can't say for certain whether this was true for each of them in the beginning or whether it was something Ricky managed to teach them all.

Anyway, the case of the young married woman in whose bed—or apartment—Ricky found that other fellow came near to causing Ricky more trouble than any of his other escapades. The fellow ran out of the apartment, with Rick chasing him into the corridor and down the corridor to a door of an outside stairway. It was not here in Farmington, you see, but out on Barracks Road, where so many of Rick's friends are—in a development that's been put up on the very edge of where the horse farms begin. The fellow scurried down the outside stairs and across a parking lot toward some pastureland beyond. And Rick, as he said, couldn't resist taking a shot at him from that upstairs stoop where he had abandoned the chase. He took aim just when the fellow reached the first pasture fence and was about to climb over. Afterward, Rick said that it was simply too good to miss. But Rick rarely misses a target when he takes aim. He hit the fellow with a load of rat shot right in the seat of the pants.

I'll never know how Rick happened to have the gun with him. He told me that he was deeply in love with the young woman and would have married her if her husband had been willing to give her a divorce. The other children maintain to this day that it was the husband Rick meant to threaten with the gun, but the husband was out of town and Rick lost his head when he found that other fellow there in his place. Anyhow, the story got all over town. I suppose Ricky himself helped to spread it. He thought it all awfully funny at first. But before it was over, the matter came near to getting into the courts and into the paper. And that was because there was something else involved, which the other children and the people in the Barracks Road set didn't know about and I did. In fact, it was something that I worried about from the beginning. You see, Rick naturally took that fellow he'd blasted with the rat shot to a doctor—a young doctor friend of theirs—who removed the shot. But, being a friend, the doctor didn't report the incident. A certain member of our judiciary heard the details and thought perhaps the matter needed looking into. We were months getting it straightened out. Ricky went out of town for a while, and the young doctor ended by having to move away permanently—to Richmond or Norfolk, I think. I only give this incident in such detail in order to show the sort of low company Ricky has always kept, even when he seemed to be among our own sort.

His troubles haven't all involved women, though. Or not primarily. And that's what I used to tell Cary. Like so many people in Charlottesville, Rick has always had a weakness for horses. For a while he fancied himself a polo player. He bought a polo pony and got cheated on it. He bought it at a stable where he kept another horse he owned—bought it from the man who ran the stable. After a day or so, he found that the animal was a worthless, worn-out nag. It couldn't even last through the first chukker, which was humiliating of course for Ricky. He daren't try to take it onto the field again. It had been all doped up when he bought it. Ricky was outraged. Instead of simply trying to get his money back, he wanted to have his revenge upon the man and make an even bigger fool of *him.* He persuaded a friend to dress himself up in a turtleneck sweater and a pair of yellow jodhpurs and pretend just to be passing by the stall in the same stable, where the polo pony was still kept. His friend played the role, you see, of someone only just taking up the game and who thought he *had* to have that particular pony. He asked the man whose animal it was, and before he could get an answer he offered more than twice the price that Rick had paid. He even put the offer into writing—using an assumed name, of course. He said he was from up in Maryland and would return in two days' time. Naturally, the stableman telephoned Ricky as soon as the stranger in jodhpurs had left the stable. He said he had discovered, to his chagrin, that the pony was not in as good condition as he had thought it was. And he said that in order that there be no bad feeling between them he was willing to buy it back for the price Ricky had paid.

Ricky went over that night and collected his money. But when the stranger didn't reappear and couldn't be traced, the stableman of course knew what had happened. Rick didn't return to the stable during the following several days. I suppose, being Ricky, he was busy spreading the story all over town. His brother and sisters got wind of it. And I did soon enough. On Sunday night, two thugs and some woman Ricky knew but would never identify—not even to me—came to his house and persuaded him to go out and sit in their car with them in front of his house. And there they beat him brutally. He had to be in the hospital for five or six days. They broke his right arm, and one of them—maybe it was the woman—was trying to bite off the lobe of his left ear when Ricky's current wife, who had been out to some party without the favor of his company, pulled into the driveway beside the house. The assailants shoved poor Ricky, bruised and bleeding and with his arm broken, out onto the sidewalk. And then of course they sped away down the street in their rented car. Ricky's wife and the male friend who was with her got the license number, but the car had been rented under an assumed name—the same name, actually, as some kind of joke, I suppose, that Ricky's friend in jodhpurs had used with the stablekeeper.

Since Ricky insisted that he could not possibly recognize his two male assailants in a lineup, and since he refused to identify the woman, there was little that could be done about his actual beating. I don't know that he ever confessed to anyone but me that he knew the woman. It was easy enough for me to imagine what *she* looked like. Though I would not have admitted it to Ricky or to anyone else, I would now and then during the following weeks see a woman of a certain type on the streets downtown —with one of those tight little mouths and with burning eyes— and imagine that she might be the very one. All we were ever able to do about the miserable fracas was to see to it finally that that stable was put out of business and that the man himself had to go elsewhere (he went down into North Carolina) to ply his trade.

There is one other scrape of Ricky's that I must mention, because it remains particularly vivid for me. The nature and the paraphernalia of this one will seem even more old-fashioned than those of the other incidents. Maybe that's why it sticks in my mind so. It's something that might have happened to any number of rough fellows I knew when I was coming along.

Ricky, not surprising to say, likes to gamble. From the time he was a young boy he would bet on anything at home. He would often try to inveigle one of the other children into making wagers with him on how overdone his steak was at dinner. He always liked it very rare and when his serving came he would hold up a bite on his fork and, for a decision on the bet, would ask everyone what shade of brown the meat was. He made all the suggestions of color himself. And one night his suggestions got so coarse and vile his mother had to send him from the dining room and not let him have a bite of supper. Sometimes he would try to get the other children to bet with him on the exact number of minutes the preacher's sermon would last on Sunday or how many times the preacher would use the word "Hell" or "damnation" or "adultery." Since he has got grown, it's the races, of course, he likes—horse races, it goes without saying, but also such low-life affairs as dog races and auto races. What catches his fancy above all else, though, is the chicken fights we have always had in our part of the country. And a few years ago he bought himself a little farm a dozen miles or so south of town, where he could raise his own game chickens. I saw nothing wrong with that at the time. Then he built an octagonal barn down there, with a pit in it where he could hold the fights. I worried a little when he did that. But we've always had cockfights hereabouts. The birds are beautiful creatures, really, though they have no brains, of course. The fight itself is a real spectacle and no worse than some other things people enjoy. At Ricky's urging, I even went down to two or three fights at his place. I didn't bet, because I knew the stakes were very high. (Besides, it's the betting that's illegal.) And I didn't tell the other children about my going. But this was after Cary was dead, you see, and I thought maybe she would have liked my going for Ricky's sake, though she would never have acknowledged it. Pretty soon, sizable crowds began attending the fights on weekend nights. Cars would be parked all over Ricky's front pasture and all around the yard of the tenant house. He might as well have put up a sign down at the gate where his farm road came off the highway.

The point is, everyone knew that the cockfights went on. And one of his most regular customers and biggest bettors was one of the county sheriff's right-hand men. I'm afraid Rick must have bragged about that in advertising his fights to friends—friends who would otherwise have been a little timid about coming. And during the fights he would move about among the crowd, winking at people and saying to them under his breath, "The deputy's here tonight." I suppose it was his way of reassuring them that everything was all right. I don't know whether or not his spreading the word so widely had anything to do with the raid, but nevertheless the deputy was present the night the federal officers came stealing up the farm road, with their car lights off and with search warrants in their pockets. And it was the deputy who first got wind of the federal officers' approach. He had one of his sidekicks posted outside the barn. Maybe he had somebody watching out there every night that he came. Maybe all along he had had a plan for his escape in such an emergency. Rick thought so afterward. Anyhow, the deputy's man outside knew at once what those cars moving up the lane with their lights off meant. The deputy got the word before anyone else, but, depend upon Ricky, he saw the first move the deputy made to leave. And he was not going to have it. He took out after him.

The deputy's watchman was prepared to stay on and take his chances. (He wasn't even a patrolman. He probably only worked in the office.) I imagine he was prepared to spend a night in jail if necessary, and pay whatever fine there might be, because his presence could explain one of the sheriff's cars' being parked in the pasture. But the deputy himself took off through the backwoods on Ricky's property and toward a county road on the back of the place. Ricky, as I've said, was not going to have that. Since the cockfight was on his farm, he knew there was no way out of trouble for himself. But he thought it couldn't, at least, do him any harm to have the deputy caught along with everybody else. Moreover, the deputy had lost considerable amounts of money there at the pit in recent weeks and had insinuated to Ricky that he suspected some of the cocks had been tampered with. (I, personally, don't believe Ricky would stand for that.) Ricky couldn't be sure there wasn't some collusion between the deputy and the feds. He saw the deputy's man catch the deputy's eye from the barn doorway and observed the deputy's departure. He was right after him. He overtook him just before he reached the woods. Fortunately, the deputy wasn't armed. (Ricky allowed no one to bring a gun inside the barn.) And fortunately Ricky wasn't armed, either, that night. They scuffled a little near the gate to the woods lot. The deputy, being a man twice Rick's age, was no match for him and was soon overpowered. Ricky dragged him back to the barn, himself resisting—as he later testified—all efforts at bribery on the deputy's part, and turned in both himself and his captive to the federal officers.

Extricating Ricky from that affair and setting matters aright was a long and complicated undertaking. The worst of it really began for Ricky after the court proceedings were finished and all fines were paid (there were no jail terms for anyone), because from his last appearance in the federal courthouse Ricky could drive his car scarcely one block through that suburb where he lives without receiving a traffic ticket of some kind. There may not have been anything crooked about it, for Ricky is a wild sort of driver at best. But, anyhow, within a short time his driving license was revoked for the period of a year. Giving up driving was a great inconvenience for him and a humiliation. All we could do about the deputy, who, Ricky felt sure, had connived with the federal officers, was to get him out of his job after the next election.

The outcome of the court proceedings was that Rick's fines were very heavy. Moreover, efforts were made to confiscate all the livestock on his farm, as well as the farm machinery. But he was saved from the confiscation by a special circumstance, which, however, turned out to produce for him only a sort of Pyrrhic victory. It turned out, you see, that the farm was not in Ricky's name but in that of his young tenant farmer's wife. I never saw her, or didn't know it if I did. Afterward, I used to try to recall if I hadn't seen some such young woman when I was down watching the cockfights—one who would have fitted the picture in my mind. My imagination played tricks on me, though. I would think I remembered the face or figure of some young girl I'd seen there who could conceivably be the one. But then suddenly I'd recall another and think possibly it might be she who had the title to Ricky's farm. I never could be sure.

When Ricky appeared outside my window just now, I'd already had a very bad morning. The bursitis in my right shoulder had waked me before dawn. At last I got up and dressed, which was an ordeal in itself. (My right hip was hurting somewhat, too.) When finally the cook came in, she wanted to give me a massage before she began fixing breakfast even. Cary would never have allowed her to make that mistake. A massage, you see, is the worst thing you can do for my sort of bursitis. What I wanted was some breakfast. And I knew it would take Meg three-quarters of an hour to put breakfast on the table. And so I managed to get out of my clothes again and ease myself into a hot bath, groaning so loud all the while that Meg came up to the door twice and asked if I was all right. I told her just to go and get my breakfast ready. After breakfast, I waited till a decent hour and then telephoned one of my golf foursome to tell him I couldn't play this afternoon. The two other members of the foursome had already called him and said they also had bursitis and couldn't play today. It's this damp fall weather that does us in worst. All you can do is sit and think how you've got the whole winter before you and wonder if you'll be able to get yourself off to someplace like Sarasota.

While I sat at a front window, waiting for the postman (he never brings anything but circulars and catalogues on Saturday; besides, all my serious mail goes to the office and is opened by someone else), I found myself thinking of all the things I couldn't do and all the people who are dead and that I mustn't think about. I tried to do a little better—that is, to think of something cheerful. There was lots I *could* be cheerful about, wasn't there? At least three of my children were certain to telephone today—all but Ricky, and it was sure to be bad news if he did! And a couple of the grandchildren would likely call, too. Then tomorrow I'd be going to lunch with some of them if I felt up to it. Suddenly I thought of the pills I was supposed to have taken before breakfast and had forgotten to: the Inderal and the potassium and the hydrochlorothiazide. I began to get up from my chair and then I settled down again. It didn't really matter. There was no ailment I had that could really be counted on to be fatal if I missed one day's dosage. And then I wholeheartedly embraced the old subject, the old speculation: How many days like this one, how many years like this one lay ahead for me? And finally, irresistibly, I descended to lower depths still, thinking of past times not with any relish but remembering how in past times I had always *told* myself I'd someday look back with pleasure on what would seem good old days, which was an indication itself that they hadn't somehow been good enough—not good enough, that is, to stand on their own as an end in themselves. If the old days were so damned good, why had I had to think always how good they would someday seem in retrospect? I had just reached the part where I think there was nothing *wrong* with them and that I ought to be satisfied, had just reached that point at which I recall that I loved and was loved by my wife, that I love and am loved by my children, that it's not them or my life but *me* there's something wrong with!—had just reached that inevitable syllogism that I always come to, when I was distracted by the arrival of Saturday morning's late mail delivery. It was brought in, it was handed to me by a pair of black hands, and of course it had nothing in it. But I took it upstairs to my sitting room. (So that even the servant wouldn't see there was nothing worth having in it.) I had just closed my door and got out my pills when I heard Ricky's car turn in to the gravel driveway.

He was driving so slowly that his car wheels hardly disturbed the gravel. That in itself was an ominous phenomenon. He was approaching slowly and quietly. He didn't want me to know ahead of time what there was in store for me. My first impulse was to lock my door and refuse to admit him. I simply did not feel up to Rick this morning! But I said to myself, "That's something I've never done, though maybe ought to have done years ago, no matter what Cary said. He's sure to send my blood pressure soaring." I thought of picking up the telephone and phoning one of the other children to come and protect me from this monster of a son and from whatever sort of trouble he was now in.

But it was just then that I caught my first glimpse of him down in the driveway. I had the illusion that he was admiring the place. And then of course I was at once disillusioned. He was only hesitating down there because he dreaded seeing me. But he was telling himself he *had* to see me. There would be no other solution to his problem but to see his old man. I knew what he was thinking by the gesture he was making with his left hand. It's strange how you get the notion that your children are like you just because they have the same facial features and the same body build and make the same gestures when talking to themselves. None of it means a thing! It's only an illusion. Even now I find myself making gestures with my hands when I'm talking to myself that I used to notice my own father making sometimes when we were out walking together and neither of us had spoken a word for half an hour or so. It used to get on my nerves when I saw Father do it, throwing out his hand almost imperceptibly, with his long fingers spread apart. I don't know why it got on my nerves so. But, anyhow, I never dreamed that I could inherit such a gesture —or much less that one of my sons would. And yet there Ricky is, down in the driveway, making the same gesture precisely. And there never were three men with more different characters than my father and me and my youngest child. I watch Ricky make the gesture several times while standing in the driveway. And now suddenly he turns as if to go back to his car. I step away from the window, hoping he hasn't seen me and will go on off. But, having once seen him down there, I can't, of course, do that. I have to receive him and hear him out. I open the sash and call down to him, "Come on up, Ricky."

He looks up at me, smiles guiltily, and shrugs. Then he comes on in the side entrance. As he moves through the house and up the stairs, I try to calm myself. I gaze down at the roughed-up gravel where his suède shoes did their damage and tell myself it isn't so bad and even manage to smile at my own oldmaidishness. Presently, he comes into the sitting room. We greet each other with the usual handshake. I can smell his shaving lotion. Or maybe it is something he puts on his hair. We go over and sit down by the fireplace, where there is a fire laid but not lit in this season, of course. He begins by talking about everything under the sun except what is on his mind. This is standard procedure in our talks at such times. Finally, he begins looking into the fireplace as though the fire were lit and as though he were watching low-burning flames. I barely keep myself from smiling when he says, "I've got a little problem—not so damned little, in fact. It's a matter that's got out of hand."

And then I say, "I supposed as much."

You can't give Ricky an inch at these times, you see. Else he'll take advantage of you. Pretty soon he'll have shifted the whole burden of how he's to be extricated onto your shoulders. I wait for him to continue, and he is about to, I think. But before he can get started he turns his eyes away from the dry logs and the unlit kindling and begins looking about the room, just as he looked about the premises outside. It occurs to me again that he seems to be observing my place for the very first time. But I don't suppose he really is. His mind is, as usual, on himself. Then all at once his eyes do obviously come to focus on something over my shoulder. He runs his tongue up under his upper lip and then under his lower lip, as though he were cleaning his teeth. I, involuntarily almost, look over my shoulder. There on the library table behind me, on what I call my desk, are my cut-glass tumbler and three bottles of pills—my hydrochlorothiazide, my Inderal, and my potassium. Somehow I failed to put them back in my desk drawer earlier. I was so distracted by my morbid thoughts when I came upstairs that I forgot to stick them away in the place where I keep them out of sight from everybody. (I don't even like for the servants to see what and how much medicine I take.) Without a word passing between us, and despite the pains in my shoulder and hip, I push myself up out of my chair and sweep the bottles, and the tumbler, too, into the desk drawer. I keep my back to Ricky for a minute or so till I can overcome the grimacing I never can repress when these pains strike. Suddenly, though, I do turn back to him and find he has come to his feet. I pay no special attention to that. I ease myself back into my chair, saying, "Yes, Ricky." Making my voice rather hard, I say, "You've got a problem?" He looks at me coldly, without a trace of the sympathy any one of the other children would have shown—knowing, that is, as he surely does, that I am having pains of some description. And he speaks to me as though I were a total stranger toward whom he feels nothing but is just barely human enough to wish not to torture. "Man," he says—the idea of his addressing *me* that way! —"Man, you've got problems enough of your own. Even the world's greatest snotface can see that. One thing sure, you don't need to hear *my* crap."

I am on my feet so quick you wouldn't think I have a pain in my body. "Don't you use that gutter language with me, Ricky!" I say. "You weren't brought up in some slum over beyond Vinegar Hill!" He only turns and looks into the fireplace again. If there were a fire going I reckon he would have spat in it at this point. Then he looks back at me, running his tongue over his teeth again. And then, without any apology or so much as a by-your-leave, he heads for the door. "Come back here, Ricky!" I command. "Don't you dare leave the room!" Still moving toward the closed door, he glances back over his shoulder at me, with a wide, hard grin on his face, showing his mouthful of white teeth, as though my command were the funniest thing he has ever heard. At the door, he puts his big right hand on the glass knob, covering it entirely. Then he twists his upper body, his torso, around—seemingly just from the hips—to face me. And simultaneously he brings up his left hand and scratches that triangle of dark hair where his shirt is open. It is like some kind of dirty gesture he is making. I say to myself, "He really is like something not quite human. For all the jams and scrapes he's been in, he's never suffered any second thoughts or known the meaning of remorse. I ought to have let him hang in some noose of his own making years ago. I ought to have let him hang," I say to myself, "by his own beautiful locks."

But almost simultaneously what I hear myself saying aloud is "Please don't go, Rick. Don't go yet, son." Yes, I am pleading with him, and I mean what I say with my whole heart. He still has his right hand on the doorknob and has given it a full turn.

Our eyes meet across the room, directly, as they never have before in the whole of Ricky's life or mine. I think neither of us could tell anyone what it is he sees in the other's eyes, unless it is a need beyond any description either of us is capable of.

Presently Rick says, "You don't need to hear my crap."

And I hear my bewildered voice saying, "I do . . . I do." And "Don't go, Rick, my boy." My eyes have even misted over. But I still meet his eyes across the now too silent room. He looks at me in the most compassionate way imaginable. I don't think any child of mine has ever looked at me so before. Or perhaps it isn't really with compassion he is viewing me but with the sudden, gratifying knowledge that it is not, after all, such a one-sided business, the business between us. He keeps his right hand on the doorknob a few seconds longer. Then I hear the latch click and know he has let go. Meanwhile, I observe his left hand making that familiar gesture, his fingers splayed, his hand tilting back and forth. I am out of my chair by now. I go to the desk and bring out two Danlys cigars from another desk drawer, which I keep locked. He is there ready to receive my offering when I turn around. He accepts the cigar without smiling, and I give it without smiling, too. Seated opposite each other again, each of us lights his own.

And then Ricky begins. What will it be this time, I think. I am wild with anticipation. Whatever it will be, I know it is all anyone in the world can give me now—perhaps the most anyone has ever been able to give a man like me. As Ricky begins, I try to think of all the good things the other children have done for me through the years, and of their affection, and of my wife's. But it seems this was all there ever was. I forget my pains and my pills and the canceled golf game, and the meaningless mail that morning. I find I can scarcely sit still in my chair for wanting Ricky to get on with it. Has he been brandishing his pistol again? Or dragging the sheriff's deputy across a field at midnight? And does he have in his wallet perhaps a picture of some other girl with a tight little mouth, and eyes that burn? Will his outrageous story include her? And perhaps explain her fascination or perhaps not explain it, leaving her a blessed mystery? As Ricky begins, I find myself listening not merely with fixed attention but with my whole being. . . . I hear him beginning. I am listening. I am listening gratefully to all he will tell me about himself, about his life, about any life that is not my own.

WHITE BOY

IVY GOODMAN

Ivy Goodman was born in Harrisburg, Pennsylvania, in 1953. Her stories have appeared in *Fiction, The Ark River Review*, and other magazines; one was included in *Prize Stories 1981*. She studied at the University of Pennsylvania and Stanford University, where she was a Mirrielees Fellow. She is now working on a novel.

She had first seen him wearing sweat socks bunched down between the first and second toes of each foot to accommodate black rubber thongs. She associated this foot garb vaguely and incorrectly with an Eastern religion. She noticed he was prettier than she. He was nice to her because he was nice, and she imagined many beautiful women he'd been even nicer to.

They were next door neighbors on the second story of an oblong efficiency apartment house. Often from her sofa she watched him clomp along the outdoor catwalk that rimmed the second story and linked the twin outdoor staircases. When he passed her windows he looked straight ahead. When she passed his she pretended to survey the parking lot. In quest of a dime he once came to her door clutching ten pennies, and she asked him inside.

It turned out he had no telephone. He'd been on his way to the booth at the nearest gas station. "No telephone?" she said, suddenly embarrassed that she had one.

"I've heard yours ringing," he said.

"How annoying."

"Not at all. May I use it sometime?"

"Peter, of course."

"Now?"

"Yes, but . . ." She glanced down at his thongs, at his mittened feet, dapper tonight in thin black socks embossed with hexagons. "What should I do? Should I leave?" she asked.

"Oh, no, Robin. Stay, unless you mind."

"The phone's over there, beside the refrigerator." She smiled. "I guess I'll go sit down."

On the sofa by the windows she pretended to read while he dialed endlessly. "Hi, this is Peter. . . . Hello, Richard? Peter . . . Peggy, it's Peter. I said I'd call. . . ." And he was a man of his word. How many people he knew whose numbers Robin would find on her next month's bill! She eavesdropped until she wearied of so much good nature. She peeked at him, seated now on her dining table for a long call. Legs crossed, he kept time to his talk by shaking his feet. Those stockinged feet gave him an air of being housebound. Where could he go in thongs and socks? Not far, certainly. Though this evening the invalid had dressed — in sporty trousers and a plaid shirt — his feet reminded that tomorrow he'd be back in bed. And yet how brave he was, as he struck his heels against his innersoles and made a sound like running to console himself because he could not run. How uncomplaining, pale, beautiful, and nearly dead. The languishing Prince! Hail!

She knew he had been hailed. She knew by the ease with which he guffawed now, pounded her table, and said, "He bit the dust, I don't believe it, who was the girl? Naw! Her?"

He was blessed, whatever he might do, and she had come to life as an immigrant, large-nosed, far-fetched, straight from the hold. If she'd been dealt her features fairly, she'd have thrown them back, forfeited a turn, and hoped for better luck next time. As it was, she remained one of the less fortunate, envious of him, and yet admiring.

He was quiet now. She watched him stand. The table shuddered. He stretched one arm toward the wall and hung up the phone. "Thanks, Robin, but it's getting late. I've got to go." Grinning, he headed toward the door and almost sneaked off.

"Wait." She lowered her book and stared at him unobstructed. "Are you sure you're done?"

"Yes, unless . . ." With one funny foot he held the door ajar. "Do you want something? It's not midnight yet. There's the corner store."

"Don't do me any favors. I'll send a bill."

"Oh, right." Nearly caught, he pretended to come forth voluntarily. "By the way — some of those were tollcalls . . ."

"By the way? Thanks for nothing. See you, Peter."

"What?"

"Just goodnight."

"Goodnight then."

She might as well have turned to him in profile and stuck out her tongue: look at how awful I am. Oh, let him think what he wanted, which probably was nothing, she realized. Days later, inside on a rainy afternoon, she watched him run through all the puddles in the parking lot. He wore galoshes. He carried a sodden grocery bag. He chose the farther set of stairs and bounded up. With his head in a hood, he hurried by. She heard his bolt click, his door whine open. She half-expected some sort of greeting next: "Look at you, you're soaking wet. Off with your clothes and into this bath." But no, her neighbor lived alone.

She neared their common wall as if it beckoned; she tilted her head. Diminishing creaks. The plaintive to and fro of metal cupboard doors. A pot lid dropped. Clatter in the kitchen. Silence in the pipes. His bathtub dry.

But would he need baths, really? She imagined his sweat would smell of pennies, damp, like the ones he'd held out. *Do you have a dime?* What would he smell on her? Onions? Fish? The back of a shop? Her shop. He'd open the door and rattle the tin bell dangling from the transom on a piece of string. At first he wouldn't see her, then he would, wiping her hands across her apron bib. "What do you want?" "May I use your . . ." "No. Ours is a business phone. The pay booth's up the street." On his way out, past the barrel in the aisle, she would falsely accuse him of theft. "Put that back." She'd grab him by the arm and pry his fist, finger by finger, until his pennies scattered on the worn linoleum. He would leave without bothering to stoop for them.

She turned and pressed her forehead to the wall. Not quite in the corner, she stood like that for a long while, as though she'd found a bearing for her head, which she rolled now and then in order to look out the window briefly.

The rain storm ended. She heard him, in his box, move closer to hers. Then, three creaks in place, hesitation, impatience, a stationary shuffle: all together signaling departure soon. As a way of getting ready, he seemed to wait for someone. *Hurry up. What's keeping you?* His door opened. He stepped out. His door shut. She watched him trot past as purposeful as a dog. Could he really have somewhere to go? something to do? His footsteps stopped. He knocked. "Robin? May I use your phone?"

In the weeks that followed, he visited often, always bringing with him his small leather telephone book. Once, when Robin glimpsed a gray-lined page, she was shocked to see addresses noted too. Had he filled that blank as a matter of form, or did he actually write letters sometimes? He sent birthday cards, he said. He was a true friend. He still had friends from the second grade.

She imagined he'd been loyal all his life, and beneficient. At two years or three, he'd probably leaned forward in his stroller to offer strangers cookies, gnawed around the edges and damp with drool. "How darling. His name is Peter? No, thank you, Peter. You eat that. That's yours." He'd laugh and shake his head and take another nibble. What were cookies to him? He could always get more from his mother, or kindly bakery clerks. "Would the little boy like a cookie? Yes? Chocolate chip?" He risked nothing, while his reputation for being generous grew.

And so he said to Robin now, "I wish I could do you a favor." He had just finished dialing, and for a moment he held the receiver aloft. Then his call went through. A thin male voice cried out, "Hello? Hello? Who's there?" Peter placated it: "Doug? Peter. Hold on a second, would you?" He turned back to Robin, who was thrilled a friend of his had to wait for her. She felt contemptuous and special, until she remembered she was paying for the call. Why hadn't she gotten up the nerve to bill Peter yet? "Anything in my apartment," Peter went on, "borrow anything, Robin, long-term. Put a lien on it." He laughed. "Though I have to admit there's nothing much there."

She laughed back. "Your call," she reminded, "your friend." She walked away to her bookcase and selected another volume to hold.

She still could not read with him there. If at first she had chosen to eavesdrop, she had no choice now. She was enthralled. Each time he knocked, she felt as though she gobbled a bowl of sugar fast before answering the door. "Peter! It's you! Hello! Come in!"

She took an aspirin soon after he arrived, and between his calls she served tea. Over tea cups, they discovered they were the same age ("Twenty-six, too!") and had gone to college in neighboring states. She grew up in the East, he in the West, and neither cared about his or her current job very much. After graduation, he had lived in Europe for a year. "Peter! Is that true? You're a man of the world!"

But was Peter a man of the world? No. More likely he was a large version of the child a mother might drag anywhere. *Nope. No problems with Peter. He's so well-behaved.* Nothing affected him really, not even indulgence. All that money Robin had spent treating him to phone calls? Wasted. She should have saved it for her first European tour.

"Robin, is something the matter?"

"Hmm? No." She looked up. And she saw again that he was beautiful and she was all wrong. He was good: that was it. She was back at the sugar bowl again, between spoonfuls thinking how good he was. "Do you know I'm corrupt?" she said.

"You? You're the most corrupt woman I've met."

"I'm serious. You're too good to understand."

"What?"

"That's right." If he ever discovered her thoughts, her deceptions, her motives. Calculations were tricks with sums to him. "Peter, you might find this insulting, but I have a crush on you."

"Robin, I have a crush on you."

"Yes?"

"We'll have to do something, won't we?" Across her kitchen table, he stared out, not exactly at her. She felt as if she'd handed him a dollar, and he was dazzled by a vision of the candy he might buy. "It would be a shame not to, still I want to think about it," he said. Sugar babies, honey bits, peppermint sticks, malted milk balls. In suspense, permutations could be worked out. "Let's surprise each other some time." He meant, let me surprise you. He was a hoarder and might save his dollar for weeks, but she would have him run now to the store.

"Would you kiss me?" she said.

"Sure."

They pushed from the table, met near the sink, embraced, bent down, and scrambled all over the floor on their knees together, kissing, laughing. Then they got up to take off their clothes.

Peter stepped back to look at her. "Around, around." He stirred his finger through the air. "Whirl."

She turned. "Am I all right?"

"All right? You're lovely."

"Then both of us are."

Love-ly, love-ly. What a lovely lie. She would believe it. In truth, they were clumsy together, and the only lovely things were his sounds, let out at last, low and lovely.

Afterwards she hoped they might lie still for a minute. But no, immediately he lifted his head and asked, "Do you want to hear a joke?" She said, "Yes," and thought, he must ruin our closeness because it frightens him. But she also thought she brought them even closer because she understood. Then again, by now he might feel absolutely nothing. She heard his joke and laughed at the rapture she had found in that deluded moment before he reared his head. He was an oaf. On the chair she saw his yellow chamois chapparal shirt, reminiscent of a dust cloth; on the floor his scattered foot wear, thongs and socks. She wanted him to dress, be gone. But then he spoke to her. With his hands he turned her head. "Here, Robin, here, here."

He left before she fell asleep. Listening from her bed, following his progress, she pretended he was merely walking to another room, not to a separate apartment.

They always slept separately. Twice a week or three times, after finishing his calls, he undressed and stayed another hour. Or else he said, "Come to my place for a while." At best, Robin decided, he was simply pleasurable. And he was very polite to her. *Say, 'Pass the sugar, please,' and do not grab, Peter.*

Even she, the immigrant, knew a little etiquette. Requesting a whole night from him would be unmannerly. Besides she only pretended to want it. Without pretense, she had no pleasure. But Peter was easy to love. He would kiss and kiss, then not kiss and with force not let her, until not kissing was better than kissing some nights. She told him, "You're tough." He hid his face in a pillow and said, "You embarrass me." He used his imagination, put it away, and in a moment was himself again, while for weeks she half-believed she loved him, though she knew better.

She listened; she waited. She could not be at home without waiting for him. Was he out? Was he in? Would he knock soon? For him, their affair just made them better friends.

"It's not passionate, is it?" he asked.

"No." She was kneeling on the floor and gathering her clothes. She stared up. "Have you ever had a passionate one?"

"Last summer, and then I hated her. But you and I, we're friends. Yes?"

"Yes."

As part of their secret, only he and she shared his slights. They had no company, though Robin imagined some: a party with Peter seated at its center, smiling, drinking, garrulous. Across the room, conscious of the air she displaced, Robin perched on a window sill. In her hand a nearly full beverage glass warmed and sweated. Even in daydreams she never outgrew herself; her time to acquire grace had passed. Peter's party-voice slid by. Though in the dark, after something arduous, he spoke just to her: "Water, water, quick, we're dying of thirst. Bring water!"

He was playful. He made up rules: they must undress each other. When she reached down her leg for her sock, he said, "No help allowed. Let me." What fun, she should have liked this, but she wanted them quickly to undress themselves and then go slowly. For him, sometimes being naked was enough. When he pushed too soon, she couldn't say, "Please wait." Instead, embarrassed, furious, she made room. Part of herself got up and watched a man and a woman on the bed.

But if pleasure was the point, she must come back; she must feel herself beneath him. His smile blew out breath across her face, and she wondered what technique of hers was laughable. In the dark his perfect, good features vanished on a plain with holes for eyes, mouth, nostrils. His brows were fine sketches of brows, and his hair, cut to look neatly ruffled, looked no more than neatly ruffled. Across his hairless chest he was so white. White boy, she named him secretly, though his skin was no whiter than that of any other man she'd known. White boy, whitest. When he became a man he would grow hair, but now he was still a boy, above her with a man's shoulders. Even a boy could make her lose herself. The hardship came in parting from him. "Robin, it's about that time. I'm really tired." "Yes, of course. Goodnight." At the door she turned to look at him, lying contained within his white, white self.

He was not simple. He was more than she knew. When she rubbed her back raw by rolling with him on the carpet, he joked about "rug burn." But after the sore scabbed he declared it "ugly" convincingly. With what ease he found the right word. How long, she wondered, had he held it ready?

Despite herself, she asked him once, "Do you like the way I look?"

"You're lovely. I told you. And exotic."

"Exotic?"

"You know, like something strange to eat."

While she drank milk from a beautiful glass, he went to the bad part of town for an ethnic meal. *The food's great but don't inspect the kitchen, and don't use the bathroom, whatever you do.* She was sure that in a matter of time she would repulse him, utterly.

When he told her he lost his virginity on a train, she asked, "Where, in the toilet?" and startled both of them with her ignorance of sleepers riding moonlit rails. She spoke too soon, too loud, and her imagination faltered. With a rank air she revealed herself, as though a door had swung open.

"And your first time?" he asked.

"On a bed. In the background I heard radio music. While in your berth you heard the locomotive." Beside him, she lay very still and added, "How romantic."

"I didn't know what I was doing."

"Neither did I, I pretended."

"Did you fool him?"

"Probably not."

"You didn't know him well?"

"We were classmates. It was nothing, really."

"I don't mean to pry, you don't have to tell me, but altogether how many?"

So, the flower had been picked and now the leaves: defoliation. "Of course I'll tell you. Let me think." Plus one, plus one, plus one . . . She liked to count them off while she walked sometimes; she liked to step on each of them. "Fewer than all my fingers and toes. Enough for a team."

He laughed at this.

"Now you," she said.

"Hmm . . ."

She turned toward the wall and felt desolate for three minutes. "Well?"

"So far twenty-nine."

"So far? You haven't come to me yet?"

"You were first. From you I worked back."

Aging, she had gone the opposite route, while he grew younger. "And you're still not sure who thirty is?"

"I just unearthed her. My first year in college. True love! I remember . . ."

Everything but her name, though he remembered other names. He had loved in sets: sisters, roommates, friends. In love, he'd corresponded, and he'd saved every envelope and letter. *Dear Peter, with all my kisses.* Love in an attic, a borrowed car, a dormitory room, an unheated cabin. All she thought love would be until she knew better, or did she? She knew he didn't love her.

"Robin, you okay? I hope I haven't said something . . ."

"Of course not. I'm just surprised to hear you're so romantic. Actually, I suspected all along." She laughed. Ugly now, or still exotic? No matter. He was in France again with a woman named Ruth. He couldn't get enough of her. "Was she exotic?"

"Who, Ruth? No, silly, you're exotic. You."

He fluffed her hair, no longer hair but rainbow plumage. He wasn't kissing, but sampling. How exotic. How peculiar. Occasionally, a taste might develop further, into distaste. *You ate it last week, Peter. I don't understand. All right, all right. If you don't like it, leave it on your plate.*

Similarly, when he decided he did not like where he was living, he moved. "I knew from the start this was temporary, or else I couldn't have stood it. My new place is in the woods. A guest house, rent-free in exchange for doing a little carpentry work in a mansion nearby."

"So you're the kind of person who gets those kinds of deals. I always wondered."

"Now Robin."

"Now nothing."

"We'll see each other."

He spoke with such certainty that she knew he meant the opposite. "Yes," she said, "we'll see each other."

She stared at his eyes. In a certain light, the outer corners showed their wrinkles: the stamp of a citrus fruit sliced open, radiating lines. Had he suffered? No, he had squinted; through his childhood he'd played outdoors every day in a hot, sunny climate. Now he slid sunglasses from his shirt pocket, unfolded them, and put them on.

Sadness, loneliness, pain. The few times he invoked those words he seemed to be drilling for tomorrow's vocabulary quiz. *Of course you'll feel uncomfortable with these new words, Peter, but you must try to use them just the same.* Rightfully, they did not belong to Robin either.

Her problems? No more serious than her landlord's. Now that Peter was gone, perhaps she should hang a sign around her neck: Vacancy. For Rent.

FAST LOVE

MICHAEL MALONE

Michael Malone was born and raised in North Carolina. He is the author of four novels—*Painting the Roses Red*, *The Delectable Mountains*, *Dingley Falls*, and the forthcoming *Time's Witness*—as well as a play and three nonfiction books. His articles and short stories have appeared in *Partisan Review*, *Mademoiselle*, *Harper's Bookletter*, *Esquire*, and elsewhere. Educated at the University of North Carolina at Chapel Hill and at Harvard, Mr. Malone has taught at a number of colleges. He now lives in Clinton, Connecticut, with his wife and daughter.

It was love at first sight out of the corner of my eye as she flew past the showroom window where I stood eating a double cheeseburger and trying not to hear Merle Longfielder bore our only customer with exaggerations about his racing a 560 horsepower Mustang down in South Carolina last Sunday. It was love in a blur, too. At first I thought maybe something rabid or mentally defective was after her. I didn't think of muggers; we don't have crime in Toomis. (As our billboard for some reason brags, "Toomis is the Smallest Industrial Town in Piedmont, North Carolina." The industries are the state mental hospital and a snuff factory. If you live here, you don't notice the smell.)

So she ran by, and when nothing else followed her, I did. Destiny can't be ignored, no matter how unlikely it may look at first sight—as my grandmother told me when she bought her bus ticket to go march with Martin Luther King, and my father caught her and put her in the (mental) Hospital. This running object of my sudden affection looked unlikely because the women of Toomis walked, on the few occasions when they weren't driving their cars, and in mid-October—whether it was forty degrees or eighty degrees—they wore wool plaid skirts with cardigan sweaters looped over their shoulders. *She* had on white shorts with red stripes and red shoes with white stripes and a sleeveless T-shirt with a picture of Margaret Mead the anthropologist on it. Her red hair in its ponytail leapt all over the place like a fire chasing her down the street.

She wasn't wearing a bra either; I don't mind mentioning that I noticed, because I'd already decided to marry her. We Wintrip males have a long family tradition of choosing a bride in the twinkling of an eye, though I believe I was the first to spot one on the run. My grandfather saw his future wife threatening a bully with a pitchfork as she stood atop a hayrick with her skirts tucked up. My father first glimpsed my mother as she and her fiancé were winning a Tri-Delta jitterbug contest. And I fell in love in a flash with the first jogger anyone ever saw in Toomis, North Carolina. I had loved only once before—unhappily—and now as I panted towards the town limits, a stitch in my side, a throb in my back, fear tingled through me: would this girl break my heart as Betsy Creedmoor had long ago?

I lost her just on the ridge of the first long upgrade of Route 55. The double cheeseburger and knee-high Frye boots did me in. After the spasms ended, I crawled along the shoulder until I felt well enough to walk back to Wintrip Motors where Merle Longfielder, my dad's other vice-president, amused himself by hurling me to the ground on the pretense that he'd already called an ambulance to rush me off for rabies shots. He'd seen the girl, too. "Nice bod," was all the oaf could think of to say.

Merle is my sex, race, and age. So much for what we have in common. His brain is thick and porous. He sports a forty-eight-long maroon polyester blazer, a crew cut, and ought to clip the hairs in his nostrils. In the summer my father and Merle lie side by side together under cars in our driveway; their legs stick out like those of Greek soldiers making love. In their time, they say, they both crunched a lot of cartilage playing high school football. I suspect Dad wishes Merle were his son. So do I. The truth is, during my youth, team sports were never that compelling. I had a weakness for learning; chess, debating, and bicycling were also favorite pastimes—all enthusiasms that struck my dad like a collapsed lung.

My senior year, when my life was in shambles over Betsy Creedmoor, the track coach lured me into a letter sweater. As it happened, I was good. But I'd always been a runner. From childhood on, wherever I was supposed to be, I ran there fast. I ran after the schoolbus. I ran after the footballs my father was always kicking at me in the backyard. I ran like the wind out of necessity. Toughs in my neighborhood, murderous with the baffled envious rage that the stupid sometimes feel for the intelligent, would occasionally bolt out at me from behind bushes or cars and try to destroy my body. When we were twelve, Merle Longfielder chased me through the Baptist nursery school playground with a branch of poison sumac he planned to rub into my eyes. I was jumping three-year-olds as if they were hurdles.

So you might say life trained me as a sprinter; now I planned to use that training to win a wife. Sunday night I pawed my old tennis shoes out from under my bed. Wearing them Monday, I was on the watch for my future bride as soon as I had finished my "real" job and hurried over to Wintrip Motors where from five to eight weekdays and all day Saturday I worked for my dad as one of his two vice-presidents. I did it for the money and for my mother who begged me. Maybe she thought that if my dad's only child refused his offer, he'd put me in the Hospital too, like he did his mother. When he first heard about my real job—state social work—he told me I was nuts. As soon as I tried to explain (on the way home from my college graduation), he let me know *social* meant socialist and *worker* meant Red Square. Then he jackknifed to a stop, swelled into a frenzy, and announced he was going to beat the Commie crap out of my head with his pistol butt. By the time he got the glove compartment opened, I'd done the quarter mile in four seconds less than my old coach's best hopes. Plus done it wearing an academic gown.

My father's response didn't surprise me. He was a man of the fifties, and in the fifties people all over the country were scared to death that the Communists might take over and brainwash

Americans into thinking they had a right to other people's property—especially that property belonging to these people who were scared to death of the Communists. Nearly all the parents in Toomis were afraid their children were going to *catch* Communism; they thought it was like polio, only there wasn't a vaccine. So when I was nine, I sold glitter-dusted Christmas cards door-to-door and the money went to help fight the Red Menace. From my father's point of view I obviously hadn't sold enough, for Russia had gotten me in the end and mesmerized me into preferring social services to the showroom of Wintrip Motors. And so, for my mother's sake, to allow him to hold up his gray (flattop) head in Toomis, and to help pay my apartment rent so I wouldn't have to live at home with him, I moonlighted at Wintrip Motors.

Thank God I did, and that Wintrip Motors hogged the side of Main Street where Meredith Krantzsky jogged. Meredith Krantzsky was her name, though horribly enough it was Merle Longfielder who formally introduced her to me. My own first try was interrupted. Wearing my sneakers, I was in a nonchalant crouch by the showroom door at six o'clock Monday when she flashed around the corner of Parritt's Diner and flew towards me. By the time we reached the end of the block I could see there were gold specks in the green irises of her eyes. She was altogether as beautiful as I'd suspected from my original blurred impression.

I tried to be casual. "Mind if I run along with you for a little bit?"

She turned, arching a copper brown eyebrow at my seersucker jacket and best paisley tie.

"My name's Blake Wintrip. Felt like. Little exercise. Just happen to notice . . ."

But then I tripped to avoid a baby in a stroller, and while I spiraled about to catch my balance, old Mrs. Etherege spied me from her bus stop bench. She clawed me to a standstill to tell me she'd spent the morning visiting my grandmother at the Hospital. By the time I could unclench her tiny relentless fingers, my bride-to-be was floating like a sunset through the intersection of Culloden and Main. But suddenly she turned, smiled at me; and then she ran on. My heart burst.

Mrs. Etherege pushed up my eyelids and stared. "Blake, are

you all right? Heaven's sake. What's the matter? Your face is a deep plum purple. Almost heliotrope." (Mrs. Etherege has been an amateur painter since Southern primitivism became fashionable; she and my grandmother—original founders of the Ladies Art League to which Mother also belonged—used to take their canvases up into the Appalachians where the gift galleries would sell them to tourists.) "Are you sick, son?"

"I'm in love," I told her. "I'm about to propose."

"Oh well, isn't that wonderful? Your folks must be so relieved. Who's the lucky girl?"

"There she goes." I pointed with a sigh as Meredith Krantzsky bounced away towards the horizon.

Mrs. Etherege's tactless remark about my parents' relief was a reference to a sorrow from which only time and an inadvertent discovery of the truth had cured me. My high school sweetheart Betsy Creedmoor temporarily lost her mind senior year under the pressure of being forced by her mother to pretend to be stupid for popularity's sake. Betsy was brainy, and in our region the intellectual life was frowned upon for females. (For males, too, as far as that goes.) Betsy's breakdown—she would sit with her bare feet in the gutter outside Toomis High, drawing designs on her legs with lipstick—was my fall from innocence. The sight of her beautiful vacant eyes was the sword that drove me from the garden into a life of social work among children of Cain. That was almost how my grandmother put it when I went to the Hospital to ask her what I ought to do. She sat at her potter's wheel, hummed her old marching song, "We Shall Overcome," while she thought. Finally, she told me to go to the state university and study injustice. Just be warned, she added, the world felt no obligation to make sense, much less be fair. Grandma was in a position to know. Here she was, perfectly sane, locked away to weave placemats. Here was Betsy Creedmoor deteriorating beyond repair, and her mother accused me of cruelty when I pleaded that her daughter needed medical help. "Blake, Blake, why do you persecute me and my Betsy so? Why are you trying day and night to lock our little girl away in a snake pit with old nutty trashy types, when you yourself have been so crazy about her ever since fifth grade and followed her around like a little puppy dog?"

Mrs. Creedmoor had never liked me; her feelings were requited. She had blue hair and leathery arms as brown as her golf bag. She smoked five packs of cigarettes a day; even when she was doing the dishes she would pinch her cigarette with a sudsy hand and stick it in a plastic ashtray over the sink. I told her Betsy was getting sicker. She'd sigh. "Oh Blake, darling, what makes you talk that ugly way? Manic-depressive? Why, Betsy's just worked too hard being a silly old bookworm, *like you,* and got herself a little run-down." And as this woman was speaking, her sixteen-year-old daughter stood weeping at her reflection in the hall mirror, then stuck her fingers in her mouth and stretched it into a grin howling pig Latin.

Betsy missed so much school because of her nervous breakdown that her grades slipped into the norm. This did, in fact, enhance her popularity. She gave up debate club and playing chess with me at lunch; instead she'd wander about the high school grounds with other girls, collecting, as she wafted by, a huddle of large retarded boyfriends—among them Merle Longfielder. With her mother's blessing, Merle escorted Betsy to the Senior Prom. There, all misty in her trance, she was elected prom queen, and by midnight she lay thrashing like a silverfish in the back seat of Merle's stripped-down Ford. A "friend" told me he saw them. At commencement Betsy was awarded the "Most Popular Girl" trophy. Eventually I began to realize that although Betsy really had lost her mind, it wasn't going to make any difference to people; the man she eventually married, a Sigma Chi pre-dental boozehound, never even noticed.

Betsy and I both enrolled in the state university. She went, according to her mother's instructions, to work on an M.R.S. degree. I went on my grandmother's recommendation. After my arrival, my father mailed me a local editorial calling the college a "radical-infested swamp of subversives, a compost heap where budding Communist homosexuals meet by night to hide their shameful scheming from God's all-seeing eye." But the truth is we were pitiably behind the times. While everywhere else they had hippies in the sixties, we had beatniks. While the New Left was ripping the ragged social fabric into headbands, we lay on the campus green playing Pete Seeger songs on our bongos. By the time we got around to burning the Marine recruiting stand in front of the dining hall, everywhere else they were back to toga parties and panty raids. I gave up running, except to the john, and passed the time drinking beer and studying injustice.

Betsy Creedmoor said only two things to me throughout our stay. My first year I stood out in the quad listening to a speech by a famous socialist who kept running for president and insisting that somebody arrest him. He told us, "Social reform begins at home. Stand still and look around you!" He went all over the world giving this speech. A group of us were greatly under this man's influence as freshmen. We were cheering him as Betsy ambled by with a weight lifter. She said, "I kid you not. Never take life to heart." That was all. And then our final term I squeezed past her coming out of the bathroom of Slaughterhouse Five, a horribly foul college bar. This time she said, "Check and mate." But her eyes weren't focused, and she may not have even been talking to me. My sole consolation then had been that Betsy had cast off Merle Longfielder for the dentist who wore colored knit shirts with an alligator over his left nipple and who lugged a golf bag to classes.

Yet now three years later all I could wish was that Betsy and Merle were off somewhere in Arizona, upwardly mobile, celebrating their wooden anniversary. The pain might have faded, and arriving at Parritt's Diner I would have been spared the agonizing sight of that hulking body in the maroon blazer leaning across two chili dogs towards Meredith Krantzsky, the girl of my dreams, whom I recognized despite the fact that she was sitting still and wearing a dress. Merle was regaling her with the news that Richard Petty's pit crew could change two tires and fill a gas tank in 12.5 seconds flat when I reached their table. He punched me chummily in the stomach, and after I caught my breath I grabbed the table edge to keep myself from stabbing forks into his cabbage-size hands.

"Merry Krantzsky, I want you to meet Blake Wintrip for about two seconds. Then forget him. He's married with six kids, impotent, queer, and he's got V.D. Say byebye, Blake." (Merle prided himself on his witty urbanity.)

"We've sort of met," she said, and looked up from her tuna

salad. "Wintrip? I've got a bone to pick with you. I know your grandmother, I spend a lot of time with her, and . . ."

"How?" My heart cramped with dread. She didn't *look* mad. But of course everyone had let poor Betsy Creedmoor run loose through life, too.

"I work at the Hospital. I'm a psychiatric social worker, and your grandmother shouldn't be in there."

"I know. But I don't think anybody else should be in there either. I'm a social work field coordinator. Nice to meet you."

Right then I could tell she'd decided there was a chance she eventually might like me.

"Merry here's a Yankee. She's been telling me about herself. Just moved down to Toomis from New Hampshire."

"Rhode Island."

"One of those little ones." Merle was holding both his chili dogs in one hand; worse, he was eating them that way as he talked. "I'm pretty sure I drove right through Rhode Island once. I wish I could remember the name of that nice place right off the highway where I ate supper. I bet you'd know it."

I found out (because Merle bragged about it) that he had simply muscled his way into her lunch booth uninvited. That evening in my old high school track shorts I was doing knee bends in front of Parritt's Diner. I'd called in sick; Merle answered the phone and I told him my V.D. was getting worse.

At last through the red and yellow leaves on the trees I saw Meredith Krantzsky jogging towards me. Saw *her*, and in a weaving line behind her, all whooping and sniffling, the eleven members of the Ladies Art League of Toomis—among them old Mrs. Etherege with a stop watch (high-stepping as an ibis), and my mother in Bermuda shorts, though she still looped the obligatory cardigan sweater over her shoulders. Crouching in the doorway, I pretended to relace my sneaker until this extraordinary procession trotted by. Later I learned from my mother that the ladies of the Art League "just loved Merry to death" and were all crazy about jogging, to which Merry had introduced them when they'd invited her to Newcomer's Day.

Reports (and there were plenty) that my mother was out every evening jogging through the streets of Toomis with a throng of elderly female marathoners hit my father like a karate chop. She was also serving broiled fish and raw vegetables for supper, and constantly talking about things like biomechanics. Dad told her succinctly, "You've gone nuts, Hattie."

"Then lucky my jogging coach is a mental health expert," replied my mother from the floor where she was doing sit-ups, her feet in their Adidas stuck under the settee.

"And I don't like the sound of that girl's name. Meredith Krantzsky. You know what kind of name that is? Krantzsky? A you-know-what, I bet. And she works in a nut house, doesn't she? Some kind of Left Wing nut, I bet."

I asked a question then. "If you don't like the nut house, why'd you put Grandma in there?"

"You're out of line, Mister." He talked as if he thought we were in a western movie.

"I think I'm going to ask Miss Krantzsky to marry me."

"Oh Blake! I love her to death." My mother looked me over. "I'm sure she'll tell you to eat less and get more exercise."

"Marry her and you're fired," my dad promised.

My curtain line I gave skipping backwards. "Hey, you better tell old Merle Longfielder she could be a you-know-what. Because he's after her, too."

Three weeks had now passed since my first sight of my fiancée, and not only were we not engaged, we had never sat down together. But we ran. November flared the trees the bright color of Merry's hair. Indian summer did its best for me, holding back the chill, keeping the evenings crisp and slow. Good jogging weather. I trained, for love, like a fiend. I went on my mother's diet. Whenever Merry wasn't running with the Art League, she and I jogged in the twilight. We exchanged life stories along the way. Her college really had bred all those radical subversives my father itched to pistol-whip. Her version of a Betsy Creedmoor had been a hippie flautist named Matthew who took a charter pilgrimage to Katmandu, where he was arrested for smuggling mescaline. She played chess.

We ran out towards the Hospital where we saw my grandmother and Mrs. Etherege trotting about the grounds as they discussed price hikes they planned to spring on their Appalachian gift galleries. The four of us crossed paths. I said to my grandmother, "What's your advice?"

"Marry this one," she told me.

Merry laughed. I raced to heaven.

That Saturday Merle Longfielder and I walked to Parritt's Diner together for lunch. Inside, he twisted my bicep with his horrible hand. "Now hey! Isn't that that girl from New Hampshire over there? What was her name? Merry? Been saving her for a rainy day. Watch this and learn something, boy."

"Forget it. I don't want you near that girl. Now or ever." I shoved him back. "I catch you around her, I'll shove your jaw up into that cavity where your brain's supposed to be."

Merle stared at me as if I had just stepped out of a UFO. He'd bullied me for more than twenty years. First he started to laugh—it was almost a giggle—then it changed to a puffing snort, and then he swung. I ducked under his basketball of a fist and socked him twice in the gut with a lifetime of injustice behind my punch. By the time he stood back up I was at the door in a prance. Just out of his reach I teased him up that long incline on Route 55. But Merle never even made it to the top.

Meredith Krantzsky and I were married in June. Grandma has the extra bedroom. When the baby comes, we'll move to someplace bigger.

Merle was always quoting Joe Namath: "When you win, nothing hurts." He was right. I feel great.

THE GHOST SOLDIERS

TIM O'BRIEN

Tim O'Brien received a National Book Award for his novel *Going After Cacciato*. A native of Minnesota, Mr. O'Brien is the author of two other novels, *Northern Lights* and *If I Die in a Combat Zone*. He is currently working on a novel entitled *The Nuclear Age*.

I was shot twice. The first time, out by Tri Binh, it knocked me against the pagoda wall, and I bounced and spun around and ended up on Teddy Thatcher's lap. Lucky thing, because Teddy was the medic. He tied on a compress and told me to take a nap, then he ran off toward the fighting. For a long time I lay there all alone, listening to the battle, thinking, *I've been shot, I've been shot*. Winged, grazed, creased: all those Gene Autry movies I'd seen as a kid. In fact, I even laughed. Except then I started to think I might bleed to death. It was the fear, mostly, but I felt awful wobbly, and then I had a sinking sensation, ears all plugged up, as if I'd gone deep under water. Thank God for Teddy Thatcher. Every so often, maybe four times altogether, he trotted back to check me out. Which took guts. It was a wild fight, lots of noise, guys running and laying down fire, regrouping, running again, no front or rear, real chaos, but Teddy took the risks. "Easy does it," he said. "Just a side wound—no problem unless you're pregnant. You pregnant, buddy?" He ripped off the compress, applied a fresh one, and told me to clamp it in place with my fingers. "Press hard," he said. "Don't worry about the baby; too late to save it." Teddy wiped the blood off his hands. "No more house calls, pal. Gotta run." Then he took off. It was almost dark before the fighting petered out and the chopper came to take me and two dead guys away. "Adios, amigo," Teddy said in his fake Mexican accent. "Happy trails to you." I was barely feeling up to it, but I said, "Oh, Cisco," and Teddy wrapped his arms around me and kissed my neck and said, "Oh, Pancho!" Then the bird took off. On the ride in to Chu Lai, I kept waiting for the pain to come. I squeezed my fists tight and bit down, but actually I couldn't feel much. A throb, that's all. Even in the hospital it wasn't bad.

When I got back to Delta Company twenty-six days later, in mid-March, Teddy Thatcher was dead, and a new medic named Jorgenson had replaced him. Jorgenson was no Teddy. Incompetent and wimpy and scared. So when I got shot the second time, in the butt, along the Song Tra Bong, it took the son of a bitch almost ten minutes to work up the courage to crawl over to me. By then I was gone with the pain. Later I found out I'd almost died of shock. Jorgenson didn't know about shock, or if he knew, the fear made him forget. To make it worse, the guy bungled the patch job, and a couple of weeks later my ass started to rot away. You could actually peel off chunks of meat with your fingernail.

It was borderline gangrene. I spent a month flat on my belly—couldn't play cards, couldn't sleep. I kept seeing Jorgenson's scared-green face. Those buggy eyes, the way his lips twitched, that silly excuse for a mustache. After the rot cleared up, once I could think straight, I devoted a lot of time to figuring ways to get back at him.

Getting shot should be an experience from which you can draw a little pride. I'm not talking macho crap; I'm not saying you should strut around with your Purple Hearts on display. All I mean is that you should be able to *talk* about it: the stiff thump of the bullet, the way it knocks the air out of you and makes you cough, the sound of the shot when it comes about ten decades later, the dizzy feeling, the disbelief, the smell of yourself, the stuff you think about and say and do right afterward, the way your eyes focus on a tiny pebble or a blade of grass and how you think, man, that's the last thing I'll ever see, *that* pebble, *that* blade of grass, which makes you want to cry. Pride isn't the right word; I don't know the right word. All I know is, you shouldn't feel embarrassed. Humiliation shouldn't be part of it.

Diaper rash, the nurses called it. They sprinkled me with talcum powder and patted my ass and said "Git-cha-goo, git-cha-goo." Male nurses, too. That was the worst part. It made me hate Jorgenson the way some guys hated Charlie—ear-cutting hate, the kind atrocities are made of.

I guess the higher-ups decided I'd been shot enough. In early May, when I was released from the Ninety-first Evac Hospital, they transferred me over to headquarters company—S-4, the battalion supply section. Compared with the boonies, of course, it was cushy duty. Regular hours, movies, floor shows, the blurry slow motion of the rear. Fairly safe, too. The battalion fire base was built into a big hill just off Highway One, surrounded on all sides by flat paddy land, and between us and the paddies there were plenty of bunkers and sandbags and rolls of razor-tipped barbed wire. Sure, you could still die there—once a month or so we'd get hit with some mortar fire—but what the hell, you could die in the bleachers at Fenway Park, bases loaded, Yaz coming to the plate. Safety is relative; it's never permanent.

I wasn't complaining. Naturally there were times when I halfway wanted to head back to the field; I missed the adventure, the friendships, even the danger. A hard thing to explain to somebody who hasn't felt it. Danger, it makes things vivid. When you're afraid, really afraid, you taste your own spit, you see things you never saw before, you pay attention. On the other hand, though, I wasn't crazy. I'd already taken two bullets; the odds were deadly. So I just settled in, took it easy, counted myself lucky. I figured my war was over. If it hadn't been for the constant ache in my butt, I guess things would've worked out fine.

But Jesus, it *hurt*. Torn-up muscle, nerves like live electric wires: it was pain.

Pain, you know?

At night, for example, I had to sleep on my belly. Doesn't sound so terrible until you consider that I'd been a back-sleeper all my life. It got to where I was almost an insomniac. I'd lie there all fidgety and tight, then after a while I'd get angry. I'd squirm around on my cot, cussing, half nuts with hurt, then I'd start remembering stuff. Jorgenson. I'd think, Jesus Christ, I almost died. Shock—how could the bastard forget to treat for shock? Diaper rash, butt rot. I'd remember how long it took him to get to me, how his fingers were all jerky and nervous, the way his lips twitched under that ridiculous mustache.

The nights were miserable.

Sometimes I'd roam around the base. I'd head down to the wire and stare out at the darkness, out where the war was, all those ghosts, and I'd count ways to make Jorgenson suffer.

One thing for sure. You forget how much you use your butt until you can't use it anymore.

In July, Delta Company came in for stand-down. I was there on the helipad to meet the choppers. Curtis and Lemon and Azar slapped hands with me—jokes, dirty names, disguised affection—then I piled their gear in my jeep and drove them down to the Delta hootches. We partied until chow time. Afterward, we kept on partying. It was one of the rituals. Even if you weren't in the mood, you did it on principle.

By midnight it was story time.

"Morty Becker wasted his luck," said Lemon. "No lie," said Azar.

I smiled and waited. There was a tempo to how stories got told. Lemon peeled open a finger blister and sucked on it and wagged his head sadly.

"Go on," Azar said. "Tell it."

"Becker used up his luck. Pissed it away."

"On *nothin'*," Azar said.

Lemon nodded, started to speak, then stopped and got up and moved to the cooler and shoved his hands deep into the ice. He was naked except for his socks and his dog tags. In a way, I envied him—all of them. Those deep bush tans, the jungle sores and blisters, the stories, the in-it-togetherness. I felt close to them, yes, but I also felt separate.

Bending forward, Lemon scooped ice up against his chest, pressing it there for a moment, eyes closed; then he fished out a beer and snapped it open.

"It was out by My Khe," he said. "Remember My Khe? Bad-ass country, right? A blister of a day, hot-hot, and we're just sort of groovin' it, lyin' around, nobody bustin' ass or anything. I mean, listen, it's *hot.* We're poppin' salt tabs just to stay conscious. Finally somebody says, 'Hey, where's Becker?' The captain does a head count, and guess what? No Becker."

"Gone," Azar said. "Vanished."

"Ghosts."

"*Poof*, no fuckin' Becker."

"We send out two patrols—no dice. Not a trace." Lemon poured beer on his open blister, slowly licked the foam off. "By then it's getting dark. Captain's about ready to have a fit—you know how he gets, right?—and then, guess what? Take a guess."

"Becker shows," I said.

"You got it, man. Becker shows. We've almost chalked him up as MIA, and then, bingo, he shows."

"Soaking wet," Azar said.

"Hey—"

"Okay, it's your story, but *tell* it."

Lemon frowned. "Soaking wet," he said.

"Ha!"

"Turns out he went for a swim. You believe that? All by himself, the moron just takes off, hikes a couple klicks, finds himself a river, strips, hops in, no security, no *nothin'*. Dig it? He goes swimming."

Azar giggled. "A hot day."

"Not that hot," murmured Curtis Young. "Not that fuckin' hot."

"Hot, though."

"Get the picture?" Lemon said. "I mean, this is My Khe we're talking about. Doomsville, and the guy goes for a *swim.*"

"Yeah," I said. "Crazy."

I looked across the hootch. Thirty or forty guys were there, some drinking, some passed out, but I couldn't find Morty Becker among them.

Lemon grinned. He reached out and put his hand on my knee and squeezed.

"That's the kicker, man. No more Becker."

"No?"

"The kicker's this," Lemon said, "Morty Becker's luck gets all used up. See? On a lousy swim."

"And that's the truth. That's the truth," said Azar.

Lemon's hand still rested on my knee, very gently. The fingers were quivering a little.

"What happened?"

"Ah, shit."

"Go on, tell."

"Fatality," Lemon said. "Couple days later, maybe a week, Becker gets real dizzy. Pukes a lot, temperature zooms way up. Out of sight, you know? Jorgenson says he must've swallowed bad water on that swim. Swallowed a virus or something."

"Jorgenson," I said. "Where is my good buddy Jorgenson?"

"Hey, look—"

"Just tell me where to find him."

Lemon made a quick clicking sound with his tongue. "You want to *hear* this? Yes or no?"

"Sure, but where's—"

"Listen up. Becker gets sick, right? Sick, sick, sick. Never seen nobody so bad off, *never*. Sicko! Arms jerkin' all over hell, can't walk, can't talk, can't fart, can't nothin'. Like he's paralyzed. Can't move. Polio, maybe."

Curtis Young shook his head. "Not polio. You got it wrong."

"Maybe polio."

"No way," Curtis said. "Not polio."

"*Maybe*," Lemon said. "I'm just saying what Jorgenson says. Maybe fuckin' polio. Or that elephant disease. Elephantiasshole or whatever."

"But not polio."

Azar smiled and snapped his fingers. "Either way," he said, "it goes to show. Don't throw away luck on little stuff. Save it up."

"That's the lesson, all right."

"Becker was due."

"There it is. Overdue. Don't fritter away your luck."

"Fuckin' polio."

Lemon closed his eyes.

We sat quietly. No need to talk, because we were thinking about the same things: about Mort Becker, the way luck worked and didn't work, how it was impossible to gauge the odds. Maybe the disease was lucky. Who knows? Maybe it saved Morty from getting shot.

"Where's Jorgenson?" I said.

"Ease off on that," Lemon whispered. "Let it go."

"Sure. No sweat, no sweat. But where's the son of a bitch hiding?"

Another thing: three times a day, no matter what, I had to stop whatever I was doing, go find a private place, drop my pants, bend over, and apply this antibacterial ointment to my ass. No choice—I had to do it. And the worst part was how the ointment left yellow stains on the seat of my trousers, big greasy splotches. Herbie's hemorrhoids, that was one of the jokes. There were plenty of other jokes too—plenty.

During the first full day of Delta's stand-down, I didn't run into Jorgenson once. Not at chow, not at the flicks, not during our long booze sessions in the hootch.

I didn't hunt him down, though. I just waited.

"Forget it," Lemon said. "Granted, the man messed up bad, real bad, but you got to take into account how green he was. Just a tenderfoot. Brand new. Remember?"

"I forget. Remind me."

"You survived."

I showed Lemon the yellow stain on my britches. "I'm in terrific shape. Real funny, right?"

"Not exactly," Lemon said.

But he was laughing. He started snapping a towel at my backside. I laughed—I couldn't help it—but I didn't see the big joke.

Later, after some dope, Lemon said: "The thing is, Jorgenson's doing all right. Better and better. People change, they adapt. I mean, okay, he's not a Teddy Thatcher, he won't win medals or anything, but the poor dude hangs in there, he knows his shit. Kept Becker alive."

"My sore ass."

Lemon nodded. He shrugged, leaned back, popped the hot roach into his mouth, chewed for a long time. "You've lost touch, man. Jorgenson . . . he's *with* us now."

"I'm not."

"No," he said. "I guess you're not."

"Good old loyalty."

"War."

"Friends in need, friends get peed on."

Lemon shook his head. "We're friends, Herbie. You and me. But look, you're not *out* there anymore, and Jorgenson is. If you'd just seen him the past couple of weeks—the way he handled Becker, then when Pinko hit the mine—I mean, the kid did some good work. Ask anybody. So . . . I don't know. If it was me, Herbie, I'd say screw it. Leave it alone."

"I won't hurt him."

"Right."

"I won't. Show him some ghosts, that's all."

In the morning I spotted Jorgenson. I was up on the helipad, loading the resupply choppers, and then, when the last bird took off, while I was putting on my shirt, I looked up, half-squinting, and there he was. In a way, it was a shock. His size, I mean. Even smaller than I remembered—a little squirrel of a guy, five and a half feet tall, skinny and mousy and sad.

He was leaning against my jeep, waiting for me.

"Herb," he said, "can we talk?"

At first I just looked at his boots.

Those boots: I remembered them from when I got shot. Out along the Song Tra Bong, a bullet in my ass, all that pain, and the funny thing was that what I remembered, now, were those new boots—no scuffs; smooth, unblemished leather. One of those last details, Jorgenson's boots.

"Herb?"

I looked at his eyes—a long, straight-on stare—and he blinked and made a stabbing motion at his nose and backed off a step. Oddly, I felt some pity for him. A bona fide card-carrying twit. The tiniest arms and wrists I'd ever seen—a sparrow's nervous system. He made me think of those sorry kids back in junior high who used to spend their time collecting stamps and butterflies, always off by themselves, no friends, no hope.

He took another half-step backward and said, very softly, "Look, I just wanted . . . I'm sorry, Herb."

I didn't move or look away or anything.

"Herb?"

"Talk, talk, talk."

"What can I say? It was—"

"Excuses?"

Jorgenson's tongue flicked out, then slipped away. He shook his head. "No, it was a bungle, and I don't . . . I was *scared.* All the noise and everything, the shooting, I'd never seen that before. I couldn't make myself move. After you got hit, I kept telling myself to move, move, but I couldn't *do* it. Like I was full of Novocain or something. You ever feel like that? Like you can't even move?"

"Anyway," I said.

"And then I heard how you . . . the shock, the gangrene. Man, I felt like . . . couldn't sleep, couldn't eat. Nightmares, you know? Kept seeing you lying out there, heard you screaming, and . . . it was like my legs were filled up with cement. I *couldn't.*"

His lip trembled, and he made a weird moaning sound—not quite a moan, feathery and high—and for a second I was afraid he might start crying. That would've ended it. I was a sucker for tears. I would've patted his shoulder, told him to forget it. Thank God he tried to shake my hand. It gave me an excuse to spit.

"Kiss it," I said.

"Herb, I can't go back and do it over."

"Lick it, kiss it."

But Jorgenson just smiled. Very tentatively, like an invalid, he kept pushing his hand out at me. He looked so mournful and puppy-doggish, so damned hurt, that I made myself spit again. I didn't feel like spitting—my heart wasn't in it—but somehow I managed, and Jorgenson glanced away for a second, still smiling a weary little smile, resigned-looking, as if to show how generous he was, how bighearted and noble.

It almost made me feel guilty.

I got into the jeep, hit the ignition, left him standing there.

Guilty, for Chrissake. Why should it end up with *me* feeling the guilt? I hated him for making me stop hating him.

Thing is, it had been a vow. *I'll get him, I'll get him*—it was down inside me like a stone. Except now I couldn't generate the passion. Couldn't feel anger. I still had to get back at him, but now it was a need, not a want. An obligation. To rev up some intensity, I started drinking a little—more than a little, a lot. I remembered the river, getting shot, the pain, how I kept calling out for a medic, waiting and waiting and waiting, passing out once, waking up, screaming, how the scream seemed to make new pain, the awful stink of myself, the sweating and shit and fear, Jorgenson's clumsy fingers when he finally got around to working on me. I remembered it all, every detail. *Shock*, I thought. *I'm dying of shock*. I tried to tell him that, but my tongue didn't connect with my brain. All I could do was go, "Ough! Ough!" I wanted to say, "You *jerk!* I'm *dying!* Treat for shock, treat for shock!" I remembered all that, and the hospital, and those giggling nurses. I even remembered the rage. Except I couldn't feel it anymore. Just a word—*rage*—spelled out in my head. No *feeling*. In the end, all I had were the facts. Number one: the guy had almost killed me. Number two: there had to be consequences. Only thing was, I wished I could've gotten some pleasure out of them.

I asked Lemon to give me a hand.

"No pain," I said. "Basic psy-ops, that's all. We'll just scare him. Mess with his head a little."

"Negative," Lemon said.

"Just show him some ghosts."

"Sick, man."

"Not all *that* sick." I stuck a finger in Lemon's face. "Sick is getting shot. Try it sometime, you'll see what genuine sick is."

"No," he said.

"Comrade-in-arms. Such crap."

"I guess."

Stiffly, like a stranger, Lemon looked at me for a long time. Then he moved across the hootch and lay down with a comic book and pretended to read. His lips were moving, but that didn't fool me a bit.

I had to get Azar in on it.

Azar didn't have Lemon's intelligence, but he had a better sense of justice.

"Tonight?" he said.

"Just don't get carried away."

"Me?"

Azar grinned and snapped his fingers. It was a tic. Snap, snap—whenever things got tight, whenever there was a prospect of action.

"Understand?"

"Roger-dodger," Azar said. "Only a game, right?"

We called the enemy "ghosts." "Bad night," we'd murmur. "Ghosts are out." To get spooked, in the lingo, meant not only to get scared but to get killed. "Don't get spooked," we'd say. "Stay cool, stay alive." The countryside was spooky: snipers, tunnels, ancestor worship, ancient papa-sans, incense. The land was haunted. We were fighting forces that didn't obey the laws of twentieth-century science. Deep in the night, on guard, it seemed that all of Nam was shimmering and swaying—odd shapes swirling in the dark; phantoms; apparitions; spirits in the abandoned pagodas; boogeymen in sandals. When a guy named Olson was killed, in February, everybody started saying, "The Holy Ghost took him." And when Ron Ingo hit the booby trap, in April, somebody said he'd been made into a deviled egg—no arms, no legs, just a poor deviled egg.

It was ghost country, and Charlie was the main ghost. The way he came out at night. How you never really saw him, just thought you did. Almost magical—appearing, disappearing. He could levitate. He could pass through barbed wire. He was invisible, blending with the land, changing shape. He could fly. He could melt away like ice. He could creep up on you without sound or footsteps. He was scary.

In the daylight, maybe, you didn't believe in all this stuff. You laughed, you made jokes. But at night you turned into a believer: no skeptics in foxholes.

Azar was wound up tight. All afternoon, while we made preparations, he kept chanting, "Halloween, Halloween." That, plus the finger snapping, almost made me cancel the whole operation. I went hot and cold. Lemon wouldn't speak to me, which tended to cool it off, but then I'd start remembering things. The result was a kind of tepid numbness. No ice, no heat. I went through the motions like a sleepwalker—rigidly, by the numbers, no real emotion, no heart. I rigged up my special effects, checked out the battle terrain, measured distances, gathered the ordnance and gear we'd need. I was professional enough about it, I didn't miss a thing, but somehow it felt as if I were gearing up to fight somebody else's war. I didn't have that patriotic zeal.

Who knows? If there'd been a dignified way out, I might've taken it.

During evening chow, in fact, I kept staring across the mess hall at Jorgenson, and when he finally looked up at me, a puzzled frown on his face, I came very close to smiling. Very, very close. Maybe I was fishing for something. A nod, a bow, one last apology—anything. But Jorgenson only gazed back at me. In a strange way, too. As if he didn't *need* to apologize again. Just a straight, unafraid gaze. No humility at all.

To top it off, my ex-buddy Lemon was sitting with him, and they were having this chummy-chummy conversation, all smiles and sweetness.

That's probably what cinched it.

I went back to my hootch, showered, shaved, threw my helmet against the wall, lay down awhile, fidgeted, got up, prowled around, applied some fresh ointment, then headed off to find Azar.

Just before dusk, Delta Company stood for roll call. Afterward the men separated into two groups. Some went off to drink or sleep or catch a movie; the others trooped down to the base perimeter, where, for the next eleven hours, they would pull night guard duty. It was SOP—one night on, one night off.

This was Jorgenson's night on.

I knew that in advance, of course. And I knew his bunker assignment: number six, a pile of sandbags at the southwest corner of the perimeter. That morning I'd scouted every inch of his position; I knew the blind spots, the ripples of land, the places where he'd take cover in case of trouble. I was ready. To guard against freak screw-ups, though, Azar and I tailed him down to the wire. We watched him lay out his bedroll, connect the Claymores to their firing devices, test the radio, light up a cigarette, yawn, then sit back with his rifle cradled to his chest like a teddy bear.

"A pigeon," Azar whispered. "Roast pigeon on a spit. I smell it cookin'."

"Remember, though. This isn't for real."

Azar shrugged. He touched me on the shoulder, not roughly but not gently either. "What's real?" he said. "Eight months in Fantasyland, it tends to blur the line. Honest to God, I sometimes can't remember what real *is*."

Psychology—that was one thing I knew. I never went to college, and I wasn't exactly a whiz in high school either, but all my life I've paid attention to how things operate inside the skull. Example: You don't try to scare people in broad daylight. You wait. Why? Because the darkness squeezes you inside yourself, you get cut off from the outside world, the imagination takes over. That's basic psychology. I'd pulled enough night guard to know how the fear factor gets multiplied as you sit there hour after hour, nobody to talk to, nothing to do but stare blank-eyed into the Big Black Hole. The hours pile up. You drift; your brain starts to roam. You think about dark closets, madmen, murderers hiding under the bed, all those childhood fears. Fairy tales with gremlins and trolls and one-eyed giants. You try to block it all out but you can't. You see ghosts. You blink and laugh and shake your head. Bullshit, you say. But then you remember the guys who died: Teddy, Olson, Ingo, maybe Becker, a dozen others whose faces you can't see anymore. Pretty soon you begin to think about the stories you've heard about Charlie's magic. The time some guys cornered two VC in a dead-end tunnel, no way out, but how, when the tunnel was fragged and searched, nothing was found but dead rats. A hundred stories. A whole bookful: ghosts swinging from the trees, ghosts wiping out a whole Marine platoon in twenty seconds flat, ghosts rising from the dead, ghosts behind you and in front of you and inside you. Your ears get ticklish. Tiny sounds get heightened and distorted, crickets become monsters, the hum of the night takes on a weird electronic tingle. You try not to breathe. You coil and tighten up and listen. Your knuckles ache, and your pulse ticks like an alarm clock. What's *that?* You jerk up. Nothing, you say, nothing. Unless. . . . You check to be sure your weapon is loaded. Put it on full automatic. Count your grenades, make sure the pins are bent for quick throwing. Crouch lower. Listen, listen. And then, after enough time passes, things start to get bad.

"Come on, man," Azar said. "Let's *do* it." But I told him to be patient. "Waiting, that's half the trick," I said. "Give him time, let him simmer." So we went to the movies. *Barbarella* again, the sixth straight night. But it kept Azar happy—he was crazy about Jane Fonda. "Sweet Janie," he kept saying, over and over. "Sweet Janie boosts a man's morale." Then, with his hand, he showed me which part of his morale got boosted. An old joke. Everything was old. The movie, the heat, the booze, the war. I fell asleep during the second reel—a hot, angry sleep—and forty minutes later I woke up to a sore ass and a foul temper.

It wasn't yet midnight.

We hiked over to the EM club and worked our way through a six-pack. Lemon was there, at another table, but he pretended not to see me.

Around closing time, I made a fist and showed it to Azar. He smiled like a little boy. "Goody," he said. We picked up the gear, smeared charcoal on our faces, then moved down to the wire.

"Let's hurt him," Azar whispered. "Pain time for ol' Jorgy."

"No, man, listen to me—"

But Azar lifted his thumb and grinned and peeled away from me and began circling behind Bunker Six. For a second I couldn't move. Not fear, exactly; I don't know what it was. My boots felt heavy.

In a way, it was purely mechanical. I didn't think, I just shouldered the gear and crossed quietly over to a heap of boulders that overlooked Jorgenson's bunker.

I was directly behind him. Thirty-two meters away, exactly. My measurements were precise.

Even in the heavy darkness, no moon yet, I could make out Jorgenson's silhouette: a helmet, his shoulders, the rifle barrel. His back was to me. That was the heart of the psychology: he'd be looking out at the wire, the paddies, where the danger was; he'd figure his back was safe; only the chest and belly were vulnerable.

Quiet, quiet.

I knelt down, took out the flares, lined them up in front of me, unscrewed the caps, then checked my wristwatch. Still five minutes to go. Edging over to my left, I groped for the ropes, found them wedged in the crotch of two boulders. I separated them and tested the tension and checked the time again. One minute.

My head was light. Fluttery and taut at the same time. It was the feeling I remembered from the boonies, on ambush or marching at night through ghost country. Peril and doubt and awe, all those things and a million more. You wonder if you're dreaming. Unreal, unreal. As if molting, you seem to slip outside yourself. It's like you're in a movie. There's a camera on you, so you begin acting, following the script: "Oh, Cisco!" You think of all the films you've seen, Audie Murphy and Gary Cooper and Van Johnson and Roy Rogers, all of them, and certain lines of dialogue come back to you—"I been plugged!"—and then, when you get shot, you can't help falling back on them. "Jesus, Jesus," you say, half to yourself, half to the camera. "I been fuckin' *plugged!*" You expect it of yourself. On ambush, poised in the dark, you fight to control yourself. Not too much fidgeting; it wouldn't look good. You try to grin. Eyes open, be alert—old lines, old movies. It all swirls together, clichés mixing with your own emotions, and in the end you can't distinguish. . . .

It was time. I fingered one of the ropes, took a breath, then gave it a sharp jerk.

Instantly there was a clatter outside the wire.

I expected the noise, I was even tensed for it, but still my heart took a funny little hop. I winced and ducked down.

"Now," I murmured. "Now it starts." Eight ropes altogether. I had four, Azar had four. Each rope was hooked up to a homemade noisemaker out in front of Jorgenson's bunker—eight tin cans filled with rifle cartridges. Simple devices, but they worked.

I waited a moment, and then, very gently, I gave all four of my ropes a little tug. Delicate—nothing loud. If you weren't listening, listening hard, you might've missed it. But Jorgenson was listening. Immediately, at the first low rattle, his silhouette seemed to freeze. Then he ducked down and blended in with the dark.

There—another rattle. Azar this time.

We kept at it for ten minutes. Noise, silence, noise, silence. Stagger the rhythm. Start slowly, gradually build the tension.

Crouched in my pile of boulders, squinting down at Jorgenson's position, I felt a swell of immense power. It was the feeling Charlie must have: full control, mastery of the night. Like a magician, a puppeteer. Yank on the ropes, watch the silly wooden puppet jump and twitch. It made me want to giggle. One by one, in sequence, I pulled on each of the ropes, and the sound came bouncing back at me with an eerie, indefinite formlessness: a rattlesnake, maybe, or the creak of a closet door or footsteps in the attic—whatever you made of it.

"There now," I whispered, or thought. "There, there."

Jorgenson wasn't moving. Not yet. He'd be coiled up in his circle of sandbags, fists tight, blinking, listening.

Again I tugged on my ropes.

I smiled. Eyes closed, I could almost *see* what was happening down there.

Bang. Jorgenson would jerk up. Rub his eyes, bend forward. Eardrums fluttering like wings, spine stiff, muscles hard, brains like Jell-O. I could *see* it. Right now, at this instant, he'd glance up at the sky, hoping for a moon, a few stars. But no moon, no stars. He'd start talking to himself: "Relax, relax." Desperately he'd try to bring the night into focus, but the effort would only cause distortions: objects would seem to pick themselves up and twist and wiggle; trees would creep forward like an army on midnight maneuvers; the earth itself would begin to sway. Fun house country. Trick mirrors and trapdoors and pop-up monsters. Lord, I could *see* it! It was as if I were down there *with* him, *beside* him. "Easy," he was muttering, "easy, easy, easy," but it didn't get easier. His ears were stiff, his eyeballs were dried up and hard, like stones, and the ghosts were coming out.

"Creepy," Azar cackled. "Wet pants, goose bumps. We *got* him. Ghost town!" He held a beer out to me, but I shook my head.

We sat in the dim quiet of my hootch, boots off, smoking, listening to Mary Hopkin.

"So what next?"

"Wait," I said. "More of the same."

"Well, sure, but—"

"Shut up and *listen.*"

That high elegant voice. That melody. "Those were the days, my friend. . . ." Someday, when the war was over, I'd go to London and ask Mary Hopkin to marry me. "We'd sing and dance forever and a day. . . ." Nostalgic and mawkish, but so what? That's what Nam does to you. Turns you sentimental, makes you want to marry girls like Mary Hopkin. You learn, finally, that you'll die. You see the corpses, sometimes you even kick them, feel the boot against meat, and you always think, *Me, me.* "We'd fight and never lose, those were the days, oh yes. . . ." That's what war does to you.

Azar switched off the tape.

"Shit, man," he said. "Don't you got some *music?*"

And now, finally, the moon was out. It was a white moon, mobile, clouded, nearly full. We slipped back to our positions and went to work again with the ropes. Louder, now, more insistently. The moon added resonance. Starlight shimmied in the barbed wire; reflections, layerings of shadow. Slowly, slowly we dragged the tin cans closer to Jorgenson's bunker, and this, plus the moon, gave a sense of creeping peril, the slow tightening of a noose.

At 0300 hours, the very deepest part of the night, Azar set off the first trip flare.

There was a light popping sound out in front of Bunker Six. Then a sizzle. And then the night seemed to snap itself in half. The flare burned ten paces from the bunker: like the Fourth of July, white-hot magnesium, a thousand sparklers exploding in a single cluster.

As the flare died, I fired three more.

It was instant daylight. For a moment I was paralyzed—blinded, struck dumb.

Then Jorgenson moved. There was a short, squeaky cry—not even a cry, really, just a sound of terror—and then a blurred motion as he jumped up and ran a few paces and rolled and lay still. His silhouette was framed like a cardboard cutout against the burning flares.

He was weeping.

A soft, musical sound. Like a long hollow sigh. As the flares burned themselves out, the weeping became raspy and painful. I sympathized. I really did. In fact, I almost trotted over to console him: "I know, I know. Scary business. You just want to cry and cry and cry."

In the dark outside my hootch, even though I bent toward him, nose to nose, all I could see were Azar's white eyes.

"Enough," I told him.

"Oh, sure."

"Seriously."

"Serious?" he said. "That's too serious for me; I'm a fun lover. A party boy on Halloween."

When Azar smiled I saw the quick glitter of teeth, but then the smile went away, and I knew it was hopeless. I tried, though. I told him the score was even—no need to rub it in. I was firm. I explained, very bluntly, that it was my game, beginning to end, and now I wanted to end it. I even got belligerent.

Azar just peered at me, almost dumbly.

"Poor Herbie," he said.

Nothing dramatic. The rest was inflection and those electric white-white eyes.

An hour before dawn we moved up for the last phase. Azar was in command now. I tagged after him, thinking maybe I could keep a lid on.

"Don't take this personal," Azar whispered. "You know? It's just that I like to finish things."

I didn't look at him; I looked at my fingernails, at the moon.

When we got down near the wire, Azar gently put his hand on my shoulder, guiding me over toward the boulder pile. He knelt down and inspected the ropes and flares, nodded, peered out at Jorgenson's bunker, nodded again, removed his helmet and sat on it.

He was smiling again.

"Herbie?" he whispered.

I ignored him. My lips had a waxy, cold feel, like polished rock. I kept running my tongue over them. I told myself to stop it and I did, but then a second later I was doing it again.

"You know something?" Azar said, almost to himself. "Sometimes I feel like a little kid again. Playing war, you know? I get into it. I mean, wow, I *love* this shit."

"Look, why don't we—"

"Shhhh."

Smiling, Azar put a finger to his lips, partly as a warning, partly as a nifty gesture.

We waited another twenty minutes. It was cold now, and damp. My bones ached. I had a weird feeling of brittleness, as if somebody could reach out and grab me and crush me like a Christmas tree ornament. It was the same feeling out along the Song Tra Bong, when I got shot: I tried to grin wryly, like Bogie or Gable, and I thought about all the zingers Teddy Thatcher and I would use—except now Teddy was dead. Except when I called out for a medic, loud, nobody came. I started whimpering. The blood was warm, like dishwater, and I could feel my pants filling up with it. God, I thought, all this blood; I'll be *hollow*. Then the brittle feeling came over me. I passed out, woke up, screamed, tried to crawl but couldn't. I felt alone. All around me there was rifle fire, voices yelling, and yet for a moment I thought I'd gone deaf: the sounds were in my head, they weren't real. I smelled myself. The bullet had smashed through the colon, and the stink of my own shit made me afraid. I was crying. Leaking to death, I thought—blood and crap leaking out—and I couldn't quit crying. When Jorgenson got to me, all I could do was go "Ough! Ough!" I tightened up and pressed and grunted, trying to stop the leak, but that only made it worse, and Jorgenson punched me and told me to cut it out, ease off. *Shock*, I thought. I tried to tell him that: "Shock, man! Treat for shock!" I was lucid, things were clear, but my tongue wouldn't make the right words. And I was squirming. Jorgenson had to put his knee on my chest, turn me over, and when he did that, when he ripped my pants open, I shouted something and tried to wiggle away. I was hollowed out and cold. It was the *smell* that scared me. He was pressing down on my back—sitting on me, maybe, holding me down—and I kept trying to buck him off, rocking and moaning, even when he stuck me with morphine, even when he used his shirt to wipe my ass, even when he plugged the hole. Shock, I kept thinking. And then, like magic, things suddenly clicked into slow motion. The morphine, maybe: I focused on those brand-new black boots of his, then on a pebble, then on a single wisp of dried grass—the last things I'd ever see. I couldn't look away, I didn't dare, and I couldn't stop crying.

Even now, in the dark, I felt the sting in my eyes.

Azar said, "Herbie."

"Sure, man, I'm solid."

Down below, the bunker was silent. Nothing moved. The place looked almost abandoned, but I knew Jorgenson was there, wide awake, and I knew he was waiting.

Azar went to work on the ropes.

It began gently, like a breeze: a soft, lush, sighing sound. The ghosts were out. I was blinking, shivering, hugging myself. You can *die* of fright; it's possible, it can happen. I'd heard stories about it, about guys so afraid of dying that they died. You freeze up, your muscles snap, the heart starts fluttering, the brain floats away. It can *happen*.

"Enough," I whispered. "Stop it."

Azar looked at me and winked. Then he yanked sharply on all four ropes, and the sound made me squeal and jerk up.

"Please," I said. "Call it quits, right now. Please, man."

Azar wasn't listening. His white eyes glowed as he shot off the first flare. "Please," I murmured, but then I watched the flare arc up over Jorgenson's bunker, very slowly, pinwheeling, exploding almost without noise, just a sudden red flash.

There was a short, anguished whimper in the dark. At first I thought it was Jorgenson, or maybe a bird, but then I knew it was my own voice. I bit down and folded my hands and squeezed.

Twice more, rapidly, Azar fired off red flares, and then he turned and looked at me and lifted his eyebrows.

"Herbie," he said softly, "you're a sad case. Sad, sad."

"Look, can't we—"

"Sad."

I was frightened—of him, of us—and though I wanted to do something, wanted to stop him, I crouched back and watched him pick up the tear-gas grenade, pull the pin, stand up, smile, pause, and throw. For a moment the night seemed to stop as if bewitched; then the gas puffed up in a smoky cloud that partly obscured the bunker. I was moaning. Even from thirty meters away, upwind. I could smell the gas: not really *smell* it, though. I could *feel* it, like breathing razor blades. CS gas, the worst. Chickenshit gas, we called it, because that was what it turned you into—a mindless, squawking chickenshit.

"Jesus, please," I moaned, but Azar lobbed over another one, waited for the hiss, then scrambled over to the rope we hadn't used yet. "*Please,*" I said. Azar grabbed the rope with both hands and pulled.

It was my idea. That morning I'd rigged it up: a sandbag painted white, a pulley system, a rope.

Show him a ghost.

Azar pulled, and out in front of Bunker Six, as if rising up from a grave, the white sandbag lifted itself up and hovered in the misty swirl of gas.

Jorgenson began firing. Just one round at first—a single red tracer that thumped into the sandbag and burned.

"Ooooooh!" Azar murmured. "Star light, star bright. . . ."

Quickly, talking to himself, Azar hurled the last gas grenade, shot up another flare, then snatched the rope and made the white sandbag dance.

Jorgenson did not go nuts. Quietly, almost with dignity, he stood up and took aim and fired at the sandbag. I could see his profile against the red flares. His face seemed oddly relaxed. No twitching, no screams. With a strange, calm delibcration, he gazed out at the sandbag for several seconds, as if deciding something, and then he shook his head and smiled. Very slowly, he began marching out toward the wire. He did not crouch or run or crawl. He walked. He moved with a kind of graceful ease—resolutely, bravely, straight at the sandbag—firing with each step, stopping once to reload, then resuming his stately advance.

"Guts," Azar said.

Azar yanked on the rope and the sandbag bobbed and shimmied, but Jorgenson kept moving forward. When he reached the sandbag he stopped and turned, then he shouted my name, then he placed his rifle muzzle directly against the bag.

"Herbie!" he hollered, and he fired. The sandbag seemed to explode.

Azar dropped the rope.

"Show's over," he said. He looked down at me with pity. "Sad, sad, sad."

I was weeping. Distantly, as if from another continent, I heard Jorgenson pumping rounds into the sandbag.

"Disgusting," Azar said. "Herbie, Herbie. Saddest fucking case I ever seen."

Azar smiled. He looked out at Jorgenson, then at me. Those eyes—falcon eyes, ghost eyes. He moved toward me as if to help me up, but then, almost as an afterthought, he kicked me. My kneecap seemed to snap.

"Sad," he murmured, then he turned and headed off to bed.

"No big deal," I told Jorgenson. "Leave it alone. I'll live."

But he hooked my arm over his shoulder and helped me down to the bunker. My knee was hurting bad, but I didn't say anything. We sat facing each other.

It was almost full dawn now, a hazy silver dawn, and you could tell by the color and smells that rain wasn't far off.

For a while we didn't speak.

"So," he finally said.

"Right."

We shook hands, but neither of us put much emotion in it, and we didn't look at each other's eyes.

Jorgenson pointed out at the shot-up sandbag.

"That was a nice touch," he said. "No kidding, it had me . . . a nice touch. You've got a real sense of drama, Herbie. Someday you should go into the movies or something."

"I've thought about that."

"Another Hitchcock."

I nodded.

"*The Birds*. You ever see it?"

"Scary shit, man."

We sat for a while longer, then I started to get up, but my knee wasn't working right. Jorgenson had to give me a hand.

"Even?" he asked.

"Pretty much."

We touched—not a hug or anything, but something like that—then Jorgenson picked up his helmet, brushed it off, touched his funny little mustache, and looked out at the sandbag. His face was filthy. There were still tear splotches on his cheeks.

Up at the medic's hootch, he cleaned and bandaged my knee, then we went to chow. We didn't have much to say. Chitchat, some jokes. Afterward, in an awkward moment, I said, "Let's kill Azar."

Jorgenson smiled. "Scare him to death, right?"

"Right," I said.

"What a movie!"

I shrugged. "Sure. Or just kill him."

THE MAN WHOM WOMEN ADORED

JOYCE CAROL OATES

Joyce Carol Oates's most recent novel is *Angel of Light* (Dutton). Her *Invisible Woman: New and Selected Poems* (Ontario Review Press) will be published in 1982. She is currently teaching at Princeton University.

The rumor was that he had died—had died of something sudden and catastrophic, like a coronary thrombosis or a stroke—or had it been a beating, in a disreputable part of the city?—but clearly the rumor was false: for there William appeared, unsteady on his feet, in the slanted acrid sunshine of early October, crossing Broadway at 14th Street. He might have been drunk. He was certainly unwell. With that elegant and slightly self-mocking gesture of his hand I remembered so distinctly he waved back traffic. The driver of a delivery van angrily sounded his horn, the driver of a low-slung rusted taxi edged forward, his fender brushing against William's thigh. I stared—I wanted to cry out a warning—for certainly he *could* be injured—but in the next moment William had maneuvered himself out of danger.

Was this derelict William? He had aged a great deal and his hair had at last gone white. But it was a coarse, sallow white, unclean. His face too was soiled, smudged: a mass of wrinkles, like a crushed glove: but the lips, and even the slightly swollen nose, still had that peculiar sculpted beauty. He wore a shapeless flopping overcoat that was clearly not an overcoat from his former life—he had probably bought it at one of the venders' stalls on

14th Street—and he walked with that dream-like precision of the drunken or the very old, his eyes fastened to the pavement at his feet, as if it were a narrow strip above an abyss, dangerous to navigate. His lips twitched, he must have been talking to himself: arguing, cajoling, explaining. I wanted to call out his name but I said nothing. I backed away. Turned away. I avoided him by ducking around a parked car and crossing the street through traffic.

I thought he called my name, I seem to have heard my name, but I didn't look back.

Do you know, I said, once, not at all bitterly (for I watched myself: and I was rarely bitter), you are a man whom women adore?

William laughed, surprised and pleased. Of course he must have *known* he was a man women adored; but he had never heard the thought so succinctly expressed. He looked at me as if, for the first time, I had to be taken seriously.

That was long ago, of course. Many years. Both William and I have changed a great deal since then.

When I first heard the rumor of his death I had a vision of a gravesite around which numerous women in black stood in postures of mourning, not joined by their common loss but further isolated by it. And degraded too: for there is something degrading in such abject surrender.

I was not one of the mourners. I never mourn anyone I outlive—that is, anyone whose attraction for me I outlive.

In the beginning, William once told me, frankly and amiably enough, it was perfectly natural that everyone adored him. He was the youngest of six children; he had almost died of a throat infection as an infant. His family was genteel and all the soft luxurious emotions—love, tenderness, sentiment—were highly prized by them, the women especially. At the present time emotions are examined with a sort of amusement, held in the palm like exotic, possibly dangerous insects, but at the time of William's babyhood emotions welled up from sources believed to be sacred, when they were not demonic. William cried a great deal as a child and he was never made to feel ashamed of his tears. He was hugged, he was cherished. He was certainly the center of the universe.

His father was a partner in one of the oldest brokerage houses in New York City. His mother's family owned, among other things, iron ore deposits along the St. Lawrence River. William's parents lived with their six handsome children in an Edwardian mansion on Fifth Avenue; in their employ were nursemaids, serving girls, a cook, a chauffeur, an English butler, and other servants. It was the 1920s and everything lay ahead.

I begged William to show me photographs from his childhood. You don't seem real to me, I said. You don't seem weighed down by history, not even personal history.

(Because of his extraordinary charm, I think. His uncommonly handsome face, his graceful manners, his sense of self.)

We were intimate at that time. But not genuinely close. I had no right to make demands but he complied, after a while, and seemed as struck as I by the packets of old photographs he brought me one Sunday—"Baby William," "William at the age of 3½," "William on his first pony"—William with his pale curls, his smile that was ethereal and pouting by turns, his rather round, thick-lashed eyes, his charming little velvet suits and ruffled shirts. William, and never Billy.

There was something legendary about the child in those sepia-tinted photographs, as if he knew very well what was his due, what his beauty required; and knew too that he would never have to insist upon it. The immense calm of *being* loved, and having to do very little *loving*. (After William left me that Sunday I discovered a snapshot left behind which I must have slipped out of the pile, must have stolen, half-consciously. William at the age of 8. Unsmiling, even a little melancholy. But very striking. A child to be cherished. If William noticed that this photograph was missing when he returned home, he never mentioned it to me. He always forgave small sins committed through love of *him*.)

Between the ages of nine and fourteen William sang in an Episcopal boys' choir good enough to travel about the northeast. He discovered that he loved music—loved singing—loved the "religious atmosphere." Describing himself as a choirboy he meant to be amusing, but in fact his voice deepened with a kind of awe, as if he had been a witness to those stately processions and not a participant. How handsome the boys were—all the boys! William had worn a long velvet robe of a deep burnished wine color; his pale blond curls had been brushed off his forehead; the expression of his gray-blue eyes was grave and demure. Angelic, everyone said. Of course they fussed over him in the family, the women especially, but he saw how, as the boys filed out the center aisle of the church, into the sunshine, the congregation—men and women both—stared at him. It seemed as if he were walking in a dream through their odd rapt faces. They looked at all the boys but they certainly looked at *him*, week after week. Quite openly, not at all rudely, but as if it were altogether natural. Of course some smiled—some were friends of the family. But others simply stared. William met their gazes shyly and his cheeks burned and his breath went shallow. What did it mean, to be so admired! So *contemplated*. When the procession of choirboys marched out of the church, clean out of the church and into the ordinary daylight, when it appeared they were only boys after all, despite their long robes and carefully combed hair, William felt a keen disappointment. Was this it? Was this all? Had he imagined everything?

He loved the choir, he said. Even the rehearsals, even the choirmaster's peevish demands.

William was sent to his father's schools—Lawrenceville and Yale—and at the age of twenty-six he married the heiress to a meat-packing fortune out of Kansas City, whom he had met in Manhattan. Within a few years he was unfaithful to her. (Technically, that is. For of course he had been unfaithful to his young wife immediately after the wedding. There are smiles which, quickly and covertly exchanged, are consummate acts of adultery; there are even occasions when the refusal to smile, the fixing of a solemn stare, is dramatically adulterous.) Women so adored William, how could he keep himself from them? He sensed too an implicit approval from certain older men, like his own father. And surely there was enough of William for everyone—his spirit was magnanimous as a Sunday buffet.

But it really began, he told me in a voice that trembled with emotion (and so many years afterward!), when a cousin of his wife's, an ordinarily pretty girl of twenty-eight, unmarried, from Missouri, came east to visit, to see their infant daughter. For some reason William and not his wife led the girl into the nursery. It was a hazy April afternoon, a breeze stirred the gauzy white curtains, the girl placed her cold, nervous fingers on the back of William's neck as he bent over the crib—and it was really the case, the girl maintained for years, that she had been unable to help herself. It happened, it simply happened, no one was to blame.

"Did you love her?" I asked.

"Oh—*love!*" William said.

"But if she was the first—"

"She loved enough for both of us," he said flatly.

The first time I saw William, he was pointed out to me at a large gathering. It was a reception held in the newly-opened wing of a museum. There he is, an acquaintance said, there, do you see?—that man? (My acquaintance was the former lover of a woman who had been, as they said, "involved" with William for a brief period of time. His voice was coarse with an indeterminate emotion—jealousy, bitterness, a curious masculine pride.)

We became acquainted that evening. There was an exchange of telephone numbers. William was struck by the fact—or the postulate—that I was an "artist" of sorts myself. "It must be very difficult to write," he said, "I mean to write about serious things, to give the kind of depth to consciousness that it really has. . . . I mean, in my own head I am going in ten directions at once, even as I stand here, but in literature or art there's a wonderful single-mindedness that allows you to go deeply into . . . into the soul. Isn't that true?"

His enthusiasm was gratifying—it was intoxicating. We are always intoxicated with the danger of being overvalued.

So I became acquainted with William, who was already legendary in his own circle and who was moving out, in this phase of his life, into wider, more experimental circles. He had money, a great deal of money, for the acquisition of art by "unknown contemporaries"; he bought books, including high-priced limited editions; he would want, eventually, to help finance an off-Broadway play. Talking with him I felt the power of his own enchantment: I was buoyed up by his intensity, his marvelous gift for exaggeration. How could I resist summoning him to me, though I was hardly the kind of young woman who "summons" men—! He had my number and did not telephone. I had his number, and did.

His eyes were a wonderful keen gray-blue, widely spaced in his strong face, rather deeply-socketed. His nose was straight, and long, with a Roman bridge. Though he was only in his late thirties at the time of our initial acquaintance (we were to see each other intermittently for years—William was always "rediscovering" me) he did give the air of being older: there was something patriarchal about him, an authority graced with kindness, affection, an interest in detail. He was filled with questions about "craft" as well as "art"—he was dizzily flattering! Does a writer *feel* things more deeply than the average person, William wanted to know, and is it dangerous?—is it exhilarating?—or merely an aspect of one's professional skill?

"Suppose you were to write about me someday," he said shyly. "And I read it. And then—"

"Yes?"

"And then—well—well I would *know*."

He never spoke of his wife to me, and of course he never spoke of his other women. (It was fairly common knowledge that he had a mistress—and the word "mistress" is not inappropriate—who lived in one of the brownstones William's family owned, on West 11th Street.) Sometimes he alluded to his children: they were "expensive" children. His curiosity about my own life, my solitude, my eccentric working hours, my bouts of despair that could shift so abruptly into hours of fierce airy energy, struck me as unnervingly impersonal. He was interrogating me, he was learning from me, yet I was not very real to him. He might have thought my "art" protected me—I could not be injured like his other women.

He had a habit, not so annoying as it sounds, of humming tunes under his breath. Cole Porter, Hoagy Carmichael, Rodgers and Hammerstein—that sort of thing. His smile could be melancholy, and then it could shift and dazzle you with—with the very fact, the impact, of good spirits—of sheer simple happiness. He liked to laugh, he liked to tell anecdotes. His stories were never original but they were wonderfully entertaining. At school and for a year in college he had wrestled and played football, and in the war he was said to have had a "distinguished" record; though he rarely spoke of that aspect of his past, as if sensing that it did not exactly represent him, I sensed in him the absolute calm that comes of a masculinity that has been put to the test and has not failed. Now he was freed of *that*, now he could give himself over simply to being adored. And the adoration, of course, had to come from women.

Sometimes he said, speculatively: "I might have been a priest, you know. An archbishop. . . ."

I understood his meaning. I said: "But you would have been an Episcopal priest, you wouldn't have had to take a vow of celibacy."

"I *would* have taken a vow of celibacy," William laughed.

Evidently he had wanted to enter the seminary as a boy. His father was disappointed but would not have opposed him; his mother was quite enthusiastic. But when the choir sang the Apostles' Creed in their high, thin, hauntingly beautiful voices, William's eyes flooded with tears because as he sang so winningly of his beliefs he knew he did *not* believe—it was impossible.

Certainly there might be God—that was reasonable enough—a presence called "God" that inhabited the universe without passion—floating through it, bodiless as cigarette smoke in a closed room—that might be true: but this presence had never taken on the contours of a personality, in William's experience. The Bible was strident and terrifying but not very convincing. As the years passed "God" became more and more abstract, more general. William shocked the chaplain at Lawrenceville by asking whether "God" wasn't a fancy word for "whatever happens." In any case God snagged on nothing immediate in William's life.

By the age of sixteen his belief had faded; and of course he had given up the choir long before.

I was sick, and William came to see me. As I lay on a sofa reeking and parchment-colored with jaundice this extraordinary man in his three-piece tailor-made suit bounded about raising windows, straightening the clutter of my life, making an attempt with a sponge—which was filthy—to clean my sink and cupboard counters. He hummed songs from *Porgy and Bess,* he whistled "Old Buttermilk Sky" so energetically one knew he had never listened to the lyrics. Though he was in his mid-forties at the time and beginning to put on *some* weight he was airy and light on his feet as a Chagall lover.

Had he been my lover, years before? He seemed not to remember. Though of course he was gravely considerate now, even courtly. He *might* have been a former husband.

He told me about his boyhood, and about the choir. He confessed that his success as an adult, and his personal happiness (for of course William *was* happy—no matter that he had caused so much grief) did not mean as much to him as those hours in church. If only he could explain—! The boys' voices lifting—the organ filling the immense church with its remarkable sound—the priest in his vestments—the sanction of the Church itself—the dizzying air of drama, meaning, intensity—

"Do you understand?" he asked, apologetically. "I'm afraid you can't understand."

But of course I did.

His second wife was said to be a gifted but erratic horsewoman, small-boned, quick and nervous and very beautiful; she brought with her, to the marriage, two young children and a $1.5 million estate in Far Hills, New Jersey. She was thirty-one and "shaky" from the experience of her first marriage, or at any rate from the protracted experience of adultery with William, which she could not have foreseen, with confidence, would develop into marriage. The divorce was mildly scandalous but did not come before a judge.

William was thirty-six years old. He loved the country, he claimed to be discovering "domestic life." (There were more than a dozen servants and groundsmen employed at the Far Hills estate.) He journeyed to the city only once a week, staying from Monday through Thursday; then he returned to the country where he cultivated a small vegetable garden and learned, with some difficulty, to bake bread. He took riding lessons at his wife's insistence so that he would be able to accompany her, eventually, on her daily rides.

But the rumors began again. There were always rumors. William this, William that. Of course he could not be blamed: women approached him: even the most gracious, the most genteel women: it was claimed they could not help themselves.

Oddly, as William grew older, and must have become less "attractive" in the usual sense of the word, the love women bore him began to acquire an increasingly desperate tone. There were scenes, there were threats, one or two attempts at suicide. A shouting match in the cocktail lounge of the Far Hills Hunt Club; a drunken street scuffle in mid-town Manhattan with the husband of a well-known actress. There was even a rumor, especially injurious because the subject was so petty, that William had put pressure on the membership committee of the Hunt Club by way of an older member's wife to get an acquaintance and *his* attractive young wife admitted to the Club. When the nomination was blackballed William was furious.

Shortly after this incident William's wife had an accident while riding, and badly smashed her right kneecap. She spent a long time in the hospital. After her recovery the two of them left for a protracted vacation—it had always been William's fancy to "travel around the world"—to Japan, to India and Ceylon—where both husband and wife became interested in Buddhism. They bought Buddhist art, took hundreds of color photographs, attended Buddhist ceremonies. It was said that they took instructions in Buddhism with a renowned teacher.

But William's wife grew ill with an intestinal disorder, so they cut their vacation short and returned to the States. She sold her horses one by one; there was talk for a while of selling much of the estate; then something happened, and William moved away to an apartment in the city—a legal separation was arranged. (I saw a photograph of William's second wife once, in a newspaper. Perhaps she had aged, perhaps the photograph was poor, but she did not strike me as unusually beautiful.)

Buddhism was one of the subjects William loved to talk about. He had memorized passages from certain sacred texts, which he loved to recite in his rich dramatic voice. *When the mind is dis-*

turbed it will strive to become conscious of the existence of an external world and will thus betray the imperfection of its inner condition. But as all infinite merits in fact constitute the one mind which, perfect in itself, has no need of seeking after any external things. . . . These were the words of Asvaghosha, a Sanskrit philosopher; William was not absolutely certain of the pronunciation of his name.

But then he loved to talk about so many things. It gave him joy simply to talk, to hear his own voice, to gauge its effect upon others. He gossiped, he recounted the plots of novels that had "struck" him, he worried aloud about the international economic scene, he criticized restaurants and nightclubs, he knew amazing little stories about government officials, exiled royalty, fashion models. Once he telephoned me simply to talk about the "extraordinary" writings of a Frenchwoman named Anna de Noailles of whom I had never heard. As he spoke I could imagine his handsome face lined with thought . . . *thought,* not worry, of the most noble sort.

He began to see me again, with more regularity. Much had gone wrong in my life and he saw it as his mission to "rouse me from despair." He loved to speak, in long rambling charming monologues, of "serious" issues—God, immortality, the soul, how to live. These were genuine issues; they were more important than anything else in life; yet no one knew the first thing about them.

William did not fall in love with me, even then, though my wretchedness, and my obvious need for him, must have been a temptation. (As he grew older these temptations were to become more difficult to resist.) But I think he was in love with—he was fascinated by—my apparent intimacy with these "serious" matters. I was a writer, after all. Not only a writer but a woman willing to live a spartan, severe, even monastic life in the service of my "art"; it was no exaggeration to say that I never went for an hour in those years without thinking of certain solemn, marvelous, slightly outlandish "questions"—the riddle of death, the paradox of our yearning for immortality encased in our mortal flesh, and so on, and so forth. I was not only willing to sacrifice myself for my art but in fact was doing so, and quite visibly.

Other women who had adored William had certainly been serious enough in their adoration of him, but they hadn't really been serious *women*—they were not obsessed with such matters. It is possible that William, though he loved them, might have believed that they deserved their misery, for wasn't it absurd of them—wasn't it an aspect of their vanity—that they should *presume* his love for them would be permanent? Sometimes he recounted anonymous incidents of a dismayingly petty nature, and we burst into mutual laughter; for wounded feelings, grief, jealousy, even rage *were* amusing. Another time he told me of scenes he'd had with his second wife near the end of their marriage: the poor woman had stopped accusing him of infidelity and had begun to claim that men were pursuing *her*. William would listen to her tales, and force himself to say, And—? Yes—? What happened—? with an air of startled and irritated possessiveness that indicated he still loved her. She would conclude her stories by saying in a small neutral voice:—Then I told him I couldn't see him again, I told him I was in love with my husband.

William sighed and laughed and rubbed his face brusquely. The great haunting philosophical questions—how are they to be linked, to be yoked, to such painfully *physical* moments? His life was becoming a riddle. He could not solve it. It seemed to him repeatedly that the women he adored in his imagination were betrayed by their counterparts in the real world. Self-pitying tears, unconscious vulgar expressions, banal or ignorant remarks . . . the mistaken notion that passionate jealousy would flatter him . . . "You're a writer," William said to me, "you must have thought about these things deeply, so perhaps you can explain: why does everything fail?"

His question angered me. That he should assume that *everything* failed—! *Everything,* when he meant of course only *women;* not even *women* so much as *adoration.* I said impatiently that it isn't the role of the writer, or of any artist for that matter, to *explain.*

"It isn't?" William asked with great seriousness. "Oh, I see. Then what is—?"

At that time I was just recovering from a long illness. Not a "medical" illness but an illness just the same. I was grateful to be alive, and resented William's tone. I said: "Well—first we survive. And suggest pathways."

William stared. He was silent for a long moment. It was clear that he admired me, and his admiration was always flattering; but it could not last. He stared, and nodded, and repeated: "I see. Yes. *First we survive.* Yes."

He was under the enchantment, or was it the curse?—of his own being. Which was one of the reasons I telephoned him a few months later, though I knew I should not be interfering with his life (he had married again, a third time, and was living on East 72nd Street, in an apartment overlooking the river).

He was in his early fifties now. He had gone through a period of intense revulsion for his work—for everything to do with finances, with money itself—but had come through. It was said that he was "happily" married at last.

I called him, though there had been a tacit agreement, on my part, that I would not bother him, and I heard his voice register surprise and disappointment and courtly patience and finally concern as I explained as frankly and calmly as possible that I only wanted to see him, to talk with him, one more time . . . I did not break down. There were no tears. He took a cab to my apartment; I hadn't needed to beg. And somehow it happened, I am not certain how or why, that by the time he arrived I had dropped off into a profound stuporous sleep, from which I had to be awakened with great effort on William's part. (Poor William! He guessed, correctly, that I had taken a dozen or more sleeping pills, washed down with vodka. That I had *wanted* and had *not wanted* to die in his arms.)

So it happened that William saved my life. He shook me awake, shouting, and hauled me to my feet, and forced me to vomit, and afterward made black coffee which he forced me to drink. He was stern, he was furious, there was nothing loving about him, and I was angry at him for saving me, and then, a few minutes later, hysterical with gratitude. Stop, stop, shut up, he said, I've had enough of you.

But he gave me a considerable sum of money—considerable

from my point of view, I mean—enough for several months' rent—and I had reason to think he paid the superintendent of the building to watch me, to do a little amateur spying. He wouldn't have wanted one of his women to die on him.

He telephoned frequently, to see how I was. In a voice meant to be encouraging he assured me that my behavior was nothing more than eccentric. He had been reading about certain "temperamental" artists lately—Gustav Klimt and Egon Schiele. (He sent me an excellent reproduction of Schiele's *Girl in Black Stockings*, saying that the figure reminded him of me!—a statement I took to be preposterous.) "Such spells, such moods," William said, "are probably quite normal for your nature and your genius."

"Genius?" I inquired mildly.

"You have to do these things," William said slowly. "I think I understand."

"But your other women do them too," I said. "Don't they? Haven't they?"

"My other women—?" he said.

"Don't you have other women?" I asked.

"Of course not," he said. "I'm happily married now."

A few weeks later it occurred to me to test William's friendship by asking for more money. Just a little more. A loan. And he did not disappoint me though I think he was hurt. (His voice registered hurt. I had called him at his office on Bank Street.)

"I'll send you a money order," he said. "But that will have to be the end. Do you understand?"

"Of course I understand," I said softly.

He was about to hang up, then changed his mind and asked my opinion of—what had it been?—a new sculpture exhibit, a new "difficult" novel? We talked for a few minutes. Again he was about to hang up. Then he happened to mention, as if incidentally, that he was having difficulties with his new wife after all. He loved her very much, he said. But for some reason he couldn't seem to make her happy.

"Do you know what she said last week?" he asked in a puzzled voice.

"No. What did she say?" I asked.

"She said—If you leave me and go to any of them, any one of them, ever again, I won't be here when you get back."

I slapped my hand over the receiver to hide my laughter.

I said, "Then you mustn't ever leave her again."

He said, "I know."

"You *mustn't* ever leave her again."

"I know," he said, his voice rising. "I know."

As William grew older and his life became more unpleasantly complicated—there were problems with his grown children, there were problems with his family's business—it happened that the women who adored him were more and more distant from his social world, and more desperate. And, except for a thirty-seven-year-old actress ("Anne-Marie"), they were getting younger.

He was still a striking man, of course. His silver-blond hair receded gracefully on a brow that was imposing; his cheeks were ruddy, as if with exuberant good health. His lips were so sharply cut as to suggest sculpture. It was not an exaggeration to say that he was a beautiful man, for his age at least, maneuvering himself about like an athlete past his prime but still in superb condition.

His wife had been an artist of some sort—or perhaps a designer or an interior decorator. It was said that she had given up both her marriage and her job for William. She loved him passionately, with a young girl's caprice. (She was in fact forty-two years old.) She could not shake off the notion—which was hardly so far-fetched as observers thought—that William's love for her began to diminish as soon as they were married and he had "saved" her from her former husband. Their quarrels were tempestuous and exciting. William had to shout her down, and then comfort her. Help me, why don't you help *me,* he whispered, but of course she did not hear, or if she heard she did not understand.

In this marriage, William declared, he rediscovered "romance" —he and his wife met for drinks in little unknown bars, saw 6 P.M. showings of foreign films, held hands in the dark, strolled along the busy avenues, stopped for dinner impulsively in restaurants they had never seen before, and often could not find again. He was very happy. His wife was a woman with whom he might discuss Shakespeare (whose complete plays he meant to read, one by one) and even Schopenhauer (whose *World as Will and Idea* he was trying to read at last—he'd heard so much about it for decades), or the latest bankruptcy scandal on Wall Street, or the mysterious meditative nature of bread-baking. (William was trying to bake his own bread again, on the weekends. It was all he seemed to retain from his Buddhist period.) Everyone said that it was obvious his wife adored him.

It was a happy time. Yet friends were disappearing from his life.

Invitations went unanswered, calls were unreturned. An old classmate from Lawrenceville, a corporation lawyer whom William saw for lunch two or three times a month died suddenly of a heart attack, on an early train from Greenwich. One of his old Yale suite-mates lost a great deal of money in real estate speculation in Long Island and committed suicide—shot himself in the head. Other friends and acquaintances drifted away because, it turned out, they belonged to William's ex-wives rather than to William, or because, remarried themselves, they found it difficult to interest their wives in their old connections. And it seemed too that William was beginning to drink too much in company, and his "charm" and "high seriousness" were becoming tiresome.

He was obsessed with the same old topics. How to live—what is love—why are we on earth. The "meaning" of death. But his voice often slurred and he was developing the habit of nervously squeezing his listeners' arms for emphasis.

A mild heart attack at the age of fifty-six. So unexpected! And unjust, for William *had* been dieting, he *had* been exercising and watching his weight. (He had joined an impressive new health club on Lexington Avenue where he swam for a vigorous half-hour before taking a cab down to work.) In his doctor's office he spoke resentfully; his face grew coarse; he knew he had been unjustly treated. His wife was blackmailing him emotionally, he said. Women had always blackmailed him. He couldn't control it . . . Couldn't understand . . .

The heart attack had been dangerously mild. William insisted for days that it had been nothing more than indigestion—only his wife's tears had forced him to make an appointment with his doctor.

He had said to her, irritably, Well—you can't expect me to live forever just for *you!*

The women were younger, scruffier, less clearly defined. One was a "psychiatric nurse" in her early twenties who was unable or unwilling to say exactly where she had trained, or where she had been employed (when William was introduced to her, by way of a friend of a friend, she was living on unemployment insurance and sleeping most of the day). Another was a "therapy assistant" who worked three or four times a week at a "clinic" in the West 40s, near the river. She was often vacant-eyed, her smile had no focus, her sentences trailed off into silence. A pretty girl, William thought, but mysteriously soiled; smudged; as if a playful giant had picked her up and smeared her with his thumb. The "psychiatric nurse" called herself Inez, the "therapy assistant" called herself Bonnie, a girl by the name of Kim Starr who struck up a conversation with William one mild June day in Washington Square was a former "ballerina." The girls had nothing in common but their youth, their vague blurry soiled prettiness, and their interest in William.

Meeting him for a very late lunch at the Oyster Bar—it was after three—one of the girls snatched up William's hand and kissed it. "You in that expensive suit—it's tailor-made, isn't it?—and your shoes!—and your fingernails manicured—and that scent—did you just shave?—oh I love you, love you—I mean it—I wouldn't lie—I'm *crazy* about you, William," the girl cried.

Inez, Bonnie, Kim. And later the young step-daughter of a business acquaintance, named Deborah. William made it a point to telephone the girls several times a week from his Bank Street office, careful that no one should eavesdrop. (The place was in disarray. The outer office was being used for storage, there was an old carpet, stiff with dirt, rolled and tied and set on end in the corridor outside William's door, that had been there for weeks.) In his address book with the worn black cover William had scribbled down two and sometimes even three telephone numbers for each of the girls, but it often happened that they were not available at those numbers. Strangers picked up the phones, shouting Yes? Hello? Who is—? Their accents were harshly foreign.

William had not forgotten me entirely. Every few months he called, took me out for a drink, squeezed my hands in his and assured me that I was lovely as always. And how was my work going? and my life?

He was happy, he said. Though after two or three drinks he would complain mildly about his wife. She had completely redecorated their apartment, had even knocked out a wall, you can imagine the inconvenience—and the expense!—yet her moods were more capricious than ever. She imagined he had a mistress. She was even jealous of his former wives, and of his grown children. (It maddened her that William should continue to loan money to his children or give it to them outright, when his own financial problems were becoming so serious.) "I will soon be sixty years old," William said with an elegant, helpless gesture, "and I assure you I know nothing—not the first thing about love and marriage and children and how to live one's life—"

It was my strategy that day to speak lightly. I said: "Too many women have loved you."

"What?" he asked, cupping his hand to his ear. "—Love? Oh, that!"

In a dark gold-flecked mirror I spied upon the two of us, seated at a pretentious little pedestal table of simulated marble. William had become an aging gentleman with hair that looked white; I was a woman with a shadowed face.

The lounge was disagreeably noisy. New customers were continually filing past our table.

"I suppose you're going to write a story about me someday," William said, raising his voice. He was both accusing and affectionate. "And if you do—I wonder: do I dare read it, or not?"

It was not long after this meeting that William happened upon Deborah, the eighteen-year-old daughter of a business acquaintance. Though in fact she was the man's step-daughter.

She was walking north on Seventh Avenue, near 8th Street,

with her arm around the waist of a slender, swarthy-skinned young man in a white shirt. She was obviously drunk, or high on drugs. She nuzzled the young man's neck, giggling, and staggering against him; it seemed awkward, it seemed rude, that the young man didn't trouble to slide his arm around *her*. William stared in amazement. He had last seen this girl at her parents' summer cottage in East Hampton, years ago. Deborah must have been no more than thirteen or fourteen at the time, yet he remembered her face distinctly. —Deborah, William whispered. Here? Like this?

On the street that day she was wearing clumsy high-heeled shoes with open toes, and jeans that fit her slim body tightly; her red-brown hair tumbled past her shoulders, snarled and matted; her pale skin was freckled as William remembered. She was wearing theatrically red lipstick but the lipstick had smeared onto her face.

William followed the couple for a block or two, and saw that they were not getting along well. Deborah's mood had changed: now she was pushing and slapping at the young man, who slapped her right back. Passersby stared at them. William came hesitantly forward. He called her name and she ignored him. She was saying something in a low rapid furious voice to the young man.

"Deborah—?"

Finally she turned and saw him. It was astonishing, it was miraculous, the stages of her *seeing* him. At first her gaze merely swung onto him, as if he were an intruder, a stranger; and then her expression sharpened; and then softened; and it was clear from the change of light in her eyes that she recognized him.

"You're— You're— Oh Jesus I can't think of your name—"

She staggered forward, she clutched at his arm.

"Oh Jesus I can't think of your name but I *know* you—"

William tried to tell her but she was too excited, too high, to hear. Her voice was all exclamation, her eyes were glittering, he could smell the odor of dried perspiration on her body. It was certainly Deborah, his friend's step-daughter; they knew each other and their behavior on the street—for now Deborah was hugging him, she had thrown her arms around his neck wildly—was really not so extraordinary as it might appear. William's face flushed scarlet and he did not know what to do with his hands.

"Oh I *know* you—I *know* you—" the girl wept.

One terrible night the telephone rang in the apartment on East 72nd Street. And William knew from his wife's voice, and her expression as she called him to the phone, that this was Deborah at last.

It was many months later. The start of November. William had given Deborah his home number but begged her not to call unless it was an emergency.

She was not very coherent on the phone. There were voices—they might have been angry, they might have been merely festive—behind her.

"Yes? Deborah? What is it? What are you saying?"

"—in trouble," she said, "I think I'm in—"

"Deborah? Where are you?"

"I'm in bad trouble," she said, "I'm in bad trouble—"

He asked her what was happening, how could he get to her, but she kept repeating that she was in trouble, in bad trouble, until she began giggling, and the phone must have been taken from her, and slammed down.

William's heart was pounding in his chest. He had to sit—had to grope for a chair. It was a long time before he heard his wife's questions. "One of your girls, wasn't it, another one of your girls, *wasn't it,* don't lie, don't you dare lie to me—!"

He did not answer her. He did not really hear her. He was waiting for the telephone to ring again but of course it did not ring and he sat beside it for several hours, numbed, in a trance of sheer despair, too upset even to heave himself to his feet and go to the liquor cabinet.

Near dawn he tried the door to the bedroom but his wife had locked it against him. So he slept, fully clothed, his shoes on, on a leather couch in the room he called his study.

The calls came infrequently that winter, though William was always prepared for them, and bitterly disappointed to hear the wrong voice. His wife laughed: "Oh, wasn't that the girl—? Oh what a pity!"

"There is no girl," William said. And then, befuddled, licking his lips: "She's the daughter of an old friend. The step-daughter."

"What old friend?" his wife asked. "You haven't any friends."

Sometimes he wandered about the apartment at night, lingering in the doorway of his study. It was alarming, the vividness with which he could recall the girl. He had escorted her along the street that day, he had taken her uptown in a cab, and once in the cab they had fallen upon each other hungrily—the girl had clutched at him, kissing him, and he had responded with a convulsive frenzy he had not known—he really had *not* known—he was capable of making. Though it was possible (as he thought afterward) that he had merely succumbed to the girl's passion.

He took her to a hotel on Seventh Avenue. Not one of the better hotels—because he hadn't much cash with him that day, and didn't care to use his credit card; and because, in a better hotel, the girl's noisy exuberance might have attracted attention.

Her arms were like steel bands around his neck and back. She screamed, she wept, she rolled her head from side to side, in a transport of passion—so clearly unfeigned!—that excited him more violently than he had been excited in many years.

And then, afterward, she had not wanted him to move from her.

"No, no," she said hoarsely, angrily, "no, I want you there, I want you *there*, I'll kill you if you leave—"

So he lay on top of her, vastly flattered, sweating, his heart hammering in his chest, his thoughts racing so crazily they were colored paper streamers, razor-thin strips of confetti.

"Don't you leave me don't you ever leave me or I'll kill you—I swear I'll kill you—" the girl shouted.

She clutched at him. Her young slender body was rancid with sweat.

"No—no—no— Don't leave me—"

But his heart, his heart!—hammering so violently. He could not get his breath. Her arms which had seemed so thin were in fact hard with muscle—hard with the violence of her frenzied need.

But of course he had to shift his body from hers. It was impossible for him to make love to her again so quickly; he could not penetrate her again; his penis had shrunken, had gone limp. . . . Fortunately she grunted and pushed him from her and fell asleep, suddenly. She fell into a thin twitching feverish sleep that excluded him.

He lay beside her for a long time, his pulses racing. She was so young—so extraordinarily young! *That* did amaze him. The bodies of young women, young girls, which they inhabit so unthinkingly—the smooth unlined flesh of the thighs, the belly—the small hard lovely breasts—

My love, William whispered, close to tears. My sweet little love.

She gave him her telephone number. But she must have made a mistake, jotting it down so hurriedly on a scrap of paper; for when he called a woman answered, speaking in a querulous Spanish-accented voice, she knew no one named Deborah, knew nothing about Deborah, what was the number he had dialed?

Fortunately William had given her *his* number. Both at the office (where he preferred her to call) and at home. And she did call—she did call—always very late at night—always in a strange mood: she was gay, she was exhilarated, she was panicked, she was very, very tired. William was so pleased, so flattered, that he refrained from asking her exactly what it was she wanted from him.

William's marriage came to an end one snowy night in February.

This was the night Deborah called for the last time, and summoned him to her.

Her voice was shrill and terrified and clear: "Could you come get me right away?" she said. "There are some people here—some men—some very strange men—"

"Deborah? What is it? Where are you?" William cried.

"Oh William I'm so afraid—oh can you help me—William—"

It was a measure of her terror, that her voice was now so clear. Despite the noise in the background he could hear her words distinctly.

"What is it," William said, "what is happening?—where are you—"

"Oh William could you come get me—come in a cab— Oh please, please—"

"Deborah, dear, tell me where you are— Can you tell me where you are—"

His hands shook so badly, he could barely write down the address. And then it wasn't a complete address—just the intersection of two streets in the warehouse district, near the river.

"Deborah," he whispered, "Deborah— I'll be there immediately—Deborah?"

But the line was dead. She had replaced the phone, or someone had taken it from her.

So William dressed, William prepared to leave, though his wife —in her nightgown, looking stunned and haggard—was trying to dissuade him. There was even some foolishness—a humiliating scuffle of sorts—at the hall closet. His wife was nearly crying. "Where are you going! What on earth do you think you're doing! It's two in the morning, it's bitter cold, how can you *think* of going out in your condition—"

On the icy street he ran, vigorous, frightened, shouting for a cab, waving his arms. It *was* bitter cold though he did not register the fact for some time.

It took him ten or fifteen minutes to get a cab, over on Fifth Avenue. By then he was shivering convulsively and his face and exposed hands ached with the cold.

And then, on the street again, he found himself hurrying along one block of darkened warehouses after another. The streets were poorly lit here; it was very hard to see. He rubbed his hands together, he muttered to himself, what would be wisest to do, what should he have done, should he have telephoned the police. . . . He dare not call her name: she might be held captive: her tormentors would be alerted.

Ice had formed curiously humped and coiled shapes on the sidewalk, upon which thin dry patches of snow lay. It was dangerous to walk so fast—the soles of his shoes were slippery—he had forgotten his overshoes—he had forgotten his gloves. A very cold wind was blowing from the river. He stared, looked from side to side, bewildered, why were there so many blank featureless doors? —windowless buildings? Loading ramps, immense sliding garage doors, an air of utter solitude, silence. No one lived here, surely. He would never find her here.

He ran from one side of the street to the other, panting, whimpering. If only he saw a crack of light— If only there was a doorway that might lead up into a loft— Piles of debris had been heaped in the gutters, and ice had formed over them. An uninhabited place. Blank featureless pitiless buildings.

"Deborah," he cried. "Deborah—?"

He could hear himself panting. And his heart, could he hear his heart as well?—queer clipped arhythmic beating—now rapid, now slow—a hiccupping sensation—no pain but a sudden surprising airiness—

Far up the street William saw, suddenly, figures on a stoop. They were just leaving a building, were they? He stared at them for a long moment before he had the sense to shout at them.

"Wait," he cried, hurrying forward, "you there, *you*—wait—don't let the door swing shut—wait—don't let it lock—"

Three or four figures. Young people, probably. They ignored him, they strode away in the other direction.

"Wait," he cried, "oh please wait—"

He stumbled forward, whimpering with the cold. His breath was alarmingly loud. He had forgotten his gloves, he had forgotten his overshoes. He could not remember—exactly—the girl's name. She was the daughter of a friend. An old friend. She would know him, of course, when she saw him. If only they had not let the door swing shut— But then perhaps it had not *locked*—

It was locked, he seized the knob and tugged at it, crying "Open up! You in there! *You!* I know you're listening!" He pounded on the door. Fist over fist, whimpering with the pain, on that blank ungiving door.

"Open up, do you hear? I know you're in there! I know what you're doing to her! I insist—"

They must have been listening to him, in frightened silence. For he heard no sound. No sound at all.

The building was a warehouse. There were enormous sliding doors made of corrugated aluminum or tin; there was a loading ramp upon which ice had formed in serpent-like coils. He could see no windows though the building was four stories high, at least. A blank featureless pitiless facade.

William's shouts echoed faintly in the streets, among the high buildings. It was remarkable, the silence in this part of the city.

"Open up!" he cried, his face now wet with tears. "I know you're in there, all of you— I've come for her— You can't deny me— She's in there and I know what you're doing, I know, but I won't let you—I've come to take her away—"

He pounded on the door until there was no more sensation in his fists.

One day William appeared on my doorstep. I had heard rumors of his death—he had been renting a room by the week in a hotel on West 47th Street, he had been found dead in the room, or collapsed in the street?—or had he died in the hospital? Obviously the rumors were false.

It was a fact, however, that he had been eased out of his partnership in the family business. But without putting up much of a defense.

A fact, too, that his marriage was over.

He had not wanted to talk about these misfortunes, however. He wanted only to talk about general things, "serious" things, the old issues of life and death and the immortality of the soul and how to live one's life. . . . He was inquisitive about me: had I accomplished what I wanted, was I happy, did I regret living alone? (For now, at my age, it was too late. Quite clearly too late.)

We talked. Beneath William's words I could hear him pleading with me, silently. Do you still adore me, he was asking.

I had not much time for him that day. It was late afternoon, I was on my way out. I pitied him because the enchantment was over—one could see that at a single glance, the poor man looked so battered, so hopeful—but I had not much patience for him. None of us do, once the enchantment ends.

Do you still adore me, do women still dream of me, William was pleading, his watery eyes fixed upon me, his fingers (which were surprisingly dirty) plucking at the hem of his suit coat.

Though of course he said nothing of the sort: he was asking about my life, my work.

I explained that I had to leave.

He walked alongside me for a block or two, before he tired. And finally he did ask, as he had been meaning to ask all along, touching my arm: "Will you write about me, do you think?—someday—?"

NEXT DOOR

TOBIAS WOLFF

Tobias Wolff is a native of Washington State. His short stories have appeared in *Antaeus, The Atlantic Monthly, Encounter, Mademoiselle, TriQuarterly,* and other magazines and reviews. He lives in Syracuse, New York, where he teaches literature and creative writing at Syracuse University. His collection of stories *In the Garden of the North American Martyrs* was published by the Ecco Press in the fall of 1981 and will be published in England this spring by Jonathan Cape. This is his second O. Henry Award.

I wake up afraid. My wife is sitting on the edge of my bed, shaking me. "They're at it again," she says.

I go to the window. All their lights are on, upstairs and down, as if they have money to burn. He yells, she screams something back, the dog barks. There is a short silence, then the baby cries, poor thing.

"Better not stand there," says my wife. "They might see you."

I say, "I'm going to call the police," knowing she won't let me.

"Don't," she says.

She's afraid that they will poison our cat if we complain.

Next door the man is still yelling, but I can't make out what he's saying over the dog and the baby. The woman laughs, not really meaning it, "*Ha! Ha! Ha!,*" and suddenly gives a sharp little cry. Everything goes quiet.

"He struck her," says my wife. "I felt it just the same as if he struck me."

Next door the baby gives a long wail and the dog starts up again. The man walks out into his driveway and slams the door.

"Be careful," says my wife. She gets back into her bed and pulls the covers up to her neck.

The man mumbles to himself and jerks at his fly. Finally he gets it open and walks over to our fence. It's a white picket fence, ornamental more than anything else. It couldn't keep anyone out. I put it in myself, and planted honeysuckle and bougainvillea all along it.

My wife says, "What's he doing?"

"Shh," I say.

He leans against the fence with one hand and with the other he goes to the bathroom on the flowers. He walks the length of the fence like that, not missing any of them. When he's through he gives Florida a shake, then zips up and heads back across the driveway. He almost slips on the gravel but he catches himself and curses and goes into the house, slamming the door again.

When I turn around my wife is leaning forward, watching me. She raises her eyebrows. "Not again," she says.

I nod.

"Number one or number two?"

"Number one."

"Thank God for small favors," she says, settling back. "Between him and the dog it's a wonder you can get anything to grow out there."

I read somewhere that human pee has a higher acid content than animal pee, but I don't mention that. I would rather talk about something else. It depresses me, thinking about the flowers. They are past their prime, but still. Next door the woman is shouting. "Listen to that," I say.

"I used to feel sorry for her," says my wife. "Not any more. Not after last month."

"Ditto," I say, trying to remember what happened last month to make my wife not feel sorry for the woman next door. I don't feel sorry for her either, but then I never have. She yells at the baby, and excuse me, but I'm not about to get all excited over someone who treats a child like that. She screams things like "*I thought I told you to stay in your bedroom!*" and here the baby can't even speak English yet.

As far as her looks, I guess you would have to say she's pretty. But it won't last. She doesn't have good bone structure. She has a soft look to her, like she has never eaten anything but doughnuts and milk shakes. Her skin is white. The baby takes after her, not that you would expect it to take after *him*, dark and hairy. Even with his shirt on you can tell that he has hair all over his back and on his shoulders, thick and springy like an Airedale's.

Now they're all going at once over there, plus they've got the hi-fi turned on full blast. One of those bands. "It's the baby I feel sorry for," I say.

My wife puts her hands over her ears. "I can't stand another minute of it," she says. She takes her hands away. "Maybe there's something on TV." She sits up. "See who's on Johnny."

I turn on the television. It used to be down in the den, but I brought it up here a few years ago when my wife came down with an illness. I took care of her myself—made the meals and everything. I got to where I could change the sheets with her still in the bed. I always meant to take the television back down when my wife recovered, but I never got around to it. It sits between our beds on a little table I made. Johnny is saying something to Sammy Davis, Jr. Ed McMahon is bent over laughing. He is always so cheerful. If you were going to take a really long voyage you could do worse than bring Ed McMahon along.

"Sammy," says my wife. "Who else is on besides Sammy?"

I look at the television guide. "A bunch of people I never heard of." I read off their names. My wife hasn't heard of them either. She wants to know what else is on. "'*El Dorado,*'" I read. "'Brisk adventure yarn about a group of citizens in search of the legendary city of gold.' It's got two-and-a-half stars beside it."

"Citizens of what?" asks my wife.

"It doesn't say."

Finally we watch the movie. A blind man comes into a small town. He says that he has been to El Dorado and that he will lead an expedition there for a share of the proceeds. He can't see, but he will call out the landmarks one by one as they ride. At first people make fun of him, but eventually all the leading citizens get together and decide to give it a try. Right away they get attacked by Apaches and some of them want to turn back, but every time they get ready the blind man gives them another landmark, so they keep going.

Next door the woman is going crazy. She is saying things to him that no person should ever say to another person. It makes my wife restless. She looks at me. "Can I come over?" she says. "Just for a visit?"

I pull down the blankets and she gets in. The bed is just fine for one, but with two of us it's a tight fit. We are lying on our sides with me in back. I don't mean for it to happen but before long old Florida begins to stiffen up on me. I put my arms around my wife. I move my hands up onto the Rockies, then on down across the plains, heading south.

"Hey," she says. "No geography. Not tonight."

"I'm sorry," I say.

"Can't I just visit?"

"Forget it. I said I was sorry."

The citizens are crossing a desert. They have just about run out of water, and their lips are cracked. Though the blind man has delivered a warning, someone drinks from a poisoned well and dies horribly. That night, around the campfire, the others begin to quarrel. Most of them want to go home. "This is no country for a white man," says one, "and if you ask me, nobody has ever been here before." But the blind man describes a piece of gold so big and pure that it will burn your eyes out if you look directly at it. "I ought to know," he says. When he is finished, the citizens are silent: one by one they move away and lie down on their bedrolls. They put their hands behind their heads and look up at the stars. A coyote howls.

Hearing the coyote, I remember why my wife doesn't feel sorry for the woman next door. It was a Monday evening, about a month ago, right after I got home from work. The man next door started to beat the dog, and I don't mean just smacking him once or twice. He was beating him, and he kept beating him until the dog couldn't even cry any more; you could hear the poor creature's voice breaking. It made us very upset, especially my wife, who is an animal lover from way back. She gives to all the funds.

Finally it stopped. Then, a few minutes later, I heard my wife say "Oh!" and I went into the kitchen to find out what was wrong. She was standing by the window, which looks into the kitchen next door. The man had his wife backed up against the fridge. He had his knee between her legs and she had her knee between his legs and they were kissing, really hard, not just with their lips but rolling their faces back and forth one against the other. My wife could hardly speak for a couple of hours afterwards. Later she said that she would never waste her sympathy on that woman again.

It's quiet over there. My wife has gone to sleep and so has my arm, under her head. I slide it out and open and close my fingers, considering whether to wake her up. I like sleeping in my own bed, and there isn't enough room for both her and me. Finally I decide that it won't hurt either of us to change places for one night.

I get up and fuss with the plants for a while, watering them and moving some to the window and some back. I trim the coleus, which is starting to get leggy, and put the cuttings in a glass of water on the sill. All the lights are off next door except the one in their bedroom window. I think about the life they have, and how it goes on and on, until it seems to be the life they were meant to live. Everybody is always saying how great it is that human beings are so adaptable, but I don't know. A friend of mine was in the Navy and he told me that in Amsterdam, Holland, they have a whole section of town where you walk through it and from the street you can see women sitting in rooms. If you want one of them you just go in and pay and they close the drapes. This is nothing special to the people who live in Holland. In Istanbul, Turkey, my friend saw a man walking down the street with a grand piano on his back. Everyone just moved around him and kept going. It's awful, what we get used to.

I turn off the television and get into my wife's bed. A sweet, heavy smell rises off the sheets. At first it makes me dizzy but after that I like it. It reminds me of gardenias.

The reason I don't watch the rest of the movie is that I can already see how it will end. The citizens will kill each other off, probably about ten feet from the legendary city of gold, and the blind man will stumble in by himself, not knowing that he has made it back to El Dorado.

I could write a better movie than that. My movie would be about a group of explorers, men and women, who leave behind their homes and their jobs and their families—everything they have known. They cross the sea and are shipwrecked on the coast of a country which is not on their maps. One of them drowns. Another gets attacked by a wild animal, and eaten. But the others want to push on. They ford rivers and cross an enormous glacier by dog sled. It takes months. On the glacier they run out of food, and for a while there it looks like they might turn on each other, but they don't. Finally they solve their problem by eating the dogs. That's the sad part of the movie.

At the end we see the explorers sleeping in a meadow filled with white flowers. The blossoms are wet with dew and stick to their bodies, petals of columbine, clematis, blazing star, baby's breath, larkspur, iris, rue—covering them completely, turning them white so that you cannot tell one from another, man from woman, woman from man. The sun comes up. They stand and raise their arms, like white trees in a land where no one has ever been.

INFIDELITIES

FLORENCE TREFETHEN

Florence Trefethen works as a book editor at the Council on East Asian Studies, Harvard University. Her column, "The Poet's Workshop," is a bimonthly feature of *The Writer* magazine.

This young woman with whom I am lunching at a French restaurant in Boston has been living for thirteen months with my only son, Giles. They are graduate students at Berkeley. Theirs is, as they say, a relationship. "Is it serious?" I demand of Giles in my stuffier moments. "Yes, serious," he tells me, "but not necessarily permanent." Serious, not permanent; I think we did not have that type of relationship back in West Lafayette.

This tall slim young woman with thick auburn hair controlled by tortoise-shell barrettes, who knows four real languages plus three computer languages, who is always dressed in a pale gray-green like a celadon vase, who cooks vegetables in a wok and plays lacrosse, may become my daughter-in-law; but, then again, may not. It's hard to predict. Like many girls in her generation, she is called Jennifer. There are no Jennifers in my age group, and, so far as I can tell, no Virginias in hers. That's why I insist on being called Gina, a little more youthful and continental, a little less like middle America in the Depression.

Our lunch is turning into a semi-annual event. When Jennifer comes east to Maine to visit her mother, who was widowed at an early age, she phones me and we arrange to meet in a chic, neutral place. We dance around each other carefully, unsure of our ground. Her man, my son, is at Berkeley getting ready for his qualifying exams. My man for thirty years, Christopher Frost, is somewhere between San Diego and Tucson, probably in bed with Faith Briscoe. Jennifer, I ask her silently, how would a woman like you react to that fact? You who have lived intimately with someone since your sophomore year at Radcliffe and are now on your third relationship? How would you react if you had been married more than half your life to the same person, then found him drifting toward Faith Briscoe?

He always drifts back. In fact, he'd been sidling off for three years before I realized it. A researcher in photographic chemicals is often on the road, and who's to know at home what's happening in San Jose, Chicago, or Rochester? The affair was revealed accidentally, unnecessarily. Chris was reading some of the poems I was preparing to send to yet another quarterly. One was called "Ex-Lover Comes to Dinner," a persona poem spoken by a woman whose former lover has animal table manners that now disgust her. Chris assumed that the "I" speaking the poem was I his wife, and went one step further, casting an old family friend who slurps his soup in the role of former lover. "I'm glad to know this," he announced to me. "I've found somebody too."

I guess he was looking for an excuse to tell me. He has a Yankee conscience—not sharp enough to keep him from deceit, just enough to make him need to confess eventually. I was surprised, and angry. We'd been seeing a psychiatrist together, to help us through a mid-marriage crisis. One of Chris's complaints was that I had not updated my sex life as much as he had, that I was rejecting some of the ideas presented in *The Joy of Sex.* "This Alex Comfort," I asked him, "why do you regard him as an authority?" Chris would not discuss it. If I wouldn't assent to Comfort, I must be frigid. "Chris," I said, "I may not know much about sex, but I know a lot about publishing. Although this book is an intentional bestseller, it is not the Old and New Testament combined, so stop giving it so much reverence."

Our psychiatrist, Ferdinand Maurer, seemed intent on helping me loosen up, become more open, more agile, more involved, more ready for change. It disillusioned me to discover he'd known about Faith Briscoe all the time. Why was he telling me to be open (including playing tapes of my voice in arguments with Chris) while he and Chris were concealing this secret: I stopped seeing Ferdinand Maurer. I'm not sure if he committed psychiatric malpractice, but he certainly made a fool of me. You've got a big reputation in Boston, Ferdinand Maurer, and I'm merely a free-lance editor who also writes poetry, so what can I do? But if ever I have a chance to get even with you, I'll take it.

I hate the way that sounds. The worst part of my situation is that it triggers in me emotions I thought belonged to Elizabethan tragedy. There are days when I keep alive only by composing scenes of revenge.

Such as this scene. Chris and I are summoned to Dr. Jason Sears, our internist and good friend. Jason says, "I have something serious to tell you; I hope you'll be brave. You, Chris, have leukemia, or cirrhosis of the liver, or a brain tumor (choose one). I'm sorry this turned up in your last annual check-up, but, after numerous rechecks, I must tell you your days are numbered. You people have some decisions to make. Chris, you can go to Mass General and be well looked after. Or, if you like, you can stay home, provided Gina is willing to nurse you through your final months." Chris wants to stay home. But am I willing to nurse? Not bloody likely! "How about in sickness and health till death us do part?" he begs, trying to make me feel guilty. "That counted while you were still observing your vows," I say forcefully. "It's canceled now. But if you'd like me to invite Faith Briscoe to come for the nursing, I'll oblige." We both know Faith won't sign on.

Or this scene. Chris comes home looking defeated. "Gina," he says, "we're wiped out. Our savings are worthless because of inflation, and the stocks I've bought have all plummeted. We'll have to retrench, sell everything we still own, and take a small house somewhere in, say Arkansas, where the living is easy and the cost is low." "Chris," I respond, "give my regards to Arkansas. As for me, I've been investing my extra money in Krugerrands, and the price of gold is soaring. See you around."

Or this scene. Chris is in Toronto, or Seattle, or Atlanta at a conference. He phones me at midnight. Instead of grabbing the receiver on the first ring because I'm so eager to hear his voice, I deliberately do not answer. He phones again at one A.M. I keep reading *The Spoils of Poynton*, declining to pick up the phone. He calls again at seven A.M. while I'm showering. I let him ring. The hell with it. If he asks, I'll say, "Oh, I guess that was the night I was up at Rockport," or "Sorry I wasn't home; there was a party at Professor Commeau's apartment."

Professor Commeau is one of my fantasy lovers. I have four. They are not exactly fantasies, since each is a real man I'm acquainted with and each has registered some interest in me. I think I would like to go to bed with one of them, or all of them, but I'm nervous. Having been only with Chris these many years and with my sex life rather dated, I lack confidence.

My best prospect for dalliance is Manfred Reutlinger, a dashing character once married to Chris's sister Elsie. Manfred and I have been waltzing together at parties whenever we meet for many years; also flirting and pretending we have a secret attachment. His third wife (a wife one wouldn't mind hurting) is sarcastic, and Manfred often gets fed up with her. I tell myself that if Manfred were to whistle I'd come running. That may be self-delusion. Two years ago he phoned to say he'd be in Boston on October 11th and could we spend the day together? I fell apart. That was the very date I'd organized a picnic at Plymouth for Giles, three of his Yale classmates, and their families. I couldn't disappoint them. I told this later to a feminist therapist. She said this shows I'm not ready for an affair—I devise family-centered excuses.

I also fantasize about Bruce Loring, Giles's godfather. We've known him and his wife Claire (whom I'd never want to hurt) since we were first married. Bruce has become thin, bald, and faded, and very conservative politically. But that old magic I remember from earlier days still tingles me. When last we dined at the Lorings, he pulled me into the cloak room for a passionate kiss. This seems promising, except that he's been doing that periodically since before Giles was born, which probably proves that he's nervous too, just fooling around. He's not ready for a Faith Briscoe kind of relationship.

Even if I had the courage, would I want to make love with a new person? There would be advantages. I'd feel less like a victimized and injured wife, more Chris's equal. But that's a mean motive for going to bed with a nice man like Manfred or Bruce. If I had such an adventure, should I tell Chris? Part of the point is proving I can do it too, so I suppose I should let him discover my affair. On the other hand, it would be delicious to have something that's mine alone, that he didn't know about. There are many difficulties. Jennifer, I wish I could ask your advice. If I posed this problem, would you stare at me as though I had just arrived from a different planet?

It *is* a different planet. I grew up not knowing much about infidelities. In my orbit in West Lafayette, everybody who was married stayed faithful, or at least seemed to. Only my Uncle Conrad strayed—to Indianapolis. He was our family's outcast because of deserting his wife and children to share an apartment with a woman he'd known before his marriage. Nowadays, lots of our friends get divorced, but those who keep together don't seem to be having affairs. Ferdinand Maurer asked me when I was screaming like a banshee (all taped, of course) after discovering Chris's unfaithfulness, "What have other women you've known done in similar circumstances?" "I don't know anybody in similar circumstances," I told him. He gave me a pitying look, as though I wasn't observant. I have lots of women friends to talk to, but if their husbands are wandering they don't mention it to me, perhaps out of shame, out of loyalty, out of injured pride. I can understand that. I don't mention Faith Briscoe to them. These days one confides only in therapists.

Frankly, I'm surprised at Chris's taste in mistresses. To introduce such confusion into a marriage after so many years, the motivation should be more potent than Faith Briscoe. Someone like Lily Tomlin or Elizabeth Drew or Joanne Woodward I could understand. But why would they be interested in Chris? He's handsome, he's intelligent, but not distinctive enough to catch the eye of a celebrity. Besides, he's still having his mid-life crisis in which he questions whether he should ever have gone into photographic chemicals. He thinks he ought to have been a surgeon. Or an architect.

One reason I like Professor Commeau is that he knows exactly what he wants to do and does it thoroughly. He's a historian, Western Europe, especially France in the twelfth century. I was a history major at Smith, which is probably why Professor Commeau keeps hiring me to edit his books. He's like a medieval cleric, dark and brooding, and wears exquisite neckties. We lunch together at the Faculty Club from time to time to discuss a manuscript. His manners are courtly, precise. He holds my coat at just the right height. And he always mentions me enthusiastically in his "Acknowledgments." Twice I've caught him staring at me in a sad and pensive way; his eyes seemed to be trying to transmit an important message. Perhaps he was thinking, "Gina, why do we keep this pretense of author and editor when we want to be lovers?" Is he waiting for me to make a move? What kind of signal should I send? Help, Jennifer! What do I do next?

In the case of my fourth lover, Joe, the obstacles are age and geography. He's only thirty-four, an archaeologist, usually digging in Turkey. He's a murky writer, so I ghostwrite his grant requests, research reports, and papers. His face is suntanned, and he has beautiful crinkles near his eyes and very long lashes. Whenever he comes to Boston, we meet for dinner with much wine. He holds my hand and kisses me hello and goodbye. But he's loaded with worries. His wife is divorcing him and asking for exclusive custody of their three-year-old twins on the argument that Joe is never around. She has a point. "But I can't abandon Justin and Psyche," he lamented when we were together last month. I wanted to say, "Joe, let's check in at the Ritz. Just for tonight, let's be loving friends." Would that have sounded corny, like "Come with me to the Casbah?" What would Joe have answered?

Though psychologically unprepared for an affair, I'm ready otherwise. Over the past two years, I've been buying up lingerie of various types. I now have six new pairs of spandex and lace pants, three new bras, two camisoles, two halfslips, and the most expensive pajamas I've ever owned. I've kept my old housecoat. It's Chinese brocade. Chris bought it for me in San Francisco, whether out of love or guilt I don't know. But it's beautiful. I've chucked out my old makeup case and bought a new one. Have makeup case, will travel—to the Ritz, to the Hyatt-Regency, to the Copley Plaza, just name it, one of you guys, and I'll appear discreetly at your door with the best collection of lingerie you've ever seen.

How do you relate to lingerie, Jennifer? I know one of your nightgowns. I helped Giles buy it. That shows how strange life has become—my son asks his mother to help him buy a nightgown for his girl, who is a serious but not necessarily permanent attachment. I took him to Filene's. It was a new experience for Giles, leafing through those racks of nightgowns, floor-length, knee-length, mini-length, in white, ecru, pink, peach, mint, aqua, powder, buttercup. He looked bemused. Finally we settled on a long white gown with lace around a plunging neckline. My feminist therapist claims Giles was trying to signal me that he now has a woman of his own, that he's no longer my little boy. O.K., Giles, I get the message; got it long ago.

In this family, it is not I with the empty-nest syndrome but Chris. Being a father appealed to him, and he did the job well. When Giles first left for Yale, Chris began to get restless. That's when he started doing all those push-ups in the morning and playing so much tennis. Another wedge between us. My right shoulder hurts when I hit a ball overhand, so I don't play tennis. No problem; there are lots of partners for Chris where we live. But he seems to think this is a flaw in me. "You should keep in shape," he says. God knows, I try. I swim and go for long walks and do stretch exercises. I am size 10. I am eight pounds heavier than when we got married.

I have another flaw. I hate to drive in traffic and will do almost anything to avoid it. When I'm on the road with cars on both sides, in front and in back, I sweat. I feel that a collision is inevitable, as though we were all in bump cars at an amusement park. It's a serious fear, and Chris resents it. "But I'm not afraid of other things," I protest. "I'm not afraid of flying. And I'm not afraid of snakes." Chris is afraid of snakes, but he blames that on racial memory so he doesn't feel responsible. "I'm not afraid of publishing things," I twist the knife once more. Chris has a block against sending papers out to journals and hardly ever does it. But he thinks that's more natural than not liking to drive because his family has always been keen on cars and gets a lot of its kicks and status that way. He has a brother with two Cadillacs, a nephew with a Cadillac and a Jaguar. Chris himself favors a white Mercedes.

Because of my faults and hang-ups, there are times when I think I'd better hang on to Chris because nobody else will ever care for me. Those are the days the black clouds roll in. Why, I ask myself, should Manfred Reutlinger, Bruce Loring, Professor Commeau, or Joe want me? They're attractive men. They can pick and choose, and they'll choose someone younger. Several men we know have divorced their wives and married younger women. One of our neighbors married his daughter's Wellesley roommate. "How can I fight this?" his wife, Myra, asked me. "How can I compete with a twenty-one-year-old kid in a bikini who is also captain of the debating team? If twenty-five years together and three children and a comfortable home won't hold him, I'm sunk, kaput." I wonder whether Myra's husband used to nag her about tennis and *The Joy of Sex*. I also wonder about that Wellesley roommate. Why would she want to marry a man of fifty? Isn't there something peculiar about a young girl like that? I know one such in the History Department at B.U. She's a new assistant professor, and she told our consciousness-raising group that the only way to get tenure these days is to attach yourself firmly and sexually to a source of power. She's chosen her person, and he's almost retirement age. I'm glad Jennifer and Giles are contemporaries. It's more honest, more natural.

It's to Chris's credit that he didn't fall for a juvenile. Faith Briscoe is our age. I assume she's updated her sex, and I know she loves to drive. I think they drive around expansively when Chris is on his business trips. Faith has no job so is free to fly to wherever Chris is. I keep in mind a map of the continental United States with a red pin everywhere they've been together. I know about Sacramento, Carmel, San Diego, Las Vegas, Santa Fe, Tampa, Montauk, and maybe Phoenix. Some of these I know because I pried the information out of Chris. Some I've intuited, like Montauk. Chris didn't phone for four days; I didn't know where he was. Finally he called from Montauk and said he'd had trouble finding a phone. I thought it must be a primitive place, but my friend Betsy, a New Yorker, told me Montauk is up-to-date.

Chris declares his affair is over, but I don't count on it. He said that before, but returned to Faith last summer. We were in California visiting Giles. I had to fly back to Boston to meet a publisher's deadline. Having more time, Chris said he'd drive down the coast and enjoy some scenery, maybe play a little tennis. I found out later he'd arranged to meet Faith in Carmel. Perhaps he'll always be like that.

I guess Faith has the advantage of primogeniture, since Chris knew her first. "Why the hell didn't you marry Faith?" I shouted at him when the affair first came to light. "I was working happily in Washington, marriage nowhere in my mind. Did I ask you to come barging into my life, to make me fall in love with you and move to Boston? Faith was available. Why me?" I think I know why. In those days, Chris had a precise notion of the person he wanted to marry. She had to be bright and well educated, interested in something more than the domestic round, with a sense of humor and lots of energy. I had all that, plus good health and good looks. Faith was also healthy, handsome. But she'd never had much education, and her only jobs have been typing and shorthand drags. She was glad to get married and give up working altogether.

I don't know whether her husband knows about Faith and Chris. Unless he's retarded, he must think something's fishy whenever she disappears to be with Chris. Perhaps she tells him she's visiting her mother or having a facelift. In my revenge fantasies, I sometimes write that husband a letter.

> Dear Mr. Briscoe:
>
> We are not acquainted, but I'm told you are a decent person. That is why you should know that you are being hoodwinked by your wife and her paramour, Christopher

Frost. Don't take my word for it. The next time she goes off on a trip, have her followed. You'll discover the truth whereof I speak.

A wellwisher

Sometimes I devise a different letter.

Dear Emmett Briscoe:

You and I have one hell of a lot in common. Are you aware that our spouses are seeing each other regularly? This has been droning on like a tired old soap opera for many years, and I'm getting sick of it. Would you care to meet and plan a joint strategy for coping with our mutual difficulty?

Gina Frost
known in pre-Liberation days as
Mrs. Christopher Frost

Naturally I send neither letter. If there's one thing I fear more than being ill-used it's making waves. I was raised in times when we were taught to smooth things over for the general benefit. Perhaps that too should be updated.

Fortunately, I still have my sense of humor and see the funny elements in my situation. For example, Chris always asks me to choose his ties when he's going on a trip. That's worse than buying a nightgown for Giles's girl! I'm tempted to make awful choices. Chris is colorblind and wouldn't know if I gave him a bright green tie to wear with a lavender shirt. Would being poorly matched reduce him in the eyes of Faith Briscoe? Who knows? Once when I was helping by unpacking his suitcase on return, I found a copy of *Hustler* under his shorts. It was very updated sexually, also nauseating. Does Faith read *Hustler?* Who knows? Anyway, she has more courage than I about getting in touch with men. I asked Chris how he happened to encounter her again after more than twenty years. He said she'd dropped in at his office and said she just happened to be in town. Tacky, yet it worked. I never drop into offices; not my style. But maybe that's why I'm not this very minute at the Ritz with Manfred or Bruce or Professor Commeau or Joe.

Humor carries you only so far. Some things cut too near the bone for laughter. When my father died suddenly in West

Lafayette three years ago, Chris was away and I couldn't find him. Giles and I tried phoning several places around Santa Fe where we thought he was. No luck. Fortunately, he phoned home and got to the funeral and to the university memorial service for Dad. Just afterward, though, he picked a fight with me, said I wasn't turning to him in my hour of grief and need. Maybe I wasn't. I felt so numb I couldn't communicate with anybody. Chris packed up and went back to Santa Fe, I thought to continue his business. Later it came out that Faith was waiting there in a motel for him to get the last rites over with and get back to her. The infidelity I might forgive, the callousness, even the deceit; but making it all seem like my fault is beyond forgiveness. We may spend the rest of our lives together, Chris, and this bitterness may wear away. Perhaps I'll be able to put on my wedding ring again without having my finger swell up and turn blue. But some things are indelible and will not fade.

The waiter is here with the dessert menu. I have not eaten dessert for many years. Jennifer debates between pastry and chocolate mousse. There is no extra flesh in her future for as far ahead as she can see. Oh, Jennifer, I do not love you yet, though I will, eventually, if you and Giles stay together. But I feel close, remembering how it was to be your age, even on a different planet. I wish we could change places now. I would bask in the freedoms you take for granted, hoping they would erase my uptightness. All loyalties seem uptight these days, but I was programmed for loyalty. Serious but not permanent may now be the only way to go. I want to learn how to have courage for that much uncertainty. I would love it, Jennifer. And I would order the chocolate mousse.

THE GREATEST SLUMP OF ALL TIME

DAVID CARKEET

David Carkeet was born and raised in Sonora, California. His short stories have appeared in *Kansas Quarterly* and *The North American Review*. He is the author of *Double Negative*, a comic mystery novel and Edgar nominee (Dial, 1980; Penguin paperback, 1982).

"Apples" Bagwell loses it in the late innings. His shoulders slump, his curve hangs, and his fastball yawns. Into the seventh or eighth he is great, almost perfect. But then he loses it, and it always takes Grammock a few more baserunners than it should to come out from the dugout and mumble around the mound and finally signal to the bullpen. Apples comes off the field looking like a puppy about to be whipped and sighs into the dugout. He just fills that dugout with his sigh.

People talk about it. He gets tired, some say. He has a fear of losing, say others, remembering his early years in the bigs. Some believe he becomes overconfident and lets up. The profile is baffling. Late innings. A lead. A stunning performance through six or seven frames.

E.T.A. Whitaker, a bespectacled first baseman with a good mind and a social worker for a wife, finally figures it out. He takes Apples to breakfast, choosing a secluded booth at the rear of the hotel coffee shop.

"Tough game last night," E.T.A. says to Apples as he gives his menu to the waitress. "For you, I mean." Apples lost his stuff in the seventh, but Butch came in and saved the game. The team is only three games out now, with a month of the regular season left.

"Yeah," says Apples.

"Grammock shoulda left you in, Apples," says the waitress, who is buxom and toothy. "He shoulda let you work it out. You're the best."

Apples shrugs and a pitiful look, one familiar to E.T.A. of late, crosses his face.

"She likes you, you know," says E.T.A., testing his theory after the waitress has gone.

Apples looks down at the table. His lids are heavy, his cheeks pale and lifeless. "Let Jaime have her," he says without feeling. Jaime is their right fielder. He has an unquenchable lust for women and an active English vocabulary of sixty-five words.

"He has," says E.T.A. "She told him she wants you."

Apples sighs and sinks deeper into gloom.

E.T.A. knows that the way out and the way in are one and the same. "The writers are talking about you for the Cy Young Award this year, Apples."

"Great," says Apples. His face doesn't say "great." Someone watching from across the room would think he was recalling famous airline disasters.

"We're all really happy for you," says E.T.A. "The whole team." Then, twisting the knife, "We all love you, Apples. Deeply. We really do."

It works. Apples begins to sob. His face turns into a contorted mass of red flesh under his hands. The waitress, who has brought his pineapple pancakes, sees what is happening and thinks he is upset about last night's game. She crawls into the next booth and leans over him from behind and begins to knead his shoulders like a trainer, whispering comforting words into his ear.

E.T.A. watches with pity which, he begins to notice with concern, is mixed with self-pity.

"Success depresses him," E.T.A. says to shortstop Scrappy Hawthorn as they walk back to the third-base line after a warm-up run. "Give him praise and he crumbles. On the mound he sees a victory coming and he folds. He's afraid of winning."

"That don't make no sense," says Scrappy. Unlike E.T.A., who is a modern athlete in every sense and an interviewer's delight, Scrappy talks like a Coolidge-era ballplayer.

"I didn't think so at first either," says E.T.A. "But then I saw that if you think you're inferior, being good at things will only make you feel like more of a bum."

Scrappy frowns and turns to him. "Apples feels like a bum?"

E.T.A. nods. They have reached the baseline and turn to run the twelve paces again, gliding easily with synchronized strides. As they slow and turn to walk back, E.T.A. says, "Maybe deep down we all think we're bums. After all, you know yourself better than anyone else does. You know how stupid and cruel you can be. Heap success on top of that and you've got a real formula for the blues." He pats Scrappy on the fanny and they turn and run once more. E.T.A. slows to a stop and turns, but Scrappy continues running in a wide arc and jogs back to the dugout alone.

E.T.A., temporarily relieved by their talk, plays well that day. Scrappy goes oh-for-five. In the field *twice* he trips over second base as he tries to make unassisted double plays, and *twice* his throw sails wide of E.T.A.'s desperate reach. The second throw is much more cautious, and much worse, than the first. Then, in the ninth, he instinctively dives to his right to make an impossible game-ending catch of a line drive, his body stretched out straight as a javelin. The cheers rain down on him in the clubhouse. That night he has trouble falling asleep. He wakes before dawn and stares at the ceiling until it is time for breakfast, when he must go into society and be congratulated again.

The next day Scrappy shares his inarticulate thoughts with Bubba Phelps, the second baseman. Bubba laughs without sympathy and apparently without understanding, and then commits a judgment error in the field and later is picked off first base—a base given to him not on the merits of a hit, but because he was too slow, too torpid, too sodden with thought, to move out of the way of a high, inside pitch that grazed him on the arm. All day, and then at night, he sees that pitch again and again, only it is higher, heading for his face, and he is even slower to get out of its way.

To ease his mind, Bubba raps with Eddie Johnson, the swift

center fielder. Eddie gives him wisdom and comfort. Later, when the team's flight is delayed by a mechanical problem, Eddie smashes two metal chairs in the airport lounge in a fit of impatience. He unburdens himself to his teammates in the outfield, Buford Ellenbogen and Jaime, and from Buford the word travels back into the infield to the fast-talking third baseman, Frank Joiner; Frank gives it to Narvel Adams, the catcher, and in no time at all Narvel is matching batterymate Apples sigh for sigh.

As the days wear on and the players collectively bring the team into first place, their symptoms diversify and specialize. Apples, of course, is the chief mumbler and moper. He has polished his flatness of affect beyond improvement. Between innings of work Grammock, a former pitching coach, criticizes and corrects him, telling him to bear down, goddammit, and push off the be-Jesus mound. He listens and feels each word adding measurable weight to his body. When he returns to the mound his motion is even more ponderous than before.

Frank is different. He plays well and looks normal, but his mind is full of spiders. He thinks people are talking about him. On the road he lurks just inside the door of his hotel room, listening to his teammates going down to breakfast, wondering why they haven't asked him to join them. He hears words that could be about him—words like "am" and "my"—and he aches for acceptance.

Narvel sighs a lot. This makes him light-headed and dizzy. Though only twenty-four, he concludes that his body is deteriorating. Two years, maybe three, and he will announce his retirement.

Bubba fears someone is going to break into his apartment on a dark night while he is in bed. The intruder will of course steal from him, but he will also abuse him with words. Bubba feels that the man will have every right to do this.

Eddie compares himself with others and comes out sub-human. The way Scrappy runs the bases, the way Jaime goes back on the long ball—he can't match them. He doesn't belong in the majors. Every day he is ashamed to see his name still on his locker.

Scrappy can't sleep. He awakens at 4:00 every morning as if

called by God. He lies awake and stares, then lurches in bed as if having sex with the air. Then he stares some more. His afternoon naps debilitate him further. The sleep he loses at night is unrecoverable.

Buford, once featured in the hometown newspaper for the way he ate four entrees in succession at a Denny's, has lost his appetite.

E.T.A. maintains that the world has gone to hell in a cardboard suitcase. His favorite word is "point," especially when it occurs with "no" or "what's the."

Jaime, newly impotent, is exploring suicide.

Narvel calls home. His mother answers and calls with elderly enthusiasm to his father, who picks up the phone in the Rathskeller.

"Narvel! How are you, boy?"

"Fine, Dad."

"Say, you guys are lookin' good. I mean good. A steady climb into first, tough resolve in the face of challenge, a widening lead in the division . . . I like the looks of it. I like it a lot. I like the whole pattern of the season. Another week of the same and I'd say you're uncatchable. I'd definitely say you're uncatchable. Of course I'm assuming lively run production from Eddie and a little more pizzazz in your starters, especially Apples. Nice play last night on that bad throw, by the way. You saved a run and kept the D.P. in order."

Narvel blinks heavily. His father is retired and lives for the game. This once gave Narvel pleasure.

"How are you?" asks Narvel. He knows his conversation is lifeless. He never could talk—not well, anyway.

"Us?" his father says loudly. "Fine, fine. Not bad for old folks. Your mom's back is giving her some trouble."

"I'm sorry—"

"It's nothing," says his mother. "Narvel, do you remember Mrs. Webster?"

"No."

"The Sunday School teacher?"

"No, I don't."

"He was too young, Ruth," says his father.

"She passed away," says his mother, ending the tale.

"Hunh," says Narvel. There is a long silence after this. Then he says, "Mom, Dad, do you remember an old diary I kept when I was little?"

"No," says his father.

"Of course," says his mother. "It's in the trunk in the attic." Her voice is chipper and sing-songy.

"Can you send it to me?"

"Of course."

"Gettin' sentimental, boy?" says his father suspiciously. "Seems to me you ought to be thinkin' of the future, not the past. Like tomorrow's doubleheader. Those guys will eat you for lunch if you let 'em."

"Yes, sir," he says, feeling reprimanded. His throat tightens and his voice thins out. "It's just that a bunch of us were talking about our childhoods and all, and I got wondering about mine and if it was, well, you know, what it was like and all, and I thought maybe the diary would help, because lately—"

"Of course, dear. I'll put it in the mail right away."

Narvel sighs in misery. His mother, as always, cooperates without understanding.

"The future is for the living, Narvel," his father says. "You guys have been lookin' pretty drab for a front-runner."

"Maybe it's our TV, Ralph. Ever since they built that high-rise—"

"I know a drab team when I see one," his father insists. "Do you hear me, Narvel? Talk to me."

"Yes, sir," he says, sighing again. His father understands but gives no support. Narvel suddenly sees himself as a soldier wounded in battle; his parents try to help him back to safety, but they arrive with a corpse mangled from mishandling.

Eddie plays with his daughter, Tina, and listens to his wife on the telephone. She is talking to Bubba's wife, making plans for the World Series. The playoffs start tomorrow and already she is planning for the Series. His resentment is like a cloak that warms him and darkens his life. He pulls it around himself tighter and tighter. She has come to expect satisfaction. She is never surprised when they win. She will never see his achievement for what it is —not just a well-paying job, but a glorious, precarious moment of trembling balance. An injury or a brief slump turning into a long one because he gives it too much thought—either of these could close it out and turn him into a regular guy with nothing more than a year or two of interesting history becoming less interesting as the years go by. And a bitch for a wife, because all baseball is to her is lots of money and a chance to shop in New York during the Series. She who has never touched a baseball in her life, who sits with the other wives and cheers in ignorance. She still doesn't know what a hit is. If he flies out four times in a game she will say he got four hits. She cannot know how good he is. Neither can Tina, because she is so young. And when she is older? He imagines her future, a product of his wife's unassisted bungling because he is on the road so much: knocked up with nine kids and no man; or maybe a good Christian who prays her bruises away while her man drinks and beats up on her; or maybe a radical feminist who uses her dead father in her speeches as an example of persistent racism in the U.S. because in spite of his brains there was no room for him in baseball management after it came to an end for him in his third year because of an injury or a slump that he gave too much thought to.

A conference on the mound. It is a key game—the fourth game of the playoffs. After taking the first two from Chicago they have dropped one and fear dropping this one. Chicago would have the momentum then and would be strong for the fifth game. They are at home, up by one, in the top of the ninth. After a disputed call on a dive by Eddie for a ball hit behind second (ruled an out), Apples has hit a batsman (who stole second on the next pitch), intentionally walked a batter, and given up an infield single—a ludicrously topped ball that dribbled nowhere in particular and advanced everybody. The bases are loaded. Apples is down, but no more than usual.

Narvel shuffles out to him. Apples welcomes the rebuke implied by his approach. The infield moves to the mound. Narvel looks at their faces and sees ghosts.

"What are we gonna do?" asks Apples.

They all look down at their feet and kick at the dirt on the mound.

"I dunno, man," says Bubba. "Don't let him hit to me. I'm blue."

"And I'm tired," says sleepless Scrappy. "Make him pull it."

They all look up at the batter to see if he is right- or left-handed. They should know this already without having to look, but they don't concentrate. He is a switch hitter, and he will bat left-handed against Apples. If he pulls the ball sharply it will go to E.T.A. at first. They turn to him and he shrugs.

"Sure," he says indifferently. "I can handle it. And if I don't?" He flashes a macabre grin and his eyeglasses twinkle in the sunlight. "What does it matter? Everyone here'll be dead someday." He sweeps his eyes over the field and then up to the stands filled with hopeful supporters. His teammates follow his eyes and suddenly find themselves surrounded by sixty thousand skeletons.

"There are people dyin' every day," Narvel says thoughtfully. "People you don't even know."

"Whatever happens," says Apples—and a quiet urgency in his voice draws their close attention—"I want you guys to know I've really appreciated your support this year."

This is received glumly by all but E.T.A. He laughs loudly. "Jesus, Apples, what do you do when you're thirsty—drink ashes?" The infield begins to chuckle grimly and a dark figure approaches. Narvel sees him out of the corner of his eye and fancies it is the Grim Reaper, but it is only the home-plate ump. He tells them to stop clowning around and play ball. Meekly, guiltily, they obey.

Two things happen that decide it. First, Apples forgets there is already one out—the disputed call and subsequent hit batsman have blurred in his mind into just one hitter—so he pitches with no expectation of victory. With the bases loaded and nobody out, he thinks, Chicago is bound to take it away from them. Then after the loss tomorrow he can stay home in bed for five months.

He puts the ball right where he should.

Second, E.T.A. gets mad. As he crouches with Apples' pitch

and watches the switch hitter he is reminded of a minor league coach who tried to make *him* into a switch hitter, ruining his average for a full year and slowing his rise to the major leagues. He complained about it frequently and got a bad rap as a troublemaker. When the coach got reassigned somewhere E.T.A. resumed his left-handed hitting and left the farm the next season. For the misery he caused him with his ignorance, that coach nearly destroyed his career.

In rage E.T.A. whirls and guns the ball to second even before he knows he has fielded it cleanly, and in the same motion he is on his way back to first to cover, because he knows Apples won't make it, and he takes Scrappy's low return throw out of the dirt to his right, stretching his leg as if convinced that to tear something in it is to tear that coach's heart out, and the ump's call and the cheers from the stands send him and his team to the Series.

It has been asked if it is possible for a team to win the big one without a big stick, or with a bullpen that is weak, or with rookies at the corners. A related question that has not been asked is if it is possible for a team to win the big one with an outfield on Elavil.

"Poppin' pills again?" asks Grammock as he walks through the clubhouse and sees Buford and Eddie comparing prescriptions. Eddie protests that it is legal—they're not uppers, he says, they're anti-downers. Grammock shakes his head in silence and stalks off to his office, feeling that he just doesn't understand his boys anymore. He has tried his bench, hoping that platooning his regulars would get them out of the doldrums, but as soon as his bench performs well they go logy on him too. So he sticks with his starters. If he's going to put nine zombies on the field he wants it to be his best nine.

Scrappy, who is in sit-down psychotherapy, challenges Eddie's treatment. He says that the outfielders will never truly know themselves if they rely solely on drugs.

"'Know thyself,' said Abe Lincoln," Scrappy informs him. "He knew hisself, you can bet."

"Like you?" Eddie asks mockingly.

"I'm workin' on it," Scrappy says with a tentativeness bordering on total capitulation. "It takes time."

"Yeah? How much time?"

Scrappy's eyes shift nervously. "A year, maybe. Maybe longer."

Eddie laughs loudly.

"I . . . I got a lotta issues to work through," says Scrappy.

"Issues?" says Eddie. "Issues of what—the *Sporting News?* What kind of word is that, you dirtbrain?" His words surprise everyone. Though big, black, and witty, Eddie has never been the club razzer. That was always Narvel's role, at least before he forgot how to talk.

Scrappy's face collapses and he begins to whine his arguments out. He says that drugs just cover up the sickness. Eddie says that if the sickness is bad only because of the symptoms, and if drugs take away the symptoms, then it's a harmless disease. It's as harmless, he says, as being allergic to moon dust: it makes no difference if you never go there.

Frank has been oiling his glove nervously and listening. He speaks up in a speedy, jerky way that is like his lateral movement at third base. "Scrappy's right. He's just got the wrong kind of therapy. What is your guy—an analyst?"

"I dunno," says Scrappy.

"How often do you go?"

"Once a week."

Frank purses his lips. "Maybe not, then."

"But he wants me to come three or four times a week."

"Ah. Does he ever talk about the here-and-now?"

Scrappy looks deeply uncertain.

"You know—what's going on in your life today," Frank explains.

"Nah. He's more, I dunno, innerested in pre-school I guess."

"Yeah," Frank says knowingly. "You got the wrong persuasion, Scrappy. You should get into cognitive therapy."

"What's that?" asks E.T.A., who has joined the group.

"It's clean and simple," says Frank. "People get depressed because they have bad thoughts about themselves. Cognitive therapy helps the patient see that these thoughts are distortions of reality. Like if Jaime here thought he was a for-shit ballplayer, if I was his therapist I'd remind him of his record for doubles last year and the catch he made on Frawley's ball last week. Stuff like that." Jaime smiles, happy to be discussed this way.

"And it works?" asks Eddie, his eyebrows dancing. He looks right at Frank, into the soul of his depression.

"Well, it's *working*," says Frank.

Eddie snorts. "And what if the bad thoughts are true? Like Jaime's batting average is way down this year, and he lost us the third game of the playoffs on that pansy throw. What does a therapist do when there's evidence that the patient is a washout?" Jaime has stopped smiling.

Frank is not prepared for this argument. "Maybe he kind of puts things in perspective," he says tentatively, gesturing broadly with his hands—hands that have been called "soft" for the way they absorb ground balls.

Eddie snorts again. "If you're throwing away money on a shrink like that you better hope we win the Series. And you better help us, like by improving your bunting, for God's sake. It stinks. Did your guy tell you that?"

"I'm just trying to get better," Frank says weakly. He is not talking about his bunting.

E.T.A. has observed this dialogue closely. Eddie's anger surprises him. He remembers his own flash of hatred for his old coach in the last game of the playoffs. He looks at Apples, Narvel, and the others. Their self-hatred is suddenly as obvious to him as it would be if they were systematically mutilating their bodies with their cleats.

"Listen up, guys," he calls out with a hint of his old hopefulness. Heads turn. The faces are pale and listless, but they are interested. He speaks. His theory is simple: depression, he says, is hatred of others turned inward. It is anger unreasonable only in its direction. "We're like a little boy whose parents have yelled at him so he kicks his dog," he says, his hand darting nervously up to adjust his glasses. "Only we're the dog. We're kicking ourselves."

Buford asks him how he gets from anger to depression. They seem to him to be different emotions.

E.T.A., suddenly losing all faith in his position, says he doesn't know. Maybe it makes no sense, he admits, and maybe no one is mad at anybody he can think of, at least not right now, but all he is asking is that they give it some thought, not necessarily right now, but—

"I hate my wife," Eddie announces matter-of-factly. He looks at Scrappy, Jaime, and Frank. He has hurt them too, he sees, along with himself. His eyes moist, he says to each of them, "Hey, man . . . hey, man . . ."

"It's okay," Scrappy says softly.

"I hate *someone*," says Narvel, banging his fist into his palm. "I know I do. I can feel it." His words are followed by a long silence. It is the first time he has spoken in two days.

"When I was a kid," Bubba says suddenly, "this other kid who was older and a lot bigger than me used to wait for me and beat me up on my way to school. He had a whip, too, and sometimes he used that. He waited for me every day."

"I was an Army kid," says Frank, "and we moved around a lot, so I was switching schools all the time. It seemed like I'd never studied what the other kids had, so I was always behind. Couldn't draw or sing, either. The teachers always found me handy as a negative example, and they would talk about me all the time in front of the other kids." He pauses, then says with a dreamy smile, "I hate a whole shitload of people."

The players form a tighter circle and continue to talk. Grammock steps out of his office and opens his mouth to ask Narvel something about the New York line-up. The words don't come out. He squints at his team—all hunched up together and muttering, as isolated and freaky as those goddamned Christian athletes in Bible study.

They win the first, third, and fifth games of the Series on skill, instinct, and constructive anger. They lose the second, fourth, and sixth games in the fog of depressive relapses. The pattern has not gone unnoticed, and the sportswriters, ignorant of the pathology, pursue a mathematical whimsy and predict victory for them in game seven. The players themselves do not know what to expect, or what to hope for. For a baseball team sickened by success, winning the World Series is definitely contraindicated. They wonder if, during the game, they will sabotage victory if they see it coming. But then perhaps a win is just the thing they need. How nice, how *insuring,* to have reached the absolute top. Good material for a cognitive therapist, that. And they are getting madder every day. Old angers grow stronger—Eddie, for example, is divorcing his wife and seeking custody of Tina—and new angers erupt: Jaime has decided that he hates women, and the nervousness his discovery arouses in the clubhouse is offset by the team thrill in the knowledge that the entire outfield, in spite of their medication, is now mad as hell.

Apples and Narvel are the only ones left to make progress. They have been slow, as E.T.A. puts it, "to get in touch with their anger." But even this changes for the good in the eleventh hour, at least for Apples. During a live radio interview in the dugout just before the seventh game, the normally placid pitcher flushes with sudden annoyance at a prying question, and as he looks back at the badly dressed broadcaster who has been tailing them all season, he recalls that it was this same man who once described him as "a tall, skinny, loosey-goosey kind of pitcher," and while Apples knows that this describes his motion perfectly, he resents the implication of awkwardness and ugliness. After all, that waitress back at the hotel wanted him, didn't she? He suddenly feels that the press has never dealt with him fairly, always suggesting that because he doesn't look like a pitcher he probably isn't. He responds to the question, not even remembering what it is, with a flurry of obscenity that leaves the broadcaster speechless. The interview is carried over the radio speakers in the clubhouse, and those players still there tying their shoelaces or looking at themselves with ambivalence in the mirror hear the words in astonishment and send out a cheer for their hurler.

As for Narvel, it is obvious from the way he returns Apples' fiery warm-up throws that he's still being blue. The team sees it. E.T.A., chewing on the bitterness of his minor league experience, knows the joy of rage, and he wants Narvel to know it too, so when the game starts he directs his encouraging chatter away from Apples to the catcher, saying, "C'mon babe, c'mon Narvel babe, get mad, babe, c'mon," and Scrappy, who has been watering with tears an ancient anger toward the incompetent and belittling grandmother who reared him, yells, "Work on it, Narvel, work on it," and Frank at third interrupts a steady stream of soft curses at a grade school teacher who said his painted trees in art class looked like apple cores to shout, "Who do ya hate, Narv, who do ya hate?"

Narvel accepts the encouragement gratefully. The game seems to proceed almost without him. He drops a few balls (but nobody's hurt), he gives some bad signs (but Apples just shakes them off), and he makes a bad throw on an attempted steal (but it's backed up by swift, dry-mouthed Eddie, who charges in from center and throws the runner out as he tries to advance to third). The game remains scoreless, the only threat coming from long balls hit to the wall in fury by Eddie, Frank, and E.T.A. New York has barely touched the ball because Apples is hot, giving up just two hits, bloop singles, into the bottom of the seventh. His cheeks are flaming red, and he gets hotter as he moves through his fateful innings. He imagines he is pitching over and over to the radio broadcaster, and he rejoices in his enemy's repeated failures at bat.

In the top of the ninth, back-to-back doubles by Bubba and Jaime give them a one-run lead. Both hits are line drives to the wall on the fly—clotheslines, ropes. It happens so quickly that they are ahead before they have time to think about it. A relief pitcher enters the game for New York, and while he takes his warm-up throws each of the next three batters waits and watches, alone with his thoughts. It *is* the top of the ninth, after all, and the more runs they score the more likely they are to win. When play resumes, Eddie and Scrappy promptly strike out. E.T.A. fares even more poorly. Remembering his minor league coach and wishing to prove himself once and for all, he bats right-handed for the first time in eight years. He ignores Grammock's baffled shouts from the dugout, and after two swinging strikes he makes contact but is called out for several of the most ignominious reasons in the rule book. His weak undercut sends the ball straight up, spinning madly but rising no more than five feet. As it drops back down it strikes his bat as it swings around in an awkward follow-through. The ball squirts down the first-base line, where it is struck again by his bat—which has slipped out of his unaccustomed right-handed grip—and then kicked by his foot as he stumbles out of the batter's box. The ump says he is out; the opposing catcher adds, "And then some." E.T.A. takes his position in the field, gloating with a strange sense of revenge.

In the bottom of the ninth Apples retires the first batter on a pop-up to Frank that Narvel should have taken, but Frank and E.T.A. have agreed to cover for Narvel because of his deep funk. The second batter hits a ball sharply down the line at third that rolls around in the left-field corner. Buford, hungry and constipated, seems to take a day or two to come up with it, and he just barely holds him to a triple. The hometown crowd goes wild: the tying run is at third. Apples, expecting to lose now, whiffs the next batter on three pitches, and the visiting fans thunder with anticipation of the final, Series-winning out. Apples, expecting to win, walks the next batter on four pitches. He studies the runner's lead at first and remembers how the press has always criticized his pick-off move. He fires the ball to E.T.A. and the runner is safe by a wide margin. He goes into his stretch and fires again, making it a little closer. He hears Grammock yell something from the dugout but ignores it. His third throw to E.T.A. is wide and E.T.A. must come off the bag to take it. The tying run at third dances down the line, itching to get home. Grammock is joined in his yelling by some fans behind the dugout. They shout, "Get the batter, Apples! Get the last out!" Unhappy with his last throw, Apples tries again and is pleased with the improvement. Yes, this is definitely a part of the game he needs to work on. No time like the present. He tries a slightly different motion and E.T.A. blocks the ball with his chest as it bounces up out of the dirt.

Grammock jumps from the dugout and a voice from the stands yells, "Tell the moron to forget about the runner and work on the batter, Grammock." The voice is familiar to Apples—it is a friend or relative of one of the players—and he smiles toward it and toward the approaching Grammock with blank indifference. Grammock chastises him further, waving violently to the rest of the infield to stay back from the mound.

Apples sighs despondently and agrees to abandon his cause.

After getting the sign from Narvel, he delivers a lackluster pitch that is outside by a foot, and Narvel surprises everyone by coming up quickly from behind the plate to try to pick the runner off at first. He too, it seems, has become caught up in Apples' obsession. But the ball doesn't go to E.T.A. at all. Instead it screams over the dugout toward the fans in the stands, and there is a shout and a *pwang!* as it flies into the tin crate of a beer vendor, knocking him backwards into a row of spectators. One voice rises above the others. It is Narvel's father, yelling, "What the hell are you doin', boy?" Beside him, Narvel's mother wipes spilled beer from her lap and softly weeps.

The runner at first advances to second on the throw. The runner at third comes home, tying the score, and he says something unkind and jeering to Narvel. Narvel does not hear him. His mind is numb. His body tingles with satisfaction.

The winning run at second is represented by a rookie—a pinch runner who nervously stands on one leg and grabs the ankle of the other, stretching his quadriceps. He chatters excitedly, and he reminds Bubba of the taunting teenage boy who always beat him up on his way to school. When Apples, inspired by the team's declining fortune, gets the next batter to hit a ground ball to Bubba for an easy play at first which will send the game into extra innings, Bubba guns the ball across the diamond to Frank at third in hopes of erasing the skinny bully once and for all. Though surprised, Frank takes the throw well—for he is good, his hands are soft, his cognitive therapist says so—and comes within inches of tagging the sliding runner. In the cloud of dust the call can go either way. Because Bubba's play was so stupid in the first place, the ump spreads his hands out wide and sticks his fanny up and yells, "He's there!"

The infield, agitated and without direction, draws together on the mound. E.T.A. says, "Well, the run that will beat us is at third."

"Yeah," says Frank. "We put him there too."

"You're a sport for sayin' 'we,' Frank," says Bubba. "It was my fault all the way."

"I put him on base to begin with," says Apples.

"And I got him to second," says Narvel.

E.T.A grins. "A team effort. That's what we'll say to the press afterward. Better yet, we'll let Apples tell them." They all chortle, producing a cacaphonous death rattle that reaches the fans in the first few rows and chills their hearts. "It's funny," continues E.T.A., "you'd think depressed people wouldn't want to be around other depressed people, but we seem to get along all right. I think it's even been good for team spirit."

"You didn't start this on purpose, did you, E.T.A.?" asks Bubba. "Jis' to bring us together? You wouldn't do that, would you, man?"

"He couldn't have," says Apples. "He didn't start it. *I* did."

"But he put it into words," says Bubba. "He made it contagious."

"Nobody started it," Frank says firmly. "It just happened. We were all ripe. Maybe everybody's ripe."

Scrappy nods slowly. "Ain't it a bitch the way it takes hold of you? And it's never over, is it? Even when you think you're gettin' better."

"It's never over until it's over," says Narvel.

As the infield pauses to ponder this, the ump steps out and rudely orders them to break it up. As he turns his back he receives a blistering chorus of illegal epithets. Their anger is like a pitching machine gone wild, spraying the ball park with vengeful sallies. The ump flinches but keeps walking to the plate. He should eject them all, but he lets it pass. His judgment has been dulled by nine innings of Narvel's sighing listlessness at his feet.

In mutual consolation for their season in hell together, and to warm one another for the long, cold off-season ahead of them, the infield forms a hugging circle and squeezes hard. With a moaning cheer they break the circle and return to their positions. Apples bends down and picks up the rosin bag. He wants to give this one some thought, and the rule book says that with a man on base a pitcher may take as long as he likes.

Meanwhile, at third, Frank and the rookie pinch runner chat, as opposing players will do, even under the most tense of circumstances. The rookie, grown cocky with his progress to third base and his instant national importance, asks Frank why his club is so weird. Apples' delay behind the mound gives Frank ample opportunity to speak about the suffering of his team. He describes the symptoms and possible origins of clinical depression, stressing his team's particular nemesis: the psychic perils of success. Frank understands the problem well and speaks about it intelligently. The upshot of their discussion is that when Apples finally goes into his stretch and looks at the rookie at third and sighs so heavily that he balks, thus automatically scoring the runner (who must trot home and touch the plate to end the game—a formality, but a necessary formality), the rookie freezes in uncertainty at third base.

GREYHOUND PEOPLE

ALICE ADAMS

Alice Adams grew up in Chapel Hill, North Carolina, and graduated from Radcliffe; since then she has lived mostly in San Francisco. Her fourth novel, *Rich Rewards*, was published by Knopf in 1980, and a new collection of short stories, *To See You Again*, was published in the spring of 1982.

As soon as I got on the bus, in the Greyhound station, in Sacramento, I had a frightened sense of being in the wrong place. I had asked several people in the line at Gate 6 if this was the express to San Francisco, and they all said yes, but later, reviewing those assenting faces, I saw that in truth they all wore a look of people answering a question they have not entirely understood. Because of my anxiety and fear, I took a seat at the very front of the bus, across from and slightly behind the driver. There nothing very bad could happen to me, I thought.

What did happen, immediately, was that a tall black man, with a big mustache, angry and very handsome, stepped up into the bus and looked at me and said, "That's my seat. You in my seat. I got to have that seat." He was staring me straight in the eye, his flashing black into my scared pale blue.

There was nothing of his on the seat, no way I could have known that it belonged to him, and so that is what I said: "I didn't know it was your seat." But even as I was saying that, muttering, having ceased to meet his eye, I was also getting up and moving backward, to a seat two rows behind him.

Seated, apprehensively watching as the bus filled up, I saw that across the aisle from the black man were two women who seemed to be friends of his. No longer angry, he was sitting in the aisle seat so as to be near them; they were all talking and having a good time, glad to be together.

No one sat beside me, probably because I had put my large briefcase in that seat; it is stiff and forbidding-looking.

I thought again that I must be on the wrong bus, but just as I had that thought the driver got on, a big black man; he looked down the aisle for a second and then swung the door shut. He started up the engine as I wondered, What about tickets? Will they be collected in San Francisco? I had something called a commuter ticket, a book of ten coupons, and that morning, leaving San Francisco, I'd thought the driver took too much of my ticket, two coupons; maybe this was some mysterious repayment? We lurched out of the station and were on our way to San Francisco —or wherever.

Behind me, a child began to shout loud but not quite coherent questions: "Mom is that a river we're crossing? Mom do you see that tree? Mom is this a bus we're riding on?" He was making so much noise and his questions were all so crazy—senseless, really—that I did not see how I could stand it, all the hour and forty minutes to San Francisco, assuming that I was on the right bus, the express.

One of the women in the front seat, the friends of the man who had displaced me, also seemed unable to stand the child, and she began to shout back at him. "You the noisiest traveler I ever heard, in fact you ain't a traveler, you an observer."

"Mom does she mean me? Mom who is that?"

"Yeah I means you. You the one that's talking."

"Mom who is that lady?" The child sounded more and more excited, and the black woman angrier. It was a terrible dialogue to hear.

And then I saw a very large white woman struggling up the aisle of the bus, toward the black women in the front, whom she at last reached and addressed: "Listen, my son's retarded and that's how he tests reality, asking questions. You mustn't make fun of him like that." She turned and headed back toward her seat, to her noisy retarded son.

The black women muttered to each other, and the boy began to renew his questions. "Mom see that cow?"

And then I heard one of the black women say, very loudly, having the last word: "And I got a daughter wears a hearing aid."

I smiled to myself, although I suppose it wasn't funny, but something about the black defiant voice was so appealing. And, as I dared for a moment to look around the bus, I saw that most of the passengers were black: a puzzle.

The scenery, on which I tried to concentrate, was very beautiful: smooth blond hills, gently rising, and here and there crevasses of shadow; and sometimes a valley with a bright white farmhouse, white fences, green space. And everywhere the dark shapes of live oaks, a black drift of lace against the hills or darkly clustered in the valleys, near the farms.

All this was on our left, the east, as we headed south toward San Francisco (I hoped). To our right, westward, the view was even more glorious: flat green pasturelands stretching out to the glittering bay, bright gold water and blue fingers of land, in the late May afternoon sunshine.

The retarded boy seemed to have taken up a friendly conversation with some people across the aisle from him, although his voice was still very loud. "My grandfather lives in Vallejo," he was saying. "Mom is that the sun over there?"

Just then, the bus turned right, turned off the freeway, and the driver announced, "We're just coming into Vallejo, folks. Next stop is Oakland, and then San Francisco."

I was on the wrong bus. Not on the express. Although this bus, thank God, did go on to San Francisco. But it would be at least half an hour late getting in. My heart sank, as I thought, Oh, how angry Hortense will be.

The bus swung through what must have been the back streets of Vallejo. (A question: Why are bus stations always in the worst parts of town, or is it that those worst parts grow up around the station?) As our bus ground to a halt, pushed into its slot in a line of other Greyhounds, before anyone else had moved, one of the women in the front seat stood up; she was thin, sharply angular, in a purple dress. She looked wonderful, I thought. "And you, you just shut up!" she said to the boy in the back.

That was her exit line; she flounced off the bus ahead of everyone else, soon followed by her friend and the handsome man who had dislodged me from my seat.

A few people applauded. I did not, although I would have liked to, really.

This was my situation: I was working in San Francisco as a statistician in a government office having to do with unemployment, and that office assigned me to an office in Sacramento for ten weeks. There was very little difference between the offices; they were interchangeable, even to the pale-green coloring of the walls. But that is why I was commuting back and forth to Sacramento.

I was living with Hortense (temporarily, I hoped, although of course it was nice of her to take me in) because my husband had just divorced me and he wanted our apartment—or he wanted it more than I did, and I am not good at arguing.

Hortense is older than I am, with grown-up children, now gone. She seems to like to cook and take care; and when I started commuting she told me she'd meet me at the bus station every night, because she worried about the neighborhood, Seventh Street near Market, where the bus station is. I suppose some people must have assumed that we were a lesbian couple, even that I had left my husband for Hortense, but that was not true; my husband left me for a beautiful young Japanese nurse (he is in advertising), and it was not sex or love that kept me and Hortense together but sheer dependency (mine).

A lot of people got off the bus at Vallejo, including the pale fat lady and her poor son; as they passed me I saw that he was clinging closely to his mother, and that the way he held his neck was odd, not right. I felt bad that in a way I had sided against him, with the fierce black lady in purple. But I had to admit that of the two of them it was her I would rather travel with again.

A lot of new people began to get on the bus, and again they

were mostly black; I guessed that they were going to Oakland. With so many people it seemed inconsiderate to take up two seats, even if I could have got away with it, so I put my briefcase on the floor, at my feet.

And I looked up to find the biggest women I had ever seen, heading right for me. Enormous—she must have weighed three times what I did—and black and very young.

She needed two seats to herself, she really did, and of course she knew that; she looked around, but almost all the seats were taken, and so she chose me, because I am relatively thin, I guess. With a sweet apologetic smile, she squeezed in beside me—or, rather, she squeezed me in.

"Ooooh, I am so *big*," she said, in a surprisingly soft small voice. "I must be crushing you almost to death."

"Oh no, I'm fine," I assured her, and we smiled at each other.

"And you so thin," she observed.

As though being thin required an apology, I explained that I was not that way naturally, I was living with an overweight friend who kept me on fish and salads, mostly.

She laughed. "Well, maybe I should move in with your friend, but it probably wouldn't do me no good."

I laughed, too, and I wondered what she did, what job took her from Oakland to Vallejo.

We talked, and after a while she told me that she worked in Oakland, as well as lived there, not saying at what, but that she was taking a course in Vallejo in the care of special children, which is what she really wanted to do. " 'Special' mean the retards and the crazies," she said, but she laughed in a kindly way, and I thought how good she probably would be with kids.

I told her about the retarded boy who got off the bus at Vallejo, after all those noisy questions.

"No reason you can't tell a retard to quiet down," she said. "They got no call to disturb folks, it don't help them none."

Right away then I felt better; it was O.K. for me not to have liked all that noise and to have sided with the black woman who told the boy to shut up.

I did like that big young woman, and when we got to Oakland

I was sorry to see her go. We both said that we had enjoyed talking to each other; we said we hoped that we would run into each other again, although that seemed very unlikely.

In San Francisco, Hortense was pacing the station—very worried, she said, and visibly angry.

I explained to her that it was confusing, three buses leaving Sacramento for San Francisco at just the same time, five-thirty. It was very easy to get on the wrong one.

"Well, I suppose you'll catch on after a couple of weeks," she said, clearly without much faith that I ever would.

She was right about one thing, though: the San Francisco bus station, especially at night, is a cold and scary place. People seem to be just hanging out there—frightened-looking young kids, maybe runaways, belligerent-looking drunks, and large black men, with swaggering hats, all of whom look mysteriously enraged. The lighting is a terrible white glare, harsh on the dirty floors, illuminating the wrinkles and grime and pouches of fatigue on all the human faces. A cold wind rushes in through the swinging entrance doors. Outside, there are more dangerous-looking loiterers, whom Hortense and I hurried past that night, going along Seventh Street to Market, where she had parked in a yellow zone but had not (thank God) been ticketed.

For dinner we had a big chef's salad, so nutritious and slenderizing, but also so cold that it felt like a punishment. What I really would have liked was a big hot fattening baked potato.

I wondered, How would I look if I put on twenty pounds?

Early mornings at the Greyhound station are not so bad, with only a few drunks and lurching loiterers on the street outside, and it is easy to walk past them very fast, swinging a briefcase. Inside, there are healthy-looking, resolute kids with enormous backpacks, off to conquer the wilderness. And it is easy, of course, to find the right bus, the express to Sacramento; there is only one, leaving every hour on the hour. I almost always got to sit by myself. But somehow the same scenery that you see coming down to San Francisco is very boring viewed from the other direction. Maybe this is an effect of the leveling morning light—I don't know.

One day, though, the bus was more crowded than usual and a young girl asked if she could sit next to me. I said O.K., and we started up one of those guarded and desultory conversations that travel dictates. What most struck me about her was her accent; I could tell exactly where she was from—upstate New York. I am from there, too, from Binghamton, although I have taken on some other accents along the way, mainly my husband's—Philadelphia. (I hope I do not get to sound like Hortense, who is from Florida.) Of course I did not ask the girl where she was from—too personal, and I didn't have to—but she told me, unasked, that she worked in an office in Sacramento, which turned out to be in the building next to mine. That seemed ominous to me: a girl coming from exactly where I am from, and heading in my same direction. I did not want her to tell me any more about her life, and she did not.

Near Sacramento, the concrete road dividers have been planted with oleander, overflowing pink and white blossoms that quite conceal oncoming traffic in the other lanes. It is hard to believe that the highway commissioners envisioned such a wild profusion, and somehow it makes me uneasy to see all that bloom, maybe because I read somewhere that oleander is poisonous. Certainly it is unnaturally hardy.

The Sacramento station is more than a little weird, being the jumping-off place for Reno, so to speak. Every morning there are lines for the Reno buses, lines of gamblers, all kinds: big women in bright synthetic fabrics, and seedy old men, drunks, with their tired blue eyes and white indoor skin, smoking cigarillos. Gamblers seem to smoke a lot, I noticed. I also noticed that none of them are black.

A large elevated sign lists the departures for South Lake Tahoe and Reno: the Nugget express, which leaves at 3:40 A.M.; the dailies to Harrah's, starting at 9:05 A.M.; and on weekends you can leave for Reno any time between 2:35 A.M. and 11:15 P.M. I find it very hard to imagine going to Reno at any of those times, but then I am not a gambler.

Unfortunately, I again saw that same girl, Miss Upstate New York, the next few times that I took the correct bus, the express at 5:30 to San Francisco. She began to tell me some very boring things about her office—she did not like her boss, he drank—and her boyfriend, who wanted to invest in some condominiums at South Lake Tahoe.

I knew that Hortense would never believe that it was a mistake, and just possibly it was not, but a few nights later I took another wrong bus, really wrong: the local that stops everywhere, at Davis and Dixon and Fairfield, all down the line. Hortense was going to be furious. I began to work on some plausible lies: I got to the station late, this wrong bus left from the gate that the right bus usually leaves from. But then I thought, How ridiculous; and the very fact of Hortense's being there waiting for me began to seem a little silly, both of us being grown up.

Again most of the passengers were black, and I sensed a sort of camaraderie among them. It occurred to me that they were like people who have recently won a war, although I knew that to be not the case, not at all, in terms of their present lives. But with all the stops and starts the trip was very interesting; I would have been having a very good time if it were not for two things: one, I was worried about Hortense, and, two, I did not see again any of those people who were on my first wrong trip—not the very fat black woman or the skinny one in purple, or the handsome man who displaced me from my seat.

Just in front of me were an elderly man and woman, both black, who seemed to be old friends accidentally encountered on this bus. They exchanged information about how they both were, their families, and then the woman said, "Well, the weekend's coming up." "Yep, jes one more day." "Then you can rest." "Say, you ever see a poor man rest?"

Recently I read an interview with a distinguished lady of letters, in which she was asked why she wrote so obsessively about the very poor, the tiredest and saddest poorest people, and that lady, a Southerner, answered, "But I myself am poor people."

That touched me to the quick, somehow. I am too. Hortense is not, I think.

Across the aisle from me I suddenly noticed the most beautiful young man I had ever seen, sound asleep. A golden boy: gold hair and tawny skin, large beautiful hands spread loosely on his knees, long careless legs in soft pale washed-out jeans. I hardly dared look at him; some intensity in my regard might have wakened him, and then on my face he would have seen—not lust, it wasn't that, just a vast and objectless regard for his perfection, as though he were sculptured in bronze, or gold.

I haven't thought much about men, or noticed male beauty, actually, since my husband left, opted out of our marriage—and when I say that he left it sounds sudden, whereas it took a long and painful year.

Looking back, I now see that it began with some tiny wistful remarks, made by him, when he would come across articles in the paper about swingers, swapping, singles bars. "Well, maybe we should try some of that stuff," he would say, with a laugh intended to prove nonseriousness. "A pretty girl like you, you'd do O.K.," he would add, by which he really meant that he thought he would do O.K., as indeed he has—did, does. Then came some more serious remarks to the effect that if I wanted an occasional afternoon with someone else, well, I didn't have to tell him about it, but if I did, well, he would understand. Which was a little silly, since when I was not at my office working I was either doing some household errand or I was at home, available only to him.

The next phase included a lot of half-explained or occasionally over-explained latenesses, and a seemingly chronic at-home fatigue. By then even I had caught on, without thinking too specifically about what he must have been doing, which I could not have stood. Still, I was surprised, and worse than surprised, when he told me that he was "serious" about another woman. The beautiful Japanese nurse.

The golden boy got off at Vallejo, without our exchanging any look. Someone else I won't see again, but who will stay in my mind, probably.

Hortense was furious, her poor fat face red, her voice almost out of control. "One hour—one hour I've been waiting here. Can you imagine my thoughts, in all that time?"

Well, I pretty much could. I felt terrible. I put my hand on her arm in a gesture that I meant as calming, affectionate, but she thrust it off, violently.

That was foolish, I thought, and I hoped no one had seen her. I said, "Hortense, I'm really very sorry. But it's getting obvious that I have a problem with buses. I mix them up, so maybe you shouldn't come and meet me anymore."

I hadn't known I was going to say that, but, once said, those words made sense, and I went on. "I'll take a taxi. There're always a couple out front."

And just then, as we passed hurriedly through the front doors, out onto the street, there were indeed four taxis stationed, a record number, as though to prove my point. Hortense made a strangled, snorting sound.

We drove home in silence; silently, in her dining room, we ate another chef's salad. It occurred to me to say that since our dinners were almost always cold my being late did not exactly spoil them, but I forbore. We were getting to be like some bad sitcom joke: Hortense and me, the odd couple.

The next morning, as I got in line to buy a new commuter ticket, there was the New York State girl. We exchanged mild greetings, and then she looked at the old ticket which for no reason I was clutching, and she said, "But you've got one ticket left."

And she explained what turned out to be one more system that I had not quite caught on to: the driver takes the whole first page, which is why, that first day, I thought he had taken two coupons. And the back page, although another color, pink, is a coupon, too. So my first ride on the wrong bus to Vallejo and Oakland was free; I had come out ahead, in that way.

Then the girl asked, "Have you thought about a California Pass? They're neat." And she explained that with a California Pass, for just a few dollars more than a commuter ticket, you can go *anywhere in California*. You can't travel on weekends, but who would want to, and you can go anywhere at all—Eureka, La Jolla, Santa Barbara, San Diego; you can spend the weekend there and come back on an early Monday bus. I was fascinated, enthralled by these possibilities. I bought a California Pass.

The Sacramento express was almost empty, so I told the girl that I had some work to do, which was true enough. We sat down in our separate seats and concentrated on our briefcases. I was thinking, of course, in a practical way about moving out from Hortense's. That had to be next—and more generally I was considering the possibilities of California, which just then seemed limitless, enormous.

Actually, the Greyhound system of departure gates for buses to San Francisco is very simple; I had really been aware all along of how it worked. Gate 5 is the express, Gate 6 goes to Vallejo and Oakland before San Francisco, and Gate 8 is the all-stop local, Davis, Dixon, everywhere. On my way home, I started to line up at Gate 6, my true favorite route, Vallejo and Oakland, when I realized that it was still very early, only just five, and also that I was extremely hungry. What I would really have liked was what we used to call a frappe in Binghamton, something cold and rich and thick and chocolate. Out here called a milkshake. And then I thought, Well, why not? Is there some law that says I can't weigh more than one-ten?

I went into the station restaurant, and at the counter I ordered a double-scoop milkshake. I took it to a booth, and then, as I was sitting there, savoring my delicious drink, something remarkable happened, which was: the handsome black man who so angrily displaced me on that first trip came up to me and greeted me with a friendly smile. "Say, how you, how're you doing this evening?"

I smiled back and said that I was fine, and he went on past with his cup of coffee, leaving me a little out of breath. And as I continued to sip and swallow (it tasted marvelous) I wondered: Is it possible that he remembers me from that incident and this is his way of apologizing? Somehow that seemed very unlikely, but it seemed even more unlikely that he was just a friendly sort who went around greeting people. He was not at all like that, I was sure. Even smiling he had a proud, fierce look.

Was it possible that something about me had struck him in just the right way, making him want to say hello?

In any case, I had to read his greeting as a very good sign.

Maybe the fat young woman would get on the bus at Vallejo again. Maybe the thin one in purple. And it further occurred to me that traveling all over California on the Greyhound I could meet anyone at all.

TO SEE YOU AGAIN

ALICE ADAMS

Like so many acutely dreaded moments, this one arrived and passed in an unanticipated fashion: the moment after which I would not again see my most brilliant and beautiful student, Seth. I looked up from the group of girl students—ironically, the ones I had least liked—who were asking me silly questions; I looked toward his seat, and was confronted with his absence, his absolute loss.

Considerably older than these kids, and especially, cruelly, older than Seth, I had envisioned quite another scene: I had imagined and feared a moment at which the students would recognize, collectively, that it was over, that this was my last class, the end of my temporary and quite accidental presence in their lives. They would never see me again, any of them. At that instant of recognition, I thought, I would have to smile and say something like "Well, it's been very nice knowing all of you. I've enjoyed this time at Cornford."

(Of course I would look at Seth as I spoke, but could I do it with no break in my voice, no catch?)

And what would they all do, my students, including Seth, I had wondered: would they smile back and maybe clap? What sort of expression would Seth wear, on that most entrancing face?

But that is not how it went at all. The class—it was in freshman composition—simply ended as it had every day of my time there. Across the campus some clear bells chimed; in the classroom books were gathered from the floor; slowly the kids began to get up and move toward the door. And some of the silliest, noisiest girls gathered at my desk, not to say goodbye or anything so formal, just to be told again what they already knew: that their final papers were to be collected from the English office. And then I looked up to the total absence of Seth.

One of the things I first thought was: If I ever see him again he'll be older. Still handsome, probably, but he won't look quite like *that*.

Seth: Red-gold curls, a wild never-combed tangle, curls that shadowed remarkably white, unfreckled skin. Narrow green eyes; a small childish nose; and a wide, somehow unformed mouth—a young mouth. And an incongruous, scruffy reddish beard. Just a messy red-haired kid was how someone else might have seen him. Whereas to me: perfect poignant beauty. And what he wrote was extraordinary—weird wild flashes of poetry, flaming through the dullest assignments. At times I considered the possibility that he was in some way crazy, at others the possibility of genius. But how can you tell with anyone so young? He might be, or might become, anything at all. Anything, in his case, except ugly or ordinary.

Not quite anguished—I had had worse losses in my life (I have them still)—but considerably worse than "let down" was how I felt as I began the drive from Cornford west to San Francisco. To my house, and Gerald, my sad fat husband, a distinguished architect—and my most precariously balanced, laboriously achieved "good life."

Cornford is about forty miles east of San Francisco, near Vallejo, in the tawny, oak-shadowed foothills. It is on Interstate 80, the main east-west thoroughfare; after Vallejo and Cornford, the highway continues past Sacramento to Tahoe, Reno, Salt Lake City, the East. Going anywhere in that direction, and Gerald and I often spend time at Tahoe, we will pass right by Cornford, again and again. Next fall Seth will be there, after a summer of hitchhiking in Spain. How will it feel, I wonder, to drive right past where Seth is, in the fall and following winter?

Or suppose he should move to San Francisco. Kids do, all the time. Just what would I do with him? What, really, do I want of him? I have asked myself that question, repeatedly, at terrible sleepless pre-dawn hours, and have come up with no answer. The obvious ones do not apply.

Meaning that it is nowhere near as simple as sex (Christ! as if sex were ever simple, or easy). If my strong feelings in his direction do have an object, it is not the act of love—I find the very idea both terrifying and embarrassing, and oh! how horrified he would be if he knew that I had even, ever, considered that. How old I must seem to him! Revolting, really, although I am in very good shape "for my age." But to him revolting—as I sometimes am to myself; as often I feel that I am to Gerald.

I reread "Death in Venice," and, with all due respect, I do not think that Aschenbach knew what he wanted of Tadzio, either.

In an earnest way I have tried to see Seth as objectively as possible—to catalogue him, as it were. I began, for whatever reason, with his voice, and right away I was balked. I could not decide whether the sound was high or deep, and I concluded that it is simply young, a little rough. Some softness in the lines of his face might suggest a plump body, but the actual body that I saw in his daily, worn, taut jeans is thin, a thin boy's body; maybe in middle age he will be heavy? I wistfully considered that. His facial expressions, too, are elusive, escaping definition—a shade of defiance, sometimes a slow smile; he is far less ready than the rest of the class to show amusement. A wary, waiting look, perhaps—is that it?

And so I was left with nothing clear, no definitions, only the weight of my own meticulous observations. And his face in my heart.

Spring and summer at Cornford, so near the Sacramento Valley, are hot and dry—a heat and dryness inversely proportional to the cold gray wet San Francisco fog, one set of weather pushing out the other. And the transition from one climate to another struck me as symbolic as I drove back and forth, in May and then in June, between the two areas. The heat of Cornford was like an adolescent summer—urgent, flushed—and San Francisco's cold like middle age. Resignation. Disappointment. Grief.

Approaching the hill where the fog always began, on my last drive home from Cornford, when everything was over, I shivered, thinking of my own, known, familiar life: Gerald, our cold clean flat. And no Seth. Ridiculously, I thought, I can't live without seeing him—what shall I do?

Gerald and I know an older man—considerably older than ourselves, that is: Larry Montgomery. As I crested that hill, for no reason that I could immediately understand Larry came into my mind. And in the next instant I saw that he had arrived there for a very clear reason: Larry is exactly as much older than I am as I am older than Seth. He has what Gerald describes as a crush on me. Larry looks at least ten years younger than he is, trim and tan, with lively blue eyes and fine silver-white hair. A forties dandy, he hums snatches from Gershwin, Rodgers and Hart, Cole Porter; he wears gold-buttoned navy blazers. His blue eyes widen and deepen, always, when I come into a room. He makes excuses to stand very near me; sometimes he touches me, but in a serious, respectful way.

Once, though, finding ourselves alone at a party, instead of beginning a romantic or even an affectionate conversation, we got into a silly argument—or, rather, he led me into it, baiting me, really. Which, as I thought back to times when I was curt with Seth, almost pushing him out of my office, I now understood: Larry was terrified that whatever he felt would show.

Once I even asked Gerald, though very idly, "What do you think Larry would do if I propositioned him?"

Surprisingly—I had supposed he would laugh—Gerald gave me a serious, considered answer. He said, "I think he would be scared to death, but very polite about how he put you off." I thought Gerald was right; whatever Larry wanted was not an affair with me; a stray motel afternoon with Larry was as unimaginable as it would be with Seth. Larry just likes to see me, to be near me, sometimes—and very likely that is what I feel for Seth, pretty much?

The accident of my teaching at Cornford came about because my friend Amy, who teaches there regularly, was suddenly, between terms, summoned to the side of her ailing mother, in New Hampshire.

"But Amy, I've never taught," I said.

"It's easy, there're just a few tricks to it. I'll teach you."

"But credentials—"

"Private junior colleges don't much care. They'll be so impressed that you've got a master's—"

"But that was just to stay on in Cambridge another year." To stay on and be with Gerald, as Amy already knew.

"How would they know that? And you got it, didn't you? Besides, Laura, it'll be a good change for you. You need . . ." For a moment Amy faltered at prescribing for my needs, then finished, lamely, "You need to get out more."

However, getting out more was surely among the things that I did need, and partly for that reason I began the twice-a-week drive, back and forth to Cornford College. I began to teach, and there was Seth, in the second row, nearest the door. Red curls, green eyes.

At first, despite the handsomeness that I noted in passing, Seth was simply one among fifteen surprisingly nice, clean young California kids—much nicer and more civil, all of them, than the Cornford faculty, none of whom ever bothered to speak to me, the substitute teacher. However, I had been warned by Amy that this might be the case. "They're incredibly rude," she had said, knowing how thin-skinned I tended to be. I managed not to mind; I told myself that I wouldn't be there for long, and that the kids were what mattered.

The first assignment I gave was a physical description of something encountered outdoors. "You want very simple, specific assignments," Amy had cautioned. "Anything else only confuses them." The papers ranged from the outrageously illiterate to the adequate; they were mostly misspelled descriptions of lakes and mountains, mountain streams and sunsets. But Seth wrote about an abandoned truck, come upon, surprisingly, in a small eucalyptus grove: the heavily stained windshield, the drifts of leaves all over, and their smell. Rotted tires, rust. A dead truck. His style was flat, specific, and yet the total effect was haunting. I, who have almost no feeling for cars, and surely none for trucks, was haunted by this mechanical death, this abandonment. I began to look closely, even wonderingly, at Seth. And I saw that he was more beautiful than I had seen at first, as well as possibly, probably, brilliant.

In fact, as my short time at Cornford passed, my feelings in regard to all my students polarized—as I might have known they would, given my propensity for extremes of feeling. Some fairly silly girls who at first I thought were just that, fairly silly, after three weeks and then four I found intolerably fatuous—the very ones who were to block out my last view of Seth. About one student other than Seth I became enthusiastic: a dark shy girl, who seemed to have read everything, discerningly, with real intelligence. And always there was Seth, about whom my feelings were strongest—were inexplicable, and impossible.

But when I was midway across the Bay Bridge, suddenly the perfect solution to those unruly feelings came to me; in effect I would domesticate them, just as, years back, I had tamed my wild mania for Gerald. Quite simply, I would make him a friend of our family; I will write him a note next fall, inviting him for dinner. With some other friends, of course, maybe people with kids of Seth's own age. In that setting, my own home ground, Seth will seem a kid like any other, perhaps slightly handsomer, a touch more brilliant, but not noticeably so to anyone else, and surely not remarkable to Gerald, my sad, successful husband. And Gerald and I will present one of our best, our most convincing surfaces to the group at large, and especially to Seth: we will portray a very adult couple, stringently amusing: Gerald and generous-to-guests Laura. I'll cook something wonderful. The two of us mildly, fondly bantering with each other.

And after dinner Gerald will say, a little chillingly, "Well, my dear Laura, I do congratulate you on your springtime of patience with the young." And then, "When would you imagine that boy last combed his hair—care to place a bet?"

And slowly, gradually, Seth will disappear from my mind—or Seth as the author of violent feelings will go, to be replaced by the messy kid I first saw, of whom I will never think.

In that good mood, having even begun to plan the menu, I drove into the city and arrived at our house on Edgewood, Gerald's and mine. And I saw Gerald's car parked in front of the house, although it was much too early for him to be at home.

My stomach and heart seemed simultaneously to clench tight. Not out of fear. I did not wonder what was wrong; I knew. One and only one condition would have brought Gerald home so early—a new depression. His depressions are as severe and as invariably recurrent as they are apparently incurable. "My sweet old Melancholia, my maiden aunt, my child, my baby Melancholia," I once heard him say, babbling his way out of the shock treatment that didn't help.

I knew what was wrong, but not why, never why, or why now—and one problem about living with someone who is depressed is that inevitably you think it has to do with you, your fault, although you are told that it is not. And I knew exactly what I would find on entering the house: heavy Gerald immobilized, immobile, on the wicker settee in the entrance hall, unable to go comfortably into the living room, or upstairs to bed. Unable to leave the house, or the marriage, as I have thought that he must, sometimes, want to do.

He has explained to me how he feels, depressed. "As heavy as boulders," he has said. "I can't open my mouth, it's so heavy. Much less move." I can feel what Gerald feels—and can do nothing about it.

And there he was, slumped down, gray-faced, barely looking up as I opened the door and then closed it behind me. I went over and placed a light kiss on his forehead—the lightest kiss—but he flinched, a little.

"I'll call," I told him.

Something crossed his face; some shadow of relief, perhaps. Not hope.

The phone is in the kitchen. As I dialed, I thought, How immaculate it is, this room. How sterile. Could I paint it red? Would that help?

"Dr. Abrams, please," I said to the voice on the other end. "Right now, if I can." And then, "Hi, Ed. It's Laura. I'm bringing him over, O.K.?"

Passing Gerald in the hall, I prevented myself from touching his shoulder.

Upstairs, I packed his small bag: pajamas, toiletries, a sweater, one change of clothes.

I got him up and through the front door, and out to my car. I drove north this time, toward the Golden Gate Bridge. Marin. The small hospital in Larkspur. Yellow fog lights lined the approach to the bridge, and it was fogged in already—summer fog, gray and billowing between the dim masses of the headlands, and swirling below the bridge, obscuring the dangerous black water. Beside me, as far from me as possible, Gerald sat, heavy as cement and as unmoving.

I turned off the highway, past developments, shopping centers, schools, playing fields, jogging courses, and a few small untouched areas of land—rough, with scattered small shabby houses.

Larkspur. The hospital is one-story, white, ranch style. It could be a motel, and there is even a swimming pool in back, for the more mobile, less desperate patients.

And there was Dr. Abrams, Ed, waiting, having recognized our car. Kind Ed, kind enough not to be hearty, or to pretend that this was a social occasion. He knows, too, not to touch Gerald. Gerald allowed me to help him from the car, and then for an instant Ed touched my hair; he must know that I love touching, any gesture of affection.

Although, driving over, I had not been aware of it, had not thought of weather, I now noticed that the day was still clear in Larkspur, a blue summer day, just fading.

The checking-in process was of course familiar, and minimal. We left Gerald in his room, and Ed Abrams and I walked toward my car, and although in a way we like each other, and surely wish each other well, we had little to say.

"Well, let's hope it won't be for very long this time," he said.

"Yes."

Then, remembering some prior conversation, he asked, "How was the teaching? You liked it O.K.?"

"It went pretty well. A couple of the students were terrific."

"Oh, good. Well, all done with that now?"

"Yes. Done. Today was my last day."

"Well, good."

I backed out of the driveway and headed back toward the almost invisible bridge, and the darkened, fog-shrouded city.

In Cambridge, a long time ago, I thought Gerald was so beautiful, so dark and thin, so elegant, so elusive that I used to trail him around the Yard: me, a silly undergraduate with a crush on a future architect who was studying at the School of Design. We had met a couple of times—I had seen to that, quzzing everyone I knew who might know him, and finally coming up with a girl with a brother who knew Gerald. But Gerald hardly had time to speak to me.

But there I always was, in St. Clair's, out of breath from following him on my bike but saying hello; and in Hayes-Bickford, or the Wursthaus. Late one afternoon I found him alone, on the steps of Widener, and with my heart in my mouth I asked him to a dance at Whitman Hall, where I lived. He came late, stayed a very short time, and left, with an abstracted frown. But the next time he saw me, standing in his way, again on the steps of Widener, he asked me up for tea, in his room, at Dunster House, and instead of tea we drank a lot of gin, and fell into bed together—for me, the consummation of a major passion; for Gerald, the onset of a habit. I stayed on in Cambridge for a master's in English literature while Gerald finished his degree, and we married; we moved out to San Francisco and we bought and remodeled the house near Twin Peaks, and we had no children. Gerald began to be a considerable success. And sometimes to be sad, then seriously depressed. Recurrently. Ed Abrams says that with age the cycle may well lengthen, and the severity of each attack will decrease. A sort of flattening out of the curve. But age could take forever; I'm not sure I have that much time.

Driving back to the city, across the bridge, I did not think in symbolic terms about my reentry into dark and fog; I hardly had to, having made that trip from Marin so many times before. I thought about supper, a glass of wine, and getting into bed to watch TV, which I don't do with Gerald at home. And in a cautious way I wondered how long it would be this time.

As always, I made it home perfectly all right. But once I was inside, the idea of cooking anything in the impeccable kitchen was so discouraging that I just nibbled on a piece of cheese—a halfhearted graying mouse.

I even thought, in a lonely way, of calling Larry Montgomery, for a friendly conversation, God knows, not meaning to proposition him. But I am not really sure that we are friends.

I washed and got into bed. I turned on the TV, and I watched one foolish thing after another—until, at about ten, a play was announced, with an actress I like, and so I propped myself up for that.

And then, Seth, there you were. A great deal older, of course, even older than I am now, curls all gone gray but the same narrow, unmistakable green eyes. It was absolutely extraordinary. In the play, Seth, you were a workman, a sort of handyman, which I suppose is one of the things you could become. The actress, funnily enough, was a schoolteacher. After a tremendous, wrenching love affair, you gave each other up, you and she, because you were married, and responsible. But, Seth, the resemblance was so striking that I thought, Oh, so that is how he will look: gray, slightly overweight, but *strong*, with a brilliant smile, and those eyes.

I waited for the credits at the end of the play; for all I knew, your father could be an actor, that actor—I know so little about you—but he had another name, and, besides, he looked more like you than like a possible father.

In any case, that sight of you was strangely cheering to me. I turned off the TV and contented myself with visions of my own.

I imagined a time when you will really be as old as that man, and as gray—when, much older still than you, I can say to you, "Ah, Seth, at last you begin to lose your looks. Now you are merely handsome, whereas before you were so beautiful that I could hardly look at you." We both will laugh.

And at that time, your prime and our old age, Gerald's and

mine, Gerald will be completely well, the cycle flat, no more sequences of pain. And maybe thin again. And interested, and content.

It's almost worth waiting for.

MAGAZINES CONSULTED

Akron Review
University of Akron, Akron, Ohio 44325
Antaeus
Ecco Press, 1 West 30th Street, New York, N.Y. 10001
Antioch Review
P.O. Box 148, Yellow Springs, Ohio 45387
Apalachee Quarterly
P.O. Box 20106, Tallahassee, Fla. 32304
Appalachian Journal
P.O. Box 536, Appalachian State University, Boone, N.C. 28608
Ararat
Armenian General Benevolent Union of America, 628 Second Avenue, New York, N.Y. 10016
Arizona Quarterly
University of Arizona, Tucson, Ariz. 85721
The Ark River Review
Box 14, W.S.U., Wichita, Kan. 67208
Ascent
English Dept., University of Illinois, Urbana, Ill. 61801
Aspen Anthology
P.O. Box 3185, Aspen, Col. 81611
The Atlantic Monthly
8 Arlington Street, Boston, Mass. 02116
Bachy
11317 Santa Monica Boulevard, Los Angeles, Calif. 90025
The Black Warrior Review
P.O. Box 2936, University, Ala. 35486
The Boston Monthly
20 Newbury Street, Boston, Mass. 02116
Boston University Journal
704 Commonwealth Avenue, Boston, Mass. 02215

California Quarterly

100 Sproul Hall, University of California, Davis, Calif. 95616

Canadian Fiction Magazine

P.O. Box 46422, Station G, Vancouver, B.C., Canada V6R 4G7

Canto

11 Bartlett Street, Andover, Mass. 01810

Carolina Quarterly

Greenlaw Hall 066-A, University of North Carolina, Chapel Hill, N.C. 27514

The Chariton Review

Division of Language & Literature, Northeast Missouri State University, Kirksville, Mo. 63501

Chicago

500 North Michigan Avenue, Chicago, Ill. 60611

Chicago Review

970 E. 58th Street, Box C, University of Chicago, Chicago, Ill. 60637

Christopher Street

Suite 417, 250 W. 57th Street, New York, N.Y. 10019

Colorado Quarterly

Hellums 134, University of Colorado, Boulder, Col. 80309

Commentary

165 East 56th Street, New York, N.Y. 10022

Confrontation

English Dept., Brooklyn Center of Long Island University, Brooklyn, N.Y. 11201

Cornell Review

108 North Plain Street, Ithaca, N.Y. 14850

Cosmopolitan

224 West 57th Street, New York, N.Y. 10019

Crucible

Atlantic Christian College, Wilson, N.C. 27893

Cumberlands

Pikeville College, Pikeville, Ky. 41501

Cutbank

c/o English Dept., University of Montana, Missoula, Mont. 59801

Dark Horse
Box 36, Newton Lower Falls, Mass. 02162
December
P.O. Box 274, Western Springs, Ill. 60558
The Denver Quarterly
Dept. of English, University of Denver, Denver, Col. 80210
Descant
Dept. of English, TCU Station, Fort Worth, Tex. 76129
Epoch
254 Goldwyn Smith Hall, Cornell University, Ithaca, N.Y. 14853
Esquire
488 Madison Avenue, New York, N.Y. 10022
Essence
1500 Broadway, New York, N.Y. 10036
Eureka Review
Dept. of English, University of Cincinnati, Cincinnati, Ohio 45221
The Falcon
Bilknap Hall, Mansfield State College, Mansfield, Pa. 16933
Fantasy and Science Fiction
Box 56, Cornwall, Conn. 06753
The Fault
33513 6th Street, Union City, Calif. 94538
Fiction
c/o Dept. of English, The City College of New York, New York, N.Y. 10031
Fiction International
Dept. of English, St. Lawrence University, Canton, N.Y. 13617
The Fiddlehead
The Observatory, University of New Brunswick, P.O. Box 4400, Fredericton, N.B., Canada E3B 5A3
Fisherman's Angle
St. John Fisher College, Rochester, N.Y. 14618
Forms
P.O. Box 3379, San Francisco, Calif. 94119

Forum
Ball State University, Muncie, Ind. 47306
Four Quarters
La Salle College, Philadelphia, Pa. 19141
Gargoyle
P.O. Box 57206, Washington, D.C. 20037
The Gay Alternative
252 South Street, Philadelphia, Pa. 19147
Georgia Review
University of Georgia, Athens, Ga. 30602
GPU News
c/o The Farwell Center, 1568 N. Farwell, Milwaukee, Wis. 53202
The Great Lakes Review
Northeastern Illinois University, Chicago, Ill. 60625
Great River Review
59 Seymour Avenue, S.E., Minneapolis, Minn. 55414
Green River Review
Box 56, University Center, Mich. 48710
The Greensboro Review
University of North Carolina, Greensboro, N.C. 27412
The Greyledge View
P.O. Box 481, Greenville, R.I. 02828
Hair Trigger IV
Columbia College Writing Dept., 600 South Michigan Avenue, Chicago, Ill. 06605
Harper's Magazine
2 Park Avenue, New York, N.Y. 10016
Hawaii Review
Hemenway Hall, University of Hawaii 96822
The Hudson Review
65 East 55th Street, New York, N.Y. 10022
Iowa Review
EPB 453, University of Iowa, Iowa City, Iowa 52240
Jewish Dialog
1498 Yonge Street, Suite 7, Toronto, Ontario, Canada M4T 1Z6

Kansas Quarterly
Dept. of English, Kansas State University, Manhattan, Kan. 66506

The Kenyon Review
Kenyon College, Gambier, Ohio 43022

Ladies' Home Journal
641 Lexington Avenue, New York, N.Y. 10022

Lilith
250 West 57th Street, New York, N.Y. 10019

The Literary Review
Fairleigh Dickinson University, Teaneck, N.J. 07666

The Little Balkans Review
601 Grandview Heights Terrace, Pittsburgh, Kan. 66762

The Little Magazine
P.O. Box 207, Cathedral Station, New York, N.Y. 10025

The Louisville Review
University of Louisville, Louisville, Ky. 40208

Mademoiselle
350 Madison Avenue, New York, N.Y. 10017

Malahat Review
University of Victoria, Victoria, B.C., Canada

The Massachusetts Review
Memorial Hall, University of Massachusetts, Amherst, Mass. 01002

McCall's
230 Park Avenue, New York, N.Y. 10017

MD
30 E. 60th Street, New York, N.Y. 10022

Michigan Quarterly Review
3032 Rackham Bldg., University of Michigan, Ann Arbor, Mich. 48109

Midstream
515 Park Avenue, New York, N.Y. 10022

Mother Jones
607 Market Street, San Francisco, Calif. 94105

The National Jewish Monthly
1640 Rhode Island Avenue, N.W., Washington, D.C. 20036

New Boston Review
Boston Critic, Inc., 77 Sacramento Street, Somerville, Mass. 02143

New Directions
333 Sixth Avenue, New York, N.Y. 10014

New Letters
University of Missouri–Kansas City, Kansas City, Mo. 64110

New Mexico Humanities Review
The Editors, Box A, New Mexico Tech, Socorro, N.M. 57801

The New Renaissance
9 Heath Road, Arlington, Mass. 02174

The New Republic
1220 19th Street, N.W., Washington, D.C. 20036

The New Yorker
25 West 43rd Street, New York, N.Y. 10036

The North American Review
University of Northern Iowa, 1222 West 27th Street, Cedar Falls, Iowa 50613

Northwest Review
129 French Hall, University of Oregon, Eugene, Ore. 97403

Northwoods Journal
Route 1, Meadows of Daw, Va. 24120

The Ohio Journal
164 West 17th Avenue, Columbus, Ohio 43210

Ohio Review
Ellis Hall, Ohio University, Athens, Ohio 45701

The Ontario Review
9 Honey Brook Drive, Princeton, N.J. 08540

Paragraph: A Quarterly of Gay Fiction
Box 14051, San Francisco, Calif. 94114

The Paris Review
45-39–171st Place, Flushing, N.Y. 11358

Partisan Review
128 Bay State Road, Boston, Mass. 02215 / 552 Fifth Avenue, New York, N.Y. 10036

Perspective
Washington University, St. Louis, Mo. 63130

Phylon
223 Chestnut Street, S.W., Atlanta, Ga. 30314

Playboy
919 North Michigan Avenue, Chicago, Ill. 60611

Ploughshares
Box 529, Cambridge, Mass. 02139

Prairie Schooner
Andrews Hall, University of Nebraska, Lincoln, Neb. 68588

Prism International
Dept. of Creative Writing, University of British Columbia, Vancouver, B.C., Canada V6T 1WR

Pulpsmith
5 Beekman Street, New York, N.Y. 10038

Quarterly West
312 Olpin Union, University of Utah, Salt Lake City, Utah 84112

Quartet
1119 Neal Pickett Drive, College Station, Tex. 77840

Quest/81
1133 Avenue of the Americas, New York, N.Y. 10036

Redbook
230 Park Avenue, New York, N.Y. 10017

Remington Review
505 Westfield Avenue, Elizabeth, N.J. 07208

Rolling Stone
625 Post Street, Box 752, San Francisco, Calif. 94109

San Francisco Stories
625 Post Street, Box 752, San Francisco, Calif. 94109

The Saturday Evening Post
110 Waterway Boulevard, Indianapolis, Ind. 46202

The Seneca Review
P.O. Box 115, Hobart and William Smith College, Geneva, N.Y. 14456

Sequoia
Storke Student Publications Bldg., Stanford, Calif. 94305

Sewanee Review
University of the South, Sewanee, Tenn. 37375
Shenandoah: The Washington and Lee University Review
Box 722, Lexington, Va. 24450
Silver Vain
P.O. Box 2366, Park City, Utah 84060
The South Carolina Review
Dept. of English, Clemson University, Clemson, S.C. 29631
The South Dakota Review
Box 111, University Exchange, Vermillion, S.D. 57069
Southern Humanities Review
Auburn University, Auburn, Ala. 36830
Southern Review
Drawer D, University Station, Baton Rouge, La. 70803
Southwest Review
Southern Methodist University Press, Dallas, Tex. 75275
Story Quarterly
820 Ridge Road, Highland Park, Ill. 60035
The Tamarack Review
Box 159, Postal Station K, Toronto, Ont., Canada M4P 2G5
The Texas Review
English Dept., Sam Houston University, Huntsville, Tex. 77341
The Threepenny Review
P.O. Box 335, Berkeley, Calif. 94701
TriQuarterly
1735 Benson Avenue, Evanston, Ill. 60201
Twigs
Pikeville College, Pikeville, Ky. 41501
Twilight Zone
800 Second Avenue, New York, N.Y. 10017
University of Windsor Review
Dept. of English, University of Windsor, Windsor, Ont., Canada N9B 3P4
U.S. Catholic
221 West Madison Street, Chicago, Ill. 60606

Vagabond
P.O. Box 879, Ellensburg, Wash. 98926
The Virginia Quarterly Review
University of Virginia, 1 West Range, Charlottesville, Va. 22903
Vogue
350 Madison Avenue, New York, N.Y. 10017
Washington Review
Box 50132, Washington, D.C. 20004
The Washingtonian
1828 "L" Street, N.W., Suite 200, Washington, D.C. 20036
Waves
Room 357, Strong College, York University, 4700 Keele Street, Downsview, Ont., Canada M3J 1P3
Webster Review
Webster College, Webster Groves, Mo. 63119
West Coast Review
Simon Fraser University, Vancouver, B.C., Canada
Western Humanities Review
Bldg. 41, University of Utah, Salt Lake City, Utah 84112
Wind
RFD Route 1, Box 809, Pikeville, Ky. 41501
Wittenberg Review of Literature and Art
Box 1, Recitation Hall, Wittenberg University, Springfield, Ohio 45501
Woman's Day
1515 Broadway, New York, N.Y. 10036
Writers Forum
University of Colorado, Colorado Springs, Col. 90907
Yale Review
250 Church Street, 1902A Yale Station, New Haven, Conn. 06520
Yankee
Dublin, N.H. 03444